I0760419

First ebook edition April 2025

Book Cover Design by Artscandre

Book couple art by Agnieszka Gromulska @aseriaart on IG

Map by Melisa Nash

ASIN (ebook): B0CVR3SM77

ISBN (paperback): 979-8-313123-20-2

ISBN (hardback): 978-1-960343-26-0

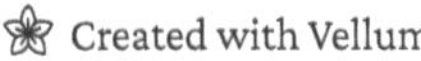

PRONUNCIATION GUIDE AND LIST OF TERMS

Creatures:

Cave rat - **Ruc'rad** (ruck-rad)

Cave bear - **Ruh'Glumdlor** (ruh glum-dl-ore)

Cave bat - **Ruc'ciel** (ruck-cee-el)

Crystal wraith - **Glacialmara** (glass-ee-al-mar-ah)

Glow spiders - **Aradhlum** (ah-rahd-loom)

Glow wyrms - **Wyrmhlum** (worm-loom)

Crystal Dragon/Mother of the Crystal Wraiths - **Drathorinna** (dra-thor-ee-nah)

Characters

GODS

Grutabela—*grew-TAH-bell-ah (Enduar goddess)*

Endu—*EN-doo (Enduar god)*

Doros—*DOOR-ose (Elven god)*

Nicnevin—*NIC-neh-ven (Elven goddess)*

Yde—*EE-dee (Goddess of the ogres)*

Khuohr—*KOR (God of the giants)*

Abhartach—*OW-er-tagh (The demon god)*

HUMANS

Estela-*es-TEL-ah*
Arlet—*ARE-let*
Melisa—*Meh-lee-sah*

ENDUARES

Teo/Ma'Teo—*TAY-oh/mah TAY-oh*
Vann—*Van*
Liana—*LEE-an-ah*
Svanna—*sv-AH-nah*
Ulla—*OO-lah*
Iryth—*EE-rith*
Ra'Salore—*Rah-sah-lore-eh*
Fira—*FEE-rah*
Joso—*JAW-sow*
Lothar—*LOW-thar*
Dyrn—*D-URN*
Velen—*VEH-lehn*
Tirin—*TEE-reen*
Niht—*night*
Faol—*fa-OHL*
Adra—*ad-RAH*
Ner'Feon—*ner-fey-own*

ELVES

Mrath—*Mu-rah-th*
Arion—*AH-r-eye-own*
Thorne—*th-OR-n*
Glyni—GLIH-*nee*

N
W
E
S
Lunara Island
The Sea of Sorrows
Iravida Point
TROLL LANDS
Enduvida
Sisterhood's Enclave
ELVEN LANDS
Shvathemar

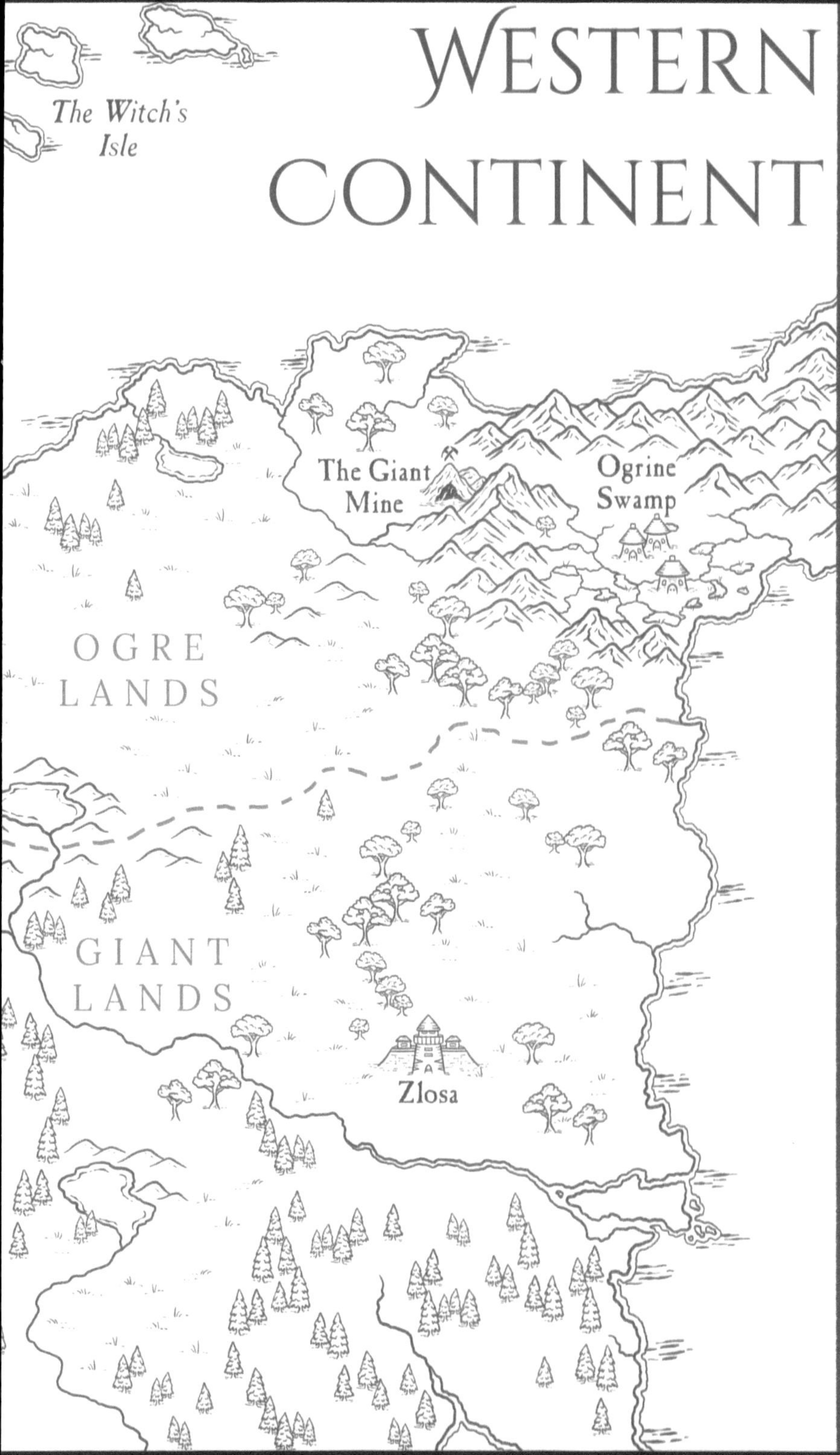
WESTERN CONTINENT
The Witch's Isle
The Giant Mine
Ogrine Swamp
OGRE LANDS
GIANT LANDS
Zlosa

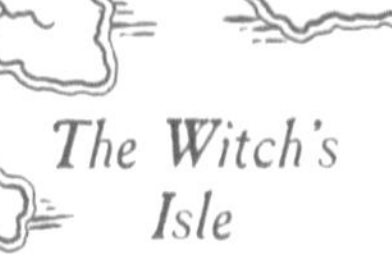

WELCOME BACK TO ENDUVIDA!

Hi! I'm Daniela.

From the bottom of my heart, thank you for picking up my novel. :)

You are about to embark on an adventure that my readers have anticipated since 2023, when I first published in this world.

Am I crying while writing this?

No. I just have allergies.

This is the start of a new series, and you do not need to read any of the novels in my other series, Entangled with the Enduar, to enjoy this one, though you might want to after finishing.

Next, I generally include Spanish in my novels. If you are unfamiliar with the words, fear not; all the important bits and phrases have been translated.

Finally, before diving in, I would urge you to check if any of the following topics are too painful for you to read. No novel is worth your mental health.

- Sexual harassment
- Mentions of slavery
- Misogyny
- Infertility

- Mentions of a miscarriage
- Death
- Blood/gore
- Self harm
- Lite bondage play
- Emotional abuse,
- Mentions of spousal abuse/neglect
- Strong language

Con mucho amor,
Daniela

For those who love fairy tales and monster tails... welcome to the unhinged side of romantasy.

PROLOGUE
ARLET

One year ago...

There are bad decisions, and then there's 'I agreed to charm a foreign sovereign with my human allure in order to win his support in the upcoming war.'

Before dread can burrow under my skin, I see the faces of my loved ones, and my nerves cool from bright embers to brittle charcoal. The crystals glowing overhead banish the creeping darkness of my path and illuminate the guards escorting me to the Elf King's chambers.

It will be fine. He's friendly. This evening won't end in tragedy. You are perfectly capable.

But I twist my fingers. I'd never been totally at ease with men, and this would be the first night I would be mostly alone with one since...

I shake my head, distracting myself.

Though I have never met King Arion, my closest friend, Estela, has painted a portrait of an elf who is aloof, cold, and maddeningly hard to read.

One might ask why a weaving woman would be dealing with a foreign official.

When Estela and I walked into Enduvida with a trading caravan a few months ago, we were the first human women to ever visit. It shocked us all to learn that Estela, the woman close enough to me to be my sister, was King Teo's mate. This meant she was goddess-destined to marry the king of the trolls.

It was a stroke of luck because the enduares, once called trolls, may be the only people with enough honor to see the gift of our matehood as not something to be exploited, but cultivated upon principles of choice and consent.

In a world where the larger, magical races thrive, humans are on the cusp of emerging as a people with a modicum of sway.

I volunteered to meet with a foreign official, though I have no experience in such matters because the elves only agreed to negotiate with the enduares for one reason. Their birthrates are also dropping, and they wish to see if they, too, might be blessed to mate with my kind.

Estela and I are the only human women in this city, and her wedding ceremony will be tonight at the Festival of Endu, the celebration of the Enduar Gods.

That left me to bear the weight of my people's future for an evening.

Two months ago, I'd been a slave shackled to a loom, weaving until my fingers bled to produce the finest clothes for the giant court, and now, I stand tall.

Free.

I was free to stop weaving when I was weary, free to speak my language openly, and free to make precarious choices that both strengthen my freedom and propagate freedom for others *just like me.*

It is a miracle for someone like her to be raised up as a sovereign and show the world we are equals. It is only right I do my part.

So here I am. Nervous. Overwhelmed. On my way to win over the elf king, potentially be mated to him or one of his guards, and to prove that my people are worth fighting for. Nothing improper is meant to occur. I will simply accompany him to the festival... and yet, sweat collects in my palms and my heart races.

The city of Enduvida buzzes with life. A small choir gathers near the bright red temple in the middle of the cavern, their voices rising toward a massive blue crystal in the ceiling that concentrates sound. This focused note is then carried by smaller crystals scattered throughout the cavern, weaving a tapestry of melodies across the open space.

Several tall white structures of murky citrine encircle the pulsing red Ardorflame temple, adding to the vibrant scene.

Dioses míos, it's a beautiful sight.

I smooth my hand over the beaded bodice of my pale pink dress as I hurry down the twisting stone corridor of the palace's east wing.

The Enduar Palace is one of many structures within the massive cavern, and, as with everything under the mountain, parts of it connect directly to the cave tunnels. Sneaking a glance at the two tall, blue hunters on either side of me, I take a deep breath to steady my smile.

They were quiet. Friendly. I liked them well enough.

Joso is on the right, with bright, silver hair that is woven into three plaits that form a thick braid, a style only worn by men and mated women. His square jaw would be severe if he didn't constantly smile at everyone who passes. He wears armor, with a tail flicking behind him.

All the troll men and women have that tail—an added appendage that extends from the base of their spines and then finishes in one tuft of hair the same color as the locks upon their head. I'd seen them used for practical things like picking up objects, but I'd also seen them used for fighting and affection.

Usually, when it was flicked like that, it showed someone's conflicted anger.

Joso is worried for you.

Butterflies take flight in my belly. He's been kind to me since I arrived, but I am still sorting out my feelings. He is the first man I've flirted with in a long time.

As for Lothar, the Lord of the Hunters standing on the left, he's harder to read. His broad shoulders make him imposing and he often wears a frown, but his tone remains caring. It is challenging yet for me to gauge the exact ages of these folk, but his paternal way speaks to me, so I choose to see him as a gentle, middle-aged man. Maybe even nurturing a family I hadn't had the pleasure of meeting yet.

The thought soothes me.

Before I came to live under the mountain, the beings inhabiting the underground city had been a chill-inducing horror story whispered around fires in the slave pens. The fires were lit to keep the huddled masses from freezing, and the stories were told to keep us in line.

Both worked well enough. In fact, I'd feared being brought to Enduvida. I didn't want to be anywhere near the bloodthirsty monsters who'd ended The Great War by unleashing a volcano upon their enemies—and the land itself. The king who'd made the order, Teo's father, possessed an indiscriminate rage. Millions died, including his own people. Only three hundred trolls survived.

The west has known nothing but sorrow since, but humans have suffered the worst. Even before the war, we had no gods, short lives, and little magic to defend ourselves. Once, giants enslaved us to build their towering cities. Now, only our spoken language remains—our last fragile tether to what we once were.

While I wouldn't call the trolls harmless, they were not nightmares. They were not anything like the giants. I was more than glad to make my home alongside them.

"I will not leave your side, not even for a second," Joso declares as we round another corner.

"Thank you," I respond with a grin of my own. "Both of you, really. It is kind of you two to accompany me this evening."

Lord Lothar grunts. "Remember, they want to be sold on the idea that some of you might be willing to help their kind bring forth a new generation." He pauses, his broad shoulders pulling back as he frowns. "That doesn't mean you should feel pressured. Remember—"

I wave my hand, cutting him off. "You will be there to help me divert unwanted advances. I am not worried."

I definitely fucking was, but he didn't need to know that. I could withstand feeling uneasy.

Lord Lothar inclines his head, pleased.

As we turn the corner down the gilded hallways and move into the dimly lit area where guests of the crown stay, my throat tightens.

Reaching up to touch my hair, I ensure that the massive pile of wavy auburn locks twisted atop my head hasn't come loose just as Joso looks back at me. My stomach flips when he gives me another lopsided smile. I wonder what he sees.

I am paler than most humans—especially after weeks underground—though my skin still retains the natural olive hue of my ancestors. Among humans, deep, unblemished skin is prized, rich and dark like polished mahogany, smooth as woven silk. I am neither.

My skin is a shade too light, an unfortunate quirk of fate that made my freckles stand out even more. They dust my nose and cheeks like spilled dye, stubborn marks that never fade, no matter how much I stay in the shade.

I'm average-height for my people, neither as slender as a silver thread nor as curvaceous as a winding riverbank. In most senses, I would consider myself just... somewhere in the middle.

But here, among the enduares, it doesn't seem to matter. Not because they find me beautiful, but because I am as foreign to them as they are to me. Their deep blue bodies, their elongated canines and sweeping tails, make human concerns about complexion and symmetry laughable. To them, I imagine I am just a strange, pale thing—not flawed, not perfect. Simply *other*.

But then, Joso cuts back into my thoughts.

"You look beautiful. Everything is going to be fine," Joso says softly, as if he could sense the unease I'd denied just moments before.

My heart stutters again, and I preen with the compliment. Beautiful. I wasn't usually beautiful for men.

"You are kind," I say, grateful.

A year ago, I would've turned down any advances from a potential partner, one of the reasons I liked the enduares was because they did not see the salvation my people offered as something to be taken advantage of, like our labor had been for so long.

These people cultivate relationships with their romantic partners in a way I'd never witnessed. They aren't regular marriages, like the one I almost had with my first love, Daniel, back in the giant capital of Zlosa; they are a joining of souls.

That is something I craved with unwavering devotion. I cannot survive being made to feel small again, and I do not share myself easily.

From my understanding, their version of matehood is meant to be *healing,* both physically and emotionally.

Thanks to the goddess-blessed gem they have put in my chest—the Fuegorra—life is not only made possible under the mountain where the sun's rays don't reach, but it is extended for my kind.

Instead of fifty or sixty withering winters, it was presumed we would live several hundreds of years along with the enduares.

And not only that... but I would be given a chance to have what I had failed at in my old life. A family.

When Joso looks at me, there are no tell-tale signs of the goddess Grutabela choosing an 'other half' for me, but the Wise Woman had explained that these things didn't have to be instantaneous.

The attention is welcome. But now is not the time for distractions.

The greatest gift the weaving mistress back in the giant capital had given me was the ability to read so I could make patterns. I was a quick learner; I'd been able to pick up the enduares' unique form of writing easily.

I know that when I see the king, I must do my best to impress him. I will greet him with 'Your Majesty' and use the formal versions of common phrases. Hopefully, the morning I'd dedicated to intense study would prove helpful.

Joso stops before we turn into the space before the Elven King's suite and takes my hand.

"Remember what I said when I came to retrieve you? The elvish folk can be brutal. I'm here to serve you," he reassures.

I look between him and Lord Lothar, who nods his head, and I feel *safe*. A beautiful, brilliant safety that radiates from the space between my heart and lungs and fans out around my ribs. Something I'd been robbed of in my old life that was given freely here.

I push onto my toes, taking Joso's hand, and kiss his cheek. The texture of enduar skin is more akin to a very fine suede than supple flesh. As our hands slide together, I can feel how the ultra-short coat is soft to the touch in one direction, while slightly abrasive in the other.

He squeezes my arm, and my breath stutters.

"I remember," I say.

A purple blush highlights his sharp cheekbones. His face grows as luminous as the crystals dotting the ceiling of the cavern. "Thank you."

Then, I break away from both of them, curving around the hallway and catching sight of the elves. They stand taller than humans, like the enduares, but they have skin tones much more akin to my kind—an entire spectrum of black, beige, and white.

Living wood, they were called in one of the scrolls I'd read. Each has one body part carved from a massive elder tree that gifts them magic from their gods at birth, though nothing like that is visible. In fact, I'd wager it's far too personal to display outwardly, though they didn't seem to be ashamed of referencing this unusual practice in casual conversations.

The guards' faces are sharp and pointed. They have elegantly angled noses, gaunt cheeks, almond eyes, and highly arched eyebrows above shining pupils in every shade. Apparently, their long fingers were impossibly adept at handling any piece of machinery the enduares allowed them to touch.

As my finely crafted shoes clack against the stone floor, the guards don't so much as turn to look at me.

Perhaps they don't want to risk a wrinkle in the shiny fabrics strapped around the shoulders of their leather armor.

My eyes catch on the cloth, and I think of the few samples they brought as gifts. That fabric is beautiful, more luminous than stone silk, but seemingly as tough as steel. It won't be easy to cut through a cloth like that.

Moving into position, I dip my head.

It's all right, Arlet. You are all right.

A voice rings through the hallway when I open my mouth to greet them and request an audience with their king.

"FIRELOCKS!"

Strong and guttural, but definitely masculine. My shoulders creep up toward my chin at the sound, and I grit my teeth, not wanting to turn back.

"Arlet!" the shout comes again.

The elven guards tighten their grips on the wooden handles of their short swords as they cast us annoyed looks.

"Forgive me. Just a moment," I say quickly and turn to see the only unsavory part about living in Enduvida.

Lord Vann, personal advisor to the Enduar King, wears a scowl as he charges toward me. I glare at the large, mountainous man with skin as blue as the cloudless sky in summer.

I can see the muscles in his forearms rippling as if he were preparing to strangle me. His silver braid flows freely behind him, and his steel-grey eyes flash as he crosses the distance with alarming speed.

"What the fuck do you think you are doing?!" he demands.

I huff up at him. *"Stop yelling,"* I grit out. "I'm about to meet with the king. Do not ruin this."

Vann's jaw muscles tense, and he lets out a growl. "The walls are thick. He won't be able to hear anything, and his guards don't seem to care."

He jerks his head toward the men in front of the door.

The one who had glared at me earlier lifts his chin in an impetuous smirk. "This is not our first time visiting the trolls. We are well acquainted with your barbarity."

The other huffs a laugh, and I watch the blue men around me cast sour looks in return.

I step toward Vann, determined to get him out of here. Fast.

"King Teo, the man you answer to, told me that it would benefit us all if we made a good impression on the elves," I say firmly. "And he didn't ask, I *volunteered*."

The first time I met Lord Vann, I was caring for Estela after a serious injury. He came to the door, demanding to see her, but I refused, as she was still asleep. As her best friend, there wasn't a chance in the bubbling mouth of the hottest volcano that I'd let someone near her in a vulnerable state.

He called me and all the other humans that'd come with me ungrateful, as if we hadn't taken up positions to help after being treated for medical conditions. I myself had spent my first week here training on enduar sitting looms, volunteering with the children, and helping to heal his future queen *out of gratitude.*

When I told the Wise Woman Liana to make him leave, he didn't like that, and he's been a burr in my side every since.

Sadly, not everyone shares my bitter feelings. Apparently, he is something of a war hero among the enduares. Some call him, 'The Cleaver', in reference both to a long, wide blade that cut through ten thousand foes and the fact that the king, who had fought at his side, was called, 'The Butcher of Giants.'

The brute shakes his head. "There are other ways to make a good impression. For one, let him observe you from a safe distance during the wedding ceremony."

I blink. This is the same man who insulted me for the color of my hair, something I had always been tormented over, and bit me when I tried to tend to his wounds after he'd nearly died. Rallying my composure, I flash him a saccharine-sweet smile and decide to spew a bit of my own venom.

"Why, Lord Vann, it almost sounds like you care."

He sucks his teeth. "What will you do when one of them grabs you and presses a knife to your throat? You come from humble means, so I'll explain this slowly: just because we seek them as allies doesn't mean they are friends."

Ugh, fuck him.

"Humble means? I can read twice as well as you." Pinching the bridge of my nose, I sigh. This always happens when we're together, and no good comes from his incessant need to bicker. I turn my head to look at Joso. "Can you take Lord Vann away?"

"Firelocks, stop this," he starts as Joso moves toward him with an apologetic expression.

"No," I bite back. "For the first time in ages, a few leaders see that my people hold power."

I don't want that power to be rooted solely in our ability to preserve other bloodlines, though I do long for a family of my own. No, I dream of more. A future where we thrive, where our history stands beside the great societies of the world. I believe Estela's wedding is the first step. The first real, lasting change.

No one will ruin that tonight.

"She knows what she's doing," Joso says firmly. "And we did get our orders from the king."

Vann grinds his teeth, turns, and then storms away like one of the children I help at the school. But not before he calls over his shoulder, "If none of you will recognize the insanity in an unarmed human spending an evening with the same man who used to collect the teeth of his enemies during the war and *wear them*, then I will just wait to clean up the mess."

I watch him disappear around the bend of the grey stone studded with golden geometric carvings and let my shoulders fall back to a normal height.

He might be the only man I've ever met that makes me feel so vexed, and yet, he leaves me, surprisingly, unafraid.

Taking another breath, I turn back and walk up to the elvish guards. The nerves mount once more, but I face the things that frighten me without hesitation. I dip my chin to my chest as I sink into a shallow curtsy.

My brief study on elven culture revealed that they appreciate the feminine art to such salutes—similar to my old giant masters.

"Good evening. I've come to request an audience with His Majesty, King Arion."

CHAPTER 1
ARLET

Present Day, or one year after the first meeting with the Elf King

"Arlet, you need to get ready, or you'll be late," Feli calls from behind one of the stone desks. She's the tall, lithe enduar woman with dark blue hair who has been helping me establish the school.

"Maestra Feli, you are distracting the children!" I tut.

She makes a clicking sound with her purple tongue, shakes her head, and goes back to organizing charcoal writing rods on the other side of the large classroom. The space is filled with stone desks, spell lights, and drawings of fungi, historical figures, and common words in both the enduar and human tongues.

I take a deep breath, and go back to reading a scroll on the second dynasty of the troll bronze age. The spot between my shoulder blades itches as my mind wanders to review the mental list of things I have to get done before leaving.

Add two scrolls to my reading roster, check.

Help Feli correct the sentences the first years wrote, half check.

Visit Fira in the weaving cavern to help her with a banner for the Mating Journey, not check.

I let out a soft groan into my hands. I have too much to do.

My ascension ceremony is tonight, and I am actively trying to ignore it. After a year of dedicated service in the face of rapid population growth, Queen Estela and King Teo had chosen me to receive an official title in their court.

Not for weaving, as Fira still held that title, but for teaching. I'm meant to oversee the development of a project I'd taken to calling The Lorepath—or a structured system for teaching a robust mix of culture, basic skills, language, and practical knowledge between the humans and enduares.

The project is exciting. The work is agonizingly frustrating at times, and brilliantly fulfilling at others. But did I feel that I had earned a title for simply doing what was necessary? *Eh.*

There is to be another festival in a few days anyway, the Mating Journey—which would help even more couples find their other half. We'd all been working on that, in between the tempest of every day life.

Wasn't enough *enough*? Why did we need to do this for me?

Around me, the children scoop up fingerfuls of glittering paint, smearing it over their canvases in a chaotic, joyful mess. The sight makes my heart swell with pride. Enough that I drop my scroll yet again, letting it fall into the chaos of my already overburdened desk, and brace my forearms against the stone.

The last year of my life has felt like a decade. First, I arrived in this city and threw myself into the complicated task of assimilating into a new culture just as war broke out between the enduares and giants. I took up a position as a weaver, and spent three months making enough fabric to cover the ruins of Zlosa, the old giant capital.

And then, nearly six months later, after two devastating battles, the Giant Kingdom fell, and thousands of humans were finally free. Most of them chose to relocate here, under the mountain, rather than have to build up a new life from nothing.

It was pure chaos for a while, but we have managed well.

Through it all, I clung to my work and let it provide order in a time of turmoil. I split my time between weaving and teaching. Each day, that decision is put to the test.

But it is better to be busy than in pain.

Especially because the outside world remains a dangerous place. One foe defeated tended to make three more rear their ugly heads, and most of our days are spent preparing for an inevitable conflict with the elves.

But war belongs to the soldiers. To the sovereigns. I belong here, either in the schoolhouse halls and behind my loom, shaping beauty where I am needed. I'd only accepted Teo and Estela's request because they assured me that my new position on the council would not suddenly make me a cog in a political machine.

My dreams of the humans changing the world would not only come because of bloodshed. I needed to speak a new language, one learned in peace, if my work was going to have the impact I hoped for.

And my one harrowing night with the elf king had shown me that my favorite place to be was not squabbling with foreign officials, but among friends, and with children. They need me as much as I need them.

"Maestra Arlet," one of the girls calls up to me.

I crouch beside her desk. "Yes, *mi amor?*"

She beams. "My mamá said there's going to be a party for you tonight. Is that true?"

Feli calls out from the back. "That's right, Sarita! And Arlet should leave soon to get ready."

I glance at Feli and correct her. "Soon."

"Now!" the head teacher insists with a laugh. *"Ilkari!"* she calls, using the enduar word for children. "Help me encourage Maestra Arlet!"

She starts tapping a beat against the desk, and the others eagerly join in. I smile at her simple song. She works with the crystal singers when she isn't here, teaching reading, writing, and numbers.

"Go now, Lady Arlet! Go now, Lady Arlet!" the children chant.

Laughing, I raise my hands in surrender, touched, despite the use of a title I hadn't officially earned. "Fine! I will leave."

As I turn to leave, a small hand tugs at my skirt. I look down to see Miti, one of the cave-born enduar children, surrounded by a group of human boys and girls.

She struggles to meet others' eyes, preferring to draw her thoughts rather than speak them.

I crouch, and she slides a piece of paper toward me.

I lift it carefully and take in the image she has drawn. In flowing lines, she's drawn me standing before the king and queen, receiving a delicate coronet reserved for members of the court. My bright red hair is twisted atop my head, and a green dress cascades down the palace steps.

Though I had planned to wear purple to my ascension ceremony, Miti's drawing reminds me of another gown hung in the corner of my closet.

"This is beautiful! Look at that. A green gown," I muse.

The corner of her mouth twists.

"Do you like this gown?" I reach out, palm up, and she slips her slight hand into mine.

It takes a moment, but she nods. My heart squeezes. *I am absolutely wearing this dress instead.*

"May I keep this?" I ask softly.

She nods again, her smile falling and her gaze moving to my desk in the corner covered with scrolls. Lesson plans that seemed to take up more time than there were hours in a day.

"I hope to see you tonight, at the party," I whisper. "And don't worry. I won't stop coming here to spend time with you, it just won't be every day anymore."

She smiles again—just a little—and then, with deliberate hesitation, raises her face toward mine. Her gaze hovers near my cheek, not quite meeting my eyes, before she suddenly leans in, wrapping her arms around my neck.

I hold her close, pressing a kiss to her temple. "I'll be back tomorrow. And maybe I'll bring you a gift."

Her arms tighten. It takes a moment before I can gently pry myself away, lifting her hands to my cheek in a show of affection before brushing out of the room.

My eyes burn as I glance at her drawing once more. Then, with a deep breath, I tuck it into my pocket and hurry out of the school.

Having a massive city in a series of enormous caves was a feat that only the enduares could do well. Parts that were blocked off or destroyed had been slowly rebuilt. Among the many changes the city has experienced, one of them is a new housing section for members of the royal court.

My new home has been carved alongside the palace, nestled in the newly rebuilt district with elegant dwellings reserved for council members and their families.

Lady Arlet.

I grimace. Today, I ascend, formally appointed as leader of education—both here in the caves and the human settlement above.

Lady *Arlet,* I repeat.

I just... don't want people to look at me differently. It would be agonizing to watch friends turn into formal acquaintances just because I wasn't *just Arlet* anymore. My desire was to be approachable.

Twisting my hands, I savor the feel of the stone silk I wove and listen to a city now-bustling with people.

Lady Arlet, I say one last time.

I never imagined this future. But, above all, I am grateful for this new life under the mountain even if it has not ended up the way I would've hoped—mated with children. But if I cannot find a mated husband, I can still nurture. Work. I can still create.

And for the gaps my duties cannot fill... well, I have recently discovered the romance section in the royal library.

As I step outside the school, a familiar figure leans casually against the archway. Lord Vann, Advisor to the King, unofficial leader of our military, and royal pain in my ass. His silver braid gleams under the cavern's light as he smirks, arms crossed over his broad chest.

"You do know your ascension is today, right?" he says. "It's tradition for the newly ascended to receive a ceremonial token from a court member."

"And I suppose that is meant to be you?" I say.

His grin sharpens. "I've been waiting a quarter hour. You're going to be late to your ceremony."

I glare. "Not yet."

Forcing myself to meet his gaze, I notice the tear in his sleeve and the smudges on his knuckles and chin. He looks tired—probably from staying up late inventing new ways to torment me.

The city clock tower strikes half-past noon. I do the calculations in my head.

"Mierda."

When our eyes meet again, his smug smile is already in place.

"Well, then, spare me the formal gift and try not to make me more late," I say, pushing past him.

"I thought you would appreciate a taste of our old traditions," he continues.

I stop and turn back, narrowing my eyes. "That *tradition* was meant for stone bending apprentices completing their first cycle of mastery. Not for court ascensions."

His eyebrows lift. "And how do you know that?"

"Because I've spent the last three months combing through the royal library all while running back and forth between the school and the weaving cave. *Because* I am ensuring that your culture isn't reduced to half-remembered myths thrown around by smug warriors with nothing better to do."

He lets out a laugh. "So those scrolls I've seen you carry around are good for something?"

"Try not to look so surprised," I grumble, resuming my journey. "And if you wanted to give a gift, I'm told there will be time for that after the ceremony."

"Like I said, this was meant to be before," he calls after me.

I don't stop walking.

He catches up to my side. I glance up to find his expression serious.

"Some advice, one council member to another, I know how uneasy you are in front of crowds."

I let out a mangled huff. "I will be fine."

"Well then. Just try not to trip in your fancy gown, Firelocks."

"I'll manage," I say and pick up my pace.

~

Even I have to admit the Ascension celebration is breathtaking.

The Enduar Palace once served as the summer home to enduar kings and queens of old. Golden in appearance, it is the only building in all of Enduvida made from the same strong metal as the signature armor the soldiers wear.

Enduar metal is strong, and it combines beautifully with the bluish gray of the cavern. I stare a while longer at the massive building, its golden facade gleaming under the shifting crystal light.

Towering statues of past enduares still stand, each with names carved underneath. The grand steps leading to the entrance are wide, easily spanning fifteen paces across, split into two tiers. They were made to create a deliberate divide—a physical reminder of the difference between ruler and subject. Now, they serve as the pathway I must ascend.

I don't want to be seen as above the others. I just want to help.

At the top of the grand steps, Estela stands resplendent in a golden gown. She is a short woman, almost a full head shorter than me, and has thick, dark brown curly hair that perfectly compliments her magically glowing light brown skin.

Teo is at her side in simple black garb that highlights his paler blue complexion and light silver hair. He's massive next to her, something I might consider threatening if he wasn't the most adoring mate I've ever met.

Behind them is the official spiritual leader of our people, Mother Liana. An old enduar woman with pure, white hair, and kind eyes. She's never looked like anything other than a benevolent goddess, one who has spent her eternities choosing to cultivate empathy over wrath. Tonight, she is dressed in a flowing black gown with hand-stitched swirling patterns of quartz.

I bite my lip, wondering if later, she'll finally share where she had gotten her elaborate dresses from.

Teo's and Estela's crowns glimmer in the shifting glow as the stone singers weave their voices through the third verse of my favorite song, *Velra'Endu*. A love ballad.

Though it holds no political significance, it is my day, and they sing what I choose.

I sit at the bottom of the palace steps, among the council members, looking up at the sovereigns. To my left, Lord Lothar—still alive and well, and raising a few orphaned children with his new mate—watches the proceedings with quiet approval. To my right, Lady Fira, the master of the weavers, offers me a warm smile. Beyond them, the other council members greet me with nods and hushed congratulations.

Behind us is a grand audience filled with anyone in the city who wished to attend. There are... a lot of people—more than I expected. My students and fellow weavers, the hunters who catch our food, the stone benders who craft and fix our tools and city. I try not to look back for fear of growing light-headed.

Teo steps forward, and the crowd goes quiet. The music shifts to a quiet hum that plays along the crystals.

The music tugs at the nerves inside of me, gently soothing them so that I can breathe. Songs that were sung into the crystals couldn't put emotions in one's soul that weren't already there, but they did a good job at bending and shaping feelings to suit any required tone.

Calm is just what I need right now.

"Good evening, friends!Before the people of Enduvida, we present Lady Arlet, who has shown great devotion to our people. Today, she takes her place among the council. Lady Arlet of the humans, approach!" he commands.

Teo, Estela, and Mother Liana look down at me from the top of the grand steps, the dais bathed in the shifting glow of crystal light. The columns stretch high above, carved with the familiar, geometric symbols of the enduares. The low hum of the stone singers blends with the hush of the gathered crowd.

I force myself to stand, despite the tremor in my legs. When I turn, the sheer size of the audience makes my breath hitch. Nobles, warriors, scholars—everywhere I look, eyes are on me.

The grand steps seem more daunting than in a practical outfit, and there are only so many places the yards of green silk can fit. Unfortunately, my path leads me straight past Lord Vann.

He watches, arms crossed, expression unreadable in my few

stolen glances. I don't slow. But his words about not tripping echo in my head.

The steps are steeper than I expected. Or maybe it's just my legs, stiff with nerves, struggling beneath the weight of my green gown. My breath tightens. The moment stretches on, each step loud in the vast hall.

At last, I reach the dais and step before my king and queen.

I lower into a curtsy, the sleek fabric of my dress pooling around me. My heart pounds against my ribs.

And then, I stand. Relief floods my chest. I made it.

Estela gestures to Liana, who steps forward. She carries a silver circlet, polished to a gleam.

"Lady Arlet," Liana calls out with a smile. "You have built a foundation of learning within the caves and beyond. You have given the people your wisdom, hands, and heart. As such, you have been called to toil longer, but now, as a lady in this blossoming court. Your sovereigns ask you to help bring our peoples together in a new age."

A dull roar sounds in my ears as the Wise Woman raises the circlet.

"Do you accept this duty?"

My heart beats once. Then twice.

Work is good. Work is grounding. I will give everything I've got to make the future brighter, despite my dislike of the title.

"I do."

She places the circlet on my brow, and the moment it settles, a gentle pulse of energy ripples through me, as if the mountain itself acknowledges the oath I have taken.

"Then turn, Lady Arlet, our Keeper of Learning," Liana proclaims.

Applause rises in a wave, filling the great hall with warmth. I lift my chin, taking it all in.

Lady Arlet.

The title rests on my shoulders firmly. There is something nice about it. It doesn't feel as bad as I would've thought.

Vann catches my eye and I realize he looks much different than he did earlier today. Hair combed. Fine tunic. My stomach clenches, almost anticipating his disapproval.

He holds my stare, and then slowly, he smiles.

For some reason, this is my day, and yet, I can't help but think of a thousand memories involving him. A year of goading and teasing and rivalries. But we would be on the council together. Not quite working together, but there would be meetings. And parties. And... well. He is Teo's closest friend, as I am Estela's.

Someone would have to make the first move in bridging the gap between us.

I dip my head toward him as he stares up at me.

And then... slowly. He dips his head back.

A smile pulls at my lips. I look away, feeling triumphant as the music starts again.

Just as I hold my hand up to wave to the people, I catch sight of the group of children making their way up the steps.

Miti stands at the front, pointing at my green dress in smiling. I grab the skirt and give it a small flourish. She squeals in delight.

The singers invite the children to join their song as the council members stand, bringing gifts to a table stationed at the bottom of the steps. My smile widens when Lady Fira stands, holding a new bolt of cloth.

She had been the woman who took me in as an apprentice upon my arrival. I missed seeing her every day, but I would be glad for the time we would spend on the council.

More people come up, leaving their trinkets as I watch, bowing my head from above, and grinning from ear to ear.

"Thank you all," I call out as loud as I can.

As the line begins to dwindle, Estela reaches out to touch my arm.

"Felicidades, querida," she says. I laugh and turn around to hug her. She pushes onto her toes and presses a kiss to both of my cheeks.

"I hate to ruin the joviality, but sadly, we must have a meeting directly following the feast," she murmurs in my ear.

My heart squeezes. Something about her tone feels ominous. Rallying my efforts, I turn back to the crowd and listen to the rest of the song.

Worry was for later.

CHAPTER 2
VANN

The queen arrives before the king and perches atop her throne. Estela smiles at everyone, her ethereal glow lighting the room. Blessed by the two goddesses, they say she shines like the swirling mass before the birth of a star.

Teo, my blood brother, sure thinks that's true.

Goddess-blessed or not, she brought mounds of trouble with her. While Teo would argue the conflicts were inevitable, I'm not so sure. We had been doing well enough—until the humans became part of our people.

In the end, my opinion on the matter of Estela and the humans was worth less than dust. She's Teo's mate, my queen, and the mother of the heir to the Enduar Kingdom. As personal advisor to Teo, my loyalty is to her.

I suppose, despite her trouble, she has earned my loyalty well enough.

Mother Liana, the Wise Woman and spiritual leader of Enduvida, stands at her right side, watching as the others trickle in.

The council chamber is hushed. Two elevated stone thrones, decorated with jewels, are the focal point of the room, but the large marble table is arranged at the bottom of the dais. Chairs have been placed around it, enough for all fifteen council members.

There are polished blue kyanite crystal clusters, cut from deeper caverns and positioned around the room, that cast long shadows across the stone walls.

Tonight, my *ailment* is relentless. My limbs are colder than usual, and the stillness of the air is pressing down on me like a blanket of snow.

I sit stiffly in my seat, arms crossed, watching as the others settle in while the post-ascension party rages outside.

I would've liked to attend, but I've been at Teo's side, going over reports since Arlet's ceremony.

The months after the war between the giants and ourselves have passed rapidly. With the giants gone, the elves have turned into the main enemy that threatens our borders.

Mrath, the sister of King Arion, leads an elven rebellion. She is our only ally, currently. Taking down the giant court would not have been possible without her and her assistance of two thousand troops. Part of our agreement was that we would help to get her the High Elven Throne when we were ready. The consensus is that we aren't. Not until the new settlement is finished and we have a secure home for every new family.

As is to be expected, Mrath is impatient. A month ago, we sent a new letter to King Arion, trying to offer solutions that would smooth our relationship over, and ensure that no war breaks out while we are still teetering along like toddlers.

According to Teo something arrived from them today, and that's why we are here.

"Welcome to your first council meeting, Lady Arlet," the dual-blessed queen says brightly. "I'm sorry it's not about a more pleasant topic."

My eyes shift to the doorway—to the reason for the celebration. If I had a heart, it would have stopped at the sight of Arlet, undone from her pristine emerald-green ceremony attire.

Her shoes are gone, her hair half-falling from the bun atop her head. A rare sight indeed—a wild evolution of a usually well-trained creature.

The corners of her mouth quirk up, pride and nerves glimmering in her eyes.

She gives a small dip. "Happy to be here," she responds.

Svanna, an enduar woman, grins. She is leader of the miners and training facilities for new warriors, but looking at her, I almost laugh. She wears simple clothes to such an important event—leather pants with a white tunic. When she begins to clap, her braid shifts to show off the two mating marks proudly glowing on her neck. The rest of the council follows.

My hands stay folded, fingers pressing into the fabric of my doublet. The weight in my limbs is spreading—a creeping numbness that starts in my fingertips and rolls up my arms like ice weaving through my veins.

"Iryth told me you still managed to dance with a hoard of men before slipping away," Svanna teases Arlet.

"It's true!" Thorne, the Elven Emissary, calls from the back. "I was even graced with a dance."

Gods, he's insufferable. Even being a half-human, he is every bit as irritating as any elf.

Arlet giggles, her cheeks tinged pink.

My mouth parts slightly, a familiar pressure forming in my chest —one I know isn't truly there. But it spreads, dull and aching, like a phantom limb trying to remind me of something long lost.

"Where is Iryth now?" Arlet asks, ignoring Thorne's flirtation as she scans the room for Svanna's mate, another enduar woman. Her and Svanna are one of the oldest mated pairs in Enduvida.

"Home with Sama. She's still spared from excessive meetings," Svanna says, casting a mock glare at Queen Estela.

Estela grins, and more people take their seats. Arlet, however, remains standing in the center of the room.

"Forgive my ignorance, but I'm not sure where to sit," she says, slipping her feet into her shoes and brushing a few wavy strands of ruby red from her face.

Ra'Salore smiles. He is the leader of a group of enduares with the ability to stone bend. Most of his days are spent tending to his new family and toiling in front of a forge, but he looks relaxed tonight. "There's no order to this chaos. Perhaps you should sit next to Lord Vann."

Her smile falters as she looks at me.

I hate bearing the brunt of her disappointment—it drudges up resentment. Most enduares accepted the humans with ease. I suppose it was their way.

But I grew up in a time when we hardly deigned to mix with our own allies.

Humans think they understand us, but they have no idea what it was like before, in the golden age of my people. The pride and glory of being enduar is dead. It will never be resurrected through books, renovations, or children's lessons.

Arlet tries too hard. Gives too much. She isn't ungrateful like the others, but she's desperate to make everyone like her.

Everyone... except me.

It's strange, given she once saved my life. A fact she doesn't seem to consider often, though it constantly plays through my mind.

The numbness creeps further through my upper body. I flex my fingers beneath the black marble table, trying to force warmth back into my limbs.

My condition always works the same. It starts with something triggering an intense emotion of any kind—anger, fear, longing, desire, irritation. Muted versions of said feelings then echo in the space where my heart once was, and a slow, crushing cold ices my veins. If I'm not careful, it will eventually lock up my joints and make me immobile.

I take a deep breath and turn away as Arlet sits down. I don't breathe in the scent of freshly washed cloth. Don't notice the way her thighs press together as she crosses her legs.

Luckily for my sanity, the door to the throne room slams shut. King Teo and Lord Lothar stride in. Teo's usual confidence is dampened by his tight grip on a thick stone slab, roughly the length of a knife.

Estela stands. "Well?" Her gaze drops to the object he carries. "What on earth is that?"

He lifts the tablet, and I realize it's been engraved.

My hands clench. The movement sends another ripple of cold through me, the edges of my vision tinged with frost.

"This is the missive from the elves," he says sourly.

Svanna sits up. "The elves... engraved a stone slab to send a letter? Do they think we don't know how to use paper?"

Thorne pipes up from the back. "Come now, you can't tell me your kind never wrote on stone tablets." He gestures broadly at the impressive stonework around us.

"Stone is impractical for records," Svanna argues. "Not only for storage but because the longer the slab, the easier it is to break. The paper we craft from rock undergoes a fine milling process. It's not unlike the paper your kind makes from wood."

"Yes, and enduares have been using stone paper for nearly a thousand years," Arlet interjects. "The insinuation is that enduar texts would be so primitive in our age is insulting."

I roll my eyes, forgetting that Arlet has become an amateur historian since starting her project, Lorepath.

Ulla, the leader of the healers, smirks at the elf to her right. "Exactly right, Lady Arlet. Forgive Lord Thorne."

"*Emissary*, not *lord*," I grumble.

Thorne is Mrath's right-hand. Even as an ally, I can't help but think she's a snake. No reason her old lover wouldn't be one as well.

"Responding to our request for peace with an insult doesn't bode well for the situation," Teo says, his voice clipped. He moves toward the throne, Lothar trailing behind to stand near the raised platform.

"The elves do nothing without careful calculation," Teo continues. "I think this is meant to show just how weak they think we are."

"From what you've explained," Thorne nods in Arlet's general direction, "I'm inclined to agree."

Teo stares the tablet. He looks at it like a man tired of war. Tired of scraping and scrimping to survive.

He has two children now. I know he wishes to be with them over charging across the battlefield.

The newest council member sits forward. Arlet folds her hands gracefully in her lap, feigning complete sobriety, as if I hadn't seen her drink three glasses of mead before I slipped away.

"Have we already begun studying its contents? I would appreciate knowing exactly what it says," Queen Estela intones.

Teo passes the missive to Lothar, who has a better understanding of elvish. The enduar clears his throat, then begins to read.

"To the rulers of Enduvida, we have received your message. Frankly, we were surprised by your request to ease tensions. Your war with the giants, and your conquests with the humans, have disturbed the balance of the continent, and without a third party to regulate your power, we worry for the future of our world. As such, we have decided to take the responsibility of peace upon our shoulders and contest your growth."

I grind my teeth, but the rest of the room remains silent. Only the distant hum of machinery filtering air into the city and the riotous festivities outside fill the void.

Lothar continues. "There is but one way to avoid the destruction of your people at the hand of our troops. It is a simple solution—a symbolic offering to prove your sincerity. King Arion requests a human virgin to bear the elven heir. We do not require time to sort through the crop and ask for the flame-haired one called Arlet. If our request is met, a binding peace agreement will be brokered, and Enduvida will be spared a second war."

"What?" I blurt out.

Every head in the room turns to Arlet.

She stiffens, her fingers pressing into the arms of her chair, as if she can root herself there.

I see the tension in her jaw and feel the dread sink low in my belly.

King Arion had met her *once*. He is a fickle sovereign. How did he muster enough power of mind to continuously think of *her?*

But deep in my mind, I understand. Arlet, in all her talent and fearless determination, is not easy to forget.

King Teo exhales through his nose.

Estela shakes her head, standing to take the stone slab from Lothar.

"That poisonous man," she hisses.

Arlet takes a sharp breath.

"I don't understand," she starts. "He wants me to marry him?"

Teo nods.

"But why?"

"It doesn't matter. No way in the fiery pits of hell will we ever let him anywhere near you. This is a trap—I'm sure of it," Estela responds.

I agree with her wholeheartedly. Arion had betrayed us before in favor of a relationship with the giants. Even with the giants defeated, the elf could not be trusted. A man who lies is bound to do it again.

My fingers curl into fists so tight my nails bite into my palms. My arms feel heavy.

King Teo exhales sharply. "Two months," he murmurs. "That's what they offer?"

Lothar nods grimly. "Two months. No more."

Thorne leans forward, eyes sharp. "King Arion does not request—he demands."

Arlet stands abruptly, her chair scraping against the stone floor.

"I—none of this makes sense," she starts, one hand pressing against her upper thigh while the other brushes hair out of her face. "Lord Thorne, you know his culture. His kingdom. What is he playing at?"

Thorne purses his lips. "Well, he is very keen to have a human. It's no secret he remains unwed, and desires an heir."

Arlet's chest rises and falls rapidly. "So I... I must be the easy choice?"

Thorne shrugs, but Estela scoffs. "Who gives a fuck what he wants?"

I grunt, finding myself once again in agreement with my queen.

Teo studies the redhead at my side, his voice low but firm. "I understand everyone's concern. However, the elves would not write something they did not intend to uphold. It would not be wise to let the decision go unconsidered."

Estela frowns. "While that is true, we have spent considerable time defining our laws and policies with personal choice in mind. The only person who can say yes or no to this offer is Arlet."

Lord Ra'Salore scoffs. "Sacrifice is a necessary element of service in the council. The trade is a human bride for ensured peace.

"Peace with Arion," Thorne interjects, his voice low. "Which would be in direct conflict with your allyship with Mrath."

As words are shot throughout the room, I see Arlet build up her defenses. Her face goes blank, and her hands still. Slowly, she sits back down, and in an act I'm sure she doesn't identify, she leans toward me.

I blink once. My tail, which had been resting on the floor under my chair up to this point, seeks the leg of her chair. It curls round as I let out a long breath. Then it pulls just a little.

Her head whips toward me, and I let go immediately, coughing once.

What are you doing?

Shifting forward in my seat, I put a little space between us and join the conversation.

"We have promised Mrath that we would assist her in claiming the elven throne. There was always going to be a war—this offer could hurt us just as much as it helps.

Estela purses her lips and returns her gaze to Arlet.

"It would be good to know your thoughts in this discussion, Lady Arlet."

The redhead at my side looks around the room, her expression unreadable.

The missive's words play through my mind.

"If our request is met, a binding peace agreement will be brokered, and Enduvida will be spared a second war."

Helping others is Arlet's addiction. It's simply too sweet for her to resist. I watch every subtle move of her body, willing her to put herself first for once in her godsdamn life.

She takes a deep breath.

"Becoming Arion's bride would support his rule, leading to a longer rule. In the long run, I think it would be more dangerous than outright refusing."

I lean back, almost smiling.

That's. Fucking. Right.

"I think it is important to know what exactly happened when you met him the first time?" I cut in, voice low. I need details.

She hesitates. Then, "I escorted him to the Festival of Endu. He told me he liked humans. I don't remember much else before the attack."

Teo leans forward, fingers steepled. "And now, he seeks you in marriage?"

"This is not a marriage proposal," Arlet says bitterly. "It's a breeding order."

A guttural growl rises in my throat, and a few heads turn toward me. The ache in my limbs sharpens, creeping up my spine, spreading through my body. My hands curl into fists against the cold stiffness taking hold.

Lothar shifts his weight in the chair. "I understand the gravity of what we're discussing, but we don't need to respond right away. We have just finished one celebration, and in a few days, we have another for the Mating Journey. Since this will not be a simple answer, I suggest we take time to review our options and speak with Mrath."

"She will not take this news well," Thorne warns. "I would tread lightly."

I grit my teeth, my breath coming slower, my veins sluggish as though something were freezing the warmth right out of me.

Another drop of hatred seeps into my mind, poisoning my thoughts. It is madness that we even have to entertain this conversation.

When I look at Arlet, something fierce scratches at my chest. I'd been too angry—too worried during the meeting—and I would pay for that. But if it meant she wouldn't consider this offer, it would be worth it.

The softer notes of the clock tower play outside, marking midnight.

"It is late, and it seems that we will not come to a conclusion tonight. If we need time to think about this and speak with our ally, then I request the meeting to end."

I feel every gaze in the room.

Teo looks at his wife, and for a second, jealousy stirs in my chest. Not for Estela, but because I miss that sensation. I miss having someone who was my partner in all things.

It is Queen Estela who speaks next. "Lothar, Ra'Salore, Vann, and Svanna, will reconvene during our regular meeting time tomorrow. You may rest for the evening."

Teo nods in agreement, and I don't wait for anyone to say another word. I stand and leave, yanking the door open unceremoniously.

I hear the sound of her shoes first—impractical little heels designed to bridge the gap between human and enduar heights.

Adra always wore slippers or boots.

"Vann!" Arlet calls.

For a second, my dull, frost-coated emotions spike again. It's unhealthy. I'll pay the price for such feelings soon.

I let out a sigh and turn, despite the stiffness in my limbs.

She's closer than I expected—almost close enough to reach out and grab. I wish I could make her swear she'd never consider leaving.

But that's senseless.

She said no.

The matter is settled.

Her brown eyes search my face. "Thank you for ending the meeting. I... I didn't want to be there."

One of the straps of her gown slips off her shoulder, the fabric dipping near the swell of her breast.

I look at the ceiling, but remember the way she shifted toward me in her seat when she felt unsafe. My hand presses into my pocket and is met with a silky texture.

Damn. The token I'd tried to give her.

"I didn't do it for you. I was tired," I grunt. It wasn't a total lie—my arms are starting to stiffen and ache.

I almost leave, but instead, I pull out the green hair ribbon with little clusters of green stones hanging off the end. "This was meant to be for you."

She blinks once, brows furrowing, and then takes the small gift.

"Thank you," she says quietly.

I incline my head toward her, just as my gaze catches on her delicate, freckled throat. The sight is enticing, which is exactly the opposite of what it should be.

Without my full control, my tail still moves towards her, the tip hitting her calf lightly. But, instead of responding, I leave her there and run away like a damn child.

CHAPTER 3

ARLET

One year ago,

I hold my breath as one of the elven guards extends a graceful hand, the color of an oak wood plank, then grasps the door handle, and twists. He slips inside, and I hear murmured elvish filter out from the open metal door. I don't make out any of the phrases.

While I wait, Joso returns from having escorted Lord Vann away, and he and Lord Lothar observe from the shadows.

The door is pushed open further, though I am not invited in. Instead, the king steps out.

He's two heads taller than me, and I look up at him, mesmerized by the otherworldly beauty. A part of me wants to shrink away.

His skin is pale gold, and his hair is so blond it is almost white. His sharp, high cheekbones cast shadows upon the lower planes of his face, and one pointed ear is decorated with a simple chain. He holds his broad shoulders perfectly straight, and his silver-stitched tunic comes to a tapered waist. A deep green cape flares out behind him, and a silver crown is laid across his brow.

I muster all the strength and grace I possess and smile. "Your Majesty, it is an honor to be in your presence. Please accept this gift."

My hand slides into the pocket on the side of my dress to retrieve the emerald-studded silver necklace wrapped in a silk cloth given to me by one of the enduares.

King Arion gazes down at me with the full force of his carved beauty. My cheeks heat under his inspection and I worry. His skin is perfectly unblemished, the opposite of mine. Did I look lowly and plain?

Though the gift is outstretched in the space between us, his crystal-green eyes don't move an inch.

"*Human*. Your name?" he asks, and his melodic voice is cold as ice shards dangling from evergreens.

I smile softly and dip my head once more. "I am called Arlet, Your Majesty."

He makes a clicking sound with his tongue. "No surname?"

I shake my head. “Humans have no need for them.”

Or better yet, we have lost our traditions around them.

He says something lyrical in elvish to his guard, and they smile in response. The same elf who opened the door retrieves the pouch from my grip unceremoniously.

Then the king holds out his massive hand. The sleeves of his tunic come to a tapered point on the back of his palm, and his bejeweled fingers point toward me.

"They told me you would escort me to the wedding. I am ready when you are," he says sharply.

I stare at his offering a moment longer, wondering exactly how I am meant to take his arm. Do I put my hand atop the king’s? Would I thread my fingers through his?

Maldita sea, I curse in my mind. *Not enough time to read.*

He shifts impatiently, causing his sleek, metallic silk to rustle, and I reach out, weaving my hand through the crook of his elbow. His brows draw together, and I'm sure I've made a mistake, but then a slight curve of his mouth causes the tension to ease. He places his hand over mine. Though perfectly smooth, his skin has a waxy, unyielding quality, like varnished timber.

"Exceptionally soft flesh, though you’ve got so many unfortunate sunspots," he says in the common tongue. Then he says something I can't make out in elvish.

I look up at him, feeling sheepish again, and cursing my lack of time to learn more about him and his languages. Of course the elves wouldn't like marks. They are... perfect.

We start to move, but I feel more uneasy than ever.

"Do you think me soft because I am not cut from the living wood?" I ask, trying to draw upon the knowledge I had gleaned from the scrolls.

He looks down at me sharply. "How do you, a human, know anything about that?"

I bite my lips together. He sounds like Lord Vann. But I was not ignorant because of my birth. I took the chances as they were awarded to me and excelled in the areas where I was allowed to blossom.

Without letting the irritation leak in, I smile.

"I very much love to read," I say.

He makes an approving sound this time.

"The humans I have encountered do not possess such an affinity for the written word," he smiles to himself. "Or perhaps, the *carved* word."

An apparent jab against the enduares, but I maintain my calm.

"They use ink and write into scrolls. It's a nice language, enduar."

He nods thoughtfully.

"Are all humans so forward?" he asks after.

A small trickle of sweat slides down my back. I don't like feeling like every inch of me is open to his scrutiny.

"No, My King, we are quite varied. In form and personality," I respond.

He nods again.

"It is *your* custom to be forward," he observes.

His tone isn't cruel, but it grates against my nerves. It's almost exactly what Daniel had drilled into me day after day—that I was annoying.

"Perhaps I shall be forward as well," he says, stretching his lips into the first grin I've seen from his people. His teeth are blunt, like a human's, with notable regular canines, unlike the enduares.

My stomach drops. Before I can respond, he says.

"I have not seen other humans in the giant court covered in so many interesting marked patterns. Were you forced to work in the sun?"

Measuring my breath, I say, "No. I weave, My King. This is a mere misfortune of my blood."

He tuts. "Fragile things, you humans. Did they present you to me because you have exceptionally virtuous qualities? Or because you are just some sort of soft, virgin sacrifice?"

I trip over a slight inconsistency in the floor's stone, and Arion tightens his grip, as if steadying me. I glance back at Joso and Lothar and see them glaring at King Arion with the force of a thousand suns.

And yet... they don't speak up.

I banish the thought because I can genuinely say I understand. This isn't about my honor. It's about saving as many lives as possible. Though, it's probably for the best that Lord Vann is far away.

Instead, I scramble to conjure up a response.

"I—"

Well, *hostia*, how was I supposed to tell him that I wasn't a virgin? Granted, I'd only ever been with my previous partner, Daniel, but Arion is a king. He's likely been entrenched in the narrow rhetoric of women's importance being manifest in their purity and fertility since he was a boy.

He doesn't know any other way. I can't fault him for that. Especially because the enduares need allies. Having allies means having troops. Troops equal more straightforward victories. Victory will result in a heaping serving of sweet freedom for my fellow humans.

"Hmm, so quiet now. Perhaps slaves rut each other like animals in the night?" he interrupts my thoughts.

I choke on my inhale. My heart skips a beat.

Don't get angry. It won't solve anything.

I can survive a night of discomfort for the greater good. King Teo promised me I would not be forced into anything inappropriate. And even with King Arion's massive, rude mouth spewing rotting bile, I didn't feel unsafe, necessarily.

I smile and do something I almost never do. Lie. "King Arion, though I have never known a man, I am sad to say this isn't a virgin sacrifice so much as a moment for you to see my people. Perhaps you will find the enduares worthy of a rekindled allyship and that will inspire you to realize us humans are worth a future that is very different from our past."

The elf continues to smile at me. "Why do you waste so much time thinking and reading when you could be home, rearing a child?"

My heart drops into my stomach. Memories return faster than I can keep up.

A child...

I would gladly be at home with a child. Tears prick at my eyes, but I never let my smile falter.

"I have been quite busy," I say sweetly.

He nods. "Yes. Well, are you not *quite* old?"

"I'm nearly thirty. Not so old for my kind."

He purses his lips and nods. "Thirty autumns is still considered a fresh babe for the elven folk—though I'm sure the conversion doesn't carry. Regardless, this has been most informative."

In the absence of a decent response, we continue to the festival in an awkward silence.

Thankfully, we emerge from the tunnel and it's easy for the discomfort to swept away quickly. When we arrive at the ceremony, the room's beauty takes my breath away.

The Festival of Endu unfolds before us, a breathtaking spectacle of light, jewel tones, and intricate song. Thousands of crystal lanterns, each glowing with a soft inner radiance, float above the revelers like a sea of suspended stars. Their lights refract against the cavern's high ceiling, casting prismatic reflections onto the carved stone walls.

The massive blue focusing crystal hums, casting out the sound of the choir to another crystal at the top of the cavern, which is then projected to thousands of red, blue, and pink quartz formations along the cavern's ceiling. The layered tunes stem from the small groups of singers stationed at each of the festival's four main thoroughfares.

The people of Enduvida are alive with celebration. Dancers clad in gossamer fabric weave intricate patterns around the towering Ardorflame temple, their steps precise, their movements as fluid as water. Flames of red and gold flicker at the temple's pinnacle, fed by a sacred molten magic that never dies.

I spot the section reserved for us to sit, but instead of guiding my ward, I pause the procession and turn to gaze at the handful of stalls that line the main avenue.

"Delicacies and crafts, Your Highness. Mostly enduar, but one of the humans has taken up a position cooking. I'm sure they would appreciate a visit," I say briefly, gesturing behind me.

He casts me a sidelong glance that makes me squirm. King Arion seems like a man who walks through life unburdened by sentiment, unmoved by tradition, and utterly indifferent to the weight of others' expectations.

He agrees through a long breath.

"Very well."

My back begins to ache from keeping my spine straight, but I hurry over eagerly.

The scent of spiced fruit and roasted meats wafts through the streets, mingling with the heady perfume of crushed amber scattered along the walkways.

"I remember the enduar markets of my youth," Arion says unexpectedly. "There was a great deal more shouting among the locals back then."

I smile up at him as he picks up a turquoise chunk carved in the shape of a snake curled around a flower.

The enduar on the other side of the stall, Flova, bows slightly. When he catches sight of the carving, his brows furrow.

"King Arion, it is an honor, but—" Flova starts, only for the elf to interrupt him.

"This is an interesting piece. Don't you think?" he asks me.

I inspect the stone. It was pretty, but I don't like serpents.

"Yes, it is lovely," I say softly.

Arion smiles again, then glances back at Flova, who is still looking slightly confused. "What is the currency down here these days?"

"There isn't one, Your Highness," Vann's voice says from behind. "Less than three hundred enduares live in Enduvida, with around eleven humans sharing our space. We have no need for shouting our wares. No need for money. This is all a gift, provided by the hard work of those around you."

Whipping around, I look at him in shock.

Please behave, I attempt to break the laws of nature and say to him through my mind.

King Arion assesses him for a few moments.

"You're the king's lapdog, yes?"

Vann smiles, saccharine sweet. *"Advisor."*

"The Cleaver, wielded by the Butcher of Giants," Arion says cooly.

I tighten my fists, and somehow, King Arion notices.

"Lord Veryl, forgive me, it seems we are making the human uncomfortable," Arion continues.

Before Vann can correct his name, the elf reaches out and tucks the stem of the flower behind my ear. The serpent's head rests on my temple, and I reach up to touch it.

I almost remove it, but don't out of respect.

"Here. A gift. *Obsequio*, in your native tongue I believe. To make you feel better," he uses his waxy fingers to trace the shell of my ear. "Ah, it looks like they are starting. Shall we?"

I hardly have time to look back at Vann, eager to make sure he doesn't do anything brash, as I am guided back to our seats.

The time passes quickly, and the conversation is quiet while I sit there.

Soon, Estela and Teo enter, dressed in complementary shades of blue. They are beautiful. A stunning pair—clearly meant to be together.

Watching Estela pledge her life to a noble king—a man devoted to giving the best life to her and their now joined people—momentarily makes me forget who sits at my side.

Tears slip down my cheeks as ancient rites weave their souls together, binding Teo and Estela in a magic that seems older than time itself.

I am so happy that it is her to take the first step in a new, exciting future. She had no easy life as the fully human daughter of an old Giant King's consort. After Daniel cast me out of our shared dwelling, she took me in.

"It was a small thing," she used to say. But it meant everything to me.

Things were uncertain right now, but I lived with this unshakeable belief the world would get better. And when they did, gods-willing, she would still have him.

The divine power surrounding this joining would bless them with children.

I want that.

I want the goddess to smile on me and heal my womb so I could have a family to raise up in a new age of human equality. To have a child that would be raised in the beauty of a crystal cavern, full of kind people caring for each other ,instead of the harsh life of a moldering home in Zlosa would be a blessing.

It would be a treasure to have someone look at me the way King Teo looks at Estela. In his eyes, it is as if the entire world hinges around her.

Suddenly, a very different time returns to my mind. A time when the wedding ceremony was called a *casamiento a la usanza.* It was a bond formed after a couple successfully conceived a child in the breeding pens and wanted to live together to raise the babe.

There were no promises made. No priestess. No rings.

Simply the act of moving one's meager things into a shared dwelling.

When I'd arrived, Daniel had made the bed look so nice. He brought a few flowers, and laid them on the cracked windowsill.

I was prepared to raise a child back then, when the world threatened to tear humans apart.

Now, I knew how much better it could be. If my body was fixed, and I was blessed with a child, I would give them a warm, safe home knowing their parents would fight for them fiercely. They would never have to wonder over their place. They would never have to wait to be chosen. I would give them a home filled with love, and work my damnedest to give them a life worth living.

Swiping bittersweet tears off my cheeks, I look to the side to see a glaring grump seated in direct sight.

Lord Vann is on the other side of the temple in a section unobstructed by citrine columns, watching Teo and Estela with his arms crossed, leaning back in his chair. His mouth turned so far down I almost laugh. His eyes find me, and watch me staring.

I bite my lip, and look away as the ceremony finishes.

Everyone moves, cheers, and shouts loud enough to shake the cavern, and then the festival starts as the happy couple slips away.

The Elf King is silent, only moving when I do. We find ourselves back down at the stalls, though I am not left alone this time. I breathe easy as Lord Lothar introduces him to the various displays.

When the time for dancing starts, King Arion draws me close.

"Be with me, my dear. I enjoy how much you smile, like a pleasant flower opening her spotted petals for me to gaze upon," he says low. "I find you... appealing."

My heart doesn't sing at the words. I feel strange. Sweaty.

We dance a little longer, then he says, "I know I have been forward with you, but I wanted to see your character. Some women snap when they are spoken down to, but you are not so sensitive as to take offense. You are clearly loyal. These are marvelous qualities in a woman."

I peer up at him. Before me is a man who doesn't care for little things and is indifferent to the small details I have spent hours combing through to ensure a successful evening educating him on humans.

"Thank you, My King," I say.

Then he cups the back of my neck, leaning down.

"This has been a most educational experience for me. Consider me convinced," his unyielding lips brush against my ear.

For a second, my soul soars. This had gone much better than

expected. King Teo would be pleased. My people would have a second chance.

I grin, about to thank him, but he puts distance between us. He starts pulling me away from the other enduares dancing. My heart gallops as he takes me to the shadowy space in front of a tunnel.

"Your Highness, we should—" I start.

He whips around and the breath is stolen from my lungs. This isn't good.

"There will come a time when—" his voice is lost in the sound of laughter and chanting from the celebration. I lean forward, trying to piece together the missing phrase.

Then I hear, "For now, just watch."

My brows draw together as my gaze snaps back onto his face. What is he talking about?

King Arion grins, slow and sharp, like he knows something I don't. His hands wrap around my shoulders holding me in place. It's forceful, and he tightens his grip when I squirm.

A scream rips through the cavern, followed by the thunderous crash of stone splitting. My head snaps toward the entrance just as the massive tunnel leading to the exit fills with movement. There are two giant warriors, bare-chested, and wearing hardened leather chausses to cover their legs. One has brown hair, while the other has pale, orange-red hair, tied behind his head.

The enemy.

Each swings his axe in a brutal arc, cleaving through two enduares before anyone can react. Blood sprays across the cavern floor, the coppery scent thick in the air. My breath hitches. My feet refuse to move.

The Elf King doesn't flinch. I try to twist out of his grip but his hold is tight. When I try to speak, he puts a hand over my mouth to silence me. Tears start to leak out of my eyes.

This is too similar to another memory. My body locks up. Terror is icy. I haven't been so afraid in a very long time.

"Just a little longer, Arlet."

His two personal guards step forward, bows already drawn, their arrows glinting in the light of the cavern. They don't fire. Not yet.

They remain poised, unreadable, waiting. The ten other elven guards spread out along the periphery, bows raised but fingers unmoving on the strings.

My heart slams against my ribs.

"Why aren't you helping?" I demand, and Arion laughs.

A roar splits the air—deep, furious, unmistakably enduar.

Vann, The Cleaver.

I take in the chaos just in time to see him close the distance between himself and one of the giants in a terrifying burst of speed. His braid flies behind him as he twists his body, his cleaver flashing in a clean, deadly path.

The brown-haired giant bellows in pain as his axe falls to the ground, along with his severed hand. The floor trembles under the force of his howl, and Vann doesn't hesitate—he lunges, a second blade sinking deep into the man's side before he can recover.

It is the first time I've ever seen Vann so deadly, and it takes my breath away—makes me afraid.

Despite how he fights, destruction falls on the city that had been so beautiful just a little before. My perfect, new home.

Tears fall from my eyes. They are cold against my clammy skin.

The elves continue to hold their ground, though everyone else is darting away, looking for shelter in homes and caves leading away from the main cavern.

It all happened so fast. Fear and the king's arms have frozen me to my spot. I look up at him, eyes wide and tremble. It'd been so long since I felt so small.

I open my mouth to speak, but am abruptly cut off.

"Now you know what I do to those who have wronged me. Keep my gift close," the king whispers in my ear, releasing me. He takes the stone flower from the spot where he'd tucked it, and hands it to me, "Now run, little flower. While you still can."

Panic surges up my spin, from my belly to my neck. I turn to run —then stumble as I dart from the tunnel's entrance. I run past one elf, then another. My heart gallops—their bows are at the ready.

But they don't shoot. When I draw closer to the Enduar Palace, I search, frantic.

Where are Teo and Estela? They'd disappeared after the festival.

I lose sight of myself, and slam into a solid chest.

Warm, strong arms wrap around me, and I look up to see Joso. His hair is streaked with dust, and his jaw is clenched so tight that it looks painful. But the firmness of his touch, the tightness of his grip, is exactly what I need right now. It awakens some part of my peculiar brain, something that cowered under Arion's grip. This is pressure plus safety. Trust. This is good.

"I'm so sorry," he bites out. His grip tightens around me, protective, urgent. "We need to get you to safety. It will be all right. You will be all right."

And then he whisks me away as the cavern continues to ring with the screams of the dying.

CHAPTER 4
ARLET

Present day, after the meeting...

After Vann left me in front of the throne room, I went to the front of the palace. There, I found my gifts had already been taken away, so I picked up a bottle of mead from the celebration and made my way home through Enduvida's cavernous expanse.

As I walk, I savor the scent of nighttime. The air is thick with the smell of damp stone and the faint, earthy sweetness of bioluminescent mushrooms clinging to the walls.

When I cross a bridge, my mind clears even more. The bottle sloshes when it hits my hip, and I long to uncork it, and take a sip.

Normally, I don't drink. Not really. Bad things seem to happen with me and alcohol, but it had been a long night, and I'd already partaken at the party. It helped me ease my racing mind. I don't want that to end.

When I enter the council residence section, I take in the dozen circular homes before me. They are sturdy, but luxurious by my standards. Though they are all similar, being built into the rock gives each one its own charm.

My steps falter as I pass Vann's home, a two-story dwelling built of dark stone. It is beautiful, like all the homes around it. Its entrance is framed by a twisting, root-like carving that gleams where the crystal veins run through it. The yard is well-kept and full of sprawling fungi that glow faintly in hues of violet and green.

A small forge sits at the side of the house, almost out of sight. I'd seen him tending to his weapons there, but at this hour, all signs of work have faded.

My fingers tighten around the neck of the bottle, and I tear my gaze away, pressing forward to my own home next door.

The words from the missive infiltrate my thoughts, and I grit my teeth.

"The solution is simple."

I can hear Arion's voice, as if it were him reading me those words. He'd made me afraid, held me to the spot. Made me watch.

A memory of screams infiltrates my mind.

I climb the steps—too fast, too clumsy, my feet catching on the uneven stone, forcing me to throw a hand against the door frame to steady myself. The mead sloshes inside the bottle. I almost laugh at myself. I never drink, and yet here I am, stumbling into my own home like I don't know the shape of these walls.

A few more words slip through.

"A symbolic offering to demonstrate the legitimacy of your request. A virgin to bear the elven heir."

The Elf King's melodic, dark voice whispers in my ear, *"Just a little longer, Arlet."*

Pushing through the front door, and into my home, I almost want to sit down right here and cry. Blood rushes in my ears, and I can only see the blur of crystal-lit stone as I press a hand against my face. Hot tears slip through my fingers.

Arion scares me.

We have an army large enough to protect our people from the vaimpír and other small threats. But we do not have enough to survive a war.

Not now.

Not now, when the children are growing up without fear.

Not now, when we have just opened a new section of our city.

"The flame-haired one called Arlet."

The king's words circle in my mind. His phrasing, his demands—they are not new. Every word from the stone tablet is something he has already said to me before. Forcing myself onward, I climb the steps to my room, open the door, and take in the cozy, familiar sight.

What the hell kind of game is he playing?

I take a deep breath. *Pull yourself together, Arlet. No one is upset with you for denying. Based on what Thorne said, it was probably for the best.*

And as for my lies? Well, I don't owe truth to a man who has betrayed me before.

But my feelings aren't so easily calmed. He wants an heir, which I would be incapable of bearing. Even if he didn't terrify me, I need strong magic to heal me. Last time I checked with Ulla, after a series of irregular bleeding cycles, my womb was still scarred.

But, she is sure that matehood would prepare me to be a mother. Grutabela's magic would be lasting, too, and potentially grant me a whole gaggle of sons or daughters.

Regardless, this is the reason the enduares are my best option. Even if humans can mate with elves, it still won't fix my problem. Their gods, Doros and Nicnevin, are focused on logic and the merit of their offspring. They don't give blessings—they enchant objects and give them to the rulers of their people.

Arion might be able to procure an object with magic strong enough to help me, but if he finds out I am barren, he is more likely to toss me aside for someone who is less trouble.

And, even if he didn't, raising a family with a being as cruel as the king?

He held me in place and made me watch the bloodshed.

I let a few more tears slip down my face.

First, I head to the table in front of a polished metal mirror, where I keep my hair brush and cosmetics. Then I pull out the hair ribbon Lord Vann had given me and inspect it. The material is delicate, and I'm struck by how thoughtful the action was.

He must've truly been assigned to give me a gift, then, because I'm not sure he would've done such a thing on his own.

A bit of blue on the table catches my eye, and I set down the bottle of mead. There, atop a silk scarf, is the carved flower, encircled by a snake that Arion had given me.

My skin goes cold, and I glance around. I'd brought the gift with me in the move, but I couldn't remember putting it here.

You're being silly. You probably pulled it from one of your moving sacks and didn't have a place for it.

Having it out feels too raw. Too unwelcome. So I grab the thing, and throw it in the top drawer of my desk.

Pressing a cold hand to my fevered cheek, I grab the bottle again and turn from all the sour memories lurking in my mind.

I cross to the stone frame loom resting against the wall in the corner, grab a jeweled goblet off the shelf, set down my bottle, and thread one of the shuttles. After a minute of threading and pushing the yarn together to tighten the weft, I feel better.

This blanket has been sitting here half finished for months. It was supposed to be a gift for my partner at the time, Joso. Now... well. That is over and I am focusing on Lorepath and weaving. I keep busy.

Still, every few weeks, I pluck away at a few new rows in the piece. What started as a simple border became a raging river—one I don't think I could cross without being swallowed alive. I've just finished weaving a sun-soaked meadow dotted with blue and pink flowers.

Each man who shaped these images in my mind flashes before me.

Daniel, my first love—the man who cut me deep and threw me out of his life.

Then Joso, the one who ended our time together because he couldn't love me. Couldn't give me what I desperately wanted.

I let out a sad laugh. The picture in front of me looked like a scene from an epic story I'd read.

Others read stories and dream of living wild adventures alongside handsome heroes and seductive heroines. They crave the wind on their faces, the thrill of rain running down their skin, and the scent of wildflowers in the sunshine as they race through open fields.

Not me.

Even considering leaving the caves makes my breath short. When

I arrived in Enduvida, I didn't mourn what I'd lost—I embraced what I could build. They won me over with the promise of a house I could turn into a home. That was something I hadn't had since leaving the breeding pens.

Here, among the furs, crystals, and small metal decorations, I have crafted an oasis. I will never willingly give that up.

My eyes land on a few clothes strewn about the floor and I pause. I didn't remember throwing those around. Had I really been so careless with my things before leaving for the ceremony? I stand and let the shuttles hang, quickly bringing the tunics to my closet. Inside, I notice one of the crates moved.

Strange.

Everything from before the ascension is such a blur, but I can't remember doing this.

After righting the small room, I return to the loom, picking up the threads, and I weave one more row of green. It's impossible not to wonder what image will take shape next.

Maybe I'll find a way to weave the king's offer into it. Perhaps it would help me feel better.

Tears prick my eyes as I stare at the rich green. It's darker than the rest of the spool, less like grass and more like evergreens or emeralds.

My favorite color.

A sharp pain stabs through my chest, reminding me that I am, indeed, alone. I set the shuttles down, pour a glass of mead, and bring a jeweled goblet to my lips.

After a life of craving, suffering, and running, I cling to the peace and promise of happiness under the mountain like a woman seeking water in the desert.

I huff a laugh, pour another glass of mead, and let out a long breath, hoping it will shake loose the ache lodged in my ribs.

I worked so hard with Joso. I thought I'd been close to having a husband. A partner. A mate to help my broken body form a family.

I was wrong.

Even the word *mate* scrapes against my already-raw nerves. My gaze drifts back to the sunlit field of wildflowers woven into the fabric.

Joso had been kind to me when I arrived. Then, he protected during the raid on the cavern. When he'd carried me, it unlocked something inside me I thought had died with Daniel. A hunger for touch and trust.

He kept close to me after that.

A few weeks later, after walking me to and from my sessions teaching or weaving, he finally asked if I would join him for a meal. He kissed me that night, slow and careful, as if waiting for me to pull away.

Soft kisses were not as enjoyable as firm ones, but I was happy to go at a slower pace. I knew it would take me time to trust again.

He took me dancing, spun me through the fire lit halls, and laughed when I stumbled over the unfamiliar steps. He helped me wind skeins of thread. And then, a part of me fell quick and fast when he admitted that, like me, he wanted a mate. A family.

I thought that I could be happy with someone so... soft.

For months, I waited for a song to begin between us. For the crystals to hum, for the world to tell me that I had been chosen in this marvelous new place. None of it came.

Now, half-drunk and alone, I think about gods and fate.

What if... whatever song they've sung into the crystals doesn't include a mate? Or a family? Or anything I've hoped for?

I let that truth roll through me, testing the sting.

Instead of accepting it, hope springs from some eternal fountain in my soul.

I picture a perfectly detailed future—one where a blue-skinned babe rests in my arms while a fire crackles in the corner of the room.

A brusque knock on the door shatters the lovely dream.

Bolting upright, I knock over the bottle at my feet. The world tilts slightly as I sway.

"Mierda," I mutter, making my way toward the front door.

Another knock. Louder.

"I'm coming!" I shout, tripping over a rug that Fira, the head weaver, gifted me after I helped her knit a new robe. Righting myself, I realize that rug hadn't been in that location either.

Before I have a chance to dwell, I hurry down the steps toward the hallway leading to the door as fast as I can without falling.

My fingers fumble around the bronze-gold handle, twisting it with more force than necessary as I yank the door open.

The moment I do, a dull roar fills my ears.

It's not real. Not sound, exactly—more like the distant echo of a river. Danger. Pain. Sadness. Desolation.

It crashes over me with a frozen chill as I stare at the man standing in the doorway.

A human. Taller than me, but only just. His blond hair is recently shorn, his tanned skin marred by scars, and his bright green eyes are alight.

I know this face as well as I know the treacherous river lurking in the corners of my mind. My stomach knots, my fists clench—just like they had when I'd pounded on the door of our shared dwelling in another life.

The man I wished never to see again stands before me, appearing like a cruel phantom.

"Daniel," I grit out.

He smiles, and my heart twists around the strings suspending it in my chest. The dimples on his cheeks had once been my favorite place to kiss. He was rugged, robust, and popular.

And many times, he had been heartless to me while the others smiled. He'd broken my trust and left me wounded.

"Arlet, they told me I'd find you here," he starts. "You looked beautiful tonight."

A cold chill coats my skin. I had no way of knowing he was lurking somewhere in Enduvida—not with the thousands of humans and enduares that joined us last in the year. I was also *just* appointed to the council, making me easy to locate. Easy to see.

This is my fault.

I move to shut the door on him. Normally, I'm not this rude, but he didn't hesitate to throw me away after I endured one of the most brutal losses of my life. He doesn't deserve my kindness.

Even as I think it, a small part of me aches.

"Not so fast," he quips, shoving his hand between the door and the jamb. "Arlet, *mi solecita,* I've been looking for you since I got to this stinking cave. Imagine my surprise to see you shine once again."

I shove against his hand, relishing the yelp he lets out.

Then... I sigh and pull the door open fully, revealing the lit street behind him. The spell lights cast a golden glow over the council district, their warmth blending with the eerie blue radiance of *lumikaps*—towering mushrooms as tall as men. Their bioluminescent caps pulse like a slow heartbeat.

Jutting from the cavern walls, massive veins of quartz catch the light, scattering faint rainbows across the streets below.

The homes surrounding us are built from a blend of stone and the enduares' signature gold-like metal, their rounded structures gleaming even in the dim cavern light. Some houses hum softly, their mechanisms still in motion.

The sight should be familiar by now. But something about it, standing here in the threshold, staring at the man I once thought would stay, makes it feel distant.

Feelings aren't things that can be neatly placed into drawers and tins.

"I'm not your *solecita* anymore," I say. "I don't want to see you again. Now, leave."

He frowns, and a part of me—it's instinct, really—wants to ease his discomfort. I don't know if it's out of habit or because of the way he treated me before.

His jaw clenches. "You want me to go? Why? Are you fucking one of the monsters?"

My buzzed mind plunges into icy water, gasping for a response. Any response.

"What are you—"

"Someone told me you were fucking one of the monsters before I got here."

My heart leaps into my throat. My lungs seize.

He doesn't get to do this. He doesn't get to act like I belong to him. He let me go—threw me away like a broken tool crusted with filth.

One breath. That's all I get before I step forward and slap him with everything I have. The sound cracks through the quiet night. Daniel staggers back, eyes blazing with fury and shock.

I have never hit someone before. It feels... *good*.

"Arlet—"

"Is something wrong?" a new voice interjects.

Behind him, two figures step into the golden glow of the lanterns —one human, one enduar. Biren, with his dark curls and stocky build, stands beside Faol, an enduar hunter on the nightly patrol.

Their gazes land on me. On the tears burning down my cheeks.

Biren squares his shoulders. "What did you do?" he demands of Daniel.

Daniel, a partner who had been as good as my husband, the man who had fathered the only child I'd ever conceived, glares up at them.

"This isn't your business," he spits.

Faol ignores him, turning his stern gaze to me. "Are you all right, Lady Arlet?"

I swallow, forcing the pain back down. My lips curve into a brittle smile.

"I'm fine, but I don't want to see him."

Faol nods, and they move. Daniel barely has time to react before they seize his arms.

His face darkens. "What the hell? Arlet. *Tell them to stop.*"

I don't. In fact, I watch.

His struggles fiercely. His voice sharpens. Desperate. Then, he switches to the human tongue.

"I swear it on our child's grave—I only came to talk. *Maldita puta!*"

Ice shoots through my veins. How dare he invoke that?

I take a slow, deep breath. A crowd gathers as others come out of their houses. Fuck, I see Melisa, and her mate Ra'Salore. Svanna. Fira. Their presence wraps around me like a suffocating fog. My cheeks burn.

And then... the people part to reveal a figure. Vann.

His bright silver eyes sweep over the scene. His voice booms, carrying over the gathered onlookers. I hate myself for feeling glad.

"What's all this?"

His gaze meets mine. Disdain flickers there—only to deepen when he turns to Daniel.

Daniel snarls, thrashing against his captors. "I just wanted to talk to my wife!"

The word slams into the crowd like the beat of a war drum.

Shock ripples across the faces of my fellow council members. Fuck. These are people who know I've been searching for a partner. People who know I was with Joso.

What must they be thinking of me?

From here, I see the shift in Vann's expression. His disdain warps into something uglier.

"Wife?" he spits, his gaze snapping back to me. I think of the meeting we'd just had hours ago.

His mouth curls.

"Shame you didn't invite me to the ceremony, Firelocks. The Mating Journey isn't for half a week."

Embers of indignation heat my skin. I won't let Daniel do this.

Not again.

I lift my chin.

"This man is not my husband." My voice cuts through the noise, ringing clear and final.

Another sentence sits on my tongue, one too private to bite out. *Whatever was between us is as dead as the daughter I once carried for him.*

"You lie!" Daniel shouts. Vann punches him in the gut, and a cold hush falls over the crowd.

I meet Faol's gaze.

"Do what you will with him. I don't want to see him again."

I don't wait to see what happens next.

I turn. I slam the door shut. I press my back against the stone, gripping the edges of my gown.

The emotions come fast and sharp, pelting me like frozen rain. I wait for the sadness, the agony, to smother the fire inside me.

But it doesn't.

Instead, I crawl across the room, reach for my bottle of mead, and take a long swig.

Then another.

The clock tower chimes a slow, beautiful tune, marking two in the morning. This day has been a million years long. I need to sleep. I need to rest. Tomorrow, there will be plenty of work.

I lean against my chair, eyes on the loom, trying to steady my pulse.

A faint sound slithers behind me.

I stiffen, then turn. The shadows seem darker now.

"Hello?" my voice is quiet.

The sound grows louder. Then—pain strikes. A sharp, electric bloom of agony moves across my ankle.

The world lurches, and everything goes black.

CHAPTER 5
VANN

The next day...

The crunch of bone sounds through the crisp early evening air as I stomp down on a vaimpír's chest. Blackened blood oozes from the gaping wound, its shattered ribs jutting through rotted flesh.

A bright light shines from the Fuegorra in my chest, warmth passing over my skin and mending the minor hurt. The scent of decay lingers, thick and cloying against the fresh bite of the wind.

I curl my lip, surveying the dozen monster corpses strewn across the snow near the forest at the base of the Enduar Mountains. The towering peaks loom behind us, their jagged silhouettes cutting into the twilight sky. The trees are deep green, much like the color of moss, and their branches are heavy with frost.

There are seven other enduar hunters with me, but I only know a few like Ner'Feon and Ra'Salore. The former is a fellow council member, appointed leader of the ocean-risen—a group of five hundred enduar soldiers that had been lost after the Great War when the sea devoured many of our great cities. By the hand of Grutabela and Endu, these men did not perish, but adapted.

Trapped beneath the waves, they stayed in bubble-like colonies sustained by the magic of the Ardorflame temples. Much like the one in Enduvida, these temples are connected to the center of the earth, where Endu is said to live.

They are gruff. Having spent decades hungering for the surface, they observe several of our more brutal past traditions. Some don't like the reminder of how sharp us trolls used to be. I think we are stronger for remembering it through them.

Ra'Salore combines his surname and full first name as the old traditions dictated, but he has lived in the caves as long as I have. He's a decent swordsman, but his real talent lies in stone bending. I brought him here to help start a fire after we finished eradicating the pests, and he stands away from the fighting, honing his concentration on a ball of magma he brought from the city's depths. He's young, incredibly tall, and has already mated to a human, becoming the adoptive father of her twin daughters.

I like them both well enough, but I find myself hesitant to let more people into my circle. Resentment comes from once having a small, tight-knit community that has transitioned a rapidly flourishing city, and it is impossible for me to learn everyone and their names.

As the king's advisor, I shouldn't even be here. My place is surveying growth, and I don't like being outside.

But sometimes, it helps to pick up my cleaver and sink it into something that isn't a stuffed bag on a pell. The act of doing what I do best, *killing*, is a welcome reprieve from moments like yesterday's meeting. I almost couldn't move from the excruciating chill weighing my insides.

My condition had been necessary for my survival once. But continuing to pay that price now? Brutal. It leaves me with the worst fucking hangover I've ever had.

And even after I had rested a few short hours, I was thrust into the proverbial frost again. I think of the man outside Arlet's home, the one who had the audacity to call himself her husband. A flash of fury burns through my mind.

I hadn't seen her all day and she hadn't made it to the council meeting. Sadness can take hold of her quickly, but it wasn't like her to avoid her duties.

Too many men try to claim her.

Another vaimpír charges, and I anticipate its feral actions, twisting around and cutting its head clean off. It falls to the snow, useless.

I take in a fresh, clean breath. Nothing like a fight to clear my head.

Except, all my head wants to think about is Arlet and that *man*. I thought we were past this after Joso, who, in his short-dicked, half-baked wisdom, tossed Arlet aside like a half-chewed bone at a feast.

"Lord Vann!"

I tear my eyes from the gore soaking the snow as Ner'Feon strides toward me, his deep blue skin streaked with drying blood. Like all of the ocean-risen, he carries the cost of survival in his broad frame, his body shaped by the depths that once held him captive. His silver hair is cropped short—something unusual for us enduares. It is damp with sweat, and his sharp features are marked with wrinkles around his mouth and eyes.

He gestures toward the meager battlefield, his brow furrowed. "Fuck," he mutters. "How many did you kill?"

"Three," I grunt.

"Shit," another one of the men starts.

"You could fell an entire army of these damned things!" Ner'Feon exclaims.

I huff a short laugh.

"I am not so impressive. I'd wager no more than ten at once," I say.

They don't laugh with me. Ner'Feon looks to the side, gauging the expressions of his comrades before meeting my gaze again. "Forgive me, my lord. I meant no disrespect."

They don't joke like I do.

"No offense taken." I inhale sharply, then grit my teeth when the breath does nothing to ease the tension in my shoulders.

It is nice to speak exclusively in my native tongue for a few hours. It used to be like this every day, but now the city has fractioned into smaller groups speaking in dialects of enduar or human, with the main tongue transitioning to the common language. A shared language didn't make these men my brothers. Not yet, anyway.

Unfortunately, most of the men I would normally spend my time with have become preoccupied. They have families, daughters, sons, partners. Everything.

And I? I have nothing. My woman died long ago. We knew, even then, that we would never have a family.

Unbidden, a shock of red hair flits into my vision. The memory of a bright laugh sings from a pair of full red lips. My mouth goes dry. I picture grabbing the back of her neck, cutting off that incessant, soothing voice with my mouth.

Arlet.

Fucking Arlet.

Get out of my head.

I exhale through my nose, forcing the thoughts away.

"Where would you like the fire?" Ra'Salore asks.

I don't respond, still staring at the blood pooling at my feet.

"My lord, we usually—" Ner'Feon starts.

As it has my entire life, I feel a touch on my shoulder. It is a small gesture, merely the weighted sensation of a palm flush against my armor. It is almost fatherly—and I have never admitted its occurrence to anyone. Even Teo.

My god, Endu, has blessed me with a meager kernel of his approval, which always leads to success on the battlefield. He's never turned me away, even after what I did to my heart, so I try to never turn from others.

I lift my cleaver high above my head, bringing it down in a single, brutal stroke. Another vaimpír's head rolls from its shoulders, landing in the snow with a sickening thud.

"Ra'Salore, put it far from the trees," I say.

Dull, lifeless eyes stare up at me, but I am attentive. These things will regenerate unless burned. Bitter bile rises in my throat as I join Ra'Salore. He lifts the molten ball of magma he's carried from the city over a stack of wood, his stone-bending abilities making quick work of the fire.

The bodies are laid out in a row, each severed head positioned above its respective chest. The others watch as I kneel beside each one, closing their eyes.

May the gods have mercy on their cursed souls. May they find rest in some version of Iravida instead of the eternal darkness of the demon god, Abhartach.

“Why do you bow your head? Do you pray for the monsters?" Ra’Salore scoffs.

"Some call us monsters," I say, tossing the words over my shoulder.

"We have our own people to mourn," an ocean-risen snaps.

"Some of these men were once one of us,” I retort.

Silence.

It’s a bitter truth, but the vaimpír are nothing more than the venom-cursed undead. In life, they could have been an enduar. An elf. A human. I want them to be put to rest for good.

"It is strange," another mutters. "For The Cleaver to mourn—"

"This is not mourning." I meet his gaze, unwavering. "This is respect for the beings they once were."

"Do you not relish killing your enemies?" Ner’Feon intones.

I pause, then say, "There are deaths I do not mourn. But again, *this is not mourning.”*

Ner’Feon grunts.

Fine. The ocean-risen may be annoying.

My fingers flex over the hilt of my cleaver as I stand. Death reminds me of the giants. The giants remind me of the humans. The humans remind me of mates. And mates... That only leads to frustration and pain.

The heat in my blood could be cured with a quick soak in the frozen lake at the new settlement. Instead, I stand. It is not becoming of a soldier to kill without cleaning up his mess, so I grab a pair of legs and hoist the body into the flames.

The orange light flickers against the now dark sky—like the ones that dance in Arlet’s hair.

She refuses to leave my thoughts. I inhale sharply, letting out a guttural sound as I throw another body into the fire.

I catch a snippet of one of the men speaking and hear the words, *"Mating Journey."*

Fuck. The next event after Arlet's ascension.

The Mating Journey is a rite that has been practiced for a millennia among my people. It is a day-long festival meant for willing, single trolls of an appropriate age to find their goddess-blessed other half by meeting as many people as possible in a short period of time. The Fuegorras in our chests did not always recognize a mate upon first sight, but it was common enough that such a ritual was effective.

In the past, when trolls were counted in the millions, it was practical. Now, it feels indulgent when people meet their mates organically at an acceptable rate.

The festival will be chaos. Tents are already lining the lower level of the city. Women will be dressed in delicate gowns or battle armor. Men will be putting their skills on full display. Old traditions. Frivolous pageantry. And at the end of the day, dozens of mates finding their other half, naked in their furs, while the rest sample the stock left behind.

The scent of sex. The heat. The fire.

It hasn't even started, and it's already choking me.

I brush the back of my bracer over my forehead, cleaning a bit of blood.

We are supposed to be preparing for a confrontation with the elves, and instead we are playing house.

Every time I go to oversee the training caves, it's all I hear about from humans and enduares alike. When I sit to eat in Hammerhead hall, inevitably someone is talking about clothes to wear and customs. In council meetings, I am inundated with talk of the organizer, Lirenne, another ocean-risen who had attended a Mating Journey just before her battalion was lost.

I hoist more body parts to be burned, and gag at the smell of the burned bodies.

Knowing that the Elvish King had sent a missive would dampen the festival, but it would also mean putting Arlet in a place for everyone to judge her decision not to be wed. I groan. Why must everything be so infuriatingly complicated lately?

I don't like it.

Finally, the last body is tossed into the fire and more smoke fills the area. Charred flesh. Blood. It all reeks.

I crouch under the smoke cloud, weary after so long without decent sleep. The cold seeps through my leathers and numbs the fire in my veins. Darkness edges my vision, almost enough to obscure the others as they finish cleaning the area and head inside.

Casting them half hearted salutes, I drop onto my ass and sit there.

Why can I not stop thinking of Arlet?

The witches swore this wouldn't happen. That my heart would be free from my body—gifted only to one woman until the day I die.

They were fucking wrong.

Gritting my teeth. I stand. Who knows how much time has passed, but the moon now makes her way across the sky, and the fire has gone cold.

It's time to light Adra's name.

My fingers, face, and feet are numb, but I ignore the sensation and stomp back toward the gilded entrance to Enduvida. There, massive golden doors are set into the mountainside. Intricately carved geometric patterns cover their surface, interlocking in a design that speaks to centuries of practice in metal craftsmanship.

Swirling veins of deep red flow through the surrounding rock, extending like lifeblood into the mountain. The familiar scent of home fills my lungs, sulfur and mineral-rich stone, but it's different than it was a year ago. There are more people. More cultures melting into something I don't recognize.

Months ago, it was just two hundred of us fighting for survival. Maybe it wasn't a life of luxury, but at least we were united.

Now, everything feels scattered. Spread too thin. And I keep taking on more and more, trying to fill the hole inside me.

No matter what I do, the emptiness remains.

The city is surprisingly quiet at this hour. Right now, the only people still awake are the enduares and humans on hunting duty, cooks, the occasional cleaning crew, and those who find solace in the silence of the late night.

As I saunter down the hallway, I turn to the left, heading toward the Wall of Remembrance. This is one of the few places in Enduvida that has survived centuries.

The glowing crystals jutting from the walls of the tunnel cast a soft light around me. I exhale slowly. Mother Liana, the head priestess and Wise Woman of our people, has been here recently. She often sets aside time to help preserve this place, using the heat of the under-earth to keep the sacred names ever illuminated.

The names are carved into the walls, stretching across the space in long rows. A sharp twinge pinches the muscle where my shoulders meet my neck. It is an overwhelming experience to stand before a list of the dead.

Many of these people were brutally murdered in the Great War. Some fell during the elvish skirmishes years before that. Thousands died quietly in their homes after a long life. And others were simply... lost.

Each name was a life, lived and ended with hopes, dreams, families. Their mates are gone. Their children. Their grandchildren. Their life's work.

Once, there was a dedicated team of artisans who preserved the dead through carving. Now, it's easy to spot the newer engravings, roughly made by those of us who survived.

Adra's name was not meant to be larger than the others. I had asked for no extra space, no adornment. But I carved it myself, and my handwriting is not very elegant.

Carefully, I pick up one of the glowing crystals from the floor and press its sharp point into the grooves of her name. Light ripples through the letters, slowly filling each indent.

Li'Adra.

A yellow-gold glow blooms across the stone, as warm as her smile. Her face floods my memory—laughing at me in my soldier's uniform. She used to call me mad with love, as if I were crazy for wanting to spend the rest of my life with her.

She was right.

The world had been simple then. I didn't need a *Mating Journey*. I needed her.

But she died in the eruption that ended The Great War, just like the others. And she took part of me with her.

As I stand here, staring at her name, I know that something else is missing. And something new keeps trying to force its way in.

My eyes burn. I take a fortifying breath, pressing my hand beside her name.

"I wish you peace, my love."

Pain stabs through my chest with every breath. I wait, listening to the rhythm of my heartbeat as unshed tears blur my vision. Finally, I let go. Step back.

A cold numbness starts in my chest, spreading along my arms.

Lifting the crystal, I press it higher against the wall, lighting a new line of names—ones that belong to those with no family left to mourn them. It feels like painting, bringing color back to something lifeless. I move methodically, frantically, not allowing myself to picture their faces. That would bring too much emotion for me to hold.

By the time I turn away, more than half the tunnel is lit.

I wonder if Arlet has ever come here. Had she seen Adra's name? I don't think she knows about her, and I have never been in the position to discuss it. It might be nice if she knew. Perhaps she would understand something inside of me.

But it is foolishness to consider this.

"Till tomorrow, my sweet Adra," I murmur. "Forgive my straying. I am a lonely old monster."

I brush past the names left unlit, knowing I will tend to them another day.

A scream pierces the air.

I stop near the entrance where the tunnels reach the open caverns. Blue and red crystal walls sing the dreadful sound back to me, momentarily quieting the hum of the city. Light blazes in the middle of the night. My head snaps up, searching for the source.

Another scream splits the silence.

Feminine. Bright. Agonized. Familiar.

Fuck.

My feet move before my mind catches up. A siren calls to me, and I have no choice but to answer. A group of humans have gathered near one of the bridges leading to the exit. I push through, scanning the space when I see her.

Arlet is curled into a ball on the floor, barefoot and sobbing.

A sharp panic grips my throat. She looks wrong. Rocking, pale against the dirty black stone. Too small. Too fragile.

This is my second time seeing her cry in two days.

"Out of my way!" I bark, dropping to my knees beside her. Grabbing her shoulder, I shake slightly. "Firelocks."

From this close, I can feel how cold she is. Sweat slicks her skin, making her look sickly. The delicate paleness of her face is almost translucent in the dim light and the freckles along her cheeks are stark against the blue veins near her temples.

She looks like she was carved from marble.

I place a hand over her brows, my palm nearly swallowing her head.

"Firelocks, what's wrong? Are you hurt?" My voice is sharp. Was she attacked? Or was it that *man* that went to her house?

She thrashes against my hand and lets out another scream.

"Fuck," I curse under my breath. "Get the Queen! Get Ulla!"

I draw her against me, my arms locking around her small frame. She shouldn't be left out here, suffering, while people gawk at her.

"GO! The rest of you back to your homes!"

Her unbound hair spills over my arms, red curls tangled and wild. I cover it with my free hand, twisting the locks to tuck them atop her head so the others don't see something meant to be private. She strains against my arms, and I notice her strength. Was she always like this?

"Arlet, I'm here." The words slip out before I can catch them.

Her eyes snap open and she slashes at me with her fingernails.

"What the hell?" I jerk back, stunned as she kicks me in the ribs. She scrambles upright, retreating on all fours like a cornered animal.

Something inside me tightens. Her wide, wild eyes flicker pure black—then, with a single blink, the blackness fades, revealing familiar cinnamon-brown.

"Vann?" she breathes, blinking rapidly as if seeing her surroundings for the first time. "What... what's going on?"

I let my face go blank.

"I found you here, on the ground. Screaming."

She wipes sweat from her brow. "I—"

"Arlet!"

I turn as Queen Estela storms toward us. My eyebrows shoot up at the fact she actually came. She's not usually available at night, not with her children to tend to.

She is small but commands a presence that rivals the goddesses who blessed her. Her braided curls look wilder than Arlet's, though her skin glows with divine power.

She barely spares me a glance before reaching for Arlet. Two guards follow her, but they stand at a distance as she comes to a stop.

"Ulla and I were in the garden when someone told us Arlet was shouting. I thought you were sick, *querida*. You didn't come to the meeting. What is wrong?" she demands.

Arlet swallows, then opens her mouth. No words come out. She shakes her head and tries again.

"I... don't... know. I went to bed. Then I woke up here."

Queen Estela turns to me, eyes sharp. "And you? What did you see?"

I hesitate. The image of Arlet rocking on the ground flashes in my mind—the way she lashed out. The way her eyes looked.

"I found her curled in a ball. She was surrounded by people. Disoriented. I worry she was attacked."

If she was attacked by Daniel, the one who had come to her house, perhaps that could explain the craze. But her eyes... Vaimpír had red eyes. She couldn't have been bit by one, I think.

Maybe an *aradhlum*? But cave spider venom was poisonous. She'd be immobile. Not running around like a madwoman.

Maybe this had something to do with Daniel.

"Thank you Lord Vann," Estela nods once, turning back to Arlet. "Were you attacked?"

Arlet looks confused. “I don’t know.”

Behind her, Lady Ulla arrives. For a long time, she was both the person who managed the meals of the city and the healer. Now, she is more focused on healing than any of the others.

She’s a tall enduar woman, with hair piled up in a mound almost the same size as her head. She’s beautiful, by my people’s standards. Worry distorts her features. She hurries, coming directly to Arlet's side, and assessing her patient.

“I see no physical wounds,” Ulla announces. "But you look pale. Fevered. We need to get you home."

I open my mouth, "You're sure there are no bruises? No signs of someone or something hitting her head?

Ulla frowns. “No." She turns back to Arlet. "Have you been sleeping well? I know we’ve all been anxious about the upcoming festival, I imagine you doubly so with the ascension.”

Arlet swallows hard. “I... haven't been sleeping.”

I think of last night in front of her home. Her crying, and a human man yelling. Daniel, I believe. *What the fuck was his problem?*

Ulla helps Arlet to stand. When Firelocks looks at me, she still seems different. There is no hint of joy in her eyes. No brightness. A part of me wishes to carry her to her house, but she would likely refuse.

“Lord Vann, thank you for helping Arlet,” Estela says, turning her head to me and tipping it forward. “Would you like to—”

“I can walk,” Arlet says sharply. Her voice is higher than usual.

She doesn’t want my help. She thinks she is fine with Estela and Ulla, even though neither of them is as strong as me.

I grit my teeth, then force a smile. “I am here to help, My Queen. Lady Arlet, I wish a quick recovery, and I hope you all have a less eventful evening."

Without another word, I turn and leave.

Rubbing a hand over my face I groan.

I need to do something. I need to know what the hell is going on with that man, Daniel, and what he did to her.

CHAPTER 6
ARLET

The morning after...

Darkness clings to me like cobwebs, despite the spell lights bobbing overhead.

I blink. Why are there lights on? There are gaps in my memory. Blotted out with a blackness that swallows small moments whole. I remember going to my bed last night, lying down—then nothing.

A little while ago, I awoke on the floor of the greeting room. Laid out like discarded fabric. A chill took hold of me then, and I haven't entirely thawed. Not as I went upstairs, drew a blanket around me, and sat in front of my vanity.

Drinking too much mead at my ascension had been a mistake. I hardly ever do it, and now I'm paying the price.

That has to be it.

And yet... after the party, after the drinking, there had been more.

It started with Arion's missive. The threat between the enduares and the elves is in the waiting for one side to make the first move. That waiting would be over if I'd allowed myself to be shipped to his doorstep. Hinging the salvation of Enduvida on my marriage to him —on me giving him a child—is a cruel cosmic joke.

Lying doesn't come easily to me. I told one lie and withheld one truth the king had no right to. Now, he wants my body to bear his heir.

And then Daniel arrived. Daniel, who promised to love me, then broke my trust in every way possible. He showed up at my house to... what? What had he wanted?

To see me? To remind me of what happened?

In the darkness of my room, sadness coils tight in my chest, familiar and sharp-edged. I remember the other time I'd been so mad with grief that I couldn't think straight.

Unshed tears burn my eyes and a memory comes to life.

I press my hand to my stomach, but there's nothing left to hold. The silence in the room is unbearable, almost as much as the braided fabric strewn across the bed had been. The torchlight flickers against the moldering wooden walls, casting restless shadows that stretch and fade.

Daniel kneels beside me, his hand covering mine, but it doesn't stop the emptiness. His fingers tremble, his breath uneven.

"What did you do to my son?"

Daughter, *I think.* It was a daughter.

I can hear the break in his voice, the helplessness he tries to swallow.

I squeeze my eyes shut, willing myself to stay in this moment just a little longer—before I have to accept the truth. As long as I don't move, as long as I don't speak it into existence, maybe it won't be real.

But then Daniel moves away, uncovering the stretch of my skirt covered in blood.

The grief settles into me like a stone sinking to the bottom of the ocean, heavy and inescapable.

I choke out a sob. There are no words, no undoing what's already been taken. There is only the unbearable stillness in my midsection where life was supposed to be.

"Daniel, it happened so fast. I told you not to go, that I wasn't—"

He looks up at me, green eyes vibrant next to the redness of his skin. "Out."

"You can't be serious," I plead. The word is so final.

"The purpose for our joining is now gone. So, get out."

He says it coldly, as if it had been my fault. As if I had been the one to bind me to the bed so I couldn't move while he went out drinking.

I blink, ripping myself away from the memory before I drown in it. Estela had found me near the doused bonfire in the center of the slave pens that night, freezing. She took me in. Cleaned me up. There were entire stretches of time after I moved into her dwelling—hours, days, weeks—that were obliterated.

King Arion's request has triggered something inside me. That's why I drank so much. That's why things are strange.

Just like before, it will pass.

I turn to the mirror, studying the crescent shadows beneath my eyes. Strange. They aren't purple or blue, like usual, but a dull, lifeless gray. My skin is strange—too pale, too cold.

My blanket parts, and something dark catches my eye in the polished metal.

I stand. I look down. And I scream.

There is a stain my nightgown. When I move my hands, I notice it's crusted along my fingernails.

Blood? Maybe this is a bleeding cycle?

I've never had a stain on the front of my body. But I'd woken up on the floor, maybe...

Gods.

Taking deep breaths, I move my hands to my face. The flakes are more purplish than crimson. If it's blood, it's not human, my mind supplies, even as my stomach twists. It's such a deep purple, it's almost black. My fingers scrape against it gingerly.

No pain. It's not mine.

Hyperventilating, I tear the gown off my body, holding it away from me like it's diseased. Cold air brushes over my bare skin. Frantic, I shove the gown deep into the bin of clothes to be washed, my hands shaking so violently I can barely feel them.

I stand there for a moment, breathing. When I turn back to the mirror to inspect my naked body, I tremble. Aside from my hands, there is no staining on my belly or legs.

My brain scrambles for solutions. A dark substance, potentially blood, coating my nightgown just like—

But it wasn't. It isn't the same as the miscarriage. You should go to Ulla.

I take a deep breath. She would be able to check out everything. I calm a fraction, just enough for different thoughts to breakthrough.

Why is this happening when the first draft of Lorepath needs to be presented in only three months? We have to prepare for a proper start to school. I'd told Fira I'd help her with fabric for furniture in some of the houses in the new mountain settlement.

And there was a whole fucking mating journey. I'd been helping to alter clothes for some of the humans.

Gods.

Instead of dressing to go to Ulla's, I hesitate. Maybe what was on my fingernails wasn't blood? Maybe it was rancid mead? Or perhaps this was paint?

Sure, it smelled worse than any paint I'd ever touched, but I'd gone to bed knowing today will be full of work. Estela had mentioned wanting to meet this afternoon.

Work first. I'll deal with this after. It was just a strange night. Nothing more.

I force myself into the washroom, scrubbing my skin raw with a damp cloth. I make a list of things that must be done. Going to the schoolhouse is out of the question. I shouldn't be near the children when I'm so anxious, so I will wait until after sessions are over to check on my plans.

I know they need help with the looms. That's reason enough to go about my day.

I take a deep breath and grab one of the cosmetics from my table. A balm-like cake, crushed with flesh-toned minerals. I press it into my skin, dulling the unnatural shadows in the hollows of my face and covering the ghastly freckles that look so much more prominent today.

The illusion of normalcy.

I give myself a weak smile in the mirror, stand, and head downstairs to grab a small breakfast. When I approach the kitchen, I see the bread that Ulla had baked me as a gift set on the table. When I grab a slice, it is hard.

Hmm.

Strange it should be so stale after only one night. The rest of the downstairs is littered with gifts from my ceremony, and I walk past them all as I pour some oil on the bread to soften it and chew.

I scan the floor, my heart pounding just in case I'll find something suspicious on the ground. There's no blood.

Satisfied, I slip on my shoes, and head to the front door just as the clock tower chimes eight.

Hostia. I'm going to be late again.

I head outside, still forcing the smile when my foot catches something solid. Something furry that catches on my shoe.

I freeze, a sick feeling clawing up my throat. Slowly, I look down.

A long, severed leg rests on my stone doorstep in a pool of thick blood, the same color as what had been on my nails and nightgown.

I choke on a gasp.

It's a cave spider—an *aradhlum,* as the enduares call them. But the rest of it is missing.

I stare at the sharp claw at the end of its glossy joint. A chill seeps into my bones.

My ankle burns.

I lift my skirt, worried that perhaps one of its offspring has emerged to bite me, but instead I reveal a strange marking of a snake curling around my ankle.

It's a tattoo, like the ones giant men would receive after battle. Enduares do not ink their skin like the giants did. Did one of the humans do this? Had I asked them to after my ascension? Maybe that's why I fell asleep on the floor.

My head pounds as I scan my thoughts, trying to fit the pieces together. Then I find a second leg further down the path.

My stomach lurches. A lightning-bright shock races down my spine.

"What the hell are you doing?" a voice says behind me.

I freeze. My breath leaves me in a rush, my lungs ice-cold. My fingers tingle, blood draining from them as if my body already knows to prepare for flight.

I turn—slowly—to face him.

Lord Vann. Fuck, I'd forgotten he is my neighbor now.

His eyes drop back to the leg.

The old me rears her head, the one who shrinks back. The one who had learned long ago how to sidestep conflict, how to soothe men's tempers before they ever had a chance to ignite.

I let my lips curve, let my voice lilt with something easy and bright.

"I—I found it on my step. Some creature must have killed it and brought it to me as a gift. I do tend to be perceived as a friendly thing."

Vann's eyes flick to the severed leg, then back to me. He all but rolls his eyes.

"Cave rats don't make friends," he says flatly. "Unless you've managed to gain the loyalty of a particularly bad hunter, I think there's a simpler explanation."

A jolt of panic laces through me, sharp as a dagger.

What does he know?

"And what would that be?" I ask.

He steps closer.

"You seemed half mad last night."

I choke. "Are you saying I did this?"

He purses his lips. "No. Maybe this attacked you? Or was someone else here?"

His voice is quieter now, more measured. Not an accusation—he's probing.

I let out a long breath. I don't want to think about this. "Say your piece and let me get to work."

For a long moment, he is silent.

Then, "I saw you yesterday," he repeats. "You were screaming. Thrashing when I tried to pick you up."

... What? Yesterday was the ascension.

My chest tightens, and my tongue acts quicker than my thoughts. "Perhaps it wounds your pride, but it shouldn't be such a surprise that if you treat someone poorly long enough, they won't want you anywhere near them."

Vann tilts his head slightly, studying me with that unreadable expression of his. A slight frown pulls at the corners of his mouth, but sweat pools in my palms.

I can't remember seeing him. I don't recall him waking me up.

In fact, he is speaking as if a whole day has passed since my coronation. But that was last night?

"I have not always treated you poorly," he says.

I blink, my worry shifting to the side as he draws near. Memories unspool, vivid as fresh ink on parchment as they pull them from the moment.

I remember his hands on my waist as he lifted me to place the bow atop the winter festival tree. Then the way we danced later.

Then there had been the night Joso humiliated me at the feast—how Vann's fist had collided with his jaw before I could even react.

A year ago, a group of vaimpír had found a way into one of the tunnels. An enduar had fallen. Vann had nearly died, too.

I remember helping him afterward. After Ulla and Estela had patched him up, they left me to care for him. He was fevered when I pressed a damp cloth to his brow, his skin hot beneath my touch.

Then his fingers wrapped around my wrist. He brought my hand to his mouth.

I remember the press of his lips against my pulse. Then he graced me with a slow, lingering swipe of his tongue before his fangs sank deep.

My breath pushes out of my lungs, sharp and uneven. My heart gallops, thundering in my ears. Warmth rushes to my cheeks, the first I've felt all day.

What the fuck is this?

I exhale, too fast, too shallow.

Vann's gaze lowers, his expression becoming something dark. He studies me, not just my words or my posture—but me. And for the first time in a long while, I can't guess what he's thinking.

I hate this feeling.

It creeps up only occasionally around him—this thing that coils beneath my skin, unsettling and unwelcome. I want to banish it, to shove it away just as I did the bloodied nightgown hidden in my room.

I should take that thing out and burn it.

"You know what I mean," I say, but the words are weak. Vann steps back, breaking whatever strange pull had settled between us.

He shakes his head, brushing past my deflection with infuriating ease. His voice is all business when he speaks again. “There is no spider blood inside the house?”

My breath catches. The stain on my nightgown flashes in my mind, stark against pale fabric.

I bite my lip. “No.” Another lie. The answer comes too quickly, too sharp to be wise. “Now, if you’ll excuse me, I need to clean this.”

Vann shakes his head. “No, allow me. You should really go to see Ulla. She helped you last night, and if you don’t remember, it would be good to check in.”

I swallow. “Right.”

Vann’s hand twitches as I step past him, but he doesn’t stop me.

I grit my teeth and keep walking. Even with my home positioned well within the council housing, reaching the looms takes nearly half an hour. The steady bustle of morning activity filters through the streets. I smile and wave at everyone who greets me.

When I pass Hammerhead Hall, the scent of roasted grains and crisped meat fills the air. My stomach twists painfully, still hungry, but I don’t stop.

I think of Ulla. What would I even say to her?

Would she see through me, hear the shake in my voice, the gaps in my memory? Would she ask how I was feeling?

Guilt prickles over my skin when I think of the spider. Clearly, I had something to do with it as evidenced by the blood on my fingernails and nightgown. But I can’t remember anything last night.

Had my subconscious protected me? Had someone who brought me back from getting a tattoo killed it?

I duck my head and press forward. When I reach the looms, I’ll lose myself in work. Everything will be fine.

It has to be fine.

The gilded arches of the weaving cavern rise ahead. The tension in my shoulders eases just a fraction. It’s safe here. Most people don’t visit—I’ll be able to hide for a while.

Some might say that being put on the council should preclude me from also serving as a weaver and actively assisting with classes.

But *some* people should be thankful for the blankets on their bed.

I cross under the arches and survey the massive area filled with over a hundred standing looms. The air hums with the rhythmic clack of carved shuttles against stone.

At the back of the chamber, Lady Fira stands with a group of stone-bending weavers, their hands working in tandem over a massive block of silkstone. Unlike regular weaving, their craft is a seamless dance between artistry and magic.

Stone benders, enduares gifted with the ability to manipulate rock, have long shaped the foundations of Enduvida. Some, like the builders, mold the city's structures with practiced precision. Others, like Fira, unravel stone itself, spinning delicate threads that no ordinary hands could weave.

I watch as she pulls at the edge of the silkstone, her deft fingers coaxing impossibly thin threads free before winding them onto her spindle. An old pang stirs in my chest. For all my skill with a loom and teaching children, I've always wished I had magic—something to let me weave as seamlessly as she does. But very few humans are born with magic, and those who are aren't exactly revered for it.

The *brujas*, as we call them in our tongue—witches in the common speech—are rarely trusted.

I glance around the chamber. Only two other weavers have arrived before me—one human, one enduar. The enduar, an ocean-risen named La'Mihni, is already at her station, her skilled hands moving over fabric more suited for a gown than a simple woven rug.

Her long, glossy gray hair is piled high above her head in intricate coils. Gems glitter across her workstation, catching the glow of the spell-lights above. Draped over her thigh is a swath of deep red fabric, rich as blood. I know exactly what she's working on. Her mating journey gown.

A frown tugs at my lips. It seems a waste when there's so much else to do.

"Lady Arlet!" Lady Fira's voice rings across the chamber. I turn, forcing a small smile at the sight of the elderly woman. She's also on the council and is one of the most respected weavers in Enduvida. She has always been kind to me.

"What are you doing here?" she asks, her sharp eyes scanning me.

I smile. "I'm here to help."

Fira lets out a long sigh, setting her spindle down with a firm click. "You already have too many duties, child. You can't keep stretching yourself thin. The city needs you elsewhere."

I lift my chin. "I just wanted to help for the day, as I promised. I haven't been here in almost a month."

Her lips purse.

"Please," I say with a smile.

"Fine," she mutters, waving me over. "But at least take that loom. Kiera won't be here today and you can sit near us while we gossip."

I chuckle, moving past the rows of empty machines to the storage cupboards where I used to keep my thread. The routine of it all soothes more of the upset inside of me. Clears away a bit of the darkness, too.

My fingers skim over the bundles of tightly wound fibers, searching for the batch I set aside for treadcloths.

When I reach the station, I settle onto the bench, my fingers brushing over the loom's sturdy stone frame. The structure is broad and well-worn, its polished columns smoothed by generations of hands before mine.

At my feet, the treadles—a set of wide, flat pedals—wait beneath the frame, their placement instinctive after years of practice. With a shift of my weight, I press one down experimentally, feeling the loom's internal mechanisms respond as the shafts rise and fall, lifting the carefully arranged warp threads.

To my right, the beater hangs heavy from its rail, its motion designed to press each new weft thread snugly into place. Above it, the castle—the central support that houses the pulleys and heddles—stands tall, holding the delicate sequence of threads that will soon take shape beneath my hands.

Every weaver knows that, in theory, all workstations are the same—but some feel different. Some pull smoother, respond better. The best ones aren't just tools; they hum beneath your fingers, ready to sing.

This one is good.

A handful of enduares at the back turn toward me, along with the only human man among them—Ariano, an older weaver with a keen eye for fine thread. He gives me a smile.

"Lady Arlet, welcome."

I return his greeting and ask, "What are the whispers in the quiet corners now?"

Before Enduvida grew so crowded with newcomers, gossip was scarce—someone finding a mate, someone falling ill, small tidbits of daily life.

Now?

There's too much to talk about. Wars. Festivals. Clashes between our people. Skirmishes. Matehoods. Children. It's usually enjoyable.

Sometimes.

Fira grins. "I went to the new section of the residential area last night. Just to see what was there. And I was *approached* by two men."

My brows lift. I respect a woman who doesn't let age define her ability to experience romance. In fact, there was this one scroll that I read a few months ago about a queen with a gaggle of lovers. It wasn't for me, but I could understand the appeal.

"Oh?"

Curiosity blooms in my chest, but I hesitate. I don't want to pry—until I see the light in her eyes. She wants me to pry.

I smirk. "Human or enduar?"

She dips her shoulder to her chin. "One of each."

I gasp. "Marvelous. Did you have a favorite?"

Fira shrugs, but before she can speak, Belia, another weaver, interjects.

"That's what we've been trying to find out for the last ten minutes."

Fira only smiles, then shifts the conversation with a glint in her eye.

"It doesn't matter who my favorite is. What does matter is what I learned from them. I may or may not have nestled myself tightly in between the two soldiers starving for affection. After it was given, they wagged their tongues like lost wolves."

"You slept with two men at once so that you could get information? You're a council member!" Ariano says, laughing.

She shrugs. "Most of the council is too busy to answer an old woman's questions."

I laugh. "I'm sure they would've answered anything you asked."

"Stop interrupting. In fact, you two should be happiest to hear what I learned. It's about the elves," she says. Her eyes linger on me, and she nods slightly. The missive comes to the forefront of my mind again. "Apparently, these soldiers are a part of the scouts that patrol the area. And... they've seen nothing. No spies lurking. And when a group of them went to check on Shvathemar, they didn't see any war preparations."

My breath catches.

They hadn't mentioned that in the meeting after my ascension, just explained what we are doing to prepare in addition to expanding and establishing ourselves once again. Perhaps soldiers did know more than I.

And really, I had little against the elves in general. Most of them were kind. And the few transplants in Enduvida integrated well.

But any mention of anything adjacent to King Arion makes my insides crawl. Darkness edges my vision. Soiling the brightness of the room.

Instead of thinking of the elves, I try to grasp at the threads of something else, and that's when I remember this morning.

In an attempt to calm my racing heart, I remind myself that I lacked for nothing in this moment.

If I chose to believe Fira, then the king's request for me was just more posturing. I could let it go. I would feel better tomorrow.

"That is good news," I say belatedly, threading up a new section and letting the rhythm of my loom take me away.

CHAPTER 7

VANN

Earlier that day,

I wake at four in the morning, ready to find Daniel before I need to report to Teo in a lower level of Enduvida. The city is still, the cavernous halls bathed in dim combination of crystals, spell lights, and giant *lumikaps*—massive mushrooms with glowing tops. Each flickers or glows like a distant star.

As I head towards the prison in the forging section, I count my steps. It's a long walk and my breath fogs in the brisk cave air.

Daniel should be there. I intend to learn what his relationship with Arlet had been and why he is still terrorizing her.

Yesterday, Faol, one of the hunters, had told me that the night Daniel showed up outside Arlet's home, he'd been detained.

He was supposed to stay for three days, and tonight, Endu willing, he would spend his time in pain.

As I pass clusters of buildings and the Ardorflame temple, I think about how, just a year ago, the caverns didn't even need a prison. There were so few of us then—just survivors, bound by the simple fact that we had each other. Now, with so many new people, we have one yet again.

It reminds me too much of the past. Of the way things were

under Teo's father. Walls, punishments, control—it all served to divide us.

There is war to worry about, but now we must also be concerned about crime creeping in like rot beneath stone.

And I don't like it. Not one damn bit.

My boots echo against the stone as I cross into the prison corridor, nodding to the guards stationed near the gate. A large, square-jawed ocean-risen enduar—Ce'Olarin—straightens when he sees me.

"Lord Vann," he greets.

I don't waste time. "I believe a human man was brought here two nights ago. I want to speak with him."

Ce'Olaric frowns. "Which one?"

I pause. "I only know he is called Daniel. He has pale hair."

The guards exchange a glance before Ce'Olaric tilts his head toward the cells. "Hmm, I don't know any humans by that name. It's a light night. One of the ocean-risen is in for running through the street naked. There should be a handful of humans, though. Go on."

I step past Ce'Olaric and walk into the cellblock. It smells of damp stone, iron, and piss. The walls are carved directly from the cavern rock, rough in some places, but smoothed by the passage of countless hands in others. The glow of embedded crystals provides dim, uneven lighting, casting long, fractured shadows across the narrow corridor lined with iron-barred cells.

Each cell is enclosed by a combination of metal gates and reinforced stone, designed to hold even the strongest of enduares. The air hums faintly with magic, the warding glyphs etched into the archways pulsing with the slow rhythm of a binding spell song.

Some of the cells are empty, their doors left slightly ajar, while others hold murmuring figures—one or two humans and several ocean-risen. I see the one Ce'Olaric mentioned, an ocean-risen sprawled lazily on a bench, still reeking of salt and alcohol with only a thin, short blanket covering his cock.

Fucking idiot.

I recognize most of the trouble-makers from previous visits. All of them are usually tucked away for minor offenses—brawls, stealing, excessive drunkenness.

I flip through my memories as I move, pulling up Daniel in my mind's eye. Yellowish white hair, flat features. He looked like someone had stomped on his face a little too hard—and I was upset it hadn't been me.

Scanning the rows, I frown. Daniel is nowhere to be seen.

A slow, burning unease creeps down my spine. I head back out into the reception room.

"He's not here," I say.

Ce'Olaric shrugs. "Someone probably came to get him during the night. I just got here an hour ago."

"Who gave the order?" I demand.

The man next to Ce'Olaric shakes his head, and I realize I don't know him. "Faol Scar-Eye. You'll have to ask him."

I look back through the doorway and stare at the empty cell, my pulse hammering. Faol told me that he had taken Daniel here, not that he'd let him free.

Gods on their stony thrones, I'm going in circles.

"Very well. Thank you," I grind out. I turn sharply and stride back into the city streets.

I had a meeting with Teo soon.

As I head toward my home, unease curls tighter in my gut with every step. But just as I reach the residential section, I see her.

Arlet stands on her doorstep, frozen. She's completely ready for the day, but her skin is pale in the dim morning light. Her breathing is fast—too fast.

Then I see why.

The thick, jointed limb of an *aradhlum* lies across her doorstep, its deep-purple blood seeping into the stone in pools. From what I see, she hasn't touched it.

I pick up my pace.

Is she all right? I myself have been bitten by the spiders on several occasions and the venom can be deadly if not treated immediately.

I reach her side, and before I can think, I say, "What the hell are you doing?"

She jolts, body seizing like a string pulled too tight. Her gaze snaps to mine, wide and unsteady, her hands curling into her palms as if to hide something. I don't see any signs of the venom on her face, and her coloring is better.

I frown when I notice the dots on her face are less visible.

"What are you doing here?" she demands.

"We are neighbors," I say simply.

Her lips part, and then she forces a smile—too bright, too easy. "Oh, this? I—I imagine some creature killed it and left it as a gift. I do tend to be perceived as friendly."

I scoff. She's fucking sunshine in this place.

We go back and forth a bit longer, but it is clear to me she's lying. She's never been a good liar. On the one hand, this spider could've attacked her. Why would she lie about that?

She needed protection, in that case.

But if she was hiding something... maybe it was because she had something to do with the death. Something inside of me, a nagging feeling, tells me that Daniel had something to do with this. Maybe there are signs of a struggle in her house. I need to get inside.

Then she says the words that draw me back to the conversation, "...if you treat someone poorly long enough, they won't want you anywhere near them."

I go utterly still.

Excuse me?

I tilt my head slightly, watching her closely. Keeping a tight monitor of my breathing to ensure I don't get overwhelmed by a numbing attack again, I carefully say, "I have not always treated you poorly."

She blinks. A flicker of something crosses her face. She looks at me for a moment longer, then breaks away, and bids me goodbye.

I tell her I'll clean the mess and watch the tension build in her shoulders before she moves with a barely contained urge to flee. She turns sharply and strides past me.

It's so different from how she'd reacted in the council meeting. That night, she'd leaned toward me when she felt danger. Why so run away now?

Did I make her nervous or safe? Or perhaps, both?

She shouldn't fear me—she'd been in my old house. Had helped nurse me back to health from an infection when I'd almost died.

Once she's out of sight, I turn to the mess. In truth, *aradhlum* blood isn't that hard to clean up, and I make quick work of it.

When the clock tower chimes eight thirty in the morning, I decide I still have time to sleuth and turn back toward Arlet's house.

Was there blood inside? Perhaps there was some threatening note from the ass-face. Or maybe a cursed object?

She wasn't ready to accept that something could be seriously amiss, so I needed to find proof. She'd listen to Teo or Estela.

Checking to ensure no one else is out and about yet, I hurry around to the door at the side of the dwelling. It's unlocked.

Really, it's her own fault for not locking both doors.

Still, a sharp pang of guilt twists in my chest the second I cross the threshold. I shouldn't be here.

Her home is... beautiful, though messy with gifts strewn about.

It feels personal being inside, like stepping into someone's mind without permission. She had only been in this home for one month before her appointment with the council, yet she had already built something infuriatingly artistic.

The walls are painted deep blue, streaked with red, orange, and emerald green accents. Light filters through woven curtains, casting soft patterns against stone.

I run my fingers over a gilded embellishment on the wall, wondering where she got such a large quantity of gold paint. Then, I think of the home I once shared with Adra.

It was different from this. The memory was perfectly intact, as all mine were. It had been smaller—for I'd merely been a soldier. It was a shame, as she was the only daughter in a wealthy family up north.

Most of what I made went to giving her jewels and dresses. She'd won my heart, and everything I owned belonged to her.

When she expressed interest in my sketches, and surprised me with a basket of paint pots, I painted everything that pleased her. And those pieces had always been displayed.

While none of those portraits exist anymore, there is artwork all over Enduvida, and yet Arlet's home is void of them.

I shake my head. She probably just didn't have time to select any. Logically, I know she takes on the work of three people.

Why should bare walls bother me? She could fill it with her own art.

I have seen her loom, her hands pulling glorious works from mere thread. She possesses a gift that would have made the master artisans of the Golden Age envious.

But still—no paintings.

Did she not think them worth her time or space?

My jaw tightens as I move through the weaving room. It isn't why I'm here.

Searching the floor for any trace of bloodstains, I move carefully.

I find nothing. The floors are clean, too clean. If there was a struggle, she—or someone else—had already erased the evidence.

Or maybe the struggle was contained upstairs?

I lift my chin, inhaling deeply. The scent of her home is distinct—it smells like her perfume, the faint trace of something floral and the lingering warmth of woven fabric. But beneath it, barely detectable, is the sharp, metallic tang of *aradhlum* blood.

It's faint, but unmistakable.

My pulse thrums and my tail twitches as I approach the staircase leading to her private quarters. For a moment, I hesitate. This is more intrusive than simply searching for evidence on the main floor. But something compels me forward—a small, barely perceivable touch.

Awareness that my god is urging me on washes over me.

I take the steps slowly, deliberately. The corridor is narrow as it leads into her bedroom. The scent is stronger up here, and the door is slightly ajar.

Pushing it open, I step inside.

Her room is... warm. Cozy in a way I didn't expect. Woven blankets drape the bed, the frame itself carved from dark stone. Shelves line the walls, filled with fabric, tools, and carefully arranged scrolls.

But what catches my eye first are the bottles of mead on the small wooden table near her bed.

Half-empty.

I walk over, picking one up, rolling the bottle neck between my fingers. Mead is not an unusual drink, but I've seldom seen her drink so much. The presence of multiple bottles suggests trouble.

Was she drinking to forget? I could relate to that.

I set the bottle down, exhaling through my nose. Curiosity pushes me onto the scrolls on the side of her bed. All of them clearly came from the royal library, and I wonder if this has to do with her work with the school. When I twist the cap on one, I see the title, *"My Tangled Desire."*

I blink.

The script is in an elegant, swirling font as though written by a master scribe. Even more so, it's written in my people's language.

Was she really so fluent in enduar? I unroll a bit and begin to read.

"He yanked down the neckline of her dress, one perfectly azure breast spilling out. With her hands bound behind her back, she could do little more than arch her body into his touch. His fingers trailed lower, tracing patterns down her stomach as his lips found purchase against her neck. Her breath hitched, and she let out a small gasp as he—"

I drop the scroll, a flush spreading up my neck and heat rushing to my groin. I wasn't a prude—but this?

After scooping up the text, I grab another. I find her marking spot —it's a metal clip with a ribbon and... the contents are similar.

Hell, I didn't even know the library stored books like this. Mind churning, I can't seem to parse this out. Wasn't the library supposed to be full of annals, maps, diaries of previous sovereigns? Scientific fact?

I hesitate a moment more, then place both back on the nightstand and look to her bed.

Did she read those words before bed? Did they stir a heat in her?

Was it a desire of hers to be bound that she might surrender to another's touch and care? Is she hungry for an intense passion borne of trust?

It... is easy to picture her enjoying that. She is a hard worker, often pushing herself to impose order on chaos. Something in me recognized that a life like that leads to few moments of respite.

I too wished for the sweet, consuming oblivion that pleasure could provide. It had been a long time since—

Clamping down swiftly on those thoughts, I turn away and adjust my pants at the groin. With another deep breath, my gaze landed on the large frame loom standing in the far corner of the room.

My chest tightens.

I approach it slowly, my fingers brushing over the sturdy stone frame. It has been a while since I've seen her working with cloth. The vertical threads are stretched taut, frozen in time, while the shuttle rests mid-weave, abandoned as if she had left in a hurry. The half-formed pattern lingers—a story interrupted.

The colors are breathtaking—deep indigos, rich crimsons, and streaks of gold woven together in intricate patterns. A river. A meadow. And... a barren mountain?

Was that blood staining the top?

No, just thread.

The craftsmanship is impeccable. Even half-finished, it is a work of art.

My fingers trace over the strands.

For all my time in Enduvida, for all the painful distance between us, I have never been allotted much access to her thoughts or hobbies. Part of that is my fault.

I wonder what she would create if she weren't carrying a thousand responsibilities. If she weren't constantly working herself to exhaustion. If she weren't... alone.

A cold ache presses into my ribs, but I shove it away. I am not here to marvel at her skill. Nor am I here to ruin my day before it's fully begun.

I am here to figure out what's happening.

Turning, I scan the room again—and that's when I find a crate filled with crumbled clothes. I stride closer, realizing the smell of blood is more potent in this area.

Pulling out a handful of garments, I spot a white nightgown, similar to the one she wore last night. I crouch as I lift the delicate fabric between my fingers. It's stained with deep purple that's nearly black.

I inhale sharply, and her scent floods my senses.

Warm, soft, something distinctly Arlet beneath the sharp, pungent tang of spider's blood. Her scent hits me harder than I expect, wrapping around my throat, stealing my breath.

For a moment, my grip tightens on the fabric. My body is betraying me, reacting to something it shouldn't.

Damn it.

I force myself to crumple it up as my fingers curl into fists. I try to steady my breathing.

Who gives a sparkling fuck what she smells like? This is about what happened last night. Daniel is missing. The *aradhlum* was butchered. And Arlet acts like she doesn't remember an entire day, nor how the spider died.

I rise to my feet, rolling my shoulders. I take one last glance at the room—at the loom, at the mead, at the nightgown—then exhale slowly.

Never in the history of my recollection has something like this happened in the caves.

I've never seen someone forget so much time from drinking alone. Never seen someone cold and pale and screaming in the middle of the night.

She wasn't bitten by a vaimpír, not with those black eyes. Maybe it was a trick of the light?

In the past, I had seen a soldier on the battlefield go mad after days without sleep paired with intense bloodlust, but Arlet isn't in that position.

Something is wrong, and that worries me.

I can't be in this state, constantly wondering if she is going to walk off a cliff. She isn't ready to face whatever is happening. But I am.

I step back toward the door, my thoughts already spinning through the possibilities. Looking down at the gown, I decide I will give her one last chance to talk to me.

And if she didn't? I would take this to Teo. She might listen to him.

If I have to go through the queen herself to get answers, I will.

I owed Arlet my life, and I'm not about to let her be hurt. Perhaps, if I can solve this mystery, my mind will stop bending toward her memory. Perhaps I will feel free from the... longing that aches in my hollow soul.

With one final look at her home, I leave head toward the weaving cavern.

CHAPTER 8

ARLET

A few hours of chatting and weaving pass, and I remember just how much I desperately miss this. Teaching is good... but *this* fills my soul.

It makes sense. Creating art is chaotic, but somehow, it always ends up working out. A part of me likes the peaks and valleys of not knowing if something will work until the very end.

After finishing three blankets, I pull my shoulders back, stretching out the stiffness just as the sound of footsteps at the door makes me turn.

Queen Estela enters, flanked by two bodyguards and a nursemaid pushing a strange cart-like contraption carrying her two sons. One is enormous—Kai. He is her and Teo's adopted son, a giant prince from the fallen kingdom. In the common tongue, adopted girls and boys are called "starling children," those blessed by the goddess and welcomed into the family.

The other, her birth son, Leo, is just slightly smaller, though still young, his skin tinged with that familiar purplish-blue hue. Her son by birth.

Seeing her, my oldest friend, usually brings joy. But not today.

Fuck. Has she come to talk to me about missing my meeting yesterday? Or... did she know about what happened outside my home?

The entire room stands at attention, bowing as the deep enduar phrase rumbles behind me, *"The stone moves beneath your feet."*

Fira's voice is loudest when she says, "Queen Estela, *Aevum Duarum*, be welcome in this place."

I take note of the enduar phrase that has started appearing more often—"Eternal One of Two." A clear reference to the fact that she is blessed by both Grutabela, the enduar goddess, and Ashra, the goddess once worshiped by humans.

But humans have not so easily returned to the idea of a deity. After so many years without divine guidance, without prayers answered or miracles granted, worship feels foreign. Ashra's name lingers like a half-forgotten legend, a whisper of something once revered but now met with skepticism.

Ashra has few shrines, but she lives on mainly through the glowing queen before me.

Estela smiles, and the whole room bends toward her. "Thank you, friends. At ease. I've come to speak with Ladies Fira and Arlet."

A twinge of discomfort spreads up my back, but I force a smile. I'm still off-kilter from this morning. "Wonderful," I say.

Not just me. This is good.

I glance at my loom, at the fabric I had just finished threading, before standing and joining Fira's side.

"What can we do for you, My Queen?" Fira asks, ever smooth and polished.

Estela steps closer, Fira herding us into the back corner of the space as the other weavers work. The clacking doesn't stop, and it drowns out the pleasantries exchanged.

Though she wears the authority of a ruler, there is still an ease between us. A familiarity that makes it hard to stay detached—especially when I see the children up close.

In the back of my mind, a voice speaks. What if I lose myself again?

Then, her and Teo's starling child, Kai, reaches toward me.

The gesture is small and innocent. And it loosens something inside my ribs. I'm in control right now, and he recognizes me—of course he does. I've cared for him many times.

Estela gives me a knowing glance before shifting her attention back to Fira. "I know that the last few days have been a mad dash to the finish line, but we still have further to go. As you know, tomorrow, the Mating Journey begins, and I wanted to check in on the progress of the banners."

I nod, glancing at Fira, who offers a small, satisfied smile.

"We finished all of the requisitions three days ago. Lady Arlet was keen to complete the list before her ascension," Fira says. "The committee you set up for the journey already took all the crates to the lower floor. I believe Mother Liana was involved."

Estela's face glows with approval. "That's marvelous. Thank you. Since that is out of the way, I have something else for you, Lady Arlet."

She turns toward her assistant, a sharp nod passing between them. The enduar woman produces two scrolls, stepping forward to hold them out to me.

I frown, hesitating before I take them. "What's this?"

Estela's smile takes on a teasing edge. "The first is a list of men participating in the Mating Journey. All nine hundred and eighty-seven of them."

My stomach twists.

"And that—" she tilts her chin toward the second scroll, her eyes gleaming with something far too amused for my liking— "is what you have somehow neglected to complete for Lirenne. Now, I know you have been busy with your new position, but remember—all unmarried members of the council are required to go. We went over this during the council meeting, but you didn't attend. In that scroll, you will find a list of questions about yourself and your preferences."

Then, she winks.

Something unpleasant slithers through me, curling like smoke in my ribs. I hadn't forgotten about the damn scroll. I had just... let it hang in the air, floating above me, unclaimed, undisturbed. Lady Fira, sensing the discomfort, returns to her duties.

Hope is a dangerous thing. I'd been in only two relationships, and neither had ended well. I purposefully didn't think of the Mating Journey because I knew my heart would start to conjure ideas, like this could be what I've been waiting for. The thing that will change everything and cause me to recognize a mate. And then I would finally have an increased measure of magic to let me get pregnant.

Right now, that thought is especially comforting because having a husband would make me ineligible for the Elf King's awful proposal.

But another part of me is tired. Exhausted from pain. Tired of betrayal and rejection. Of being an option, never the choice.

I clutch the scrolls, feeling their weight, the jewels glinting in the floating lights. Lirenne is the enduar in charge of the festival, and she has been sorting scrolls for over a month. She has developed a mathematical system to help her match potential couples together while still preserving a flexibility that would let everyone at the festival at least see each other.

The week after would be spent filled with mating ceremonies. It is to be a long month for me. It would be a kindness to let me just... skip it all.

Estela's voice softens. "Given our friendship, I have told Lirenne to accept your scroll at the beginning of the festivities. And I think it would be a good idea if you made note of any men who seem to stand out." Another knowing look. "Perhaps it will lead to a more successful day."

Well, ouch.

Something pinches inside my chest, a quiet, relentless ache. I don't covet Estela's power nor her husband. But the idea of what she possesses? Love. Family. Trust.

She has always had that, and it has always hurt. I hunger for such things.

This isn't helpful. I know she means well, that she wants me to move forward. To heal. But this—this isn't the answer.

I twist my hands and her expression changes.

Her brows furrow, a crease forming between them. "Arlet? Was I too forward?"

I hesitate. Then, finally, I say it.

"I don't wish to attend."

She blinks. "But you must, it—"

"A foreign king wants to carry me away as a bride. I don't know if I'm in the right state of mind to find a mate," my voice snaps, sharp as a blade.

It's a mistake.

The air changes, crisping at the edges.

Estela exhales slowly. "*Querida*," she says firmly, "you don't have to do anything that doesn't feel right for you. I know you are overwhelmed."

The words should be soothing. But instead, they crack something inside me.

Daniel. Joso. King Arion. They all swirl before me. Of the two lovers I'd had in my life, both had broken my trust and it came down, sadly, to one thing. My inability to give them a family.

I lost Daniel's child, and my crystal never produced a song for Joso. Not only was I not barren, I was not chosen by those I chose.

The one person who had chosen me is dangerous.

Damn it all.

I rub my temples, feeling a headache coming on. I need to focus on my work.

For so long, everything inside me has felt like one or the other. All or nothing. Hope or despair. Love or rejection.

I don't know what I want anymore. A family, yes. But... what about love?

For too long, my love has been measured by what men wanted from me—whether or not I was meeting their expectations. Arion only wants me because he believes I've never been with another.

Daniel wanted to waltz back in after everything.

Joso avoids me.

I can't take it.

Estela watches me carefully. "Just say the word, and I won't make you go," she says.

I open my mouth. "I don't..."

Then, footsteps sound behind us. They are heavy and measured. Familiar.

A deep, rumbling voice cuts through the tension.

"Queen Estela."

The sound filters across the now-crowded weaving hall.

Vann.

Silence follows his words. Every single person pauses then turns, watching as he moves through the rows. And despite the way I study his face, he never once looks at me.

Yet he commands the room.

The way he saunters into my work, my place, makes the rows of weavers watch him with equal parts awe, desire, and fear. He has never been a charming man—not by any stretch of the word—but he is a force.

A figure larger than life.

He holds people in place around him, like our planet holds the moon.

Which begs the next question: What the fuck is he doing here, and why does he look like he wants to set something on fire?

A clammy sweat covers my skin. Has he come to ask about the spider again?

"Lord Vann, what a surprise. Is something wrong with my mate?" Estela asks.

Vann bows before her, his gaze sweeping over the room with an intensity that makes my stomach tighten. He reaches into the cloak draped over his shoulders and pulls out a long white nightgown.

My nightgown.

My spine locks straight, my breath catching in my throat. The gown soaked with Aradhlum blood.

No. Not here.

My pulse hammers. What is he doing? He opens his mouth, and before he can speak, I lunge forward, grabbing his wrist in a desperate, instinctive motion.

The second our bodies make contact, he freezes. His eyes, sharp as winter's edge, lock onto mine.

I've never looked into them for this long.

Something shifts behind them, the solid silver turning fluid, bending, tilting—or maybe it's just the world around me spinning. His wrist is cold but heat from his skin seeps into my hand, spreading up my wrist like an infection.

"Arlet?"

Estela's voice feels far away, but I can't look away from him.

"Can someone tell me what is going on?" she tries again, sharper this time.

I rip my gaze from Vann's, forcing myself to breathe. "Lord Vann seems to want to discuss something better left to a private conversation." My voice is tight, my fingers still clamped around his wrist.

Together, our small group heads to the area carved out of the back of the weaving room. It's full of tools, threads, discarded scraps, metal buttons, and a dozen crates filled with other supplies.

I let go of Vann's hand as Estela turns.

The queen's face solidifies into something cold. "What was so urgent?"

He shrugs, but I don't miss the way his fingers flex—how his grip tightens on the gown.

"Do you remember last night," Vann says, his voice calm, controlled—but cutting. "When I found Arlet screaming in the middle of the passageway?"

My breath stills.

Estela's face pinches in concern. "What?"

Vann lifts the middle of my nightgown, the fabric stiff with dried blood. "I found her outside, standing over a dead *aradhlum*."

Estela gasps. "Were you attacked?"

I hadn't even thought about that. My mind races, flipping back through blurred memories, searching for something—anything—that makes sense.

Vann continues before I can answer. "This is its blood. I found her disoriented outside her house this morning, standing over a severed leg. Two nights before, a man named Daniel was seen near her home. I went looking for him today, and he's gone. I think he brought the creature there. Maybe he poisoned her."

"You don't think... I attacked the spider?" I ask.

A cold sweat breaks over my skin. My heart pounds too fast.

"Why would we think that? You are not a violent person, Arlet," Estela says softly.

I remember the blood on my fingernails.

"She needs to get out of here and go see Ulla," Vann snaps, his jaw tight. Then he hands the nightgown to me.

Estela glares at him. "Lord Vann, I think it's best you leave. I'm sure there is plenty that must be done before tomorrow."

Vann's gaze lingers on my face. He doesn't speak, but I feel his stare before he turns and strides away.

The second he's gone, I take a deep, shaky breath and clench my fingers around the nightgown. Estela watches him leave, still frowning.

"He can be overbearing," she says a moment after. "And forgive me for pushing so hard about the Mating Journey. I didn't realize how difficult the past few nights have been for you. Are you all right?"

A heavy weight presses on my temples. I need to rest. But my mind is frayed, a live wire ready to snap. I also need to work. There is so much to do. The new program, the blankets, the meetings... It's too much.

"Arlet," Estela starts, but I barely hear her.

"Sorry. I am fine," I say a moment later. "And you are right about the Mating Journey. It's my job as a new council member. I will fill this out and bring it with me."

She pulls me into a hug. "Oh, I'm so glad. Now, take the day off—*rest*. I will see you at the festival."

I nod absently, force a smile, and slip out of the room. Estela leaves first, called away by the cry of one of her sons. Once she's gone, I throw the nightgown into the scrap bin, then sit down and resume my work.

"Everything all right?" Lady Fira asks a moment later.

I turn to her and smile. "Yes, sorry. It was something about the Mating Ceremony."

She nods. "Of course. Gods, he's handsome. Don't you think?"

"Lord Vann?" I ask.

A few others grin, giving their own versions of "yes."

I bite my lip. Vann is... untouchable. Handsome? Perhaps. But very much not mine.

"I don't know, I've never noticed?" I say. Another lie. *Hostia*, what is wrong with me lately?

Everyone around me begins to chatter and gossip once again. I need to go to Ulla's in a little while, but I should finish this project first. I don't want to rest. Apparently, I'd rested enough in a day that is entirely lost to me.

There is work to be done.

CHAPTER 9

VANN

After Queen Estela banishes me from the weaving cavern, I go to find Teo. We were supposed to meet two hours ago. He'll be upset at my tardiness, but I had more important things to tend to first.

I walk through the heated forges ringing with the sound of hammers. Past the forges is the third tunnel that leads down to the lower level of Enduvida.

The city is similar to a hive in many senses. The main section of the cave system where we lived, aged, forged, and partied was the largest cavern, but deeper, other useful pockets of space could be used for anything.

A crowd is gathered outside of the entrance of the tunnel.

I let out a huff of a laugh. Where there is chaos, Teo must be nearby. He's got a talent for organizing it.

This section leads down to a lower cavern, an open expanse where the Mating Journey will take place tomorrow. The passage is narrow, the steady flow of people carrying crates, food, water, and crystals making it feel even tighter as I push forward.

When I emerge, the cavern widens into a vast, open space, bustling with movement. Nearly a thousand people worked to clear this area, and now, hundreds of tents stand in neat rows, their vibrant colors striking against the deep gray basalt walls. The jewel-toned fabrics ripple under the shifting glow of overhead spell-lights, casting shimmering reflections across the cavern floor. The ceiling arches high above, making it the perfect space for the festival.

My eyes skim over the textiles. Has Arlet touched these, too?

I can't help but think of the image on the loom in her home. Beautiful, bright, and then barren—streaked with threads representing blood.

Enough, I insist.

I walk past workers carrying supplies—food, cushions, banners—grimacing at the excessive use of precious materials. Then, I spot the king.

Teo stands in the center of a group of ocean-risen, overseeing the preparations.

I approach, extending my hand.

Teo breaks away from his conversation and clasps my palm, pulling me into a firm embrace before clapping a hand across my back. Then, he gestures toward one of the ocean-risen women beside him.

"Brother, this is Lirenne."

She is striking—tall, elegant, half her face marked by a white birthmark that stands out against the deep cerulean of her skin.

She smiles at me, and I catch a hint of flirtation. I nod, but don't return the gesture.

If she thinks I don't know who she is, she's mistaken. Her name has been spoken more than ten times in council meetings leading up to this week.

"Lord Vann," she says smoothly. "It is an honor to finally meet the king's personal advisor."

I incline my head. "Lirenne. Your work is commendable." Then I turn back to Teo. "What do you need?"

My blood brother lifts his brows, giving me an amused look before shifting his attention back to Lirenne. "Our gracious coordinator was just filling me in."

"We were discussing the matching strategy. My team has worked tirelessly to ensure everyone has equal opportunity to find their mate. Forgive my forwardness, Lord Vann," she says quickly. "But as part of the festival, we are making recommendations for both men and women—matching them based on their preferences."

"Novel," I say flatly.

She laughs softly. "I myself will be participating. I would love to know more about you."

"Why?"

She hesitates for only a moment, but Teo answers first.

"Funny you should mention that," he says. "Lirenne tells me you haven't presented the council with your scroll."

I go completely still.

"Strange," he continues, watching me carefully. "Seeing as how that means you probably haven't touched it. Even more so, knowing you've already been assigned a tent. Vann, you know that every unmated member of the council will be participating. There will be people coming through, visiting tents, and you will be one of those ensuring the men and women are served on their journey."

My expression hardens. "Why the fuck would you do that?"

A flicker of irritation passes over Teo's face, but Lirenne is the one who answers.

"Excuse me," she says, tilting her head. "I had assumed—well, you are unmated, are you not?"

A sharp pulse of anger rolls through me, but my attention stays focused on Teo, even as my limbs grow cold.

"You know I had a woman," I say coldly. "Adra. Her name was *Li'Adra*. We loved each other. We were partners in every sense of the word. Why do you constantly ask me to dishonor her memory?"

Lirenne falters. "I—"

His nostrils flail when he exhales. *"Brother."*

I freeze. I've overstepped.

"Forgive me, My King." I turn to Lirenne, "Forgive me as well. I am merely tense. Please allow me a moment with His Majesty."

She bites her lower lip, but turns and walks away.

Alone, Teo shakes his head. "You know that Arlet will be attending."

"What does she have to do with anything?"

There's an awkward pause.

"You told me you wanted to kiss her once. You practically crushed the stone missive from the Elf King. You have admitted that you and Adra were not mated."

I pull up the memory from the battle at the Giant Mines. We were half-dead, lying in a rotting battlefield. I was half-mad with pain and hunger—I was delusional.

Teo had asked if I had regrets. Nonsense had poured from my mouth.

"Arlet and I. Are. Not. Mated. *Either*. There is no song. No marks on my neck. My crystal does not warm near her. I said that in a moment of weakness. Forget it."

Teo exhales, some of his irritation giving way to regret. "Very well, Vann." He rubs a hand over his jaw. "You can choose to fill the scroll out or not. Just... take it. And then go to the men in the back. I'm sure they'll have something for you."

I don't respond.

Instead, I take the unfinished scroll from the table and shove it into my pocket.

I'll burn it later.

Or throw it into the lava pit beneath the city.

CHAPTER 10

VANN

Hours of moving, lifting, and manual work have made my body tired, but my mind is more alive than ever.

When I'd broken into the kitchens, I found one of the human men cleaning up—Luiz—who handed me a bottle of mead. It felt wrong to drink in front of a man still working, so I left, mead in hand, wandering home.

The lights in Arlet's dwelling are off.

Good. She needs rest after what she's been through. She better have gone to see Ulla.

Pushing open the door to my own house, I look around, seeing it as if for the first time. The inside of my house is simple, functional. A circular space with smooth stone walls, reinforced with the golden-toned enduar metal that lines much of the council district. No unnecessary decorations, no flourishes—just what I need.

I recognize the easels lining one wall, and the row of paints and brushes stored in baskets. But then I look at the large, sturdy wooden desk, which takes up one side of the room, a place for maps, reports, and the occasional untouched letter from Teo. Above it, shelves hold weapons and tools, a mix of old and new—blades honed from ancient obsidian, a hunting spear, a few small mechanical trinkets from the city's metal benders that I have yet to throw away. Above all of them rests my cleaver.

I've killed so many with that blade. It's almost an extension of my person. My identity.

Across from the display, a stone hearth keeps the space warm, a low fire still smoldering from the morning. A single chair sits beside it, worn from use, angled just enough to watch the flames. A habit, more than anything.

My sleeping area is upstairs. It's the most pleasant area to look at, draped with furs and woven blankets. The scent of the mountain lingers here, sharp and mineral-rich, mixed with the faint trace of the oils I use to clean my weapons.

Who the fuck was all this for?

I didn't need so much space. I was happy in my old house.

My tail jerks to the side, slapping against the wall. I uncork the bottle, throwing my head back as I take a deep drink. The sweet, honeyed liquid burns, trailing fire down my throat, but I welcome it.

A little pain to remind myself that I am alive.

To live without a heart is to have every emotion cut in half—distant, muted, like sound underwater. Still there, but dulled.

I drop into one of the gold-trimmed chairs by the table I never requested, slamming the bottle down before pulling the scroll from my belt and letting it fall beside it.

Then I take another drink.

I stare at the damned parchment before finally, ripping the twine free and unrolling it.

The usual nonsense is there. Name. Pastimes. Preferred scents. Favorite meals.

Then I see the last line.

"Sexual preferences."

Fuck.

I choke, nearly laughing at its absurdity. But my mind is already there, it has been since I picked up that stupid scroll in Arlet's room.

"You know Arlet will be there," Teo had said.

Arlet, with her unwavering dedication, friendliness and goodness. Arlet with her perfect, pink lips, wild red hair, and intriguing desires.

Arlet. The bronze-freckled woman with a soft body that fits perfectly in my arms.

She needs someone to care for her, to consume her. And then return the broken pieces of her soul, all while helping her smooth over the jagged edges.

It's been so long since I'd been with Adra. No other woman had touched me since.

The heat lurks at the edges of my soul, waiting for an outlet. And suddenly, it floods my system.

A rush of blood passes over my skin—hot, sharp, demanding.

The sensation shoots straight to my groin, tightening into something dark and insistent.

Fuck. It's potent.

I stand abruptly, and the stiffness in my pants is uncomfortable. I need to cool off. To relax. I could stay here—take care of this like I have before.

Or I could leave.

Even half-drunk, I know the answer.

I burst out of my house, gulping in the cool cavern air. The deeper I walk into the city, the less suffocated I feel and the more the heat recedes.

I let out a few musical notes when I reach the tunnels at the end of the residential section. The crystals around me, quartz, amethyst, and citrine sing back. They hum in my bones, trying to soothe me.

Tunnel six was dedicated to public pools. They are often occupied, even at night, but a new room just opened, one crafted by the ocean-risen. It was usually empty past midnight.

They call it a salt room, whatever the hell that means.

I head toward it, wondering if salt crystals will sing as prettily as quartz.

Each step drags me away from the thoughts I don't want and the chill in my chest that leads to pain the following day.

Arlet didn't need me thinking about her constantly. She has

always been predisposed to fight twice as hard against me when I'm the one bringing up the issue.

I should have left the matter of the nightgown alone.

But I can't.

Not when I found her standing over the severed leg of an aradhlum, her hands shaking, her expression blank—like she wasn't even inside her own body. Not when she barely remembers a full day. Not when Daniel was seen lurking near her home, and now he's gone.

The pieces don't fit together cleanly, and it's driving me mad.

And if I don't figure out what is going on soon, I'm afraid I'll find her in the same position again—except next time, she won't be the one left standing.

Dragging my hand across my face, I turn down a new path and find the entrance, and I untie the tunic around my shoulders. The room is warm, glowing with the soft orange hue of salt crystals, and I didn't want to get overheated. For some reason, they insisted on a door. I push it open, stepping inside... and stop dead.

A woman's form stretches across one of the slabs, entirely unclothed.

Flame-red hair cascades over smooth shoulders, curling over freckled skin. She's bathed in the soft amber light, as if sculpted from the same mineral around her.

A single arm drapes over her eyes, shielding her from the glow. She doesn't stir.

I go rigid.

Then, a soft snore escapes her lips.

For a moment, I can't breathe. Can't think. The rush of blood, of heat, of want comes like a wave, knocking the air from my lungs.

She is delicate in a way that is entirely different from what I have ever known.

My mouth parts, my chest tightens, and I tear my gaze away, cursing myself.

What is she doing here, alone? Where are her clothes?!

Gods, this is not helping. She's putting herself in danger, I swear.

I should wake her up before anyone else comes in.

Now.

I clear my throat, making my voice louder, rougher than necessary, and continue to avoid looking right at her.

"What in the name of my gods' stony feet are you doing here, disrobed?" I growl.

The reaction is instant.

Arlet bolts upright, her unbound hair spilling over her bare back, eyes wide, startled.

For a split second, I don't recognize her.

Her lips are parted, her face unguarded, her pupils blown wide—so wide they swallow the brown of her irises.

"Turn around!" she screeches.

I whirl immediately, clenching my jaw.

"How long have you been standing there?" she demands, her voice still edged with sleep.

I swallow, the image of smooth, bare skin flashing through my mind. I let it pass, knowing it's wrong to keep such things near my thoughts.

I am good at ignoring memories. It's how I've survived.

"Hardly a few seconds," I respond, my voice betraying the lack of air in my lungs. "But, again, why are you here?"

I hear movement behind me, fabric rustling as she redresses.

"I went to see Ulla after work, but she was gone. I waited for an hour, but she didn't return. One of her assistants checked me quickly, then they told me to come here. They said that being nude would help the salt crystals clear out the cloud of negative energy surrounding me," she mutters, quieter now. "No one ever comes at this hour—I thought I was safe."

Then, after a pause.

"Did you look?"

Her voice is small, unsure.

I exhale slowly, jaw tight.

"No."

Another moment of silence. Then, softer—"You hesitated."

Damn it all.

I scrub a hand over my face, willing my body to calm the hell down.

"You startled me," I admit. That much is true.

She sighs. The tension in the air shifts, but even then, I don't look directly at her.

"Vann," she nudges me with her voice.

"I didn't look, Firelocks."

What good would come of telling her that I had?

I've kept her at arm's length, despite every person in my circle constantly throwing us together.

She seems pleased. Arlet lets out a shaky breath, the soft rustle of fabric filling the room as she ties the cloth around herself. It's an absurd sound, far too erotic for what's actually happening. My muscles lock, every part of me willing this torture to end.

"How long does it take to tie a thin strip of cloth around your waist?" I grit out.

She makes an irritated noise, as if I'm the problem here.

I push further. "All decent?"

"Yes," she hisses.

I turn.

The heat in the salt room is heavy. It's not unbearable, but sweat beads at my brow, slipping down the back of my neck.

And Arlet is glaring at me like she's ready to set me on fire.

"What?" I grunt out.

"I didn't expect to see you tonight. And I just remembered how angry I am at you."

"Why? Because of this?"

"Did you forget you broke into my house?" she snaps, arms crossed tight over her chest.

I let out a slow breath. "I wasn't trying—"

"I don't care," she cuts in, stepping closer. The flush on her cheeks isn't just from the heat now—her temper burns. "I don't like getting angry. But you invaded my house. My nightgown was in my room! *With my soiled clothes.* You—" Her voice catches, her fingers shifting at her sides before she clenches them into fists. "That is my home, Vann."

Something in my chest pulls tight. I didn't want to violate her space. I just—I just needed to make sure she was safe.

That's the part I can't say. The part I don't even know how to put into words.

Guilt churns in my gut, twisting like a blade. I exhale sharply, rolling my shoulders, trying to shove it aside—but it sticks.

"I'm sorry," I say, the words gruff, unpracticed.

Arlet blinks, clearly startled.

Good. Maybe that'll be enough.

But then I make the mistake of looking past her, to the polished marble slab where she had been lying, and my attention snags on something that shouldn't be here.

A Mating Journey scroll. The same damned kind that's sitting on my table at home.

I move before I think, pushing past her, reaching down to grab the parchment just as she lunges for it.

"Why are you going through my things *again*?" she snaps. "I'm leaving if you don't stop."

"Come now, this is not so personal. I was given the same one. You can read it if you'd like," I say, smiling to myself as I unroll the stone paper. She would find nothing on my scroll, but I might be able to get her to have a drink with me. We could talk about what was happening.

Then, I consider she might be looking for another partner. So soon? With everything else?

"You are... going tomorrow?" she asks.

"They keep asking me to," I return.

"Because you are unmated?"

"I am alone," I deflect. I flick the scroll back toward her, my patience thinning. "You know, the Mating Journey is like having your heart pulled out through your nostrils."

"I'm already familiar with the sensation."Arlet snatches the scroll from my grip, eyes flashing. "And what were you doing here again?"

"I could ask you the same thing."

Now it's her turn to brush past me, walking toward the glowing salt walls and trailing her fingers along the delicate mineral bands.

“I already told you. But I guess I came here to relax. Specifically at midnight to avoid... annoyances."

The light gilds her skin, making her glow as she looks back at me. Her unbound hair is one of the most beautiful things I’ve ever seen. It looks so soft.

I like that I see it so often, despite having no right.

Smirking, I ask, "Am I an annoyance?"

"Yes." She doesn’t even hesitate.

Well, I suppose it is warranted. I’ve been an ass the past two days. But I didn’t always want to be one, especially not to her.

I step toward her, closing the space between us. "You wound me."

Reaching out, I tap the top of her scroll, letting my fingers land dangerously close to hers. There’s a lot I want to ask her. I want to know about Daniel, if she remembers anything from the night before, why she continues to work even though she’s not well.

But instead I say, "Now tell me—are you really planning to go to the festival tomorrow?"

She turns fully, only realizing just how close I am when she looks up.

"Of... course I am," she says, eyes flicking—too quickly—to my bare shoulders.

"Why?"

The Mating Journey is pageantry. A performance. One even worse than the mockery I was forced into during the Queen’s Festival months ago.

In the old enduar customs, the Mating Journey was held every year. Some returned year after year. Some never stopped searching.

I only went once.

For me, it had been hours of self-reflection and physical preparation wasted. Even thinking about it now has me irritated with the way I had to shape myself into something palatable, something a mate might want. I spent so much time crafting that version of myself, forcing my rough edges into something smoother.

I hated myself for it. But I hated myself even more when it didn’t work.

Why would she subject herself to that? She is fine as she is.

"Enough," she snaps, frustration creeping into her tone. "You've had your fun—barging in here while I was in an embarrassing position. I'm tired. Definitely not feeling up to your mockery."

But her words lack their usual sharpness.

My brows pull together. I want to push. I study the dozens of shades of red in her hair, making note of the warm and cool tones—the exact colors I would need if I were to paint it.

I shouldn't be thinking about that.

"I had no intention of mocking you," I say softly.

Her eyes widen, just slightly.

Her lips part.

"Oh."

She did make me angry from time to time, but the edge I sported around her was something else. Something unsure of how to be... friendly. Upon meeting, she didn't like my commanding tone, but she also didn't even try to understand my position as the king's advisor. From there, the sourness between us had been a long string of my inept ability to speak my mind. That caused growing resentment.

I knew it was happening. I just didn't know how to stop it.

Instead of fumbling this moment, I tap the top of the scroll again.

"So why?" My voice is calm, but there's an edge beneath it. "Why parade yourself around to find a partner? Surely there's enough interest elsewhere."

Everyone loves Arlet. Even if not romantically. When she'd been with Joso, I hadn't liked it, but he was far from the only one gazing upon her with stars in their eyes. It wasn't her fault she picked someone as useful as a sword with no edge.

As my thoughts unfurl something dark and dangerous twists in my gut. I didn't like talking about potential suitors.

She pauses, fingers playing with the tie around her waist. The one that holds the thin, barely-there fabric to her skin.

Stop. Thinking.

"You know how cruel that statement is, Vann. You saw what happened with Joso. He—I wasn't what he wanted. It's not the first time it's happened."

A sharp, icy stillness spreads through me. First, knowing I've said the wrong thing again, but then I'm angry at Joso. I should have done more than punch him.

"Call me foolish, but I want to be loved. Just once." Her voice is quiet, raw. A delicate silver line appears along her bottom lashes. "It could be easy to find someone at the festival. So many people. So many options."

Every part of me pauses.

Too many options.

Her words sting against the cold, empty space where my heart should be. I wonder, if I actually had one, would this feel worse?

"Hmm."

She looks away, brushing her fingers over the scroll.

"Estela is making me go," she admits. "And I've just been lugging this around all day."

I bark out a laugh.

"Yes. They are insistent we all go."

Her eyes brighten, her mouth quirking in amusement.

"So you are joining me?"

I think about finding her earlier. The blood on her nightgown. That small spark of joy tamps down any warmth I might have felt.

"Aren't you afraid they'll find out your secret?" I murmur. She was so set on not letting anyone know what happened in front of her house. How will she even be able to tell someone she's in danger?

Her expression twists, true hurt flashing in her eyes.

Damn. Another misstep. Another crack in the fragile ground between us. There must be a way to fix this—to untangle the threads before they fray beyond repair.

I need to show her I mean well.

"How dare you—"

"It might be best if you tell me exactly what you're looking for in a husband. I could be of help... especially with the matching system." I grin, broad and sharp.

"Maldito idiota," she breathes. An insult in her tongue. "You don't want to help me and I don't want to be mocked." She tucks the scroll against her chest and steps back, clearly moving to leave.

The warmth vanishes, and something in my belly lurches.

Before I can think better of it, I grab her hand.

She stiffens, her fingers caught in mine, the heat of her palm grounding me in place.

"I know I don't say things the right way," I murmur, twining my fingers with hers. "I know I keep making mistakes."

She looks down at our hands, pulling away again, but instead it changes the position of our limbs and our small fingers interlock—hers, the ones that had been stitched back on. Mine, the ones I lost half of in the war.

My gut clenches.

I squeeze lightly, almost as if I were still holding her hand to create a proper vow. "But I want to do better. I will do better at being kind, so you know we can be friends. That's a promise."

Arlet's eyes flick to mine, searching.

I don't know if she believes me. But she doesn't pull away.

"Help me?"

I nod.

"Why?" Her voice is unsteady. "You keep doing that—you keep helping me. But you also seem to hate me."

"Maybe I don't want you wandering around the city with a frown." I purse my lips. "So, what do you say? Will you let me help?"

She bites her lip. Her small finger twitches.

"Fine. But I will leave if you're rude again," she says.

I grin.

"What male friends do you have?" I ask after a moment.

She pauses, unsure.

"I am acquainted with many, but friends with few. I've always felt more at ease around women. Estela has been my primary confidant for as long as I can remember."

I knew that. While I wouldn't say she avoids men, she is... different in their presence.

"So, what are you looking for?" I press.

She inhales slowly, her breath rising against the silence between us.

"I want to make someone happy. I want to have someone to create a home with." A pause. "I want to give someone children."

Her words exist for someone else. To give. To be a part of another's story.

Didn't she realized she deserves her own?

"It sounds like you want to make someone incredibly happy," I murmur.

She nods, the sadness retreating.

"Yes," then she bites her lip. "I'm sorry. I think I've misjudged you because I didn't expect you, of all people, to understand that."

But maybe I do.

I bite my lips together. A thousand blunt-edged responses dance through my thoughts, sharp and unrelenting, but I hold them back. It would be a lonely evening if she left.

And while she's here, I can look after her.

"So how would you phrase this...?" she trails off.

"Yes?"

"I want to say that I want someone who will stand beside me, not just expect me to follow."

I smirk. "So... 'I seek a man who won't mistake me for a decoration'?"

Arlet rolls her eyes. "That sounds combative."

"Good. It'll weed out the weak ones," I grin up at her.

She bites her lip.

"Very well." Then she produces a piece of charcoal from her robe pocket and scribbles down notes.

"All right. Now, there will be men who only see my status. How do I phrase something that makes it clear I won't tolerate that?" She looks up at me and tucks a strand of hair behind her ear.

I think for a minute.

"Try 'I am not a stepping stone. Walk over me, and you'll fall off a cliff.'"

Arlet laughs and the sound is sweet. It's one of the only times she's ever laughed at something I've said. "You enjoy this, don't you?"

"I enjoy watching you consider hurting me," I say without thinking, my ears eager to be graced with another laugh.

She merely smiles. Then writes again. After, she taps her lips.

"Anything else?" I ask, thinking about the list of words.

One prompt in particular, *sexual preferences*, returns to my thoughts.

I won't ask about that.

Shouldn't ask about that.

I suck in a sharp breath, and she speaks, graciously breaking me out of my buzzed thoughts.

"You'll laugh at the next one," she says.

Straightening, I shake my head. "I will not."

She purses her lips.

"I want children. As many as I can have. But I—" she breaks off. Her face turns away, as if she were hiding something. She clears her throat. "I—I don't want someone to just *use* me for that."

Like Arion. Fucking prick.

Her words both stun me and don't. I could picture her as a mother as easily as I can remember her scooping up children and playing childish games. The shock comes when I think of her with a rounded belly.

That sight... I swallow.

"Then don't. Say you want a partner in building a home, that you're not just a womb to fill."

"That's blunt," she says quietly.

I step closer to her, hand itching to reach out and touch her clothing. "You want a fool who can't handle blunt? Or do you want someone who knows exactly what you mean?"

A slow smile spreads over her face, and then she writes.

When she looks at me, I feel a little dizzy.

"You know," she starts, "I think this is the first time we've ever spoken without fighting."

"No it isn't," I retort.

She opens her mouth, and I bite back a smile. Then, realizing my joke, she laughs again.

I luxuriate in the sound. It washes over me like warm water.

We talk for another hour before she thanks me and says she would like to go to bed.

I oblige her request, feeling... light. Lighter than I have in a while.

No sharp, emotional spikes to ruin the night. No lingering tension waiting to snap.

After so much talking, the walk back is quiet, and my mind circles around things I don't want to name.

She leaves first, disappearing into her home, and then I find my own dwelling.

When I shut the door behind me, my eyes immediately land on the scroll. It sits on the desk. Mocking me.

My house is quiet. Always quiet.

The only sound is the faint hum of the city beyond the door, and the scratch of my calloused hands against the wood of the desk as I pick up a pen and go to retrieve the scroll.

Staring at me.

"Just go," Teo had told me when we talked about the Mating Journey.

I bite my lips together. My fingers brush the pen. I roll it between them, stare at the parchment, and—after a pause—set it down.

I don't need to go to the festival.

I don't need the pageantry, the spectacle, the false smiles from strangers who don't really see me. But I could go for Arlet.

I wouldn't have to see anyone else. Wouldn't have to talk, wouldn't have to pretend. I could just be there in case she needs me.

Daniel is still out there. And that thought alone makes my decision.

I sit back, exhaling slowly.

And then, I smile.

CHAPTER 11

ARLET

When I wake, I am not surrounded by a large, shirtless blue enduar, but by the gentle press of my handmade blankets.

I am glad to be here, in my bed, not some other strange place, with my memory fully intact. And what a memory it was.

I roll over and sigh, thinking about meeting Vann in the salt room last night. Vann was an ass to start, but then he turned so kind... it was almost a dream.

Wiping my eyes, I let out a long breath.

This is one of those mornings where the weight of the day's tasks pulls me from slumber easily, but actually making it out of bed—leaving the warm, familiar mold of my mattress—is a different battle entirely.

Then the hour strikes six, and one by one, the spell-lights bob to life above my head. The room is bathed in warmth.

Today is the Mating Journey.

Today I might actually meet someone.

That single, dangerous flicker of hope sends my thoughts spinning, weaving visions too beautiful to bear—a mating ceremony beneath a lush, golden canopy, the sound of crashing waves mixing with the scent of salty pine. A home, a loom by the window, the echo of a child's laughter chasing their sibling too close to the hearth. A man's deep chuckle, and music winding through the air.

It's the kind of dream that hurts. Some things are so beautiful that they only serve as a reminder of what is missing. Like the ache left behind after a song ends or the scent of smoke clinging to an empty fire pit.

I rip myself from the tangled threads of the thought before they can weave more pain.

Maybe nothing will happen.

I throw back the blanket and plant my bare feet on the cold, flat rug Fira had gifted me. Another deep breath, and I'm on my feet, reaching past my scrolls for the gilded hairbrush and the collection of crystals by my bedside.

I tap each one, tracing their meanings in my mind. Amethyst—for deep sleep. Yellow Jasper—for creativity. Jade—for… hope. Jade has always been my favorite.

I have no magic, but I can feel the stones as well as any enduar thanks to my Fuegorra. This one… this one makes me feel whole. Like it holds some unseen vein of warmth, something eager to absorb the ache inside me.

I pick it up, squeezing it tightly in my palm, trying to patch up the hole in my heart. By the time I reach my polished metal mirror, I set it down, feeling lighter until I see my reflection and remember finding myself in the nightgown.

A shudder crawls up my spine.

It's over now, Arlet. And anyone who knows is worried about you—not what you could have done. You are all right.

Still, many of the sweet feelings inside of me evaporate. I tear my fingers through my hair, undoing the silly plaits I'd woven before bed. Women with a male mate almost never braid or unbraid their own hair. It's a sacred task, meant for their partner.

But when he'd helped me write in my scroll, I'd been so at ease.

I want to be his friend.

My cheeks heat. Just be his friend?

When he'd grabbed my wrist, a thrill shot through me. How long had it been since I felt *that*? Vann wasn't someone I'd considered a romantic option in the past, but I would be lying if I said I didn't miss closeness.

I brush my hair into a tight, neat bun, my hands moving on their own, letting my mind wander far from babies and mates and the king's advisor.

In my closet hangs the loose, stylish gown in red with orange beads I'd pulled out the night before. Beneath it are soft slippers, with a few jewels set on the table near the soiled clothes bin.

First, I start with powdered cosmetics to dust over my skin, covering the speckles on my nose, cheeks, forehead, chin, and shoulders. Then I pull on the gown, tying it to compliment my figure. Layer by layer, I build myself back up.

But a shadow lingers in the corners of my mind. I can't help it—I'm a worrier.

After heading downstairs, I grab the Mating Journey scroll from the desk near my door and step outside, feeling the cool air against my flushed skin. A part of me expects Vann to appear with a big smile like the one he'd worn last night.

There is no one waiting outside and I tuck a loose curl behind my hair.

No matter. We're all busy.

He said he might go to the Mating Journey as well. Maybe I'll see him there, though definitely out of duty. He doesn't want anyone. He'd said so himself.

Gripping the scroll tighter, I walk down the path between the houses in the council district. The path widens as I pass the palace, heading over a bridge that will take me to the area of Enduvida where the forges are.

Near the forges, there are a series of tunnels. The third leads down to where the mating ceremony is to take place. Hand woven and painted banners are hung up, and crystals decorate the entrance.

Several groups of people have already arrived, many coming from the residential district inside of the massive cavern, and several others heading down from tunnel six, which leads to the outdoor settlement.

Most people walk in Enduvida, but there are a few *glacialmaras*—

long, floating serpent-like creatures with razor sharp tails and eyeless faces that enduares use as mounts. Some humans like to call them 'crystal wraiths.'

I've never ridden one. Flying seems like it would paralyze me, even from a safe distance above the ground.

As I approach the crowd, my heartbeat picks up. This section of the cavern is alive, the energy light, humming, full of anticipation. There are no children nearby, just adults. My eyes go wide—so many of them I've only glimpsed in passing, but there are enough strangers I've never even seen.

Some live in Enduvida, some have come from the settlement above.

That bitch called hope pops up in the back of my mind. Maybe this won't be awful.

Lady Ulla, the main healer in Enduvida, pops out of a cluster of humans.

"Arlet!" she calls.

I grin, looking at her fitted, silver dress. Her silky, straight hair is fanned and tucked at the nape of her neck. As soon as she's close enough, she holds out her hand to take mine.

"No one was spared attending, I see," she says with a laugh.

"Well, Estela made it clear what my duty was," I say.

She takes in my dress. "This is amazing. You're going to float through the festival with a gown as comfortable as that. I should've considered that before..." she gestures to her tight bodice.

I grin. "With any luck, you won't have to stay all day."

She laughs a little. "Well, I am not anticipating a mate. But I have never done this in the past, so who knows."

Before I can respond, she gestures back to the tunnel.

"Shall we?"

"We shall." My heart is pounding harder than before as we descend through the tunnel.

It takes a while to get to the bottom, but when we arrive, we are let out into another vast, open cavern. The sheer energy of the place grips me.

Incense curls through the air, thick and heady, mingling with the faint bite of minerals from the stone. The glow of glittering crystals refracts against jewel-toned fabrics stretched across the sea of tents. Their colors are vivid under the combination of crystals and spherical spell lights. Mats and banners are laid out and hung up, their designs woven by careful hands—some of them are mine.

The sight of them makes a quiet warmth settle in my chest. A mark of the work I did in the past, before I became a part of the council and spent more time with the children than my weaving.

Laughter rises, chaotic and electric, filling every empty space as people flit between the tents, moving in waves through the festival grounds. There is no hush, no hesitation—just joy.

But beyond the heart of the festival, my gaze catches on the roped-off section. That's the place where we will gather waiting for the Mating Journey to begin.

A pressure curls around my ribs.

I inhale sharply, nearly dizzy from the sheer life of it all. But I cannot ignore the insecurity sitting in my chest. The joy starts to turn shrill, and I feel uncomfortable.

Am I getting sick? Gods damn.

Ulla's assistant didn't see anything wrong last night.

No matter how much I want this to feel real, I cannot change the fact that I feel wrong. I feel like I am being pulled back.

I paste a smile on my face when I see the royal throne, stationed at the front and flanked by the entire Teo and Estela. Mother Liana stands nearby, fussing over an ore-chime. It hangs from a sturdy wooden stand, and the long cylinder is forged from enduar goldstone, a rare dark metal streaked with veins of molten amber.

I've seen a few of these before. When struck, their luminous bands glow faintly.

My excitement mounts, and I say a quick goodbye to Ulla before pushing toward Estela and Teo.

Teo is dressed in a deep black stone silk ensemble that catches the cavern light with faint glimmers. His long coat, embroidered with silver filigree, drapes over his broad shoulders and extends down the front of his body, the design mimicking the flow of molten metal. His high collar is fastened with a clasp of dark quartz, and the only color on him comes from the crimson sash tied at his waist.

Estela stands beside her mate, her golden gown flowing like liquid light, the fine brocade woven with faint sigils of her two goddesses. The bodice is fitted, accentuating her form, before spilling into cascading layers. A chain of moonstones sits across her collarbones, luminous against her light brown skin, and her dark curls are swept into intricate braids, adorned with delicate golden charms.

Together, they are a contrast—midnight and sunlight—yet they undeniably make a whole.

As I approach, I realize the royal children are also here. Estela picks up her youngest son, Leo, and his small hands clutch the gems on the bodice of her gown.

"Arlet!" she calls, beaming as she pulls me into a side hug. The warmth of it seeps through me, erasing some of the gloomy shadows following me around.

"I'm so glad you've made it," she says, her eyes immediately landing on the scroll in my hands. A knowing look lights her face. "Are you ready?"

I nod slowly. "As ready as I can be."

“Lirenne!” she calls over her shoulder. The enduar woman who organized the event comes forward. She’s much taller than Estela or I, and she wears a white gown that trails on the floor behind her. Her shoulders are exposed by thin straps, and only her ears have jewels. A large, white birthmark covers her left cheek, vivid next to her vibrant blue skin and grey hair.

“Yes, My Queen?” she says with a bow, her tail curling into a circle.

With her free hand, Estela touches my back and says, “Lady Arlet is ready for her assigned numbers.”

Lirenne dips her head, taking my scroll and using a bit of magic to write something in the top corner of my paper.

I take a moment to scan the crowd, looking, just for a moment, for Vann. I don’t see him or his familiar frown.

“There you are, Lady Arlet. We are so happy you are here,” she says. Then excuses herself.

Estela lets out an excited sound. “All right, have fun. I won’t be here the whole time because I’m told some couples get very scandalous, and I don’t want the boys around that.”

My cheeks heat. I know exactly what she meant.

“But, with any luck, tomorrow we shall have breakfast, and you will have good news.”

Before I can respond, my friend, the queen, ushers me forward, away from the throng, and toward the section where a group of men and women prepare to enter the tents. I take a deep breath, studying the signs outside each tent with a number written in geometric enduar script, and then open my scroll to reveal the suggested matches.

Enduar script is my third written language, behind the common tongue and my limited giantese. The human tongue exists only in speech—its written form lost to time, something I’ve been trying to restore in Lorepath.

I recognize the letters well enough, but the first is a little hard to make out.

"I'll be honest," a human woman in a long, red dress murmurs beside me. "Even if I don’t get a husband out of this, I’ll be happy if I just get fucked."

I look over as she smirks. Her dark hair is braided over one shoulder, and a thin golden cuff gleams against her upper arm, catching the flickering light.

Sharp eyes the color of aged amber, glint with amusement, and there's a confidence in how she carries herself—unhurried, self-assured, like she already knows the outcome of any game she plays.

I can’t relate, though I wish I could.

She catches my stare, then grins. The movement sends the jewels along her neckline shimmering under the spell-lit cavern, glinting like firelight.

"Lady Arlet, isn’t it?" she asks.

I am taken aback by the title. It’s still strange to hear it on a stranger’s lips. Dipping my head forward, I manage a small, "Yes."

She holds out her hand. "Dashia. I live in the settlement.”

"Lovely to meet you."

Her smirk deepens. "Good luck today."

The room hushes as King Teo rises from his throne. His voice carries with effortless authority.

"Brothers and sisters, blood of the stone, life of the ocean, children of the over world—welcome." He pauses, sweeping his gaze over the gathered. "We have fought, we have bled, we have built, and now we must grow. Today, you will endeavor to meet each person in this room. At the end of the day, let us celebrate bonds—new and old, forged in fire and fate. Let this journey bring not only mates, but strength to our people. May your Fuegorras burn bright, and may your hearts sing true. At the sound of the tone, we shall begin."

CHAPTER 12

ARLET

My heart pounds so loud, I'm sure the enduares can hear me. We wait for the sign to start.

Then, Mother Liana strikes the ore-chime and a deep, metallic toll rings out. The sound is rich and layered, rippling across the crowd.

The murmurs return like a rushing tide. I smile just as the first wave of women pushes forward, their scrolls in hand.

Inspecting my scroll once more, it takes me a moment to realize the first symbol is *fourteen*. Since that is the closest to me, I set off there first, winding my way through potted plants from Estela's magical underground garden, carefully placed alongside artfully arranged crystals that hum soft, ringing tones. The cavern is bursting with color—flowers, jewelry, food, mead—so much that it makes my head spin.

When I arrive at tent fourteen, a small crowd of women has already gathered, admiring the man inside. I shouldn't be surprised by the lavish arrangement of jewels hanging from towering crystals.

Jewelry is very common in the under mountain, but sometimes I forget just how much of it there is. Humans aren't used to such finery, so we mainly bring it out for special occasions.

My eyes land on the tall, ocean-risen enduar inside, wearing nothing but a loincloth. His broad shoulders gleam under the warm light. He's got the darkest blue eyes I've ever seen—so much so that they are almost black, and his hair is also exceptionally smoke-grey. My mouth parts.

I blink, sure I didn't see him waiting in the group of people. In fact, I don't think I've ever seen him before. His muscles look like they are carved from stone and his legs are built like pillars. He greets each woman with a slow, reverent kiss, and they *actually swoon* at his touch.

My feet move before my mind, and I take a step forward to join the line. But then I look at the other women in front of me and remember how hollow I feel receiving affection from a man also charming other women so openly.

It is fun to be adored and pampered. I couldn't blame anyone for wanting that. But I wasn't totally comfortable with casual. Definitely wasn't open to sharing.

Being honest, it ruins the moment for me. He's attractive, but I don't think this will work. I want to be wanted so desperately that it feels like I am slowly losing my mind. I want someone who sees only me, burns for me, doesn't look at another when I am near.

I want that person also to be my mate, so I could have another chance to be a mother.

I exhale, staunching any disappointment, and glance down at my scroll for the next number. Number thirty-nine.

I move on down the passageways between rows of tents.

As I weave through more stations, another chime sounds—this one higher pitch and twinkling. A low moan follows, throaty and desperate, and I whip my head around just in time to see the human woman from earlier, Dashia, pinned beneath an enduar man I don't know, caught in a frenzy of lust, their passionate kissing fully on display.

Assistants rush forward, cloaks held high to shield the scene and a few humans laugh uncomfortably around me.

The announcement rings through the cavern, voices lifting with it. "The first matehood has been made!"

The words leave me hollow and burning all at once. That happened so fast. *What the hell? She wasn't even looking for a mate.*

I scold myself for the unkind thought, and press on.

We are all different. We all have different needs.

My breath is uneven, the damp warmth of the cavern crawling along my spine. I wipe sweat from my brow, swallowing the frustration curling in my gut and hoping my makeup doesn't show off my freckles.

Reminding myself I mostly only came here for Estela and to support the council doesn't help. I just feel... behind?

I reach tent thirty-nine almost hoping for something miraculous to occur, but the result is the same. The decorations are different, but the enduar man inside is equally stunning, and the ritualistic gathering of potential partners is just as familiar.

But this time, I don't leave. I wait until I'm standing before the man, and smile.

"Lady Arlet," he says. "It is an honor."

My lips twitch. We're both fully clothed, but I feel so exposed. There is no place to talk or see if we might have shared interests. No place to have a few minutes to get to know each other.

This feels shallow.

After a few seconds, I realize neither of us have spoken.

"Sorry. Hello. Uhm, how are you?"

"Fine, thank you," he says.

There are a few giggles behind me and my skin burns.

The man, who's name I don't even know, looks down at me and I can practically hear what he's thinking. *No song. No pull. Next please.*

My eyes burn. This is happening too fast. He's decided I'm not worth it before I ever had a chance.

Another chime strikes, and I flinch. More lovers giving their joy to Grutabela and Endu. And there's me—sweaty, restless, empty.

"I wish you luck," I say, moving out of line, and sucking in as much fresh air as I can muster.

I don't want to feel this way anymore. I need to finish visiting my tents so I can leave.

The press of bodies around me, the warmth of laughter, the electric hum of the Mating Journey spinning onward—it all tightens around my ribs. Too much sound, too much light, too much expectation.

It hurts to try and to be rejected. It breaks another piece of my heart, despite all the time I'd spent mentally preparing. I try to focus on the joy in the air, the celebration, but my thoughts twist inward, sharp and unrelenting.

I catch the eye of a few enduar and human men while walking, exchanging flirtations, letting myself pretend—just for a moment—that I don't need to feel pressure.

Each time, I draw near. I feel a flicker of expectation, and then—moments in—both of us would realize there was no song. It didn't matter that not all songs started immediately. With only one day to meet as many people as possible, they all want instant results.

Each moment curdles, shifts, and I watch as their expressions soften, and they would excuse themselves.

That is worse.

Ulla had told me once that I needed matehood to have a child. That memory burrow deep, clawing at a wound I can't seem to close.

More couples find each other and form bonds that will grow into something more. And I am spinning, spinning, spinning—drifting through a ritual that is not meant for me.

What the hell was Estela thinking? What was *I* thinking?

I turn away, pretending I don't care, pretending it doesn't sting like an open wound. Wiping my hands on my dress, I swallow the emotions and start walking again.

Just one more tent.

I turn down another row, head down, my temples throbbing. Then I hear a laugh that makes my heart stutter. I look up to see Joso standing in front of his tent, a few women lined up to meet him.

He looks just as he always does. His silver hair is neatly woven into three plaits, thick braids falling over his shoulder the same way it had when he used to walk me home at night. The same way it had when he twined his fingers with mine under the festival lights, kissed me, and told me he wanted a mate.

Back then, I had thought it could be me.

The women waiting for him are eager, hopeful, and I'm not surprised to see a few men also interested. He greets them with that easy, lopsided smile, the one that used to make my stomach flip. The way he stands, relaxed but engaged, is familiar—the same way he had stood when he first asked me to join him for a meal.

Hostia, he even wears the same deep blue tunic embroidered with silver thread, fitted at the waist with a belt of braided leather that he wore the night he ended things.

That night, I remember him jovial. He'd had a few glasses of mead—and his tongue came loose.

Vann had come to join us. He'd started a string of uncomfortable questions after talking about his experience in the battle a week before.

I remember how Vann looked at Joso, smiled a bit, and said, "War changes your perspective. Makes things feel more urgent. You see what's important, no?"

A strange look had passed over Joso's face. "You're right." When he set his drink down, he exhaled like a decision had been weighing on him.

I shifted in my seat. Something about Joso's tone made a familiar emotion creep up. Panic.

"And what has felt important to you?" I asked, not looking at Vann.

He pursed his lips. "We don't have to do this right here."

Ice coated my skin. Wrong. He had been marginally less affectionate than before, but the retreat of his warmth had me feeling anxious. The same switch had been abrupt with Daniel. He went from being so attentive to distant and absent.

It was happening again and I couldn't handle it. I stood, walking away from the table. Joso followed me, grabbing my arm. It wasn't aggressive, but I reacted. Pulling away, almost hitting him.

"It's over, isn't it?" I said, looking up at him as my throat burned.

He frowned, processing slower than normal after all that drink. "I want a mate, Arlet."

My skin had gone cold.

“Our song hasn’t started,” he continued. “You are beautiful. And fun.”

“And it’s over,” I said with finality. “I can’t give you what you want so you will cast me aside.”

I couldn’t help but cry. And Vann, seeing my reaction, had come over, and punched him. It all happened so fast, I don’t even remember why he’d been so abrupt.

Joso and I didn’t see each other afterwards. I was humiliated but he hadn’t deserved the hit.

And now, as his eyes sweep over the crowd, he looks the same.

Until he sees me.

For a split second, something flickers in his gaze—maybe hesitation. Then, he offers me a small smile.

I grip the fabric of my sleeve and step back. Slinking into the crowd, I hurry until I find the next tent listed on my scroll.

Two more and I can go home.

No men or women are waiting at the front of this particular space. I hesitate before going in. Then, a friendly face emerges. A very *human* face.

The man has an open, easy expression. Atop his head are dark curls cropped short, sun-kissed umber skin, and a smile that reaches his eyes. He’s a bit taller than me.

I smile, relieved. It’s been a while since I’ve felt at ease around another human. Especially a man. I approach, pleased to find him alone. Maybe this time, I won’t feel the weight of expectation. Maybe the ritualistic shame won’t cut quite as deep.

"Hello," he says, smiling. "I've seen you before."

I tilt my head. "Yes. I'm Lady Arlet."

"No," he says, eyes flickering with recognition. "I think with the children. You volunteer for my nephew."

I beam. The children.

"Yes! Who is your nephew?"

"Aiden."

"Ah—yes. He’s torn his pants more than once on the playfield,” I laugh.

The man laughs, too. "It's nice to see you have such a nurturing heart."

I consider how he talks about his nephew. “It's not common that I see humans that stick together in families from before arriving in the city.”

He grins. "I'm cut from a lucky cloth."

Something inside me tenses. That phrase. A *human phrase.* The kind steadiness in his voice creeps up my neck, settling deep in my chest.

It feels like he understands something inside of me.

Without thinking, I step closer, letting my fingers brush against his as I take his outstretched hand. His thumb strokes the back of mine, a slow, absent motion.

"Well, my name is Diego," he says, voice warm. "Can I interest you in something to drink? I've been instructed at least twelve times to make sure anyone who visits is well-cared for.”

I smile, letting him guide me inside.

"I'd love that."

The tent is large, sturdy, stretched over a frame of bone and substantial wooden supports. The walls are made of cave bear skins, cured and stitched together, and their deep brown fur brushed smooth. The entrance flap is tied back, allowing the light from the glowing cavern crystals to enter and flicker against the armor displayed along the inner walls.

Diego moves with practiced ease, reaching for a clay vessel on the nearby table. He pours deep amber mead into two cups, the scent of honey and spice rising in the warm air.

"Work with old Flova in the forges?" I ask, tilting my head. “He’s a good craftsman. I’ve seen his work.”

He nods. "Yes. In Zlosa, I used to..." He trails off, his lips pressing together. "Well, that is something for another time."

His presence is solid behind me, warm, but not demanding. I turn, watching him carefully, and take the goblet from his hands before sipping. There’s something confident about him.

As Diego tells me about his family, I lean in, listening intently. His voice is warm, and his stories are full of vibrant colors. I'm shocked how happy his life had been serving under the giants. He had a family that stayed together and a childhood of shared meals and kindness aside from the brutality of the giants.

I like imagining that. I smile when he does, nod when he speaks of his sister's wedding shortly after coming to Enduvida, laugh softly when he shares a boyhood memory of mischief gone wrong.

It is nice to talk to someone without so much pressure finally.

Then, his voice dips, turning thoughtful.

"May I see your scroll?"

I pause, then oblige. This is the first time that's happened. It is not easy to hand over a piece of paper that reduced all of me to a few simple answers.

"Let me know if you need help." I'm not trying to be condescending, just... realistic.

He smiles, clearly not offended. Then begins to look. I fidget and let my gaze wander.

"A woman of wit, I see," he says with a grin.

My smile softens, and I think of Vann. Those words he helped me come up with.

"I suppose so," I respond, thinking about last night again. How nice it had been. It is good to be Vann's friend.

Diego looks up with a smile. "I see you want to be a mother. I've always wanted children," he admits. "A family of my own. Someone to build a life with. Someone to share it with."

The words sink deep, lodging in my ribs and reminding me of the sad truth. I swallow, fingers curling against the fabric of my skirt.

I have heard this before. I have lived this before.

Well then, if there is no song with Diego, I should do us both a kindness and leave. My breath feels too tight in my chest, but I force a smile, nodding like nothing inside me has shifted. Like I don't already know how this ends.

He reaches the bottom part, where I was meant to share a few thoughts about sexual compatibility. I included my preference for men, and then very lightly skimmed over some of the things I was still too nervous to share. Joso hadn't liked some of my fantasies, and I worried that it wasn't common in Enduvida.

Then he finishes reading my scroll and meets my gaze.

"Can I kiss you?"

I swallow. Am I ready for that? This doesn't feel hollow to me. He is nice, and I like talking to him.

It is just a kiss.

"Yes," I say with a nod.

He comes near. His lips hover over mine, waiting, before finally pressing against my skin. It is soft, chaste, fleeting. And when he pulls back, I feel...Nothing. No heat. No surge. No song.

A quiet, hollow disappointment sinks in my chest. His hand slides gently around my waist, but I shift back, forcing space between us.

No matehood, no family, I say. *If that's what he wants, you have to give him time to find it.*

Spare the both of you pain. Go.

"Did I do something wrong?" he asks softly.

I shake my head. "No. You are lovely—it's me. Thank you. I just... have others to meet."

A faint frown flickers across his lips, but he doesn't pull away immediately. His hand lingers over mine, holding me there, as if he is waiting for something more.

I look back at him, offering one last smile.

"If you don't find a new partner, come back to me," he says, his grin warm and hopeful. "I'd love nothing more than to spend the evening soaking up your presence."

Then, with a slow, deliberate movement, he lifts my hand to his lips and presses a kiss to my knuckles.

A part of me wants to stay.

Instead, I push out of the tent, stepping into the swirling chaos, and realize a crowd has formed while I was in the tent.

I catch the gaze of a few other women waiting in line. A sharp twinge of jealousy blooms in my chest, but I swallow it and keep walking.

With all the sincerity in my heart, I hope he finds what he is looking for.

I barely pass two tents, head down, before I collide—hard—into a broad chest.

Solid. Unyielding. A head and a half taller than me.

His arm slides around my back, steadying me as I step back, breath catching as I look up—right into Vann's scowl. His gaze shifts, following the path I'd been looking at before moments ago.

"Your cheeks are flushed," he says bluntly.

The world around me spins. I can't even manage a response.

"Why haven't you come to my tent?" he demands.

I frown. "So you did decide to come. Good for you. Meet any interesting women?"

"I thought you would at least visit," he continues.

I smooth out my skirts, taking another stuttering breath. "Which number was your tent?"

"Twenty-four," he says abruptly.

I pull my list from my pocket, scanning the numbers. "It wasn't on here. I would've visited if I'd known."

Before I can react, he snatches the paper from my hands.

Again, he takes my things. He crosses into the bubble I keep around myself.

"Vann—"

He groans. "Whoever wrote this had atrocious script."

I roll my eyes. "Oh?"

He narrows his gaze at me, flipping the page toward my face. The fourteen is poorly written, nearly unreadable. And now I see the gentle curve at the top of the first character.

"Oh."

He rolls the paper up and hands it to me.

"No matter. We will go back now. Are you hungry?" He takes my hand and starts moving.

I stare at him in utter disbelief. "Wait," I quip.

He stops, turning.

"You can't be serious. You don't need to entertain the idea of this silly ritual for me. I know we're friends now, but I am weary. I want to go home. You should do the same, I know you didn't want to come."

"Who told you that?"

"You did."

His jaw tightens, but then he mutters. *"Dalkhir von torath."*

My brow furrows, not fully catching the heavily accented enduar. "What does that mean?"

"Come with me to eat before you faint," he grumbles.

I stand my ground.

"No. It's been a long day."

His stare darkens. "Why won't you come? Surely I was agreeable enough last night. I promised to be kinder."

"Because going with you would mean something to the others looking."

The air goes still.

Vann freezes, body preternaturally tense. He turns, his movements slow, deliberate. My stomach flips over itself a half dozen times.

"There is more to life than endlessly chasing matehood" he says, voice low.

I meet his gaze, unflinching. He doesn't know what being blessed and chosen means to me. He doesn't know all the scars I carry.

And I am not sure I want to tell him.

"But the purpose of this festival is just that. Since we don't have any signs that we are to be bound, I would like to leave now and we can talk later, when I feel less overwhelmed."

He just stares.

Disbelief lingers in his expression, but I step back, taking my hand back. A long moment stretches between us before he straightens, composing himself.

"Fine," he says coolly. "I will see you later."

"Until then," I murmur. Then I turn, pushing into the crowd, willing the weight of his stare to fade.

But it doesn't.

And as I approach my final tent, my heart plummets.

It is empty.

Another man gone. Another missed chance.

My stomach rumbles, and I realize how hasty I was with Vann

earlier. He was being kind, and I wasn't. I should apologize, and perhaps he'll offer me something small to eat.

I retrace my steps to the start of the tents. My breath is unsteady, my hands curled into fists at my sides. When I finally reach Vann's tent, several women linger, but he is gone.

What if... he found someone?

I don't like the thought, but the more logical part of me doubts it.

Out of curiosity, I turn toward the displayed parchment, the one where tent patrons had written their desirable qualities for a woman to see.

I step closer.

I scan the page.

Desires to be a father.

I wince.

Would be exceptionally good at caring for a wife.

Enjoys painting.

Interested in intelligent women with a hunger for reading and weaving.

My breath catches. My hand tightens around the scroll.

Something inside me twists—deep and sharp. This has to be a joke. An iteration of the conversation we had last night. Slowly, my eyes drift over the tent's decorations and land on the details arranged for viewing.

There are fortune-telling crystal cards, slivers of razor sharp obsidian formed to look like a playing card, catch my gaze first, lined up neatly along the side of the tent. I follow their carefully painted images—underground caverns studded with jeweled mushrooms, a breathtaking enduar woman I do not recognize, and then...

A red-haired human woman standing beneath a starlit forest. Her back is turned, but her unbound hair spills down her spine, curling at the edges in a way I know all too well. An ache blossoms inside me.

Is this meant to be me?

No.

No, that would be *ridiculous.*

Aside from last night, Vann has spent the better part of a year avoiding me, oscillating between helping me when it suits him and acting as though I am a thorn in his side.

My mind spins. If we were mates... We would know by now.

It has been almost a year.

If fate had meant for us to be bound, we would have felt it.

This? I think, looking at the tent again. *This is a joke.*

He must have copied my own words, the ones he helped me write, and twisted them into something to get under my skin.

My hands curl into fists, and without thinking, I march away, only to run into the human man from earlier. Diego.

He is carrying armor, smiling.

"Hello, lovely. Sad you didn't take me up on that offer?"

The arrogance is almost too much. But it is warm, teasing, effortless. It smooths over the raw ache I've been trying to ignore.

I haven't been with anyone in months. Haven't felt wanted in longer than that. I'm tired of being lonely, of watching everyone else find warmth while I stand in the cold.

I exhale sharply, forcing a slow, easy grin onto my face. "Who said I didn't take you up on it? I was coming to find you."

His smile widens. "Well then, let's not waste time." He looks away back at his tent a few rows away, but I don't want to be there. I don't want to be heard. I don't want to hear anyone else.

"You'll like my dwelling. Come,"

He follows me, weaving through the crowd, up the tunnel, across the agonizing distance, until we reach my house. I step inside, shut the door, and turn to face him. The armor barely clatters to the floor before his lips are on mine.

And it is enough. Enough for now. I like knowing that this—this moment, this pleasure, this choice—is mine.

It will be a nice night, one that does not have to be forever—because I don't even know if forever is in the cards for me.

It certainly hasn't been up to this point.

CHAPTER 13
VANN

Perhaps it is guilt from attending the Mating Journey, but Adra's face lurks in the corners of my mind, haunting me as I move through the tunnels of my dreams.

I find myself at a wedding ceremony that never happened. We were a couple cursed before we could even begin. There is a blue gown, a chain of thousands of crystals, each one shattered, useless. Blood is staining the floor, and Adra is beside me, our bodies sprawled against the cold, unyielding stone, unable to stand, to move, to reach the place that should have bound us together.

This isn't real, but it feels like it when the stone presses into the back of my skull, sharp enough to numb my face. This dream has come to me before. I don't want to watch what comes next. Don't want to hear her sadness.

"My Vann," her voice whispers. "My strong, mad love. Time robbed us of something we borrowed. Be happy and let me go."

I open my mouth, trying to argue. But the rock beneath us comes to life and spreads over my mouth, encasing me, trapping the words inside my throat. I scream against the stone, thrashing, fighting—until it consumes me completely.

The pressure mounts and crushes me beyond repair. I wait for death, for the moment I will finally be free to return to her.

Then a true scream rips through the silence.

Not my own.

Real.

I bolt upright, my chest heaving as I choke on nothing. My tongue tastes of dirt, my throat is raw, and my lungs burn as I hack and cough, trying to force out something that isn't there.

Another scream shatters the silence.

I am out of my bed in a second, grabbing the knife I keep under my pillow, my body already moving before my thoughts catch up. The house is cold and there is a lingering scent of old smoke and mead.

Then I hear a final, gut-wrenching scream of a man dying. I'd heard it a thousand times on the battlefield.

It comes from nearby.

Was it Arlet?

Has Daniel come back? My skin is colder than usual. I throw on some clothes, pound down the steps and run out my front door. The distance between my house and Arlet's house is short and I shove her door open without hesitation. She could get mad at me for intruding later. The scent of blood hits me first.

The darkness is thick, but the metallic tang coils through my gut like a knife.

Damn it.

I surge forward, leaving the door open and pushing through the hallway, my feet too fast, too desperate. I feel lightheaded. The cold that creeps through my limbs, that sick, creeping circulatory collapse, is already starting.

I reach the stairs that lead to the second level where her bedroom is. Light spills from the open door.

Taking two steps at a time, my vision narrows to the scene inside.

Arlet stands over a mangled body, gore gumming up the tip of her red-stained knife. Who the fuck knows where she got that from?

Her chest heaves, her fingers dripping red. A new smell takes hold and I recognize something I haven't tasted in months. Pure, dark magic.

I freeze, unable to comprehend what I am seeing. In the time I'd known her, she'd never exhibited any magical qualities.

When witches had come to the cavern, they hadn't recognized her.

Until a week ago, there had been nothing to alert that her aura was tainted. And even after her strange behavior, I hadn't noticed any trace of a curse—not when she was in the cavern, nor after the spider incident.

I suspect Daniel, but the body on the ground doesn't look like him. I gape in horror at the poor human.

"Arlet," I say

Her head snaps up.

Black eyes meet mine.

Not brown. *Black*.

A deep, abyssal void where warmth should be.

"Get out of my way," she hisses. Her voice is lower and darker than the bright, familiar tones I know.

And then she moves. The blade slashes through the air, too quick, too precise.

I dodge, barely. The jagged edge catches my arm, slicing fabric and biting into flesh. I hiss, but it is not the worst pain I have felt.

This isn't her. *Gods on their stony thrones,* this isn't her.

She lunges again, the weapon poised at my throat.

I catch her wrist, twisting the shard out of her grip, securing her arms as I yank her against my chest.

"Let me leave!" she shrieks, thrashing, her strength unnatural.

When her teeth sink into my arm, white-hot pain rips through my body.

I nearly drop her.

"Help!" I bellow. There should be others nearby, hopefully a patrol. It seems like they didn't hear the first scream, but hopefully they will hear this.

My eyes return to the man near the bed. He's definitely dead. I wish I could cover the body, so it wasn't strewn about so disrespectfully.

Commotion comes from downstairs, but I don't feel relief. Not while surrounded by tragedy.

"Vann?" Ra'Salore calls up. Gods damn it, his house is just a few rows down.

"Get Teo!" I shout back, as Arlet gouges her fingernails into my skin again.

I didn't mind the pain, I would heal, but I don't know what this curse is or how to make her wake up. She continues to thrash.

Soon, Faol arrives carrying a weapon. His expression is that of horror as his eyes land on the man, and then Arlet.

"Go, find someone else! I need help restraining her," I grit out before he can comment.

It doesn't take long for Faol to return with two hunters, but they linger near the door. A glow of light precedes the arrival of Queen Estela and Teo, and they are the first ones to enter.

Teo looks right at the body half on the bed, and half on the floor.

"Oh gods, who is that? Where is Arlet?" he demands.

Estela lets out a mangled cry, stunned when she looks at Arlet, who still thrashing in my arms.

"Who did this?" she asks, voice high with shock.

I say nothing as the queen moves. It's an awful scene, and I don't know how to tell her her friend did this.

Teo wraps his arms around his wife, pushing her behind him.

"Don't look, *mi amor,*" he says as he approaches the body. He kneels, but doesn't touch the blood, carefully inspecting the person when Arlet hisses.

I watch Estela look at her friend. Arlet scrapes at me and the queen presses into the wall, confused and scared.

"I am sorry, Estela," I start. "Arlet did this."

"No," she says, eyes wide. "She couldn't..."

Arlet thrashes harder, kicking at me until her foot connects with my groin. I curse, pain shooting up my spine, and she drops to the floor, scrambling away from Estela's light.

I stand just as Estela steps forward.

"*My star*, no," Teo clips.

We grab the queen at the same time, each catching an arm, and stilling her movement. Estela takes in a sharp breath.

“Stay back,” I growl.

“Wait. She fears me. She... whatever she is right now needs to be restrained before she hurts anyone else again. I think I can scare her, be ready to put her to sleep,” she says firmly, looking at Teo.

We release her arms, and she reaches into her pocket, producing a crystal. Amethyst, for sleep.

“You know how to sing, yes?” she asks me.

I nod once. “I can put her to sleep.”

Arlet makes another hideous sound. The air around her is twisting, warping, as if something unseen is curling its fingers through her. The edges of her form seem too sharp, her breath comes in ragged gasps, and her blackened eyes glint.

Teo walks with Estela as she moves forward. "Arlet, are you in there?"

Arlet hisses. Then she lunges.

Estela's magic acts faster. Light erupts. It floods the space, blinding and hot. For a second, I worry that Arlet is hurt. For a single, fractured moment—I see fear.

When the light dims, Arlet is cowering in the corner of the room.

I hurry forward, grabbing her and pressing the crystal to her temple. Arlet lets out an awful sound, trying to get away. My sleeping song is short and clipped, but the moment the crystal glows against her skin, her body goes limp against me.

The silent room is filled with horror.

Estela uses her finger to conjure another spell light that better illuminates the bed. It’s covered with tangled sheets stained red.

Her breath catches.

"Lord Vann." Her voice is raw. “Do you know who that is?”

“I don’t,” I say, reverently. Words pour through my mind—begging for a peaceful journey to the afterlife.

This is all wrong. Why was Arlet with anyone at all? And how did she turn into a monster?

“We must send someone to try to tend to the body and prepare it for burial," Estela continues, then her throat bobs. "Ulla could..." she trails off, and presses a hand to her forehead.

Teo steps forward, wrapping his arm around Estela's back. "I will find Ulla. Vann, I think you need to leave. Take her to the throne room. We will decide what to do from there."

"All right," I croak.

I stand, breathing through my mouth to avoid taking in more of the scent of blood and dark magic, and turn to leave.

CHAPTER 14
VANN

Even without seeing the room, it is burned into my memory. It's... impossible to believe she could hurt someone like that. That she took this man into her bed—and then tore him apart like some unfeeling predator.

Moving out of the house is a blur. Faol walks at my side, guiding me back to the throne room.

It is quiet. Chairs are positioned from another meeting, and a marble table is at the right foot of the thrones. I approach the table, laying Arlet down.

Gods only know how much time passes as Ra'Salore, Teo, Estela, Liana, and Fira trickle into the room. A few guards have been positioned around the back, and then the doors are closed and an uncomfortable silence hangs over us all.

Then an unexpected person joins the group. Thorne, the Elven Emissary. He doesn't saunter in like usual, he walks with purpose, a frown on his face.

"What are you doing here?" I demand.

He looks at me and narrows his eyes. "I heard that Lady Arlet is not well."

"Who the fuck told you anything?"

Teo appears on the other side of the table and looks at me, his face guarded. He shakes his head at me.

"Vann," he warns.

I suck in a hot breath. Thorne was important to the alliance with the elven rebellion, but that didn't mean I had to like him.

Thorne holds up his hands. "I meant no disrespect, friends. I was with Ulla when King Teo came to tell her she was needed. I only wanted to offer my help."

He looks back at Arlet, and I try to move my body to shield his view.

"What is wrong with her?" he asks.

Estela comes to my side. "Lord Thorne, we appreciate your concern. But she isn't well, and we would appreciate it if you would allow us some privacy for a while longer."

He hesitates, then bows with a flourish of his hand. "Of course. Whatever you say, My Queen."

Then he disappears out of the room and the doors are shut tightly.

The silence returns, and I watch Estela stare at her friend in quiet horror. I note that Arlet's hair is still streaked with drying blood.

"Vann," Teo says softly. "Please tell everyone what you saw."

I recount what happened, but my words clipped and mechanical.

When Lady Fira asks for the victim's name, one of the guards steps forward.

"Lady Ulla informed us that it was one of the new arrivals from the liberated camps. Diego," he reports. "Unmarried, but he has family in the residential section."

I grit my teeth, but close my eyes for one beat, speaking his name to the gods in my mind, giving him the same respect I would offer any soldier.

Teo takes a deep breath.

"Lady Arlet is a member of the council, but she killed an innocent person. She will need to be punished."

Estela steps forward. "Punished? We don't know all the facts yet. If she did this, then something is deeply wrong. We owe it to her—and to Diego—to find out why."

"While I do mostly agree," I start. "I was there. I saw her holding the knife. I am sure that her body, cursed or not, caused that awful scene."

Mother Liana joins me at the table. She's draped in jewels, her presence almost as bright as Estela's.

"I do not know how I didn't see this coming," she says.

No one responds for a second.

"When I was held captive in Zlosa, I spent time with The Six, a group of *brujas*," she starts. "I remember what the magic felt like. What I felt in that room was the same, oily and sticky."

I incline my head. "Yes. Dark magic. I've seen it on the battlefield."

Teo looks at me, nodding once in agreement. There was a demon god, one who some didn't even consider an official deity, Abhartach. Many of the human witches had begun to worship him. He offered eternal life in return for gifting him souls.

The thought of Arlet sullied with his darkness was abhorrent. It couldn't be true.

Estela looks up. "So when did a *bruja* come in contact with Arlet?"

The air shifts.

Liana approaches the queen's side. "From what I know of this magic, we would be able to tell if there is a mark. Some sort of curse glyph."

I grind my teeth as Teo and I are pushed away from the table. It is impossible to be parted from her in this moment, so I shield her from anyone else as they move around her nightgown, searching her blood-stained skin.

"Vann, can you find me a blanket to help cover her?" Estela asks.

"Ask someone else," I manage. I don't want to leave her alone again.

Estela and Mother Liana exchange glances, their unspoken language shifting between them in flickers of expression. Liana moves out of the room swiftly. When she returns, she holds a covering.

They drape it over Arlet, and then Estela continues searching her skin.

"Liana" Estela starts, no longer speaking to me. "I don't see any bite marks or words."

Mother Liana joins her, pulling back the hem of Arlet's night gown, exposing a delicate, freckled ankle.

There, above her bone, is a small, twisting snake etched into her skin.

Queen Estela gasps.

"No..." She looks up, color draining from her face. "The witches in Zlosa had a snake."

My breath hitches.

The black is deeper than shadow, absorbing every trace of light that touches it. It's like a void pressed into flesh. The more I look, the harder it is to tell where the ink ends and where the world resumes.

"That's a tattoo, no?" Liana asks, voice edged with curiosity. "Like the ones the giants wear."

"No, I'm sure. This must be the mark," Estela says immediately.

My hands clench so tightly my nails bite into my palms. A chill rises up my neck, my vision sharpens.

"Curses are vicious things," Liana starts. "If that is a mark, then it could be activated from time to time, putting her in a state of frenzy. It would be like a tool—one our enemies would use to get to you. They could kill you and Teo?"

Liana looks at Estela.

The queen stares at her, processing. Teo curses under his breath.

"Do you think a remnant of the giant court asked for her to be cursed? Or one of the witches? Or the elves? Gods, why must this be so complicated?" She rubs her forehead.

I stand frozen, seething. Someone used her—controlled her like a puppet and twisted her hands into a weapon. I want to rip them from this world for what they've done.

Mother Liana steps forward, her gaze sharp. She turns, gesturing toward the edge of the room. "Bring me a piece of quartz, I want to try to remove it."

A guard hurries off, returning moments later with a long, pale quartz, cut smooth like a tower. It's a stone known to draw out darkness, to force tainted blood to the surface.

Theoretically, it could pull the curse from her body.

Teo watches closely from where he stands, his expression unreadable, but I recognize that his mind is already turning. Calculating.

Liana takes the gem and steps toward Estela and Arlet. "Hold her still," she instructs.

The queen shifts, securing Arlet against her chest, while Teo stands at her back. Teo murmurs something to his wife, holding her shoulders.

Then, Liana presses the quartz stone to the tattoo, chanting something quietly.

The stone rests against her skin, unmoving, unchanging, but the crystals glittering in the walls light up.

A single, thin tendril of darkness unfurls from the mark, winding above the quartz and then vanishing.

Liana pulls back, frowning. "Damn. It is a curse mark. But it cannot be easily removed."

Ra'Salore lets out a long breath, standing up. "All right. She is cursed, but there is also a casualty. Then let us do as the king asked and proceed with solutions."

"Yes," Teo agrees.

"I think we should start with the crime. She killed someone. We have not made any laws that dictate how to proceed when a council member does that," Ra'Salore starts.

The words grind against me. I can't be objective right now.

Fira shakes her head. "But this is a curse. You all scented dark magic. The report was that she was hissing and biting. Vann said her voice and eyes changed! If we punish her, then we would be punishing the wrong person and neglecting to castigate the one who *did this to her*. You do not blame the puppet for the master's sins."

Ra'Salore frowns and shakes his head. "But we do not even know who that is. Her hands injured a fellow council member and killed an innocent man."

"I was not hurt," I growl.

"According to our law," Ra'Salore continues, "murder is someone taking a life that was not freely given. A life stolen must be accounted

for. We all agreed that the guilty party must restore balance. So either, Arlet must offer her own life, or she must step down from the council and assume a life debt to his surviving family in whatever capacity they wish."

Mother Liana shakes her head. "No. I agree with Fira. She did not know what she was doing. How can we impose such a harsh sentence on her?"

"How can the people trust us if we do not?" Teo interjects, breaking his silence.

Estela speaks up next. "It would be a greater disservice to everyone if we punish her without finding the person truly responsible."

I grit my teeth. If only I had found Daniel. If only she had stayed with me over that man, maybe none of this would've happened. I could've prevented this.

"Lord Vann? You look like you have something to say," Teo says, picking up on my displeasure.

I exhale slowly, clenching my teeth. She was so private sometimes. Did she want me bringing up Daniel in front of everyone?

And yet... this is serious, and if I don't help argue for a lighter treatment, she could wake up in prison, on the other side of the city. Alone and suffering.

"Could this have anything to do with Daniel?" I say, directing my question to Estela.

Her head snaps up, eyes narrowing. She tightens her grip on Arlet, her knuckles white where they press against the fabric of her gown.

"What do you know of *Daniel*?" she spits the last word.

I straighten under her relentless tone. "The night of the ascension, he went to her house. I found him yelling and her crying." I pause. "Supposedly, he was taken to the prison, but when I went to see him almost two days later, he had been released. I still haven't found him, but I have been concerned for a while that he would come to Arlet's house. And now... *this*."

Estela's expression shifts—not fear, not worry. Rage. The kind that burns slow and deep. The kind that has festered for years.

"That filth," she murmurs.

Teo watches her carefully. "We don't know exactly what he did yet."

She shifts, adjusting Arlet carefully before lifting her chin to face Teo. "But if he is to blame, we have to know. Send a guard to find him that we might question him."

Teo places his hand on her shoulder. "Yes."

I wanted to be in that room. They could argue over the leftover scraps.

"Lord Vann, you said that she told you to let her go? Was it because you were restraining her?" Fira asks, changing the subject.

I frown as I consider.

"I don't think so. It was like she wanted to get out of the room."

"Likely to get to the king or queen," Ra'Salore insists.

He could be right.

"Does this have anything to do with the missive," Lady Fira asks.

Queen Estela shakes her head. "The more I think about it, the more it seems impossible. I was in Zlosa when King Rholker forged an alliance with the elves. Arion hated the witches. He was disgusted by them, and this is their magic as far as we know."

Teo watches, taking in all the opinions. "Is there a way to find out exactly who did this?"

Mother Liana gives a slight shrug. "Perhaps? If I can remove it, I can consult the gods."

I suck on my teeth before continuing, my voice steadier this time. "So if we do not want to impose the law upon her, what can we do?"

"Some part of her killed someone. She needs to be put in prison," Ra'Salore says.

Fira glares at him. "Arlet has cared for our children and woven our clothes. While I understand the threat she poses in this state, she deserves more respect than what you are giving her. Put her somewhere better. I offer my own home, and we can restrain her against something."

I nod my agreement.

Ra'Salore throws his hands up. "If what you say is true, she is not in control of herself when she is *in that state.* She needs to be restrained, because if she wakes up again she could kill. Do you want her to be killed out of self defense?"

The responding silence is tense.

"I understand this situation is delicate, for myself included, but Lord Ra'Salore is not wrong," Teo says firmly. "In my experience, we need to demonstrate to our people that we will not put friendship over collective gain."

Estela closes her eyes. "This isn't solely about friendship. Arlet's character is well established and we have evidence of her curse. I will not condemn her for actions she did not make, even though I do agree she is dangerous. I prefer her being under the watch of someone trusted. We can figure this out. *We will figure this out.*"

She looks at me, but I notice Liana and Fira nodding.

"A prison cell is not so awful," Faol says. "She can rest."

"She'll be humiliated! And her position will be undermined. Who's to say she won't hurt herself if we leave her alone? And is it right that we subject anyone in the prison to her curse?" I say. "I agree with the queen's proposal that she be detained with one of us. I also offer my home. Anyone at risk can be temporarily vacated from the nearby houses."

Ra'Salore frowns. "And go where? I have a wife and two children, plus a wolf. We can't just move."

I step into the middle of the room. "It won't be a move, you will merely stay somewhere else for a few days. I will help you myself. Three days, please. We will fix this."

Ra'Salore raises his brows, tilting his head to the side at my offer.

"So you will oversee the troops, go on hunting patrols without asking, tend to the king, and help our families move for a few days while also taking care of Arlet? You stretch your time too thin, Lord Vann. You cannot let your affection for her cloud your judgement," Ra'Salore says.

I grit my teeth. "I will not be alone in watching her."

"She will stay in my house," Mother Liana says with finality after watching the discussion. "I am the only one with a chance of breaking the curse. I have spent months weaving protections over my home. It is safe. She won't ever get as far as the palace."

Estela, Fira, and I voice approval.

Teo rubs the bridge of his nose. "And what of the mating ceremonies that are meant to take place tomorrow? Lirenne dropped off a report, and there are more than six. What do we do for them? How do we balance that alongside a funeral?"

Estela takes a deep breath. "You and I will speak to the family first thing in the morning. We will bring mourning offerings. Liana and I will oversee the ceremonies after." She looks up at her husband. "We can make this work. And, as Vann says, if she is not healed in three days, we will take more extreme measures. But this is not so cut and dry as some might think."

The ideas are reasonable, and I am satisfied with the solution. But a question lurks in my mind. "When you tell the family what happened, what will you say?"

I look back at Arlet, still dirty and covered in blood, and my throat tightens.

The queen straightens her spine, "We will call him a tragic, unnecessary casualty of growing tensions. We can confidently say the *brujas* magic did this, and those witches have been shown to collude with our enemies. Thus, they too can be considered hostile to us and our city."

"Well said," Lady Fira intones.

Teo considers all of the information. "Very well. Lord Ra'Salore, do you have anymore thoughts?"

The man in question shifts. "I don't want to leave my home."

"If you stay, and the king and queen accept our proposed offer, you will be at risk," I say.

He frowns. "What of Sama? Svanna and Iryth will hate being outside."

"I will help them, too. It will only be three days," I reply. "Maybe less. Mother Liana is a resourceful Wise Woman."

When I meet Liana's eye, I glimpse a sliver of uncertainty. Strange. But she nods.

"Yes, we will sort this soon."

Estela takes a deep breath. "If we do this, we will also be able to offer an explanation for Arlet's behavior. Hopefully one that will not sour her image entirely."

"It will be all right," I grit out.

Everyone is silent.

"My King, My Queen, do you find this solution acceptable?" Lady Fira asks.

Estela nods enthusiastically, but Teo hesitates. He looks at his wife, and I can almost see the silent conversation they share in their minds, mate to mate.

Teo nods. "Three days. Let us fix this and find the infiltrator."

Relief floods through me, and I look around.

"Can we get something to clean her up? She shouldn't wake with —" I start when a small sound cuts me off.

All eyes snap back to Arlet.

Teo straightens, pushing his wife to the side and jerks his head for me to come. I take my position at the top of the table, cradling Arlet where Estela had been before.

The queen also tries to move, but her husband holds her back.

"You are my mate. I won't risk you." Then, to me he says "Vann, be at the ready."

Arlet stirs in my arms, her crusted, bloodied fingers twitching, body shifting. My fingers curl around her shoulders, holding her down, just as a weak groan escapes her lips. Her face twists and scrunches as her eyebrows draw together and her chest rises abruptly.

A second later, a soft sob escapes her mouth.

"Arlet, I am here," Estela says, gently straining against Teo's arms.

I want to say something, too. But I don't.

Instead, I watch as she blinks awake, her delicate lids fluttering open to reveal her regular eyes.

"Vann?" she says. Her hand comes up to touch her face, but it is still crusted in red. She sees her hand and her face twists into a picture of raw, unfiltered horror.

"Gods. Gods, no. Please—please, no."

Her voice splinters through me, cold as ice, heavy as stone.

"Where is—?" Her words catch, her breath hitching. She bolts upright, looking around the throne room, and seeing, in full, the blood covering most of her body.

Fira and Liana gather round, as a guttural sound tears from her throat. Without thinking, I wrap my arms around her chest, and pull her towards me. I feel the sound ravage her small body. The screams turn back to sobs. She is shaking, breaking, unraveling.

It is the most awful sound in the world. I have heard it before. On battlefields. In burned villages. From families clutching their dead.

It is ancient. It transcends the differences between humans and enduares.

And we bear witness.

The women surrounding us touch her shoulders and legs, but no one speaks. We watch the destruction of a piece of her soul.

It doesn't matter that my body surges with a frost that threatens to make me immobile.

I realize that perhaps losing my heart made me forget the purpose of pain. Perhaps this is the first time I have wanted to remember.

"Mother Liana," Teo says behind her. "Put her to sleep. It would be a kindness."

I don't protest as she takes out a new crystal and does just that.

CHAPTER 15

ARLET

"I *am so pleased you didn't get rid of my gift,"* a voice slithers through my dreams. *"It's time for you to come back."*

I open my mouth to speak and my jaw hurts.

"What?" I croak.

No one responds.

Dark walls loom around me, but I don't know where I am. The bed is warm, but my body refuses to hold the heat. I hear people moving, their footsteps slipping in and out of my awareness like whispers in a dream.

They aren't safe.

None of them are.

Water had scoured my skin clean, washing away the evidence of blood, but not the filth. They thought a bit of soap could erase what happened, as if cleansing my body would cleanse my soul. But pieces of memories are scattered like shards of glass in my mind.

Diego was gentle.

I remember the warmth of him, the quiet, fleeting comfort of another body against mine. When he made to leave, I asked him to stay. I hadn't wanted to be alone.

The world outside my door had felt too uncertain, too unsafe. And he—he had been something solid, something strong. Someone who, for a moment, could have shielded me from the void of terrible uncertainty swirling inside of me.

I just wanted to forget.

To not be the one left behind while everyone else moved forward. A few red flashes take over my thoughts. I see Diego under me, a knife in my hand. It slashes. Sinking deep into his stomach.

A dull roar fills my head. The blood. Trying to run from the images is impossible, and I am forced to stare at the truth head on. My eyes burn as the truth slaps me across the face. I was having problems, and I waited too long to go to Ulla. I shouldn't have settled for her apprentice, I should have waited.

And now... my selfish neglect has resulted in a death.

The world wasn't unsafe.

I was.

"Arlet."

Estela's voice is soft, careful.

I don't look at her.

"Something is wrong with you, and we'll find out what."

Her words shatter me.

I had been lying in a pool of my own blood once when Daniel had told me those exact words—*Something is wrong with you.*

I grit my teeth.

Maybe Daniel is somewhere nearby. Maybe he will reappear to remind me of how awful I was. How broken I was.

I already know. I *know*. But can anyone actually fix this?

"I'd like to be alone," I murmur.

Estela steps forward, coming fully into my line of sight.

"I don't think—"

"I AM DANGEROUS!" The words rip from me, jagged enough to tear at my throat. "Leave me be!"

Estela's eyes widen. Then she steps back. Instead of pressing, she lets me go.

For a moment, the silence is suffocating. But she returns into view. She always does that.

"Arlet, we need you to stay still."

Her hand closes over mine, warm and steady.

I squeeze my eyes shut, feeling the burn of unwanted tears.

Voices hum around me—questions, theories, but they are distant. I am lost in the black swirl of my thoughts, desperately clawing for memories of what happened.

My mind fractures.

Violence is seldom my answer when it comes to solving problems. How could I have killed someone? It is different from the spider or the day I spent lost.

I can remember parts of this act.

The world spins and my head throbs. I can't breathe. I can't think. Time passes, but I can't tell how long.

"Arlet?" A voice pulls me back.

I press my lips together, wading through the black mist in my mind, searching.

"Sh, my child." Liana's voice wraps around me. "You are in my home now. Can you hear me?"

I force my eyes open, blinking against the dim glow.

Instead, golden crystal light pulses along the walls, casting shifting patterns across the stone. The air is thick with the scent of dried herbs and something metallic, like crushed minerals.

I shift, my body aching, and take in Mother Liana's home.

There are shelves carved into the rock that hold vials of tinctures, bowls of crushed powders, and polished gemstones. Bundles of hanging plants sway faintly, caught in an unseen draft. A heavy wooden table sits in the center, scattered with scrolls, mortars, and fragments of uncut crystal.

Veins of deep violet quartz twist through the ceiling, glowing softly. Unlike the throne room, these stones do not speak of war, but of healing.

My heart beats unevenly. I had always loved the minerals and stones in Enduvida. Through the Fuegorra, the enduares taught us humans that stones have energies—some more than others. I'd spent months learning their potential to heal, unify, and mourn. In Enduvida, life felt like a fabric—woven from the threads of loss and love.

But something is ripping me from that fabric.

I want to scream at whoever will listen—at the Human Goddess, locked in her prison, shackled and silent, refusing to help me. At the fates that had neglected to give me a simpler life.

"Liana." My voice is hoarse. Unyielding. "What exactly do you think is wrong with me?"

Silence spreads through the room like a slow-moving tide.

"There was dark magic around you after what happened last night," Liana says carefully.

Last night. Wow.

"How long have I been asleep?"

"Around one day," Liana says softly.

More time lost. I focus on keeping my breaths even. "And... what is wrong with me?"

"You have been cursed, Arlet. We think it comes from one of the human witches. Have you been in contact with any recently?"

I furrow my brow. I hadn't seen any since... since before the battle against the giants half a year ago.

"No. Not at all." To be honest, I'd almost forgotten they existed.

"It will take time—"

"It can't," I cut her off. "What if I hurt more people?"

I shift, attempting to rise—but hands close around me, firm.

My breath catches.

"What are you doing?" I twist my neck around, trying to see who's here.

Vann steps into view, standing next to Estela. His expression is carefully blank. Why is he here? Is he angry?

He holds up a few silk ropes.

My skin goes cold.

Maldita sea. It's too soon. I'm not ready.

"This is for your safety," he says, voice gruff. "We don't want—"

"No," I beg, voice cracking. "Don't bind me again."

He looks confused. "Again?" His voice is softer now. "Arlet, this is the first time we've done this."

Estela takes my hand. "We are here for you, *querida*. We'll make this better."

I press my lips together. "Please, find another way."

They each take on their version of an apologetic look.

"Forgive me," Vann says, threading the rope through something on the bottom side of the table where I lie, and passing it around my wrist.

A sharp, icy press meets my forehead.

Liana's voice fills my ears, a melodic hum that snakes its way into my thoughts.

Darkness surges up to meet me. Its claws fasten around my arms and throat, dragging me back. I try to call out again, but all that is left is darkness.

CHAPTER 16
VANN

Nearly two days after Arlet woke up...

It's as if the world around me has tilted.

I am unbalanced.

It's too quiet, too dark.

Few know the truth of what happened in Arlet's house, and even fewer are speaking of it. No one else remains in the council section except Liana and me.

All the other houses are dark.

We have one day left to fix her, and I am useless. Daniel is still missing.

There is still no enemy to slaughter yet. What good is a warrior against magic? I am not a great reader, nor do I know how to consult the stones of fates. Even Endu has been silent during the last two days.

I did not attend any of the mating ceremonies, nor did I go with Liana and Estela to speak with Diego's family. A hollow feeling opens in my chest, but I push it away. Instead, I shirk sleep and other responsibilities to head to the only place that I feel like I can breathe. Liana's dwelling.

To Arlet's side.

The Wise Woman and I have cultivated a friendship over the years, helping to run Enduvida. She is the one person who indulges my joy of painting.

I like the way she toils to ensure the old customs are actively practiced. One of those traditions is the Seer Cards, or obsidian shards, sharp enough to split flesh. Their edges bleed fate, speaking of futures yet to unfold. When used, Liana can see images in her mind, just as she does with the Fuegorra. I've already given her several decks, but she continues to ask for more.

Estela also performs the ritual from time to time. It's a pleasing idea, but I have never partaken. I don't need someone to tell me that my future is dark.

As I climb the steps to Liana's home, brushing past the glowing *lumikap* mushrooms and towering crystals, I have a harder and harder time breathing. One foot after the other, I tell myself.

I'll feel better once I see Arlet—once I know she's alive and safe. And then I can paint until sleep taps on the windows of my mind.

I knock twice against the door.

It doesn't take long for the door to swing open.

Liana stands there, her silver curls half-loose and her robe threaded with starburst crystals. She looks less like the Wise Woman and more like a woman exhausted from too many questions and insufficient answers.

"Extra informal tonight, are we?" I raise an eyebrow, nodding to her hair. It is a custom that only mated pairs or lovers see each other with their hair unbound. A tradition that grows looser and looser with each passing month. I don't like it.

I frown at the sight and she narrows her eyes. "Oh, keep your mouth shut. Elaborate hairstyles give me headaches. I'm old. Let me live."

I huff a laugh, lifting the bundle of brushes in my hand.

She exhales through her nose. "You came to... paint."

I nod.

She mutters something in Old Enduar and steps aside. "Stubborn youngling."

I enter. The moment the door closes behind me, the pressure I felt walking through the city falls away. Liana's home is filled with glyphs and wards to keep Arlet in. The outside world is completely silent here.

"Arlet has stirred once or twice, but I always put her back to sleep to be cautious. Her curse has shown no signs of activating," Liana says, leading me through the hall.

I frown. "Any progress in removing the mark?"

Liana shakes her head. "I've tried everything. The Fuegorra does not speak to me. The seeing cards are jumbled, and my mind conjures no pictures. I've consulted every text I could find, searching for an answer. I bathed her in blessed oil, chanted, prayed, even sang the old songs meant to cleanse the afflicted. And when I used the cleansing stone..." She turns to face me fully. "It came back clear. As pure as a newborn's aura."

Something icy slips down my spine.

I don't like that answer, but Liana sounds exhausted. She was a thorough woman. She doesn't skip steps, and she is probably exhausted. "When was the last time you slept?"

Liana levels me with a sharp look before turning back down the hall. Crystals are stacked from floor to ceiling, their songs vibrating through the air like a million whispered voices, a harmony that's usually calm, peaceful.

Now, it's urgent.

"Stressed?" I ask.

"You are not here for me." She scoffs. "Come. I'll show you the redhead you pretend to ignore."

As we walk down the hallway, I relax. Liana and I were not friends until after the Great War, but she had filled the line of feminine guidance lacking in my life. Our friendship was treasured, despite our relationship being crisp to the outside spectator.

She brings me past the dining room teeming with scrolls and crystals, and then, to the back of her dwelling where she opens a door. Sound pours out into the hallway.

I step inside.

Dark-colored crystals—obsidian, black tourmaline, smoky quartz, hematite, and onyx—line the room in a circular arch. Each one hums, their deep vibrations working in tandem to help ward off dark magic.

In the middle lies Arlet. She is still dressed in a new nightgown, and a blanket is pulled up to her waist. Her skin looks thin, blue veins snaking beneath the surface, luminescent under the soft light. Her hair is brushed and braided to the side, strands of auburn woven like delicate threads of silk.

The sight clenches something in my chest.

I glance back toward the exit, as if considering leaving.

Instead, I move forward.

When I finally reach her, my hand extends, resting atop one of her delicate feet.

She doesn't stir, and a part of me is disappointed.

A year ago, I nearly died after being bitten by a vaimpír. For some reason, she had been there to take care of me—memories of her are threaded into my fevered dreams like a song stuck in my head.

When I awoke, half-mad, she was at my side.

She shouldn't have been. But she was.

And now—I am here. My, how easily I let my thoughts stray from Adra around her.

"You took longer than expected to visit again." Her tone is wry, but I catch the flicker of uncertainty in her expression. Then she tilts her head, studying me. "I wanted to consult the Fuegorra one last time. If it still refuses to give me answers, we will need to have a new sort of conversation. Will you watch your woman?"

I narrow my eyes. "I have no allegiance to her, other than the fact that we serve in the royal court together."

Liana hums, unconvinced but too tired to argue.

"It's all right," she says, arranging one of the dark crystals at Arlet's bedside. She hums a few notes under her breath, shifting the placement of an obsidian shard. Each stone responds, glowing faintly as the entire arch shimmers with a soft hum, colors shifting in waves of violet and gold.

"No one should bother you while I am gone," she says.

The rainbow light dances along Arlet's cheekbones, highlighting the soft curve of her jaw.

If my heart were still inside my chest—if I were a man whole and unbroken—it would be cracking in half right now.

I exhale, steadying myself, then say, "Travel safe. I'll stay with her."

Liana gives me a long, knowing look before nodding. She gestures toward a plush chair in the corner, one stuffed thick enough to nearly pass as a bed.

"Try not to haunt the bedside too much," she says dryly, then disappears down the hall, her robe trailing behind her in a whisper of silk and crystal.

"Don't forget to put your hair up!" I call.

Liana cackles.

I lower myself into the chair, letting my body sink into the fabric, but I keep my eyes on Arlet.

A stack of the obsidian future reading cards sits on the table beside me. I smirk, barely, acknowledging the small act of anticipation. Liana knows me too well. She sees the things I refuse to acknowledge, even to myself.

For a long moment, I don't move. I let my mind wander, something I rarely allow. To live in the past is to suffer.

I know that.

And yet... I see my life before.

The home I built with Adra, the warmth of her presence. She was always there.

I remember coming back from the military academy, exhausted and half-starved, only to find a meal waiting. She had learned my preferences and memorized them. And I had done the same for her—listening, watching, giving. We made a language without words—crafted an instinctual love.

It had been so easy, and it had been enough.

Now? Every person in Enduvida has sacrificed something. Why should my happiness be any different?

My life was once beautiful beyond measure.

That should be enough.

And yet...

My eyes betray me.

They shift to the red-haired woman lying on the inclined table, red hair braided neatly over one shoulder, chest rising and falling in steady rhythm.

I tell myself I am only looking. Only studying. But I notice too much.

Freckles scatter in faint trails across her, the bluish-cream tone of her cheekbones. But my eyes follow the darker spots—on her collarbone, her shoulders, her hands.

The urge to connect and trace them like constellations is overwhelming. Would I find a pattern? A hidden map of her soul?

Suddenly, Arlet's eyelids twitch. It's a small movement, barely perceptible, but I feel it like a jolt of electricity through my veins.

I sit forward. Liana had wanted her to stay sleeping. But she's been lying there for so long. Maybe if she woke, I could find out something helpful to Liana.

There is nothing about Arlet I can't handle.

"Arlet?" I try, my voice quieter than I mean it to be.

She doesn't move.

I want her to wake up.

I want her to see the power she's had over me since the moment we met, and watch as it soothes her soul.

"Firelocks," I say next, testing her, wondering if irritation would bring her back faster.

Her eyelids flutter again.

A small victory.

I bite my lip, uncertain. I have never been one for comforting words or touches.

You already touched her and nothing happened...

But my skin made no contact with hers.

Instinct moves me. I reach forward.

I cup her cheek, fingers hovering before they touch warm, fragile skin, and hold my breath.

Her head tilts into my touch, her eyelids fluttering like the delicate wings of a moth. Something hot and territorial floods through me, pouring over my skull like molten gold.

It submerges me wholly, drowning me in something old and

instinctual—a feeling that I have no name for. Even now, in this fragile state, *she knows me.*

And physically, I am not cold for the first time in half a century.

My thumb brushes over the dusting of freckles, and I let my pointer finger trace one of the fine lines near her eye—the kind that lingers permanently from a lifetime of smiling. I like it. I like that it exists. That she has lived enough, felt enough, to have these faint traces of joy etched into her skin.

Suddenly, her eyes snap open.

I jerk my hand away, startled.

The flicker of hurt across her features nearly destroys me. What an unwelcome sight I must be.

She yanks at her bindings, her body tensing, her breath coming in ragged gasps. Then—her face twists and a broken sob rips from her throat.

"No. Please. Please. Remove the ropes."

The panic in her voice slices through me. I don't know what to do. I can't fathom what is going through her mind, can't bear the way she pleads.

Just moments ago, I was sure I was the one person who could help her—that my presence, my hands, could offer her some kind of peace.

Now? Now I'm the one tightening the ropes around her wrists and drowning her in a nightmare.

It's a feeling that finds the severed heart in my chest—locked in a box, beating somewhere far away—and rips it in half all over again.

I need to fix this. I need to do something.

Frantically, my eyes search for the amethyst crystal they used in the throne room, desperate to put her back into the numb embrace of sleep. Anything would be better than this. Anything.

She cries again, and I abandon my search.

"Sh, sh," I start to say.

"Vann, I'm begging you," she sobs. "Please, just... loosen the ropes. I can't bear it," she pants, looking up at me with those fear-struck eyes. "Take me to the prison. I don't want to hurt anyone else. Please."

It kills me to see her like this. Not fierce nor fiery, but lost and small. I know it's dangerous. I know. But I tell myself I'll put her back to sleep after.

"I'm here, Firelocks. I will loosen them," I murmur, crossing to the foot of the table bed and pulling on the ties. *"Ald'kar finthira, A'delor imduri."*

You are not alone. I will not abandon you.

Her body eases, shoulders slumping as the sobs quiet into silent streams of tears sliding down her cheeks. I reach up to loosen her right hand.

"Gracias, mi cielo," she whispers.

I pause, frowning. "What does that mean?"

She sniffs, regaining some of her spirit, and then—without missing a beat—she smirks weakly. "It means: thank you for not being an asshole for once."

I arch a brow, but say nothing.

Some part of her is still her. That should be a relief.

One by one, I move around the table, loosening the knots at her wrists and ankles, watching as she relaxes. The ropes leave behind faint red imprints, and I clench my jaw against the irrational urge to run my fingers over them, to erase the damage.

Then, standing by her head, I murmur, playing her game and use my language again. I speak pretty words into the air, even if she doesn't realize it, I want her to be at ease, *"Grath'ardorien morflamara."*

Do not worry, my flame.

She blinks, eyes flicking toward me. "What does that mean?"

I smirk, lowering my voice as I think of her laughter. That was what she needed. "I'm cursing your bloodline."

She frowns, and I realize my insensitivity. Again. I'm so fucking careless with my words.

"That was a joke."

"You're lucky I can't shove you into that wall right now," she says weakly.

"I'd consider it foreplay."

She scowls, but there's no heat behind it.

"What the hell is wrong with you? This is not the time for jokes," she bites out, voice cracking.

"Arlet," I start. There was too much tenderness in my voice. All of this was a betrayal to Adra's memory, and yet, I couldn't stop. Not after I saw her tears. "I have endured through more battles than you have endured human years. If there is one thing I've learned, it's that there is always time to make a situation lighter. No one believes you are a monster—least of all me."

"Why?" she croaks. "I knew something was wrong, yet dragged my feet to seek help. If I had..."

Ah *yes*. Regret. I understand this emotion well.

"You sensed something was wrong, but you didn't know what. Did you think you would kill someone?" I ask.

She bites her lip. "I didn't want to be around children. I was... cautious. But no, I didn't believe myself capable of this."

A hollow smile tugs at my lips.

"I didn't think so. We tell ourselves that being good means always making the right choices—but that's fucking exhausting. We are all going to make mistakes. Maybe some of the blame is yours, but you didn't choose to kill that man."

I hold her gaze, steady. "You can claw at the past, Firelocks, but it won't change. What matters is what you do now."

For the first time in many months, my eyes burn. Why did this make me feel like, for just a few seconds, I had a heart?

It was a cruel thing to do to Adra, who must be watching me care for another woman from the afterlife in Vidalena.

She deserved better than me, but I owe Arlet a debt.

"I need to put you back to sleep," I say, my voice gentler this time. "But you can rest easy knowing you are watched."

Her jaw clenches, and for a moment, I think she'll fight me.

"I don't want to go to sleep again, Vann."

The way she says my name makes me pause. I reach down to the only binding I didn't loosen—the one securing her hand with scarred fingers. As I had done in the salt room, I hook our weakest fingers together.

"I promise to take care of you."

Her eyes fill with tears and her lower lip wobbles. “All right.”

I don’t move my hand as I press the amethyst against her temple, watching as she inhales sharply. Her lips part, and for the briefest second, I see something raw in how she looks at me.

“Thank you,” she breathes, the words barely a whisper. “For being here.”

I ignore what those words do to me. Instead, I focus on humming a soft tune, letting the melody connect with the crystal.

“Don’t leave,” she says just before her eyes flutter closed. The strain marring her face eases as she rests fully against the table bed.

I stand there, frozen.

Of course I would stay. I wish I could promise her this would be the last time she’d have to fall asleep in fear.

Instead, I let go of her finger and sit back down. I pick up a covered paint pot from beside my brushes, along with one of the obsidian cards. Before applying the paint, I reach for a bottle of alcohol to clean the surface and ensure adhesion.

I inhale deeply, letting the scent of oils and minerals fill my lungs, grounding me.

“This will be all right in time,” I murmur into the open air, my voice quiet. I’m not sure who I’m saying it to. Her… or myself.

CHAPTER 17
ARLET

My dreams are less foggy than before. The suffocating, immobilizing darkness no longer holds me captive, but a swirling gray mist still infiltrates my mind, billowing around me like an unspoken warning. I walk forward, compelled by something I can't name—an itch at the back of my thoughts pushing me on.

I pass through the city in my dream, moving through Enduvida's familiar tunnels. I see them—the successful mates from the Mating journey sharing their blood and promising their lives before Mother Liana, their forms flickering through the haze like ghosts.

Both laughter and the smell of roasted meat spill from Hammerhead Hall and the songs of celebration echo down the corridors. I hear the clash of weapons, the rhythmic whir of a whetting stone grinding against golden enduar metal as the warriors train in the newly renovated practice barracks.

I hear the songs of death from a funeral I would never attend.

The city moves on without me. My students play and chant and sing. Sweet Miti from class. Heat spreads over my skin I promised her a gift, and then didn't go back. Feli, my teaching assistant, stands over her. The young girl is leaning over a large sheet of stone paper, painting.

Enduvida doesn't need my teaching or my weaving.

I follow the paths downward, deeper into the Fuegorra caverns. The air hums with the songs of the crystals—thousands of them, vibrating, alive, and ancient.

I wonder—not for the first time—what it must be like to speak through the stones to the gods. To be heard.

But then the mists reveal my bedroom.

The blood stains the bed. Diego's body is mangled beyond recognition. A knife appears in my hand.

I stand over the corpse. I'd stabbed him so many times that his flesh was pulled apart in strips. So much blood has spilled over the bed that it's soaked the floor beneath in red.

No. No, gods, no.

This is wrong. I shouldn't be here. I shouldn't be seeing this. Vann told me he'd protect me. Where was he in my dreams?

I turn and run. My breath burns as I sprint through the tunnels, searching for the exit. I move faster than I should—faster than I ever could in waking moments. The tunnels shift around me, remolding themselves in unnatural shapes. Walls break apart and rebuild, stone folds in on itself like a living thing.

One path opens. A single arched entrance.

I lunge toward it. As soon as I push through, my body jerks—like being pulled backward through water—and I wake.

My eyes snap open and I gasp for air. It takes me a second to remember where I am—in Liana's house. And then I remember Vann was with me the last time I was awake.

My arms pull against the restraints, my fingers twisting—they're loose. That's right. Vann loosened them. Something warm sparks in my chest. He had been kind again. I turn my head, heart pounding and find the man in question asleep.

The sight of him takes me off guard. His broad frame leans back in the chair, his breathing slow, steady. His tail is laid over his lap, curled around a paint pot. The flickering spell-light casts soft shadows across his deep, blue face, and his braid falls over his shoulder. Neatly stacked beside him are painting supplies, brushes still wet with pigment.

In front of him, half a dozen painted cards are laid out on clear display.

What was he thinking, sleeping around me?

I wiggle my hand against the silk rope again and realize I can pull myself free. The thought is intoxicating. I could get out of here. Run away from the memories.

But then what? Go home? Risk killing someone else?

The people I love live in this neighborhood. Svanna, Iryth, and their son. Ra'Salore has two daughters with his mate Melisa. Teo and Estela are in the palace, not far away. I could run to their children's rooms right now.

What happens if I wake up covered in blood again, and it turns out to be Vann's? My heart skips a beat.

I work the ropes against my skin, rolling my wrists until one finally slips free. I pause, looking back at Vann and watching for any sign of movement. Nothing.

Unusual.

The question from before slams into me: *What now?*

Only one answer stares back at me. Leave Enduvida. It doesn't matter if it feels like a boulder crashing into my chest. I have to go.

Blood rushes into my numb limbs and burns. I flex my fingers, my muscles sore from hours of tension.

I loosen the bindings at my ankles, rubbing the circulation back into my legs. Then, as quietly as possible, I slide off the makeshift bed-table, my feet hitting the cold floor.

I don't let myself hesitate. I open the door quietly and slip out.

The hallway in Liana's home is filled with books and crystals and fungi of various species. I linger, walking quietly toward the exit. I'm barely halfway when the door creaks open and I freeze.

Liana stands there.

She looks tired, her usually pristine robes rumpled, her hair loose. But the strangest part is the lack of surprise on her face. She takes me in without alarm.

"You're not going to kill me, are you?" she asks dryly.

A painful ache hollows out my chest.

I lift my hands slowly. "I'm awake. No weapon, either."

She raises a brow, glancing toward the pointed crystals lining the walls. Any number of them could, in theory, kill someone.

I clear my throat. Her frown deepens.

"I just came from the Scrying Grotto," she says.

I recognize the place. There, a giant Fuegorra crystal is housed, surrounded by thousands of towering citrine shards. Each one hums, tuned perfectly to the harmonic resonance of her magic.

It is a potent connection between the Wise Woman and her gods. Sometimes it tells of the future, other times it may be used for information. If she was there, she was looking for a solution to my problem.

"It was..." She doesn't finish.

"Liana. Please."

Her jaw tightens. She looks at me, then away. For the first time, she looks defeated.

"I don't know how to break your curse. I've tried everything—prayers, cleansing, crystals. Nothing has worked," she finally says, soft, solemn. "I am... so sorry."

I swallow hard. I had sensed this, but hearing it out loud makes something inside me crack.

My breath burns as it pushes up my throat. "Then that means I need to—" I stop. My voice breaks and my lips quivers.

Liana holds my gaze.

"You need to find someone who can help," she says, gentle and certain. "If there's an answer, it's with the ones who gave you the mark. I believe that is one of the human witches."

Reality sinks into my bones, pressing down on my chest until I can barely breathe.

Leave. Venture to find women who had actively worked against us in the last conflict. The *brujas* might kill me before I can even plead my case.

But what Liana says is true–there are no options left.

"I don't want to go," I whisper. "But I can't keep putting everyone around me in danger. I'll go alone."

Liana watches me closely. Then she exhales, her shoulders rising and falling as she takes in my words.

"I know you're made of tougher stuff than most, but going alone is dangerous. Do what Melisa did—make someone escort you."

She references Ra'Salore's mate. Melisa had asked for a bodyguard when she returned to the Giant Capital, Zlosa, in order to spy on the giants. It was a different situation. The danger was external then.

This is all me.

I shake my head sharply. "And kill them, too?" My voice wavers, but I don't back down. "I can't control myself. I won't ask someone to risk their life for me."

Liana nods once, her gaze solemn. "I know when a woman has made up her mind. If you feel this is best, I will not stop you, but you cannot go empty-handed. Let me help you pack."

I hesitate, my instincts screaming at me to move quickly, but I know she's right.

"I need to leave soon," I murmur. "Can you tell Estela? Mikal? Teo?"

Vann...

Her eyes flick toward the room where I was housed, as if she expects someone to come bursting through. She raises her hand, and the door shuts quiet. "We will not be heard now." Then she meets my gaze. "I'll deal with everyone else."

"Thank you," I whisper.

She ushers me toward the kitchen. "First, you should go to Mrath. She will be grateful since we have helped her with the *Cumhacht na Cruinne*. Her spies seem to know a little of everything."

Mrath, the leader of an elven rebellion, has spent years infiltrating practically every corner of the continent. Though her alliance with Teo is new, she has always expressed her disposition to be of help after King Teo and Queen Estela recovered the *Cumhacht na Cruinne*. This divine artifact helps to determine the next sovereign.

It was lost for generations, its absence left the throne in chaos, but Teo placed it in Mrath's hands, giving her a powerful foothold in the struggle ahead.

I nod once.

Liana extends her hand, the long billowing sleeves of her nightdress flowing like mist as she reaches for me. "When you leave the cavern, head south. The Enduar Mountain Range will shift from black to grey, and once it does, keep close to the base of the mountains. A thick forest should surround you. The Sisterhood's Enclave is there."

I nod, trying to absorb every detail.

Liana, seeing my overwhelm, steps closer. "Come, my child. We'll prepare you to leave. It's going to be all right."

I nod again and let her lead me.

But she doesn't take me to my old room. Instead, she brings me deeper into her home, past the kitchen, and to a small side chamber I rarely entered. I freeze in the doorway, my breath catching.

So many of my things have been brought here. My clothes, my scrolls, my shoes and boots—they are all neatly folded and tucked away.

I step forward on unsteady feet, running my fingers over the familiar fabrics, the worn scrolls I'd been studying. "Why do you have so many of my things?"

Liana straightens. "They only gave us three days, but Lord Vann insisted that you wouldn't want to return to your room for a while."

I swallow the lump in my throat, forcing myself to focus. I can't afford to fall apart now. Instead, I reach for one of the scrolls I had been reading, running my fingers along the edges before my gaze drifts toward the clothes. I see a fur coat, leather leggings, gowns, everything.

"Arlet, what do you want to take?" Liana asks from the closet.

"Mostly clothes, I think. A knife. A dish. Something to start fires. A bedroll? And perhaps a few preserves," I respond. She exits the room and I dress quickly, putting on woolen socks, pants, a woven tunic, a brown fur coat, boots, and finally, bearskin gloves.

When Liana returns, she nods at my attire. "Very wise."

Then I grab an old pack, beginning to stuff it with the assembled bounty. Liana moves quickly but methodically, tucking a few extra items neatly into the bundle. I notice her leave a few more times, but think nothing of it in the flurry of packing.

After a few minutes, she reappears at my side. “You need to go slow. Drink water. And don’t forget—”

“I’ve survived worse,” I cut in gently. “I know how to be outside. I know how to live in the cold.” I’d done so in the slave pens.

She presses her lips together, then nods.

A heavy silence settles over us.

Then, without thinking, I embrace her.

Liana isn’t a woman who takes easily to touch. She stiffens for a moment, caught off guard, but after a breath, her arms wrap around me, holding me close.

When we part, her eyes soften, but her voice is steady.

“You cannot leave without a *hlumrynna*.”

I recognize the term immediately—a Parting Ceremony.

The Enduar Wise Woman presses a cool stone into my palm, a small citrine crystal wrapped in silver wire. It hums against my hand.

“Our gods will watch over you, my child. And we will miss you while you are gone. Come home quickly. Come home healed.” Then, she takes back the gem, and my throat burns.

“I’ll miss you all,” I whisper.

"Your loss will be felt for many. Now come, I will escort you to the exit."

The city is silent. Sleeping. We move through the council district, past the houses of people I’ve loved.

My pack is heavy, but I grit my teeth and bear it. Reaching the edge of the space, I see the steps of the Enduar Palace and keep going. It takes time to cross to the tunnel that will lead me out of the city, and every step feels like I am ripping myself apart.

Liana walks beside me the entire way.

When we reach the tunnel entrance, I see two guards. Do they know what I've done? Will they take me away?

I start to speak, but Liana lifts a hand, stopping me.

“Lady Arlet has business to attend to outside,” she tells them firmly. “Let her pass.”

The enduar guards hesitate, glancing at one another, but they do not argue. They step aside.

Liana turns to me, studying my face as if memorizing it. "Go," she says softly. "Know that you will be missed."

I nod, gripping the bundle tight, and step into the tunnel.

The incline of the tunnel is steep. It's been so long since I'd been outside for more than a few hours. When I reach the exit, I squeeze my eyes shut, putting one foot in front of the other to avoid looking back. Instead I picture the massive golden doors and the red veins swirling around the entrance.

The ice floes floating on the ocean to the distant left creak. Fear pricks at the back of my neck. The cold night air bites at my skin, burning against the heat of the tears threatening to fall. I keep them back, knowing they will freeze if I let them spill over.

The worst part of leaving is not knowing if I will ever return.

But Enduvida has given me everything. How could I not do what was needed to protect it?

I press forward until the last traces of black stone fade from view. The mountains slowly shrink behind me.

Ahead—the forest waits.

I scan the shadows, wary. For the first time, I remember vaimpír could be near. The thought makes me hesitate, but I see nothing. No movement in the midnight mists. Cursing, I grit my teeth. I'm not used to being on my own, despite what I said.

I keep going.

I say goodbye to the sight of the ocean as I enter a ravine called, *El Paseo de las Nubes.* Towering walls of ice rise on either side with veins of bright white running throughout.

The passage is narrow, like a frozen canyon carved by time and storm. The moonlight shifts strangely here, refracted through the translucent walls, casting long shadows that stretch and distort with every step.

I haven't been here since the slave caravan took Estela and me to Enduvida for the first time.

The early spring winds bite at my cheeks, strong enough to make walking difficult, especially since the Enduar Mountains are high enough to almost always be frozen. The air hums with something strange—a faint, whispering song.

It isn't unpleasant.

"FIRELOCKS!"

A voice roars behind me.

I freeze.

Every hair on my arms stands on end.

"Arlet!"

The sheer force of the sound gives me goosebumps.

I whirl around. The fur of my coat whips against my face.

Vann runs towards me. His messy silver braid is loose, and the strands ripple in the wind, his cloak billowing. His chest rises and falls, breath labored.

I step back, bracing myself.

"Arlet, what the hell do you think you're doing?"

My heart pounds. He'll take me back. *He can't do that.*

How did he find me so quickly?

I turn—and run into *El Paseo de las Nubes.*

My boots pound against the frozen ground, my breath comes in sharp bursts, and my pack slaps uncomfortably against my spine. Every sound I make echoes on the walls. The ground turns to ice and I slide across it more than once, almost falling.

I feel uncoordinated and slow, but he mustn't catch me.

His footsteps thunder behind me. A quick glance over my shoulder is fruitless, as I can't quite see him through the mist and winding path, but I can hear him. He's gaining.

Then, an impact hits me hard. It's a blur of motion, and I'm turned around just before I slam onto my back. The air rushes from my lungs at the awkward angle of my pack and the world spins as Vann looms above me, his weight caging me in. He is dressed in black, and a cloak settles over both of us.

His breath is ragged. "What the fuck do you think you're doing?"

I snarl, shoving at his chest. He grabs my wrist and pulls one of my hands over my head, as I say, "I'm leaving to save the people I love."

His expression doesn't soften. No. It *darkens.*

And then—he leans in, cupping my chin with his thumb and

forefinger. His cloak shifts and I see more clearly through the fog as it reveals his own pack.

My mouth parts.

He is close enough that his breath fogs the space between us, leaving only his burning silver eyes visible. My arm burns where he holds it, but I don't try to move.

"And you thought you were going to do it alone?"

I only manage to get out, "I have to."

He shakes his head and my weight sinks onto the blanket of snow under me.

"When I was poisoned and dying, you risked everything to stay by my side—even when my very presence was a danger to you,"

He's so close I can't breathe. He's as big as the whole sky—beautifully blue. The weight of him on top of me feels good. It feels safe.

"Do you think I'd let your kindness go without repaying it? I am coming with you."

He stands abruptly, pulling me up with him. I am breathless at his goodness. Tears burn in my eyes.

"Now let's go," he says.

CHAPTER 18

VANN

We trek south from Enduvida, and the cold gnaws at my bones. Our path makes us stay close to the mountain ranges' base and walk through terrain that rolls in a jagged rhythm, sharp-backed hills rising over winding ravines. It's as though nature itself could not decide between ascent and descent.

It might have been wise to take a more direct path, but we cannot be caught by King Arion's patrols as we draw closer to the elven lands. The threat of him has been far from my mind lately, but a distant threat was still dangerous.

I'm sure he would just love to find Arlet out here. It's my job to ensure she doesn't have to go anywhere near the egotistical knave.

Wind blows over me, carrying flecks of ice that sting against my exposed skin.

But it's nothing compared to the sensory memory that burns in my chest from when I'd tackled her. I remember her small frame trapped between my thighs. Her hips pressing against my stomach, her breath warm against my ribs as she squirmed beneath me. Strands of red hair splayed across the ice, vivid against the frozen white like spilled embered silk.

A full day later, and the effect Arlet had on my body still lingers like a phantom touch that refuses to fade, though now we walk shoulder to elbow. The memory remains in every taut muscle, in my sensitive skin.

"Vann," Arlet grumbles.

The name is mine, but I've almost forgotten how to use it.

After waking up alone in Liana's home, I worried Arlet had escaped and tragedy would strike again. But then I found a note scribbled on the door in glittering, magical letters.

She's left Enduvida to find a cure.

Beneath it was another pack, with my cleaver lying atop.

The hand of Endu tapped my shoulder, reminding me that I owed her my life for the time she'd cared for me. I do not take debts lightly.

Even though I'd grabbed the things, I had run out of the city with the hope of bringing her back, but her explanation for leaving touched me. She was right—if she was out of options in the city, she needed to seek elsewhere.

It was not an easy choice for me to make, as it meant leaving the others to pick up my duties. But it wasn't as if I'd planned this. It simply happened because I owed her.

The woman standing at my side is not a small consolation, though. It was uncomfortable to admit, but I liked being alone with her.

I tighten my fists and recall how it felt to have of her hand trapped in my grip and pinned near her head. The image flickers behind my eyes.

She's beautiful. I've always known that. But now, alone in the wilderness with her, I am confronted with it in ways that are difficult to ignore.

When I glance down, she swallows hard. That throat—gods.

"All right, I will talk, then. You listen. The plan is to find the Sisterhood's Enclave, get information about the *brujas*, and then go find them, yes?" Arlet breaks the silence, discussing the plan we had made the night before.

A grunt escapes me, and I shove the thoughts away to the sound of snow crunching beneath my boots. But then she stops walking, and I let out a low groan before turning to face her. My vision shifts, and momentarily, I see her sprawled on the ice again—vulnerable, enticing.

"Yes, that is what we agreed upon," I respond, irritation bleeding into my voice as I haul myself over a large chunk of rock. Then I feel bad, knowing that it comes from my own traitorous thoughts and not her. Before the night the curse killed Diego, we were starting to be friends.

I promised I would be better.

"I'm afraid I might not be the most pleasant to travel with," I say. "I slip into an intense focus while hiking, which makes me quiet. It is not easy for me to strike up a meaningful conversation."

Arlet crests the same rock, and then puts her hands on her hips.

"That is good to know," she says. "I... like reassurance. Sometimes it makes me irksome, I think."

I soften. "Just remember that the terrain will not ease, and we are still many days from the Sisterhood's Enclave. I will try to manage my tone."

She glances at the rugged rocks scattered between trees, uncertainty flickering across her face.

"I like... reassurance," she had said.

I bite my lip. *Very well.*

"Arlet, you are doing very well. You move quickly for someone who isn't used to this," I thrust my hand toward her, waiting.

Her mouth parts, and she looks up at me with dilated pupils. She liked the compliment. Her fingers wrap around mine without hesitation—strong and sure despite their smallness. My chest tightens at the contact.

I feel as if I have won a prize. Learned a bit about her. I will remember this reaction.

"Are you sure it is a good idea for you to be here?" she says as she straightens, brushing ice from her clothes.

"Why? You don't think you need me?"

She shakes her head. "Vann, I would love nothing more than a companion, but we can't forget I killed someone."

"I won't sleep," I grumble.

"That's insanity."

"I'll sleep lightly. We can keep you tied up."

A shadow flickers across her face. "I—" She stops, her gaze flicking toward the rocky mountain path stretching endlessly ahead. Then, she exhales sharply. "Is there any hope I can persuade you to leave?"

I shake my head.

"All right, then," she says, resigned. "I suppose we continue onward."

I nod and gesture for her to lead the way. Sadly, my words run out and I decide silence is better. Silence is easier. Less torturous.

One of the hills slowly gives way to a brittle forest, skeletal branches draped in ice, the weight of winter heavy upon them. The cold intensifies under the shade. I wonder if the war had been this cold. If I had ever been this cold, despite the sweat sliding down my back.

The sun drags lower in the sky, painting the ice-tipped peaks in bleeding hues of gold and crimson.

We have walked for days, and for the first time, Arlet starts to huff. I can't blame her, I too am struggling against the unforgiving landscape.

A labored, rattling sound escapes her lips. I glance at her, watching the effort etched into her face. When she catches me looking, I turn away.

We keep hiking, but the sound Arlet makes returns—a soft, pained noise. I glance again.

She grits her teeth, her gaze snapping up to mine. "My moderate training sessions didn't account for climbing mountains and crossing frozen ravines. Mind yourself—I will keep up."

"I just want to make sure you are all right," I say.

She pauses. Then, she smiles. It's small, but it catches me off guard. Something shifts inside me, unfamiliar and unwanted.

And when she stops walking, leaning against one of the evergreen trees on the side of the hill, gulping down air like she's drowning, I know I can't ignore it.

I pull out a animal skin filled with water, take a swig, and then hold it toward her.

"Would you like to rest?"

She looks up at me, her brown eyes glistening, her cheeks flushed with effort, and she takes it.

"I swear I can do this," she insists. "We haven't even made it that far."

"We have made it far enough. And you aren't well, Firelocks. We should rest."

She doesn't respond.

Eventually, I turn away, and find a spot to think. What is Teo thinking right now, two days after my departure?

Out of the eighty years we have known each other, I have never done anything without ensuring it was all right with him. We'd been each other's confidants for as long as I could remember. He knew everything about me.

And yet—I didn't tell him I was leaving.

A deeper, more tragic realization settles in my chest, heavier than the cold.

I hadn't said goodbye in Adra's name.

I hadn't lit her stone.

My shoulders curl forward, and for the first time, I wonder what the hell has come over me. I had rules. *Order*.

Arlet coughs again, and I turn back to the woman I've chosen to follow blindly away from my home. The horror of the situation dawns on me like the glow of her flushed skin.

I've chosen her over everything else that once mattered to me.

My mood, my plans, sink like a stone landing in sand—final, without ripple or recourse. I let out a long breath, draw myself up, and seal my lips together. Then, I move toward Arlet and wait.

She regains her composure and begins walking again. I don't goad her.

I made a choice, and whether it was the wrong one no longer matters. I'll send a message to Teo when we reach the elves.

I glance back at the trees. Carving Adra's name into wood is unnecessary, but there are stones everywhere. I could use one of the knives in my pack.

Something in me eases. It will be like bringing her memory with me across the continent. She would love that—she always wanted to travel far from home. A quiet reverence settles over me. I can do this for her.

My eyes flick to the side as Arlet walks ahead. Something tugs at me, an unseen thread drawing me toward her.

No. I correct myself. It isn't a pull.

She is vulnerable. Prone to dying. I don't want something as innocent as her swallowed by the depths of this cruel world.

"You think so intensely, it's almost as if I can hear the words cross the distance between us," Arlet says.

I stop dead in my tracks. Hear thoughts? That's something that belongs to mates.

We aren't mates.

"You don't know anything," I snap.

"Dioses míos, I didn't expect you to shift moods faster than a storm wind over the Enduar Peaks, yet here we are—grumbling and brooding once more."

"We should rest," I quip, still a bit raw after thinking of Adra.

That does the trick to silence her, but now I berate myself for my actions. Maybe she's right. Maybe I am mercurial. She doesn't know how to treat me because I've never given her a clear indication.

I went to that cursed festival for her. I brought her into my space the night before and then cast her out. We were there for each other when we suffered.

I all but kissed her in the salt room.

I close my eyes. The more I think about this, the more I'll convince myself of things that do not matter. I need to let go. Let the past be what it is instead of begging for more.

Deep breaths.

In and out.

We will make it through this journey, and we will go home. If Liana believes the Mrath and her elves will have the answers, then they will. I just need to trust the path the god of stone has laid before my steps.

~

The first night alone together is quiet. Once the camp is set up, the fire lit, and the food roasting, I finally look at Arlet.

She sits perched on a flat rock near the flames, her hands resting lightly on her lap. The flickering glow highlights the soft angles of her face, the warmth of the flames chasing away the last traces of the day's chill.

Earlier, I had taken down a wolf—a clean kill. Arlet hadn't flinched at the sight of the body or its blood when I dragged it back to camp. Instead, she had wordlessly helped me gather the right branches, lashing them together with a practiced efficiency to create a sturdy tripod over the fire.

Now, the rich scent of roasting meat curls into the air, mingling with the crackle of burning wood and the distant sounds of the chilly forest settling into night.

Tomorrow, we should be out of the snowy areas. The white blanket has already started to grow more patchy.

I shift my weight, stretching out a hand toward the warmth. "You've done this before," I say, not really a question.

Arlet tilts her head, a small, knowing smile flickering across her lips. "I used to help Estela cook. In our section of the slave pens, our foreman let us forage and hunt for meager rations."

I hum. "It is a good skill. During the war, I spent a lot of time in the over world," my hand gestures around me, "and I picked up a few tricks as well. Life under the sun is no enchanted haven, but neither is it a cursed wasteland."

She stands, and grabs a stick to help her turn to food. Her head turns to the side and says, "I'm sure you've seen more of the world that I will ever."

"Most of what I have seen is the battlefield." I furrow my brow. "I remember pausing to take in a sight or two while marching, and, believe it or not, I like trees, but my memories from those days are soaked in red. By the end of this journey, I may be a new man."

She lets out a bright laugh which cuts off. "Wait, how long do you think it will take to heal me?"

Arlet goes rigid, shifting away from the food, and she pulls on her fingers, nervously.

"I can't give you a specific time, I only know I will be with you."

She relaxes a little, soothed by the words, much to my delight, then turns to finish the cooking. Once it's done, she fishes a knife and dish from her pack, then exclaims when she finds a second plate.

"Mother Liana..." she mutters. Then she cuts and arranges part of the meat.

"Here you are," she says, handing me one. "The rest of the meat can be smoked, I think."

"Yes. I will tend to that as soon as I'm finished. Thank you, Firelocks," I say, digging in. Hunger was not new to me, but I forget the ravenous way my belly can get after walking long distances.

Arlet returns to her stone and sits. She moves the meat a little, picking up one piece before letting it fall.

"You're not eating," I observe, keeping my tone neutral.

She looks up, fighting. "I'm not hungry."

I snort. "How? We have walked a long way. You must eat to keep up your energy."

Her lips part, but no retort comes. Instead, she lowers her gaze to the ground, putting her plate on her knee, and using her stick to trace patterns in the snow idly. The way she avoids my eyes sets my teeth on edge.

I see her lying on the table, screaming and begging for me to loosen the ropes. She is terrified of herself.

"You can't keep running on nothing, Arlet," I say, the words coming out sharper than I intend. "You'll collapse before we even reach the enclave."

"I'll be fine," she mutters.

"No, you won't," I counter, leaning forward. The firelight casts shadows across her face, accentuating the tension in her jaw. "You're pushing yourself too hard, and for what?"

Her eyes snap to mine, burning with a sudden intensity that makes me sit back. "I want this curse gone. I want to go back *home*."

I stiffen at the word home. It's possessive, agonized, filled with longing. I remember feeling like that during long stretches in the over world during the war.

We both stand, and I tower over her.

"Are you angry at me?"

She bites her lip, cheeks red.

"Yes."

"Then tell me why," I push.

She shakes her head.

"I don't want to."

I grab her wrist. "If you live your life skirting around the feelings of others, resentment will build in you. I know. Tell me why I've made you angry. Don't just take jabs at me."

Hot breath pours from her lungs. She swallows, but doesn't answer.

"Someone used your body to do awful things. They took away your power. Is that part of what angers you?"

Tears line her eyes.

"Let the anger out, Arlet. Yell at me. Scream. Slap me. Do it, and then speak plainly," I push her.

Her mouth wobbles. "I—"

"You can. You can do anything—I've seen it. So stop hiding," I insist.

A tear slides down her face.

"Why, exactly, are you mad at me?" I demand, stepping even closer.

"Because you *followed me*. You're the king's advisor. You help oversee everyone—the soldiers, the builders, the cooks, the hunters, the benders. You are so used to having some level of control over every situation. But you don't control this, Vann. Someone wants to hurt me and used my body to kill another. I slaughtered Diego. I—"

She goes silent.

Another moment passes, and I wait for her to continue. When she doesn't, I say, "I'm not so foolhardy that I believe an iron fist alone will manage the darkness that lurks in you. I want to help you."

Her laughter is bitter, humorless. "I know you plan to tie me up again. It's not good enough—what if you doze off and I gnaw through the ropes like some rogue monster?"

"Remember, you aren't a monster." Then I frown. "And I thought you agreed it would be wise for you to be bound?"

"I said nothing!" she shoots back, her voice cracking.

The tension between us coils tighter, and for a moment, the only sound is the crackle of the fire. Her gaze drops again, and she hugs her arms, curling into herself like she's trying to disappear.

"Why does being tied up bother you so much?" I ask quietly. The scroll in her room spoke of such things with pleasure. I can't make out how this is different.

Her shoulders tense, and I know I've hit a nerve. She doesn't answer right away, and I'm not sure she will. But then, so softly I almost miss it, she says, "It's nothing."

"This again? If we are to be both travel companions and friends, then I think it is best we speak honestly."

She looks up at me then, and there is something raw in her expression, something that makes my heart stumble. "Surely you have scars that you don't show anyone."

The statement catches me off guard. Of course I did. Sometimes... the way she challenges me makes me feel things I thought I had buried with Adra.

But I can't say any of that. I don't even want to admit it to myself. In the last two weeks, things have changed. Accelerated.

So, instead, I shrug and say, "Of course. But if they applied to a mission, I would disclose them. As it is my duty."

Her mouth falls open, and for a second, I think she might tell me. Then, to my surprise, she laughs—a real, genuine laugh that makes the corners of her eyes crinkle.

"You're an ass," she says, shaking her head.

"Maybe," I admit. "But I'm not wrong."

She sighs, the laughter fading but leaving a hint of warmth in her eyes. "I don't want to tell you yet. But I'll eat."

"You don't know how happy that makes me," I murmur.

As she picks up the plate, and I let the silence settle between us again. This time, it feels less empty, more... companionable. I watch her out of the corner of my eye, noting the way the firelight softens the angles of her face.

Later, when the fire has burned low and she yawns, stretching her long neck, I clear my throat.

"How about a deal?"

She raises one red eyebrow. "Go on."

"I won't tie you up if you tell me why it causes you such panic," I drawl.

She stiffens. "Not yet."

I sigh. "Then we will proceed out of safety."

She scrambles to her feet, stepping back, but she's too slow. I catch her wrist, careful not to grip too hard, but firm enough that she knows I won't back down.

"Vann," she whispers, her voice shaking.

I hesitate for only a breath. "Just tell me and I will bind you with nothing more than my arms."

She bites her lip, her entire frame trembling, but she says nothing. Not a single word.

I exhale through my nose, and my decision is made. Gently, I pull her toward the nearest tree. She resists, but there's no real strength behind it.

Then I leave her there, waiting, as I gather supplies. I take my time, setting up a stone at the base of the trunk and covering it with her sleeping mat, so that she might sit. Next, I tie the rope around her wrists and position her back against the tree. Once she is comfortable, I secure her torso to the sturdy trunk.

The moment retreat, she lowers her head, her shoulders trembling. A choked sound escapes her, and my stomach twists.

She's crying.

Damn it.

I kneel beside her, wiping the tears so they don't freeze on her cheeks.

"Arlet, please don't weep." I cup behind her neck. "I don't want to be cruel."

"It is all right, Vann. I know this is all we have to keep you safe."

I step back, mind churning over the conflict in her.

"I'll start smoking the meat and then I will keep watch," I murmur. "Get some rest and try not to..."

I trail off, not wanting to be crueler than I already have been. I grab a few more blankets, covering her face, legs, and hair. Everything should be insulated enough not to melt the snow around her.

Once I'm finished, she doesn't speak, and instead turns her face into the coverings.

I sit beside the fire, knife in hand as I begin to cut strips of meat.

After a few hours, I hear her snore softly.

Then I retrieved a rock, and begin carving my Adra's name, all the while, thinking of Arlet.

CHAPTER 19
ARLET'S CURSE

I awake for the first time in several days, tied to a tree and sitting in front of a fire burning low.

More cursed light.

Meat is being smoked alongside the flames.

Where am I?

The cold bite of the rope restraints cuts into my wrists, the bark of the tree is rough against my back, and my breath comes out in ragged snarls. My body is soft and weak.

I cannot break free, despite the need to move. To run. My legs and feet tense as I fight against the restraints. The world around me blurs, pulsing with red light, shifting between shadow and fury.

The forest is vast, and the trees stretch upward around me. The air smells like frozen earth. Wind rustles the canopy, sending fragmented beams of moonlight dancing over the area where I am tethered, and every flicker of light feels like a predator moving just out of sight.

I need to break free and go south. It is a direction that I would understand even if my eyes were closed. I will go as far and as fast as necessary, tear down any pillar of flesh that stands in my way, until, at last, I reach my destination.

A voice slithers through the darkness.

"Arlet."

The sound cuts through the haze of instinct and rage. A masculine tone momentarily calms the wretched, hunger gnawing at my belly and the urge to run.

"You wake at last. It is good to feel you. Continue your path, darkness will guide your steps."

A pull, like talons sinking deep into my chest, drags at my soul. My vision swims, the hunger to run surging again, and I thrash against my bindings. I kick off the blankets covering me. My limbs strain and my body contorts.

Whoever tied this was cautious. A growl builds in my throat, vibrating through my bones.

Movement draws my attention to the side, and I see the blue-skinned warrior with silver hair and a gaze like that of tempered steel. He was there the last time I awoke, intruding in my room. He stood in my path just as he does now.

I... think I know him.

His presence tugs at something buried deep, but he is not the one I seek.

He is in your way. Kill him, as you did the other. Use a knife, and I will guide you. Or better yet, use your fingers.

This voice is different from the first that spoke to my mind. Deeper. More ancient.

You will like the feel of his blood on your skin.

My lips peel back, exposing my teeth. My body lurches against the restraints. Rip. Tear. Kill—just as I had the other one.

I salivate for his death.

Then—another voice, fragile, distant, yet familiar.

Stop!

It is my voice. The words flicker at the edges of my mind, an ember in the storm of my thoughts. My breath hitches.

"Arlet," the man before me murmurs, his voice impossibly soft. It is strange that a thing so delicate engulfs me so entirely.

The sound wraps around me, tugging me back from the precipice.

And then I slip, my focus breaks.

I FLINCH, PANTING AND SHIVERING. MY MUSCLES LOCK AS THE MONSTROUS desire inside me fights to reclaim its hold. I am trapped between control and ruin.

Vann crouches beside me, the moonlight catching the silver in his hair. The glow casts long, flickering shadows over his sharp features, his expression unreadable yet unwavering. He does not flinch. Does not step back. Instead, he reaches forward, his hand pressing against my arm, solid and warm.

I snarl and try to bite him. It is involuntary.

"Easy, Firelocks. I see your eyes. I know the darkness is retreating." His voice, quiet but unshaken, slips through the madness and settles deep in my soul.

I shudder. My body trembles, my instincts scream, but I do not lunge. I do not snap.

Tears burn, hot against the cold sheen of my skin. I am so tired. "Vann, I—"

"I know."

His fingers curl gently around my neck, grounding me. The hunger writhes. He brushes a loose strand of hair from my face, his touch so cold and careful that it sends a sharp pang through my chest.

"You're going to be all right," he says, not as a question, but as a certainty.

The exhaustion surges forward, dragging me down like a wave. The voice in the dark still whispers, but it is fainter now.

Exhaustion from a full day of walking returns. It almost makes me forget I am tied up.

The thought of ropes bound around me again should make me afraid, but I find myself welcoming the barrier between me and Vann.

Ropes symbolized a lack of power in my life—something that had resulted in a loss. Now, something lurks inside of me so frighteningly powerful that I must be restrained to avoid killing.

"Vann, I heard a voice," I murmur.

He studies my face. “I know. It spoke to me.”

I furrow my brow. He heard the person calling me back?

“What did it say?”

“Stop,” he responds easily.

The memory of awaking in my cursed state is not total darkness, as other memories like this had been, but I remember the thing inside me recognizing him.

It wasn’t the same voice I heard.

“Your eyelids droop, Firelocks,” Vann says. His tail retrieves the blankets I’d kicked off, and he places them over me, using his hands to tuck it into my sides. After, his tail curls around my covered foot, and squeezes. “Sleep.”

It’s so comforting. I want to continue talking, but every muscle in my body is sore.

My lashes flutter, and the last thing I see before I succumb to the weight of sleep is Vann, still watching over me, his touch burned into my skin and anchoring me to the now.

I should have said thank you.

CHAPTER 20

ARLET

The sound of scraping draws me from a dreamless sleep. When my eyes open again, it is to the early-morning light straining through a flap of leather. A blanket is pulled up high enough to cover half of my face.

A rush of anxiety pumps through my veins, and I bring out my hands to inspect them for blood. Flipping my ungloved hands over and over, I see nothing.

They are clean, save the dirt building up under my nails.

Nothing.

My whole body relaxes at the word, yet I still feel my heartbeat in my ribs. I blink once, glimpsing blood behind my eyelids. Wringing my hands, I feel over the bumpy scars on my fingers. While the movement in those fingers is mostly normal, they always tend to be a bit colder than the rest of my hand.

Pushing up onto my side, I look around at the brown, leather tent. Cave bear leather, likely.

My brows draw together. I definitely didn't fall asleep here. My boots are set near the front of the tent, and the rope Vann used to bind me is laid there.

I suck in a sharp breath.

Last night hasn't faded totally. It's shrouded in a dark red veil, but it's there. The rage, the hunger, the way the world narrowed to the single, overwhelming need to destroy and run.

And Vann had been in my way.

Thank Endu I'd been bound, and thank Vann he'd brought me inside.

When I push out of the small dwelling, I find Vann kicking ice over the fire, the sun's rays casting restless shadows over his face. I watch him carefully, searching for something to tell me what he's thinking.

"Good morning," I say gently.

He looks up, and for a moment, he stares. His silver brows pull together, and his jaw tightens, as if he's bracing for something. Then, in two strides, he's in front of me, kneeling to bring himself to eye level.

"You're awake," he says. His gaze drags over my face, searching.

"I am," I murmur. I should be angry about last night. Maybe I am. But mostly, I'm exhausted. Tired of not understanding what's happening to me. Tired of feeling like something inside me is twisting and pulling in ways I can't control.

I know he wants honesty, but I don't know if I am ready to tell him that.

His throat bobs. He exhales sharply, raking a hand through the loose hair above his braid. "Are you well?" he asks, low and rough. "Last night I tried—" He stops himself. "When I went to check on you, you were ice cold, even with the fire. I brought you inside."

With you? I wonder. The thought sparks something inside my chest. I reach for his wrist, and he flinches—not away, but as if the warmth of my touch is startling.

"Thank you," I whisper.

He covers the spot where I grab him with his other hand, and then moves my hand.

"You... are welcome."

"Did you sleep?" I ask, reaching back and pulling the blanket tighter around me. The morning air is cold.

He nods once. "We did not touch while you slept, if that is what you wonder. I would've asked before bringing you in, but you didn't stir."

I smile a little. "I wouldn't think you would do anything inappropriate."

He smiles, and I'm just so grateful to have him here. It wasn't *that* common to have a friend that was willing to risk their life for another.

Moments like this made me trust him. My most important emotion.

"We need to get moving soon," he says. "Will you help me clear out the tent?"

"Of course." I push out of the space, and squint, shading my eyes. "Maldita sea. The sun is bright. Does it bother you?"

He frowns. "No? I do not notice it so much." Then he turns back to the stretch of leather he'd laid out, with strips of meat laid equidistant apart, and rolls it into an easy-to-travel bundle.

I take a breath, then duck back inside. Raking my fingers through my tangled hair, I am grateful that Vann hasn't mentioned how I look. Being in the sun would make my freckles worse, and it was hard to manage my hair with few materials.

A bun was impractical without a mirror, so I quickly braided my locks, and then pulled on fur gloves. I rub my hands together, grateful for the warmth, and then start winding up the bedrolls.

Something rolls out of Vann's blanket.

I suck in a breath, turning the stone over in my fingers. The name is carved in enduar, the etchings worn but careful. *Li'Adra.* The letters mean nothing to me at first, but a memory stirs. Vann's woman, the one who passed on.

I glance toward my traveling companion, a strange unease curling in my chest. Not fear, not jealousy—just a reminder of how little we know each other.

The stone is warm from where it had been resting, as if it still holds the memory of his touch. I press my thumb against the name and wonder about her.

Then I slip the stone into his things.

No sooner than I exit the tent, he begins to take it down. He folds it into nothing, wrapping the leather in the blankets and then tying them to two rods supporting his bag.

Once everything is cleaned and I've eaten, I stand there quietly.

"We're two days from the Sisterhood's Enclave," he explains, walking slightly faster than my natural stride.

I huff along, letting the heat exercise brings zap through me.

After what feels like an hour, I stop, panting.

"Vann, about last night—"

"We don't need to speak of it anymore. I know it upsets you." Then he continues walking. His silver hair catches in the sun's glow as he moves past endless trees.

Gods, he moves fast.

"Wait! I just... wanted to thank you."

Vann exhales slowly, rolling his shoulders before flashing me a grin. "Again?"

"...Yes."

"We are friends, aren't we?"

I swallow against the lump in my throat. Despite his arrogance, a sick feeling coils in my gut. "I know I tried to hurt you."

He raises a brow. "I'm not easy to hurt, Arlet."

I exhale sharply, shaking my head. "Maybe not. But that doesn't mean I shouldn't worry." My fingers tighten at my sides.

He stops, then grabs one of my shoulders. "If anything, it is I who should worry over you, Firelocks." Then, softer, almost reluctant, he says, "And I already do."

TWO DAYS PASS WITHOUT INCIDENT. EACH NIGHT, HE TIES ME UP BEFORE BED only for me to wake on a bedroll.

The forest thickens the closer we get to the Sisterhood's Enclave. Snow thins until it disappears, and the trees grow larger and older until their roots tangle across the ground like the veins of some ancient creature.

Mist curls around our ankles, and the air is cool and damp,

carrying the faint scent of moss and wildflowers. Still, it is better than the frost. I only need to wear my coat and gloves at night.

Vann also opts for fewer clothes, and proudly displays his cleaver strapped to his pack. His white tunic clings to his skin when it grows damp with sweat and mist.

Sometimes I stay back just to watch him move. He's quiet, and I like the way his tail flexes in time with his ass.

But that is a secret I will take to my grave.

I know we're getting close when the trees begin to change. Their bark shimmers faintly in the low light, and their leaves glow, casting everything in an ethereal green hue.

Though they are beautiful, sometimes the hair stands up on the back of my neck. I sense something—like the trees peer out at me with unseen eyes.

Vann had explained we hadn't taken the common path as to avoid any other travelers, especially ones linked to King Arion.

The Elf King is a threat to me, but he's lower on my list than removing this curse.

I stop in my tracks as a clearing comes into view. Three enormous trees circle the area. Their trunks are so wide, they seem to go on forever in both directions.

I've never seen anything like it. Not in Zlosa, with the dangerously tall trees, nor in Enduvida, where the city is ruled by fungi rather than traditional flora.

Approaching one, I lean in closer to inspect the trunk. The bark is rough and gnarled, etched with lines and grooves that look like a language I haven't learned to read.

The branches stretch high into the sky, disappearing into a canopy of glowing leaves that pulse faintly, like a heartbeat. Recognition flickers. This is where Mother Liana told me to come.

We've made it to the Sisterhood's Enclave.

From my studies, there were many factions of elves, but the vast majority adhered to the rule of the crown. Elves produce fine wood makers and expert archers, which I suppose could be expected from a land filled with hills, mountains, and tall trees.

I had no more than glimpsed Mrath in passing during her visits in Enduvida, but I know that the sisterhood was home to a great deal of deadly elven women. Assassins, thieves, spies. Even though they are our allies, I wasn't totally at ease with the idea of being surrounded by them.

"We're supposed to just walk in?" I glance at Vann. "Where?"

He hesitates, something I'm not used to seeing from him. "I've never done this before."

I blink. "You don't know how to get in?"

His jaw tightens, and he gives me a withering look. "From my understanding, someone should come to greet us."

I chew on the inside of my lip. "What do you need me to do?"

Vann looks at me with an appraising expression as he moves to another tree, presumably searching for clues.

"Your current actions are adequate."

"I just stand here and wait?"

"Yes."

"For how long?"

He groans from, obscured behind a tree. Then his head pops back out, his eyes shining through the thin lace of grey mist.

"As long as it takes me to find something useful."

I sigh, crossing my arms and shifting my weight from one foot to another. The air around the tree is too silent. I can hear my thoughts stretch on, broken only by the rustling of leaves and the occasional creak of a tree's massive branch.

When I think I can't stand the stillness any longer, a figure emerges from the shadows of the forest.

At first, I gasp, cowering at the larger-than-life image. But then the feminine form steps out of the mist, returning to a more normal size, and I instantly recognize her.

"Glyni," Vann says, his voice low and tense.

This is one of the elves that lived under the mountain in Enduvida for several months. She's a decent hand taller than me, with a cascade of auburn strands, braided and twined with tiny glowing flowers, and fierce amber eyes.

She is one of Leader Mrath's archers, but that never stopped her from showing a kind smile to any enduar. She shared a flask of mead with me on more than one occasion.

Rumor has it, she also had a decent series of romps with one of the enduar men, Niht. She knows Enduvida's culture well—but I feel uneasy out here.

Seeing her here in the forest makes her look different than how she did in the under mountain.

The elf who approaches is almost otherworldly. Her skin is the pale, cool color of a maple tree. It's unblemished and even.

When she moves closer, her amber eyes sparkle with amusement. She looks between us, her lips curving into a sharp, knowing smile.

"Arlet," she says, her voice smooth and lilting. Then she turns to my companion. "And Lord Vann! I didn't think I'd see you again. We've been expecting just this lovely human."

She jerks her head toward me.

"Expecting her?" he replies, his tone clipped.

She laughs, a low, melodic sound that sends a shiver down my spine. "Oh yes. We received a message from Emissary Thorne that Arlet has a problem, Mrath might be able to solve." She purses her lips and shrugs one shoulder. "Mrath does tend to clean up a lot of your people's messes."

Her gaze shifts to me, and I feel pinned under her scrutiny, despite how she reaches for my hand. "So, my dear, what ails you?"

I open my mouth, then close it. Visions of Diego. Blood. So much blood. Ropes. The voices. My stomach roils and the hand she holds turns clammy.

"She's cursed," Vann interjects unceremoniously. "It's dark magic, likely from one of the human witches."

She frowns and drops my hand. "Abhartach, then?"

Vann nods. "Likely."

When Glyni looks at me again, her face is full of pity. "We cannot fix that."

"No, but you can help us find someone who can," Vann counters.

She smiles. "Well, let's get you inside to see what we can do."

As she steps forward, the ground rumbles. Leaves part, revealing a gnarled wooden face emerging from the soil, its massive form embedded in the forest floor. Large, glowing green eyes blink open amidst the branches, and its wooden mouth creaks open to speak in old Elvish.

Glyni bows before the door and murmurs, *"Oscailte."*

"Bím i gcónaí ar fáil duitse," the door responds in a low, lilting accent.

I glance at Vann, catching the way his shoulders stiffen and his jaw tightens. His usual stoicism falters for a moment, and I see something sharp flicker in his eyes.

He doesn't like elves.

"Oh, come now. We don't bite," and then she grins broadly. "Not you two, anyway."

They certainly didn't seem like a species that was instilled with a morality as black and white as the enduares. Their sense of right and wrong shifted like the wind through the trees.

The wooden face groans again, the mouth stretching wider, revealing a hollow interior bathed in a warm, golden glow. The scent of wildflowers drifts toward us as the opening solidifies into a tunnel.

Vann hesitates, just for a moment, before stepping forward. I follow closely, my heart pounding as we approach the massive, living entrance.

The door watches us. Its gaze lingers on me.

Inside, the space opens up into a vast chamber grown from living wood. It is lower than we were outside, but not so far down that we are underground.

Golden veins pulse along the walls, giving off a soft glow. Vines curl along the floor, shifting as we step forward, whispering against our boots. The scent of damp earth and fresh blossoms fills the air, mingling with something older, something untouched by time.

Bridges made from intertwined branches stretch above us, connecting to higher platforms where elven figures drift through the shadows. Their eyes shimmer in the dim light, flicking to us before they vanish deeper into the tree.

I spot a few dryads. *Protectors of the forest,* they'd been called in one of the history scrolls. They look like they are made entirely of wood.

Ahead, a grand spiral staircase winds upward, its steps formed directly from the tree's heartwood. Glyni gestures for us to follow, her footsteps light and soundless.

"Not a single piece of cut wood," Vann murmurs, almost impressed.

When I look back at the scenery, I realize he's right.

As we start up the stairs, Vann moves warily. His shoulders are tense and his hand never far from his blade.

The higher we go up the tree, the more the air hums with magic. I can barely glimpse the sky beyond the canopy of leaves. The feeling presses against my skin, seeping into my bones, whispering secrets in a language I don't understand. I turn back as the leaves flutter. My breath catches.

There is no wind in this place. Everything is alive, and it's watching us.

CHAPTER 21
VANN

Glyni leads us deeper into the Sisterhood's Enclave. As a young man, I'd visited the elven capital, Shvathemar. It was a gleaming, wooden city. But this... it is unlike other places I've seen carved from trees.

The Sisterhood's Enclave is woven together by magic, not blade nor chisel. The branches arch overhead, forming walls and corridors that creak, their shapes shifting ever so slightly.

It's warm, too. The pack is heavy on my back, and I pull on my shirt to cool myself down. I can even see a few stray strands of hair curling along Arlet's neck.

Glyni leads us toward a structure that seems to have grown from the earth itself. The walls are woven from gnarled vines and sturdy branches. Flowers bloom in the eaves, glowing faintly, their petals sparkling as if they'd just been watered.

The elf presses her palm against the twisted frame of the entrance. The wood sighs, shifting under her fingers, and the doorway unfurls, revealing the space within. The air temperature is pleasant compared to the rest of the enclave.

"I have prepared two rooms for you," Glyni says. A brief relief washes over me before she continues, "Ah, my common tongue is lacking. I suppose I should say, two spaces."

I step inside first, immediately noting the organic curves of the room, its walls forming seamless shelves of roots and vines. The soft glow of bioluminescent leaves gives the space a gentle radiance, but it's impossible to miss that there are only a few furnishings.

A lavatory is open in the back with what I can only assume is a door similar to the entrance, and there is a tub nestled next to a flowing fountain. A folding partition constructed by leaves covers part of the bathing area.

And then... in the middle of the room, there is a bed. *One wide bed* covered in a blanket woven with shimmering threads.

"One bed?" I ask flatly, turning toward Glyni.

"Two spaces on either side." She smiles, unbothered. "A generous arrangement, considering the Sisterhood does not often extend hospitality to outsiders. Even your king did not spend the night when he visited. You should be grateful."

Arlet's expression is unreadable as she moves past me, her fingers ghosting over the bed coverings. She doesn't protest, nor does she look at me.

"Rest," Glyni commands. "You'll see Mrath in the morning."

I step forward, brows furrowing. The canopy of leaves covers most of the sky, and there are no windows in this room. "How will we know it is morning?"

Glyni smiles. "I will come to wake you."

Something slithers through my insides. I didn't trust the elves here—they are not strictly honorable.

"Are you sure there is no way to meet with her sooner?" I ask politely.

"She does not want to see guests tonight," Glyni says, though there's a flicker of something in her gaze—amusement, perhaps. "Enjoy your time together."

Then the door folds shut and we are left alone.

"Well, that wasn't the least bit helpful," I grumble.

Arlet laughs behind me. "What did you expect? The elves are rarely forthcoming. I'm just eager to speak with Mrath—I miss home."

There's that word again. It sounds so sweet to my ears.

"Come, you should prepare for sleep," I say, holding out my hand.

She doesn't protest as I ease our packs to the ground and guide her to sit on the bed. As soon as she does, she starts pulling at the laces of her boots, her fingers fumbling slightly.

I crouch in front of her, reaching for her shoes.

Her brow furrows. "I can do it."

"I know you are active, Arlet, but preparing for a trek like the one we've endured the last few days is hard. I know you are tired—fuck, even I am ready to sleep," I loosen the knots. "Just let me help."

She exhales, something between a sigh and a grumble, but she doesn't push me away. Not really.

My fingers slide through the laces. One boot slips off, then the other.

"Vann, go away. I'm dirty. I stink," she mutters, shifting uncomfortably.

She's wrong. I have travelled with unwashed troops—this is not a *stink*. It's a light odor.

When she tries to move, she pulls her grimy sock half-way down. It reveals her curse mark.

"Wait." My hand curls behind her ankle.

It's the first chance I've had to really look at it—the dark lines winding around her skin in the form of a serpent poised to strike.

Seeing it settles like a weight on my shoulders, unease prickling at the edges of my thoughts.

Arlet tugs her foot away. "Thank you, but I don't like looking at it. It reminds me of Diego."

"I can understand why," I respond. I had things I didn't like remembering.

I change the subject, placing her boots beside me, and sitting against the wall. My legs stretch out, and I cross one over the other.

The position, her on the bed and me on the floor, is casual. I feel comfortable around her. Despite her looking tired, she is studying the room.

"What do you think of this place?" I ask.

She pauses. "That is a little hard for me to answer."

"Why?"

Arlet looks at me, almost wary. “The first thirty years of my life, I was confined to the same small area. Then Estela brought me with her to Enduvida. The journey was... brutal. We were cold. Poorly dressed. Some of us were whipped along the way. I don’t remember much of the scenery.”

She lets out a long breath, then looks up again.

“Enduvida was the most beautiful place I’d ever seen. More beautiful than any glimpse of finery I saw in Zlosa. But now I’ve seen the sunrise, and the way the forest looks covered in mist, and living trees that morph themselves into what seems to be an entire town, and I can’t help but think the under mountain’s beauty has its rivals,” her lip curls at the corners.

I like the way she speaks. It’s poetic—and I liked reading the poets of old. But she still speaks like she’s doing something wrong.

“Why do you say that like it’s a bad thing?” I ask. “There are many beautiful places around the world. No enduar would fault you for that.”

“Because I owe everything to your people. I feel ungrateful for even considering to love anything else. And...” she pauses. “The only reason I am seeing any of this is because of something I did that was wrong. Perhaps, even more than what I just said, I feel guilty for seeing anything lovely when I did something so awful, such a short time ago.”

Well, fuck. That first part, about gratitude sounds exactly like something I used to say. I had been such an ass back then.

“Arlet, do you think you are ungrateful because of ideas I used to spout?”

She shakes her head, but then pauses. “Perhaps in part, but I felt it before you said anything. I guess... it is simply how I see things.”

I exhale, then lean forward. A few lines from my favorite poet, Lo’Niht come to my mind. I translate the words from memory.

“Regret clings too easily, like burrs in the hem of a weary traveler—
A weight that asks nothing but to be carried.
But beauty? Beauty is lighter, fleeting, slipping through open hands,
Yet it does not demand to be earned.

It simply is.

You have walked far enough beneath heavy skies, let your step, for once, fall upon something soft."

Arlet goes entirely still, but her gaze is unyielding as she watches me. There is a slight crease between her brows as she considers the words.

"That was... beautiful. What is a man like you, the Butcher's Cleaver, doing reading poetry?" she teases.

I huff a laugh. "I know for a fact you can weave, sew, teach, read, write, heal, and cook. You do not need to be just one thing, why should I?"

A smile stretches over her face. "And the paintings at the Mating Journey?"

It's my turn to pause. "Those were..."

I don't know what to say. I'd brought some of my recent pieces, and there had been one of her. I hadn't set out to make the painting *of her*, per se. But it came out beautifully.

"You have unusual hair," I murmur. "It pairs well with other colors."

Her brows shoot up, surprised. "That is so sweet. Are there any other parts of me you'd like to paint?"

My mind goes dangerous places before circling back to a simpler answer. I lift my hands, pointing to her freckles. "Your spots."

Her smile vanishes, and she brings a hand up to cover them.

"What?" I ask.

"Humans don't—well, technically, I didn't think anyone liked sunspots. They are blemishes. Ugly. I try to cover them."

I frown, pushing onto my knees to position myself in front of her. She draws back as I assess her face. "They are not, and you shouldn't."

Silence stretches between us, but I don't move. It is lovely here, close to her. Maybe it's the room, but I feel warm with her.

"You are surprising," she says. "The poetry, the paintings, and... this. I think I finally understand how you've been Teo's closest friend for so long."

I tilt my head to the side. "What about it was not clear?"

She shrugs. "Teo is extremely kind and open. You are the opposite."

"Not all people open like unlocked doors, Firelocks. Some take time—like winter-bound rivers, slow to thaw, but no less deep."

She nods slowly. "I think I'm seeing that."

Her answer doesn't sit right with me. *Seeing that*, as if it was not something she instinctively understood, as I have come to understand parts of her.

She squirms under my gaze.

"I think you always knew."

She sucks in a breath. "What?"

"You've never noticed how you lean into me when there is danger? How you seek me in a crowd? Perhaps you do not always love to see me, but you always want to know if I am there."

"I—" She blinks, chest rising and falling rapidly. "I think—"

Heat pulses between us and I walk the line between action and inaction. I could touch her.

My fingers *ache* to touch her.

My blood is hot in my veins, for the first time in gods know how long.

But that would be cruel to both of us. I shift out of the way, giving her a bit more space.

"It is fine, Firelocks. I am merely making an observation."

We are silent for a time. Then her body angles from me and she stands, "Thank you for this. Really. I don't want to cut it short, but —" her gaze goes to the tub in the corner. "I would like to bathe before you bind me again."

My pulse jumps and I sit up. "Here? We should talk about the morning."

"Technically there," she says, breathless, nodding toward the hollow basin large enough to fit a human. Next to it, a stream of clear water pours from the wall. "I know you think I should stand around while you craft a master plan, but we've been walking for days. We can't do anything until morning. It's been a very long time since I was this dirty."

"With me in the room?"

She purses her lips. "There's a covering. And I think you have more than earned my trust that you won't look." Then Arlet casts me a devious smile. It's playful, not at all sexual.

But I *have* seen her naked. I had a very strong reaction. The thought of her undressing near me...

"I don't think it's a good idea. What if we need to leave quickly?"

She groans.

"Mi Cielo, I promise you, I will not manage to open the room to this door and wander outside into the cold, misty forest so I can freeze to death."

I say nothing, forcing my gaze to stay fixed on the floor.

Mi cielo.

My sky.

Hmm. Why would she call me that?

She walks past me, close enough that I can smell her—salt and wind and something faintly sweet. I clench my fists.

"You could probably use a wash, too," she says over her shoulder, teasing.

"I'll pass," I mutter, mind churning.

Arlet laughs softly, the sound trailing behind her as she moves toward the basin. I don't look. Hearing the water splashing is bad enough. It makes my mind conjure images I have no right to think about.

A sharp ache spreads through my limbs, radiating from my chest, heavy and numbing all at once.

I have no heart. That means no circulation. No warmth with her gone. My limbs feel slow and stone-heavy.

I move onto the bed, and start to look through the items stacked on a table. Under a few books written in elvish, I find a tome with blank pages. A small slot is on the front where a bit of charcoal is placed.

Books were not totally foreign concepts to me, but I found them less effective than scrolls. Even still, the charcoal scratches nicely over the page. I spend a few moments, sketching out a few basic trees. It helps ease the tension that comes from hearing Arlet wash herself.

I count my breaths, forcing control. One. Two. Three. Then I sketch a bit more.

A sharp curse snaps me from my focus.

"Maldita sea," Arlet mutters from behind the screen. There's a rustle, a splash, and then a frustrated sigh.

I glance up at the partition, hiding the book beneath the pillow. "What?"

"I forgot to grab clothes," she grumbles. "And I'm not about to put those filthy things back on."

My gaze flicks to the small table near the wall—a neatly stacked pile of folded garments rests there. I push to my feet, crossing the room. Without a word, I pull a fresh gown from the pile and walk toward the screen.

I pause just outside it. "Here."

A moment of silence. Then a damp hand peeks past the divider, fingers curling around the fabric as she takes it from me. *"Gracias."*

I return to my seat against the wall, reclaiming my book. But I don't focus on my sketching this time. I stare at the page without seeing it, listening to the quiet sounds of fabric shifting as she dresses.

When she steps out, her damp hair clings to her shoulders, water trailing down the curve of her collarbone. I drag my gaze away, clearing my throat.

"I—" My voice falters. I hesitate, about to gesture to her hair. It's long. Adra had long hair and found it hard to style when she was weary.

But Arlet doesn't hear me, instead a dark look comes over her face.

"What's wrong?" I ask.

She doesn't meet my gaze. "I was just wondering when you will tie me up?"

The words land between us, sharp, quiet.

"I think you are safe for tonight." My voice is steady, but I see something flicker in her eyes when she looks up—fear, not for herself, but for me.

"But what if I wake up and—"

"I'll be here," I cut in, my voice firm. "Tomorrow will be stressful with Mrath. You should rest."

She exhales, her shoulders losing some of their tension. "I really don't know how to express the depth of my gratitude."

I'm graced with another smile, and then she climbs onto the bed, turning away from me. I wonder if I should be here.

Normally, I would sleep on the floor without thinking. But she likes to be asked. Likes it when I talk.

"Do you mind sharing the bed with me?"

She turns her head back to me and smiles.

"I trust you."

Trust. What a sweet, precious thing. A heady thing. A sacred thing.

I watch as she settles beneath the blankets, damp strands of hair fanning across the pillow. So informal. So... familiar. Someone... some man would be very lucky to see her loose hair every day.

For a long moment, I just sit there, listening to the steady rhythm of her breath as sleep claims her.

Hours later, the room is quiet. Arlet is asleep, curled up on the bed with her back to me, her breathing slow and even. I sit on the bed, keeping watch.

Was I tired? Yes. But I'm also on edge. I'm very protective of Arlet tonight. I don't know why.

I don't dare let my guard down. Not here. Not in a place where the walls seem to listen, where the air hums with power I don't trust.

I close my eyes briefly, not to sleep, but to steady myself. The soft rustling of blankets draws my attention back to Arlet.

Then, just as I think she has drifted into deep sleep, she shifts.

A breath. A whisper.

"Gracias, Vann."

My name.

It slips past her lips so softly I almost miss it.

The sound of it curls around my memory. My hands tighten into fists, my jaw clenching against the strange, unwelcome warmth that spreads through me.

She doesn't wake. Doesn't say anything else. I don't move for a long time.

The glow from the bioluminescent leaves dims, but it still casts shifting shadows across her face, softening her worry lines and highlighting the curve of her cheek. The steady rise and fall of her breath is soothing.

In sleep, she looks unburdened, free of the weight she normally carries, and something about it makes my chest ache worse than the cold ever has.

Being in the elven lands makes me think of the missive. So far, we had been lucky, but I wouldn't rest easy until we were out of Arion's kingdom.

If Arion ever managed to take her, I was almost sure he would destroy her. Men like him broke beautiful things. They cut wood for their castles, kept precious artifacts behind lock and key, and stomped on rotting corpses to make their way to wherever they deemed important.

I exhale slowly, but it does nothing to ease the pressure building inside me.

Longing is a foreign thing, an emotion I thought I had buried long ago, and yet here it is, clawing its way to the surface, undeniable in its presence. She shifts slightly, curling deeper into the blankets, and my throat tightens. I want to reach out, just once. Just to feel that she's real, that she's here, warm and alive beneath my fingers.

But I don't.

Instead, I press my back harder against the wall, letting the cold anchor me. Wanting is dangerous. Wanting leads to weakness. And weakness, for me, has always led to pain.

So I stay where I am, watching, sketching, listening to the steady rhythm of her breath. And when the pain becomes too much, I close my eyes and pretend I don't feel it at all.

CHAPTER 22

ARLET

I wake up warm and blissfully unbound. A slow, creeping sensation spreads through my limbs before my mind fully registers where I am. The blankets are heavy with residual heat from my slumber, and the air is still, carrying the faint scent of damp earth and stone.

Then I feel a person—solid and unmoving, pressed against my back.

I liked the firmness. I couldn't stand light touches—they made me feel anxious.

Then a blue tail with a silver tuft rests over my hip

My breath stills in my chest as awareness sharpens. *Vann.*

At some point in the night, he must've moved closer. His form is curled near mine. My skin prickles.

Of course, he needed to sleep at some point.

I knew that—I'd told him to lie with me on the bed.

It made sense. We'd slept near each other before. But I didn't expect his arm to drape around my waist.

Cautiously, I shift just enough to turn my head yet not to disturb the delicate balance between us. I've never seen him truly rest, only sit still in his unnerving way. His silver hair has fallen out of his braid and spilled over his face, strands ghosting over the sharp cut of his cheekbone, over lips that part slightly with each steady exhale.

But his skin is cold.

Strange.

He'd touched me a lot lately. My face. My hands. The small of my back. My ankle.

Somehow, I hadn't noticed how his body felt, how the cold lingers beneath his skin like frost that never melts. I shiver.

If I couldn't see him breathing, I'd worry he was dead. But then his hand flexes before pressing against the soft curve protecting my lower belly.

The action moves my ass right into his lap, and my core clenches.

Oh, I think. *Oh... yes.*

He's holding such a particular spot, the space right above where I would carry a child.

My mind swims, but I don't move away. I don't *want* to.

He had been so kind last night. There was something about talking to him that made me feel better. Safe. And... beautiful?

I didn't think he would ever be affected by a human. But he likes my freckles and my hair.

I study him, my gaze trailing over the way his shoulders rise and fall. He looks different like this. Less like a warrior or an unyielding force, and more like...

My fingers twitch against his hand. The back of his palm heats, and he nuzzles closer, pressing his nose to my throat. The sensitive skin tingles, and my mouth goes dry.

I don't know if I had ever been held so tightly—definitely not since the night I lost my daughter. Before then, I used to luxuriate in moments like this. Being caged in until I was trapped.

I liked abandon. Loved the way my skin tingled with the roughness.

It had been a decade since the sad night. So much of my soul had changed and healed in that time.

While I wasn't ready to say I liked being bound again, I definitely like this.

But a part of me wonders if it is because of time, or the man behind me. He holds my trust like it is a precious thing.

My eyes flutter closed as his breath tickles over my neck and collarbone. More heat pools between my legs.

His words from last night play in my memory. *"You have walked far enough beneath heavy skies, let your step, for once, fall upon something soft."*

This is more than soft.

This is... peaceful. Something about beautiful words and firm, possessive hands ignite my skin. I was hot next to him. And a slickness accompanies the ache deep in my cunt.

Many of the men I had been attracted to were because of their friendliness or their handsome features. Safety was important to me.

Vann provided that... but there was something else. An intellectual side to him I had never experienced with another partner.

The first time I saw him, I had thought he was beautiful, almost untouchable, like something carved from moonlight and stone. Then he opened his mouth.

He was sharp-edged and cruel, and so many of his words cut me as deep as any blade.

But that was before his tongue turned sweet. Before he followed me away from Enduvida, or called me beautiful, or asked to be my friend. Before he held me *like this.*

Does this mean he... wants me?

If Mrath knows where the witches are, then we could be home in a few days. A thrill snakes through my ribs.

Vann and I could go home together. Maybe, then we could—

A knock makes me jump. Glyni's voice carries through the walls, and a bright light appears overhead. "It's time to go!"

Vann shifts, his chill retreating as he removes his hand and sits up, putting space between us. I stay there for a second, frozen, and still aching. I feel the absence of his presence like a cold gust of wind against my spine.

When I do shift, my now dry hair falls precariously around my shoulders and he meets my gaze. His pupils dilate, and he lets out a ragged breath.

"Beautiful" he murmurs in his native tongue. My mind translates it perfectly. Then he straightens, pushing away to fix his clothing. "We have to go, Firelocks."

We ready ourselves quickly, neither speaking, even though my mind churns with questions. Does he remember how he held me?

Glyni waits for us outside, her sharp eyes sweeping over us with amusement. "Sleep well?" she asks.

Vann ignores her, stepping past without a word, and I follow, a little sad to leave behind the moment with him.

The court of the Sisterhood is chaos incarnate. Long tables stretch across the massive hall, groaning under the weight of golden platters overflowing with food. Elves lounge in their seats, draped in silks and woven garlands of leaves, their laughter sharp. The air smells of incense, something being roasted, and sparkling wine.

And then, there is Mrath. The leader of the rebellion.

She is precariously perched atop a throne of thorns, each cruel barb twisting beneath her. A crown of the same jagged thorns rests upon her brow, dark and glistening against the silvery blond hair that cascades down her back.

She looks entirely at ease, legs crossed, a blade strapped to her thigh, and her fingers drumming idly against the armrest. Her green eyes find me immediately, and a slow, predatory smile spreads across her lips.

"Well, well, well," she purrs, clearly amused. "More trolls come to visit. Step lightly, I only respond to begging." She winks.

Vann moves forward, his voice steady. I notice his height. Was he always so tall?

"We're not here to beg, Mrath. With all due respect, we seek information."

Mrath tilts her head. "Oh? And what could possibly bring the great Cleaver and this lovely human to my doorstep? Could it have anything to do with the message I received from my darling Thorne that said, and I quote, *'A cursed human comes to darken your door.'*"

Then she leans forward. "I don't mind a visit from my allies—in fact, I welcome it, so long as it is good news about your efforts to slaughter my brother. I doubt this is that. So, why should I care about a cursed human?"

Vann's jaw tightens. "The enduares are grateful for your assistance, as we have made clear several times, one of which risking the lives of both our king and queen to retrieve an artifact precious to you."

Mrath smiles, then nods her head. "Ah, yes. Well, I suppose you may explain."

Vann dips his head forward. "Thank you, Mrath. Arlet is a member of our council, and she is important to our people's growth. Within the last two weeks, she was cursed. It seems to turn on or off at random, and only when she sleeps. At that point, she turns violent. We believe that it was a human witch. We do not know how to locate one, but you are skilled in trading information. We would only ask you to tell us where one is, that we might reverse the curse."

I straighten, pleased with Vann's words. He has a talent for diplomacy, when he needs it.

The mirth in Mrath's expression vanishes, and her idle drumming comes to an abrupt stop. The entire court seems to hold its breath.

"Was Arlet cursed in Enduvida?" she asks, voice low and measured.

"Yes. She was marked by dark human magic. The mark is a snake curling around her ankle."

Mrath's eyes narrow as she considers his words. "A snake? The human witches are fond of the ugly things."

She purses her lips, her mind clearly churning over the revelations. Had Thorne not already told her everything?

"Go on, little ruby. What else does this *curse* entail?" she snaps, this time directing her words to me.

I swallow, uncomfortable, and move closer to Vann without thinking.

"It was after a night when I'd gotten drunk. At first, there were stretches I could not recall. But then, during one of the nights when the curse stirred, I killed a man."

She grins. "I was older than you the first time I'd killed someone. Did the man hurt you?"

My heart races. How could she be so... cavalier about death? The memory tears me apart every time I touch it.

I clear my throat.

"No. He was a friend."

She looks disappointed. "Ah, well. Pity. Anything else?"

I take a deep breath, not wanting to talk to this woman anymore.

"A few memories remain—a hunger, a desire to kill—and a voice."

Mrath raises one perfectly pale eyebrow.

"A voice?" she asks.

In the corner of my eye, Vann looks down at me, confusion etched on his face. I shift my gaze from him to Mrath and nod. "Yes."

"What did the voice say?"

I furrow my brow, glancing at Vann again. Should I tell her everything? I doubt he hears my thoughts, but he offers a reassuring nod.

My gaze returns to the leader. "It told me to return."

"And you have no idea where you are to return to?" she asks.

I shake my head as distant voices filter around me and the light overhead grows uncomfortably bright.

"It told you no name, no location, no direction?" she presses.

I reach into my mind. The memories are slick and hard to grasp. But the thing inside me was pleased with our direction. It wanted to go faster.

Mrath clears her throat, impatiently demanding a response.

"Maybe?" I start, "It seemed to like where we were. It just wanted me to go faster."

A dryad, with skin like polished bark and hair woven of shimmering leaves, glides forward gracefully bearing a crystal goblet filled with ruby wine. Mrath leans over, gesturing to a few women at a nearby table.

The leader begins a long stream of elvish. I catch a few words—*fragile* and *cock*. She grabs the goblet, then drinks deeply.

Finally, she looks back at us, and point a finger at me. Her tone turns brisk.

"Emissary Thorne has also told me that King Arion has declared he will hold off on a siege if you, *specifically you*, would be his bride."

My skin goes cold. I didn't want to talk about this.

"We considered Arion, but we have reason to believe he would not work with the witches. We are seeking other options," Vann says.

Mrath huffs.

"Well, I have no hard proof other than being raised alongside the cuck, but Arion doesn't let requests go unanswered. He would have claimed you without delay if he truly desired you."

"What do you mean?" Vann says.

"The magic may belong to the witches, but what if he has stooped to the Giants' level and asked for Abhartach's help?"

The room spins around me. Vann thought it was Daniel somehow. Liana believed it was just the witches. Now Mrath thinks it is Arion.

Facts spin through my mind, but no matter how much knowledge I have acquired, it never seems to be enough.

Elves did not look for their brides among nobility since the daughter of a courtier is just as likely to stab her husband on the wedding night as a snake is to strike when cornered. No, they found women in the mountains and fields. They threw them over their shoulders, and ran to be married.

Is my curse some version of that tradition to Arion?

"I... I do not know. We met for one evening—I did nothing to encourage *this*."

She frowns. "You didn't have to. The world has gone mad for humans, and with the dwindling numbers of women in the elven court—lost to death or defection—I'm sure Arion is afraid," Mrath says. "Can't promise a new supreme reign of the Elven Empire without soldiers. Believe me, I despise it like a weak fuck, but you humans are the only ones left who can bear so many races' children."

My stomach twists violently. The urge to tell her I can't sits on the tip of my tongue—not without the magic that comes with matehood.

"I wouldn't bear his child," I fumble.

Vann stiffens beside me, his head snapping in my direction, but I can't meet his gaze.

Mrath tilts her head, her voice hardening. "And you think that matters?"

A bitter laugh escapes me. I still can't believe this is happening. My time with the Elf King lasted one night? He called me pretty. Loyal. And—

Suddenly, fragments begin to coalesce in my mind. It's like I am transported to his side at the festival a year ago. We'd just finished dancing. There was something he said—something I couldn't catch. I'd thought of it a few times since then, but it comes to me now, clear as the dawn.

"There will come a time when I will need you. Fear not, for I will bring you to my side without injury."

Oh gods. My hands go numb.

After I'd killed Diego, I'd heard a voice upon waking.

"I am so pleased you didn't get rid of my gift."

A gift. *Hostia.* He'd given me a stone with a snake on it. It'd been on my dresser the night I got cursed. And now, I realize the whispers, the fleeting promises—they all point toward this. Arion is controlling me like a puppet.

Vann, likely noticing the tremor in my hands, reaches out and cups my wrist. It is a small thing, but it gives me strength to speak again.

"It doesn't make sense that he would fight so hard for me. It's trivial. Kingdoms should only wage wars over things far greater than me and my womb."

Mrath's gaze sharpens. "Trivial?" she echoes. "To give life, to create something where there was nothing—that is not trivial, girl. It is power. The most sought-after power of all, as it is one a man cannot carve out himself. A man is nothing if his line dies with him."

Her words pierce me. What she says makes sense. But, if that is true, what does it mean about me?

"I think you might be right," I declare, even though bits and pains are pricking at my conscience. Small cuts that never healed—that make me wonder about my place if I can't easily do this thing that others seem to be able to do with painstaking ease.

A slow, frown spreads across Mrath's face. "Then we have a problem. I do not keep company with witches any longer, and there are none in my Enclave."

Disappointment curls in my gut. If she didn't know, what was I to do? This was my only plan? The only other option could be going to King Arion.

"But, fear not. Mrath to the rescue," she chimes back, and a few other elven women titter. "The last I heard about the witches, they had retreated to some small speck of an island in the Sea of Sorrow. To reach it, you must go west. There is a city, I will inform my contact there to find you. They will take you to see the witches."

I swallow hard, my mind racing with the implications. Another journey means I'm not returning to my home for a while longer. In scrolls, heroines seemed to be so adaptable under such conditions. But I feel like weeping.

I wanted this to be over faster. I wanted to be whole.

Instead of crying, I lift my chin and ask, "What if we get to the island and the witches refuse?"

Mrath smirks. "Then you had better learn how to be persuasive, little ruby."

I almost think she's done, as she takes a long drink from her neglected goblet, but she sets it back on the dryad's tray and says, "A word of advice—Stay as far away from Shvathemar as possible. My brother must not have any claim to you; if he sires a child, my own bid for the crown will become that much harder."

She fixes Vann with a piercing stare. "And you, Lord Vann—you are not a king, but you have his ear. I was serious when I told your king that we should've killed Arion immediately after the war with the Giants. I will not be patient much longer, nor will I be so generous as to indulge other little *favors*." Mrath sits back on her throne.

She exhales sharply, then makes a shooing motion. "If my brother has cursed you, he might figure out where you are if you linger longer. Leave now. I have matters to attend to, and you are using my people's resources."

"Wait," Vann exclaims. "I need you to send a message for me to the king. Tell him where we go, that we are well."

Mrath rolls her eyes. "I'm not a messenger."

"Please," Vann pleads.

She sighs. "No." Then she snaps her fingers once, and the world around me goes dark.

CHAPTER 23

VANN

The cold morning air outside of the Sisterhood's Enclave bites at my skin and the mist curls between the ancient trees.

"Yrelajd vol'chtu," I grumble in enduar—*Damn this mess.*

I feel like a godsdamned fool. I'd been so focused on my theory that Daniel had hurt her that I failed to realize who the true villain was.

King Arion.

You clueless bastard.

Then I think of Teo.

Gods, I should have thought of some way to send a message back to him. Brought speaking stones, a fucking magical voice projector. *Something.*

I fear he will never forgive me.

Sucking in another breath, I sort through the packs Mrath had also haphazardly transported out of her enclave.

We will both need to make sure that our belongings are still intact. I open my mouth to tell Arlet, but looking up causes me to pause.

She stands there. Deflated. Her arms are crossed over her midsection. Her breath billows out from her nose, which has turned beryl red from the chill.

I straighten. The conversation with Mrath had gone as well as I could've hoped. She didn't maim either of us, and we had a genuine direction.

But still, Arlet had come here with hopes of returning home sooner. That is delayed, and it must hurt.

I suck in a breath. Especially not her.

A few more moments stretch on, and she gazes at the trees, breathing slowly.

It is time to leave this place and let everything go. Instead, I listen as the silence between us is punctuated by the steady rhythm of the forest.

"Firelocks," I start. "Are you upset?"

She glances up at me, face expressionless, and I wish I could stop the way that my mind memorizes the movement, cataloging it with a dozen others that help me to interpret and read her.

"I am fine," she replies, though I see how her lips turn down after each word.

"I am sorry they did not have useful answers for you. I know you seek to be free of the curse," I try. "I know you want to go home."

She looks up at me, and the world stills. I was a fool around her.

"Be happy," Adra had said to me in a thousand dreams. But was that her, or was it simply my manifestation of what she would say if she could communicate from the afterlife?

I don't know if it was a betrayal to turn away from Adra and our life together for a new one.

Sucking my lip between my teeth, I think of pulling out Adra's name tonight to say a prayer before I go to sleep.

I would do it now, but Arlet looks like she is spiraling away under her calm exterior. Someone needs to hold her together—she seems like she needs an embrace.

We are friends.

This woman serves with me on the council. Attends every function by virtue of our chosen family. She deserves more than what I have given her.

I had embraced each of my friends. Many times.

Carefully, deliberately, I cross the space between us. There is no hesitation in the action. Surprisingly, I feel no inner battle.

From this moment, I would not look back. Firelocks would always be my friend.

When she looks up at me, her jaw tightens and her lip quivers.

"Would it be alright if I held you close?" I ask.

She must be very sad, for she nods instantly. Then she sucks in one last breath, face breaking, and I pull her into my arms.

She is warm, impossibly so. Her body melts against mine, the tension in her shoulders unraveling when I press her close.

I hold her firmly, my arms locking her against me as though I can shield her from disappointment.

She is small in my grasp, fragile in a way that unsettles me. Her hands, hesitant at first, curl into my tunic and grip the fabric as though afraid I might disappear if she lets go.

Her sweet scent fills my senses, grounding me. The weight of her against my chest is pleasant.

"For better or worse, I am here for you."

She buries her face against my arm, and I feel the warmth of her breath through the cloth.

My fingers slide up her back, resting just beneath the curve of her neck. I don't want to let go first—she can take as long as she needs.

"Thank you," she says, though her voice is muffled. "I would like that."

I pat her back once.

"It is not easy to come far only to learn the journey is not yet over. There were days during The Great War that I feared never seeing my home again. I imagine you feel similarly," I murmur. "But fear not, our threads are woven together in this, and I will not unravel from our task."

She laughs. It's a watery sound. "That was quite good."

Something close to a smile pulls up my cheeks.

"Textile wisdom is just one of my many talents."

She laughs again, and then pulls back. "It's time to go, isn't it?"

I nod, lips pressed together. "Don't worry, we will go at the pace you need."

"I like... reassurance," she'd once told me.

"You really have impressed me with your strength during this journey. I've never seen someone fight against their fears so viciously."

Her chest sinks as she lets out a surprised gasp. When she gazes at me, I see a hungry woman.

Starved for connection and touch.

Then she swallows and looks away.

"But what about Enduvida? I was hoping we would solve this quickly, but now this means more time away from everyone. Lorepath, my pupils," she puts one gloved hand over her eyes. "*Hostia puta,* I have blankets to make. People need blankets!"

It's strange to think I would hear someone's mind rioting and their heart galloping, but I do.

"*Arlet.* The river does not carve the mountain in a day, but with enough streams, even stone yields," I murmur. "All I'm saying is no burden is too great when carried by many, and make no mistake, many hands are ready and willing to shape the future of our home. What must be done, will be. You are allowed a rest."

For a second, my throat tightens as if the words spoken to her were also meant for me. We'd both been working ourselves to the bone. We both needed to be careful.

Strange how that could happen.

She gives me a peculiar look. "Have you been reading De'Rahn?"

My brows shoot up. "How do you know about him?"

De'Rahn is another popular poet from the Golden Age. He'd been popular when I was in the military academy. I'd never met him but had enjoyed his work from time to time.

She purses her lips. "*Mi Cielo,* I've been reading enduar literature since I arrived in Enduvida. And... you never seem to invent such an eloquent turn of phrase by yourself."

I narrow my eyes. "I am an excellent speaker."

She casts me an incredulous look, then snarks, "Yes, and all the crystals in the cavern sing at your every syllable."

I laugh. "Forgive me, I only thought you read scrolls full of pleasures best enjoyed behind locked doors."

The words fall out before I can stop them. Arlet looks up at me, and a scene from one of the scrolls I found on her bedside plays in my head.

"How do you..." her eyes widen. "You went through the things on my bedside when you broke into my house?"

I smile.

"It was for a good cause."

"Well, friend, let me know if you would like recommendations," she says, though her cheeks flush a deeper shade of red in embarrassment.

It's my turn to be speechless.

"You seem to be in better spirits. Would you like to lead?" I manage.

"I'd prefer if you did it. I'm... weary." She dips her head toward me, then, taking another breath, begins to gather her pack. I do the same.

"Where are we going, exactly?" she asks.

"West." I grin. "But in truth, I don't know. It's an adventure."

She bites her lip, hoisting the pack onto her shoulders.

"You know, I'm not one to crave adventures."

My brows draw together.

"Really? I would've expected you to seek them at every chance."

She shakes her head. "You know I wish to have a family. I like being home and making a home."

Then she begins walking.

"That doesn't mean you can't enjoy a quick escape from time to time," I retort.

She looks up at me, but something clouds her vision. "Perhaps." Then her eyes fall back to my face and she says, "Why don't you like the elves? Recent history aside, your discomfort around them seems... deeply embedded."

"I don't hate them. I just don't trust many them," I bite my lip. "Our peoples have not always gotten along. They killed a great many of my people."

She curses. "Fuck, sorry. I knew that. In the war before The Great War, I read they killed tens of thousands. I should've remembered."

"Books can't always help you," I retort. "And, believe it or not, Arion's father was worse. Even still, it is their way of being arrogant, like Mrath. Even the half-blood, Thorne, is insufferable."

She frowns and looks at me. "I like him. I think he is interesting, and open. He helps Ulla from time to time. It is sweet."

I grit my teeth, and grunt. There is something about him I don't like.

We fall back into silence only broken by our boots crunching over damp leaves and gnarled roots.

It stays like that as the early morning shifts to afternoon and we watch the towering Elder Trees swallow the last visible remnants of the enclave behind us.

The further we go, the denser the forest becomes, the canopy overhead darkening as the sunlight filters weakly through the tangle of branches.

I wait for more conversation, but she doesn't offer anything else.

"Do you feel any different?" I ask at last, remembering how she'd revealed hearing a voice. I think she'd tried to tell me that.

I needed to listen better.

She finally turns her head slightly, meeting my gaze. "What do you mean?"

"You said the voice wanted you to keep moving forward. Toward Shvathemar," I remind her. "If we're taking a different path, do you think it would still—"

"I don't hear it right now," she cuts in quickly, but a tightness in her voice makes me uneasy. She looks away first, exhaling sharply.

I nod, though the discomfort settles deep in my gut. She stops walking suddenly, and I tense. But she doesn't look afraid. Instead, she turns to me, jaw tight, shoulders squared as though preparing for something unpleasant.

"You should tie me up," she says, blunt as a blade to the ribs. "Tonight, when we prepare for sleep."

I study her, waiting for her to take it back, or, at the very least, look afraid. But she stands firm, waiting for me to agree.

I exhale, nodding. “That is wise.”

“I don’t like it,” she admits. “But until we know for sure... it’s the safest option.”

It was a respectful thing to do. A wise thing. A selfless thing. I didn’t expect anything less from Arlet.

So I honored her choice with silence, not asking any of the probing questions about ropes or scars running through my mind.

When we reach the beginning of the mountain, she gives it a long, appraising look, and grimaces.

“Well, here we go,” she mutters in the human tongue, and starts up the path.

My eyes follow her. I know how hard this must be. Her feet are probably sore and his joints must ache, yet she doesn’t hesitate—she forges ahead with a quiet, steadfast resolve. In this moment, I see her so clearly.

She faces every fear head on and tackles challenges even when they seem impossible.

I follow behind, regretting any negative thought I’ve ever had about her.

~

AFTER A DAY OF CLIMBING, WE ARE BOTH SWEATY, DESPITE THE BITING WIND tearing through the trees.

“I thought spring was supposed to be warm,” she gripes. “In Zlosa, we had four distinct seasons.”

I shrug my shoulders. “The mountains are always colder than valleys or hills. We’ll need to watch for ice patches.”

She exhales, long and slow, her breath forming little clouds in the crisp air. “Great. Another thing trying to kill us.”

The wind shifts, carrying the damp scent of earth and pine.

Night is creeping in, and the sky deepens into shades of violet and gray. We make camp, set up the tent, and cook a small feast of boiling dry meat and preserved mushrooms from Enduvida.

She finishes eating first.

I glance at her, watching the way she keeps adjusting her gloves. She's anxious.

After I finish my food and clean my plate, I reach for the length of rope in my pack. My stomach twists as I hold it between my fingers. I grab her bedroll, spreading it against the tree, then place a blanket on top.

"It is time," I murmur after readying the place.

Arlet obeys, and I begin tying the knots around her wrists. She winces. Her pain makes it impossible for me to remain silent.

Maybe now...

"Will you tell me why you don't like being bound now?" I ask yet again.

She stills, readying to refuse me.

"Remember that we trust each other. I will repay your honesty with anything you'd like to know."

"But why do you insist on knowing?" she asks.

"That first night, after we found you, you asked me not to bind you *again,* but it was the first time I'd done such a thing."

When she finally speaks, her voice is quieter than before, as if she's fighting to keep it steady.

"I—Gods it is humiliating. And sad," she starts.

I leave the rope to dangle, then I touch her arm gently, and I move so we can see each other. Her warm brown eyes study my face.

"What?" I ask, thinking of all the situations involving being bound in ropes that would be humiliating.

"You are aware of the breeding pens, yes?" she asks.

I nod. The giants treated humans like chattel, subjecting women to horrendous conditions with other male slaves to ensure there were enough workers in each generation.

"Well. The man you saw outside my house, Daniel, had grown up with me. He was my first love. We were assigned together in the breeding pens," she says, pausing to take a deep breath. "When we were successful, we were given a home to raise the child."

I freeze. That meant... Arlet had been... pregnant.

She doesn't look at me, her gaze fixed on the tree line ahead.

Clearly, she doesn't have a son or daughter now. What happened?

"I'll spare you the gory details, but the fear of ropes came in between all of that," she says softly.

I close my fist. I should let her be and not force her to relive the pain. But she bites her lip, and glances at me as if she wants to keep speaking.

"If you want to tell me, I want to know," I respond. "I am not afraid of gory things."

Her glassy eyes look to the sky and she blinks. Gods, she was so good at expressing herself. I envied that.

"Everyone adored Daniel," she says slowly. "He was the charming rogue of my youth—jovial, amiable, and fond of drink. One evening, after a grueling day in the fields, he wanted a night with his friends. I have never liked revelry—even less so when I was pregnant and feeling unwell. I asked him to stay and help tend to our dwelling instead."

I know the look on her face—the hurt mixed with a quiet resignation. I feel protective, aching to shield her from the memory of that night.

She continues, "Daniel didn't like being told no. I had noticed it first in small moments. Like, if I told him he couldn't leave his shoes on our bed, he would. Silly things."

She takes a deep breath.

"But that night was different, he was angrier than I'd ever seen him. Pregnancy was not easy on me, and he felt I kept him home more than I should have. When I insisted he remain, yet again, it was like a candle was blown out. He changed."

I grit my teeth.

Then she swallows hard, her eyes distant. "In his anger, he tied me up. When I cried out in pain, he told me I was dramatic, claiming the ties would help me rest by keeping me in one place."

A cold silence falls between us. I squeeze her hand gently, trying to offer comfort with a touch that says, *"I'm here."*

"Sometimes," she murmurs, "when I think of that awful night, I like to believe he was so utterly drunk that his judgment was lost to madness. Because otherwise, he willingly—" Her voice falters, and I feel a surge of protectiveness wash over me.

I lean in, pulling her into another hug. In the quiet, I vow that I will never let her suffer such pain again.

Endu must hear because he extends a light, godly touch to my shoulder.

"I was halfway through my carrying term," she says. "I had a lovely little belly and a drawer full of clothes I'd hand knitted. And I —" She swallows hard, shifting her bound hands behind her back. "I couldn't get loose. Something was wrong, and I couldn't move. I was so scared. He came home, and I was lying in my own blood."

She looks at me, face red, and eyes glossy.

"It was a girl. I had a daughter," her voice breaks, and tears spill down her cheeks. "Vann, if I break loose before this is finished. *If I am killed*, then bury me in light layers. Comfortable clothes. If I wake up in the next life, then I want to be able to find her. To be a proper mother."

"Arlet—" I say. The rage starts in my chest, and I feel as if I am borrowing a grain of her pain, and placing it where my heart belonged. It beats and pulses, as a heart should. It fuels my anger.

Firelocks, *Arlet*, had been betrayed and lost what she wanted most.

Gods, if I didn't understand that.

When I first asked her to tell me, I'd made a deal. Honesty for no bindings.

So now, my hands find the rope around her wrists, and I start untying the knot.

"He was so angry, he cast me out. I didn't see a healer soon enough, and when I did they said there was scarring and I couldn't get pregnant again."

More pieces of her lock into place before me, and I pull away the rope.

When she'd been preparing for the Mating Ceremony, she said she wanted a family.

Fuck. How much agony did she hide in those words?

How did it feel to watch Estela have two children while she had none?

For dozens of pairs to be mated while she went home, cursed?

She leans into me, her hands gripping my shirt, and continues speaking. I don't want to stop her. I want to collect more pieces of her soul.

She looks down at her hands, unbound.

I grab her face, swiping away the tears that had fallen.

"Arlet, that wasn't humiliating. You were humiliated by someone you trusted," I insist.

She stares at me. Her eyes pierce through my defenses.

"I think that Daniel was sad for doing it. But those with children were given their own little dwelling. He didn't want to be shoved into a barracks with the other men, and he couldn't stand the shame he felt because of me. After he'd thrown me out, he found someone else. I tried to ignore him. The first time we'd spoken in years was that day in Enduvida."

My breath scorches my lungs.

"Firelocks. That spineless, self-indulgent wretch wouldn't know the weight of a life if it was chained around his own worthless throat. He is not a man—he is a festering stain on the world, a leech masquerading as something worthy of breath." More frozen emotions pump through me, too fast, too quickly, but I hold her tight and *she holds me right back.*

I would pay for the overuse of emotions tonight. If I wasn't careful, I wouldn't be able to move soon.

"If I had known this when I saw him outside your door, I would've killed him."

Her jaw goes slack. She searches my face, watching me with unfeigned hope like I had spoken the moon into existence.

"Please, don't pity me," she says abruptly, expression shifting. "I like my life. I like who I am. I just... Arion wanting me to bear a child has reopened deep wounds."

She looks away from me then, her expression tired but resolute. "I know you told me I wouldn't have to be bound if I told you, but I... think it's a good idea. It doesn't bother me so much anymore."

My jaw tightens, and I force myself to nod. "I'll be careful."

She nods back, but I see the way her hands tremble.

I move to grab the rope, then wrap it around the nearest tree. This time, I leave her sitting.

A crushing weight is pressing onto my limbs and a searing cold blankets my skin. My regret returns.

And then my right foot goes numb.

Fuck, it won't be long before I can't feel my hands. My vision blurs, black frost creeping into the edges of my sight.

Not now.

The world tilts, and my body refuses to obey. I need to lie down before I collapse.

Arlet turns just in time to see me sway. Her eyes widen in alarm. "Vann?"

I can't answer. My throat is ice. My breath is ice.

My fingers twitch and my vision flickers, narrowing to a pinpoint of light through the trees.

Arlet says something else, alarmed.

"I... need... sleep," I manage through clenched teeth, every word scraping like a blade against my throat.

Her lips part like she wants to argue, but I hear myself wish her a good night.

I need to take care of her, make sure she is secure against the trunk, but instead, I stumble toward the tent and barely manage to lower myself before my body refuses me entirely.

CHAPTER 24

ARLET'S CURSE

When I awake and find we are yet again far from our mark, I grow angry. This is not where my task should take me.

I am surrounded by mountains and a thinning forest. It is cold, and that chill is only remedied by the warm, sticky wolf blood that coats my hands and fingers.

My legs pound, one after the other. The cold bites into me, and the blood dries, but there is something more powerful than the discomfort—the need to run, and the hunger.

Each step in the right direction causes a little thrill to snake up my spine. But then something reaches my tongue on the wind.

"I have sent help, fear not, little flower."

The first voice returns. I slow, and the scent of others reaches my nose—elves.

But why? The deeper, ancient voice asks. *They are the obstacle. I have need of them.*

I furrow my brow, confused at who to follow.

They stand in your way. Crush them, and then you can reach the voice and complete your task.

"I cannot kill them," I whisper back, even as my mouth waters. "I have no weapons."

The deep, second voice inside me chuckles.

You do not need weapons. Let me show you.

My fingers curl into fists, and my teeth gnash as the bloodlust surges within me. It's familiar, the need to rip and tear, to spill the life from others. My legs respond, driving me forward in a run.

Five elves stand at the base of the mountain. Three hold swords, two with bows.

They share the same glossy, unnatural features.

I should be afraid, and yet I am not.

"Little flower, wait," the first voice says. *"They are friends. Go with them!"*

Instead, the rage builds inside of me, and with one violent motion, I lash out. My arm strikes like a whip, and before any of them can react, one elf falls. My hands grip his throat with unrelenting force. His windpipe collapses and I tear out a chunk of his neck. Blood sprays across the snow, warm and thick.

The remaining elves freeze, their eyes wide in shock. The scent of blood sates my hunger, and I can feel the fear radiating from them. They hesitate, but I do not.

I charge again, but this elf grabs me. Before he has time to think, I shove but he doesn't let go.

I roar, my voice a violent storm inside the body, but the elf does not relent. He pushes me into the ground and brings out a blade.

It is pressed into my throat.

"Stay still," he grits out.

A searing pain shoots through me.

"You do the king's bidding, human," the elf says with cruel certainty.

I writhe. The elf's smirk widens, but it doesn't last.

Thud, thud, thud.

The ground trembles. A familiar, powerful force pounds through the trees. My vision clears just enough to see him before I retreat entirely.

I know him. Vann.

~

I snap back into full consciousness and find myself pinned under an elf. But King Arion's soldier isn't looking at me.

No, he looks up as Vann charges down the mountain. Vann leaps from a boulder with a roar, his cleaver raised high, his gaze dark and fierce. His tail whips behind him, cutting through the air like a living extension of his will, helping him balance as he lands with a heavy thud.

The elf with the knife to my throat snarls. Then he pulls me to a proper standing position. "We must go!" he demands, trying to move me.

But before he can pull me further, the first elf raises his sword. Vann is fast, his cleaver cutting through the air with deadly precision. His tail sweeps out behind him, steadying his posture as he slashes downward, parting the elf's chest in one clean stroke. Blood sprays, and the elf crumples onto the dirt. Vann doesn't stop.

Before I can even take a breath, the second elf swings his bow at Vann. But Vann is too fast. He arcs his cleaver downward, slicing the elf's arm off. His tail lashes out in a whip-like motion, helping him pivot with fluid speed, and he drives the blade deep into the elf's chest.

The third elf raises his bow, and just as I think he's too late to react, he lets loose an arrow. It strikes Vann in the shoulder, the force of it shoving him back. He falters, but his tail snaps out again, pushing him on.

My breath catches, and the elf holding me captive yanks me again, trying to force me to run.

I dig my heels in, watching as my companion growls. He rips the arrow from his shoulder with a savage roar. Blood pours from the wound and the Fuegorra flares to life in his chest. It is bright enough to shine through fabric, and it causes the exposed flesh knit back together.

Arrow in hand, Vann charges. With a single, brutal motion, he stabs the shaft directly into the elf's face. The point sinks into his skull, and the elf crumples, lifeless, before he even hits the ground.

The final elf, the one yanking me on, is quick to react, pulling me into his arms as if he's going to carry me away. I barely have time to register the movement before I hear the sharp whoosh of metal cutting through the air. Vann is there—his cleaver flashing—and in a single, fluid motion, he decapitates the elf.

I flinch, but Vann's strike is so precise that it misses me entirely. The man's head falls with a sickening thud, and his body crumples beneath me.

I am unharmed but Vann immediately pulls me into his arms, lifting me effortlessly as though nothing had happened. The rush of adrenaline leaves my heart pounding.

Vann's cleaver thuds to the ground and the clearing falls silent. His breath is heavy, and his Fuegorra still glowing though the wound in his shoulder is already closed. It leaves a faint, blue scar where the arrow once was.

His eyes meet mine, and he offers a look of reassurance that I don't deserve but desperately need. Then he pulls me close. So tight he practically holds me together.

He is the exact shade of the sky right now. He is stunning.

"Are you all right?" he breathes. "I woke up and you were gone. I couldn't... Fuck, I'm so glad I found you."

I nod, breath still short, and hands still numb, but he looks like he's falling apart.

"I am all right. I am here," I say. "I am safe. With you, I am safe."

He presses his lips to the top of my head. The action is rough.

"Always."

I close my eyes at the word and sink into him.

We stay like that a moment longer.

Then I break the silence. "Arion spoke to me again. The curse forced me to kill a wolf. And then it made me walk until I met the elves. They tried to take me, but it doesn't like them. The one—" I run out of breath. "Did you see what I did to that man?"

"You did what you had to do."

"I hate this," I sob.

"Don't worry. We will stop this," Vann murmurs.

The words strike me hard.

"We need to leave before someone else comes. But first, I must tend to the bodies."

I close my eyes. "Whatever you need to do."

He walks me to a tree, but then hesitates. I can feel his gaze on my face. His arms tighten around me, and I feel the shift in him—the change from practicality to something deeper, something vulnerable. He doesn't speak right away.

But then he says, "I don't think I can let you go. Not like this."

I blink. His words wrap around me like a warm blanket.

"It is all right, I am here." I thread my dirty arms around his neck. He shifts me to one side as if I weigh nothing, then stabilizes my legs with his tail.

"Close your eyes if you don't want to see the blood," he murmurs.

"I am all right," I reply.

He doesn't say anything else as he goes to stand over the bodies.

It is a gruesome sight. Crimson liquid and parts are scattered the ground, but he doesn't look away. He quickly scans each elf carefully and his posture stiffens, and he moves almost... reverently.

He kneels beside the first elf he killed, and begins to check the body for any weapons or supplies. He moves efficiently, removing anything that might be valuable to us later.

Then, with a careful touch, he closes the elf's eyes and murmurs something in his language—something I don't understand, but it sounds like a prayer.

"Do you pray for the dead?" I ask, unsure of the answer I expect.

Vann tilts his head to the side.

"In a sense. They died serving their king, and I cannot fault them for that."

"But Arion is the enemy," I argue. "These men tried to kill you and take me to him."

His expression tightens, his eyes darkening for a moment. "Yes. And they were wrong, which justifies the consequences of their actions. But they weren't evil, not in the way some like to think. They are just people, much like us. Subjects to a poor ruler, caught in the machinery of something much larger than themselves. They have families and lives outside of their work." His voice softens. "Their families would appreciate their bodies to be handled with respect."

I pause, taken aback by the way he speaks. He reminds me that war is never just black and white, that we cannot reduce those we fight into mere monsters.

He thinks for a moment, but his words seem to hang in the air. "I was like them once. Under Teo'Lihk's rule, during the Great War. I was raised in a time of insecurity, violence, and survival. It was the reason I became a soldier. When there's someone at the top, they create the rules—the negative ideas, the stories that fuel their followers. Most people accept them without question. And then, what?"

He looks away.

"Again, I'm not saying we're not responsible for our actions, but I can't help but think that bad leaders are the root of a poisonous society. They are the ones who create the environment that breeds violence and war."

His voice drops, and I can feel his thoughts swirling in the space between us. "Perhaps something greater than me will teach them one day—though I did all I could."

Vann stands straighter, his posture returning to the familiar composure, but his eyes remain distant, thoughtful. "We are similar in the fact that neither of us take joy in killing them, but I've come to understand the necessity. They were a threat, and that's what we had to do—what *I* had to do."

His actions speak volumes of the man he is—honorable, even in the most brutal of moments.

I find myself drawn to him. The weight of the violence is still heavy on me, but his presence offers me a strange sense of peace.

Not just like a friend. *A partner.*

"Would you like to close the eyes of the man you killed?" Vann asks.

I don't know.

"It might help."

My mind churns for a minute, and then I nod. He sets me down and I approach the elf with the torn throat.

God, it hurts to look at. I close my eyes, then kneel.

The sight isn't better up close, and I reach out, gently pulling down his eyelids.

I look up at Vann. "Now what?"

He presses his lips in a flat line. "Now you wish him well in the next life."

It takes me a moment, but I do. Somehow, it feels as though the wind passes through me as I say the words.

I feel... changed. Lighter.

Once finished, I stand on wobbly legs.

I clear my throat. Then, as if it's the most natural thing in the world, the words slip out in enduar, *"Veyán dorath vel thun."*

Thank you for teaching me.

Vann's gaze flickers to my lips, and I wonder if he misses hearing the old tongue spoken freely. I remember the comfort of coming home after a long day of speaking a language that wasn't my own and settling into familiar phrases like soft pillows.

Perhaps we are similar in that way, too.

He swallows, his throat tight as he watches me. "Forgive me for sleeping last night," he says, his voice low.

Then he picks me up again.

I shake my head and nestle into his arms. "You are allowed to rest."

He grunts. Then says, "We need to go back to camp so we can keep moving. I can carry you for now, do not worry."

Without another word, he stands.

I don't resist. My body is heavy, my limbs ache from everything we've just endured. I rest my head against his chest as he begins walking us back toward the camp.

Strange, I think. I can't hear his heart very well. But I let myself enjoy the moment. We needed to continue.

Arion wants me at his side, and I need to be fixed so that never happens.

Normally, I would panic, but right now, I feel a strange kind of safety that I haven't felt in a long time. In a world that's often been cruel to me, he's a rare thing—someone who's both the storm and the calm.

CHAPTER 25
ARLET

We move with haste after the tent is packed up.

The terrain grows rugged, the incline steepening with every step, and in certain places, the path is barely wide enough for one person to pass at a time.

I ask Vann to put me down, knowing that my body is capable of pushing itself hard. Trying to find a way to walk with him carrying me would only slow us down.

I want to be far from Arion and his men.

It doesn't take long to find a tall pass—a jagged scar cut through the mountains, its mouth yawning and swallowing the light of the afternoon sun.

"Should we go over it?" I ask, eyeing the steep slopes rising on either side that are covered with loose scree.

Vann shakes his head. "We'll go through. It will be faster, which should please you."

I bite my lip, but say nothing as I follow him inside.

It's worse here than I imagined.

The air is thin, and each breath is sharp in my lungs. The path itself is treacherous. It's narrow. Loose rocks skitter beneath our feet with every step, some tumbling into deep cracks. They vanish before I can hear them land.

The wind howls through the passage, blowing between the towering walls of stone, tugging at my coat, and whipping my hair across my face. The further we press on, the darker it becomes. Shadows stretch long and eerie across the path, and the sound of the wind is broken only by the occasional distant crack.

I force myself to keep walking, my hands brushing against the stone wall for balance.

My heart pounds against my ribs. The cold seeps into my bones, and the tension in my muscles only makes everything worse.

Vann moves ahead of me with sure steps, unaffected by the shifting ground. His silver hair contrasts starkly against the dark stone. I focus on that, on the steady rhythm of his movement, using it to ground myself as we continue forward.

A scream shatters the silence.

It's high-pitched, desperate. And it echoes off the stone, ricocheting through the narrow pass. I'd spent enough time in the school house to recognize a dozen different types of shouts.

That is a child, and they're in danger.

My heart leaps into my throat. Throwing down my pack, I don't think, I just run.

"Arlet!" Vann's voice call behind me, but I'm already moving. My feet pound against the uneven ground, and my breath is ragged as I sprint toward the sound.

As I round a sharp bend in the path, more fear sears through me. There is still enough light for me to spot a small form swathed in green fabric. A child is huddled against the rocks, barely more than a blur in the distance. I push harder. It doesn't matter that my legs sting and there is a sharp bite of cold air in my lungs.

Vann halts just behind me, cursing under his breath. His pack is also gone, though he holds his cleaver.

"What the hell is a child doing here?" he grumbles.

His eyesight is better than mine, and I turn to ask more questions, but a low growl rolls through the pass.

I freeze mid-step, my body locking up as my ears strain.

Another sound echoes off the stone, vibrating deep in my bones. My pulse pounds, each beat faster than the last.

"A wolf?" I barely manage to get out. Could it be stalking the child?

Vann shakes his head. "No, that wasn't a wolf."

Before I can respond, another sound comes from above us. I glance up just as a few pebbles dislodge from a shelf of rock, tumbling down in lazy spirals.

The child screams again in a language I don't know, and a cold shock slaps across my shoulder blades.

Vann moves, silent as death, holding out his cleaver. He moves like he is the predator—lithe, aware, stealthy.

I hold my breath and scan the cliffs, waiting.

Then, the creature comes into view.

Its tawny coat blends almost perfectly with the sun-soaked rocks, and its muscles ripple beneath its fur. Golden eyes lock onto us, unyielding.

It's feline and undeniably powerful. A mountain cat.

"Arlet, get behind me," Vann commands, his voice low and steady.

I obey, breath shallow as the creature prowls closer, gracefully leaping down a series of sloping formations. Its tail lashes, muscles coiling beneath its sleek frame, ready to strike.

Vann stands firm, blade raised. His body is drawn taut like a bowstring. Every movement is controlled.

Then, in an instant, the lion moves—not at Vann, but to the side, toward the pile of rocks where the child hides.

I dive before my mind catches up. The world narrows to the space between me and the child. The lion turns, golden eyes flashing as its focus shifts to me. Vann shouts something, but I don't stop.

The child—an elven boy, no older than what I would consider five in human years—looks up, terrified. The child's skin is the deep, warm brown of polished walnut, and he's wrapped in a finely woven green coat. I reach him just as the lion lunges, throwing myself between them.

Pain explodes in my side as the creature's claws rake across my ribs. White-hot, agony sears along the space. The air is punched from my lungs, but I manage to shove the boy behind me. His hands tug on the back of my coat, throwing me off balance.

My Fuegorra heats in my chest, working in record time to heal the deep wound faster than the tears on my face can fall.

"Vann!" I scream, grabbing the first rock my fingers find and hurling it at the beast.

The mountain lion snarls. It crouches, tail flicking, preparing to strike again. I brace myself for the killing blow.

And then Vann is there. His blade flashes like silver lightning.

The child sobs and seeks my hands. He repeats something over and over in what I assume is an unknown dialect of elvish.

The fight is brutal. The lion's snarls mingle with the sharp clang of steel on rock. Vann moves with deadly precision; his strikes are clean and relentless. The lion lashes out. Its claws scrape against the leather on his forearms, but he doesn't falter.

Vann thrusts one last time, and the beast collapses at his feet, blood soaking into the rocky ground.

I slump against the cliff wall, gasping for breath, pain radiating from my side despite the bleeding having stopped. The boy clings to my hip, tiny hands fisting into the fabric, shaking.

Reaching out, I pull him close.

"It's all right," I murmur into his impossibly shiny brown hair.

Vann turns to me, breathing hard. "Are you hurt?"

I hesitate.

"Firelocks."

"Yes," I say. In truth, the wound was already closing, but the Fuegorra's effort is taking its toll. My body needs rest, and soon.

Vann curses under his breath, kneeling beside me. His hands are rough, but his touch is careful as he inspects the wound.

"You're lucky," he mutters. "Nothing too bad."

I smile weakly, but the boy whimpers, his body trembling against mine. I exhale, forcing the pain aside, and brush my hand through his dusty hair.

"It's all right," I murmur. "You're safe now."

His wide, tear-filled eyes meet mine, and something inside me breaks when he leans into me. For the first time in days, I feel like I've done something right.

"I'm Arlet, are you well?" I manage in my meager grasp of elvish.

He looks at me, clearly confused and then starts spouting a stream of unfamiliar words.

I look up at Vann, slightly bewildered.

He kneels next to both me and the boy, then begins to speak. The words are clearer, and the lyrical grace surpasses anything I've heard before.

The boy responds.

"What language is this?" I ask.

He shoots me an amused look, "I thought you know a little about everything."

I frown. *"Vann."*

"This is a mix of the old northwestern wood elves dialects. I don't know it fully. I think he's saying he's lost."

"Clearly," I say, and then the boy stands, pulling on my hand. "Would the elves we encountered by searching for him?"

Vann shrugs and the child starts to run.

"Ask him his name," I say to Vann.

He does, and the boy responds with, "Lorien."

I smile down at him, and gesture to him. "Lorien."

My hand presses to my chest. "Arlet."

He says the name slowly, but fear is still shining in his eyes when he looks at Vann.

"Don't worry," I say, even though I know he can't understand me. I turn back to my companion, and find him watching the two of us with a grim expression.

"I'll go for the packs, then we can leave the pass."

I nod, the boy squeezing my hand as Vann returns to where I carelessly threw my belongings.

Lorien remains silent.

I kneel and speak softly, "It's all right. You're safe now."

He looks at me, confused, and we wait for Vann to return.

When he does, I explain that the child seems uneasy. Instead of responding, Vann crouches beside him and speaks in the unfamiliar language, his tone calm and steady.

The boy listens, still unsure, but the fear in his posture softens.

After a brief exchange, Vann glances at me and, in a gentle motion, scoops the child into his arms, murmuring a few more comforting words as we begin to walk. The child relaxes, though his grip on Vann's tunic remains tight.

In the distance, the air blows with an unnatural gust. It begins to move faster, with a rumbling sound like thunder.

"*Mierda*, is that a storm?" I ask Vann.

He is already looking at the sky, confused. It is growing darker, but there aren't clear signs of clouds.

"Perhaps. We'll go fast, and try to find his parents," Vann responds, the boy burying his head into his shoulder.

The noise comes and goes for the next hour. I watch as Lorien looks to the sky, worried.

"Is he all right?" I ask Vann.

Vann asks the boy, and he just nods.

"Where would his parents be, I wonder," I continue.

Vann conveys that, too, then takes a sharp breath after the boy's response.

"He says he doesn't want to tell you, for fear you will be angry."

The shock on my face must be apparent, because Vann laughs. I am not scary, nor do I grow angry quickly.

Then a few images of blood and gore flit into my mind. I push them away, soothing myself by knowing that I'm not *usually* dangerous—and not during my waking hours.

"Relax, Firelocks. My powers of translation are not so strong; he probably meant me."

I flash Vann a small smile, and we continue. It takes a good hour before we reach the end of the passage, and I am itching to find this child's parents.

What is he doing out after dark?

A dozen other scenarios play out in my mind, from a runaway child, to traveling caravans accidentally leaving the little one behind.

Vann shoots me a sharp look as we exit the pass, as if to say, *Now what?*

Another sharp gust of wind sweeps through the air, and with it, it carries the sound of wings beating.

A shadow moves above us, sweeping across the jagged cliffs. Then a massive scaled form descends. Atop it is a dark-skinned elf cloaked in furs, his silhouette framed against the early evening.

My eyes go wide and my heart races.

A... *dragon?*

In Enduvida, there are crystal wraiths. They hum with the rest of the underground city, but they are as much a mystery as the song of the Enduar Gods. One was ridden into battle by Estela, they call her Drathorinna. The mother of wraiths.

But this is flesh and bone and *scale.*

Dragons existed in stories, but I'd never seen one—never even considered I would cross paths with one.

A glance at Vann shows him similarly shocked, though the boy curls further into Vann's shoulder, as if he could hide.

My braid whips around my face, as I squint and look up.

The dragon's wings flare wide as it lands upon the rocky ledge.

The beast is enormous, its scales gleaming like polished onyx, with sharp, curved horns protruding from its head. Its four powerful legs end in talons, gripping the stone beneath. Its vast, leathery wings fold close against its armored body. The rider slides from the saddle with practiced ease, boots crunching against the rocky surface.

He is tall and clad in dark leather and thick, dark spectacles to cover his eyes. I notice he has many of the same features as the boy: long, sleek hair, a curving nose, deep skin, and fine clothing, though markedly older.

Lorien says something else I don't catch.

"Is that his father?" I ask Vann.

"Lorien says it's his uncle, Theren," Vann says quickly.

The dragon tilts its head back and lets out a high-pitched call.

Three other dragons, each a different hue, appear. One is a deep crimson, another is a stormy gray, and the last is a striking emerald green. Each dragon lands with a tremor in the ground.

I swallow hard, instinct screaming at me to move, but I'm too exhausted, too caught in the sheer presence of what's before me. Luckily, Vann steps closer, partially hiding me from view.

Theren's gaze bears into us—piercing, assessing. Then, his voice cuts through the frozen air.

He uses the dialect I don't understand. Vann steps in front of me, calling out answers back at him, gesturing at Lorien.

Lorien looks like a child properly scolded. These must be his people, and I relax feeling my previous scenarios melt away.

Vann continues to argue as I stare at the dragons, mesmerized by the lethal strength in every shift of their feet.

My gods, what would it be like to ride atop one?

When I'd looked at crystal wraiths in Enduvida, I thought I would be afraid to ride them. But I am not the same person as I was then—I'd traveled across the continent, fought the enemy, spoken to a formidable leader and won the trust of a man fierce enough to be called *The Cleaver.*

Fear stems from the unknown, but the world felt less so to me each day. Slowly, that fear is being replaced with curiosity.

My bold new attitude dissolves when the elf atop the green dragon strings an arrow in a bow and points it at Vann and me. I yelp, shifting back in the face of the threat.

Lorien yells out something, and Vann's voice turns soothing.

Theren, the rider with the onyx dragon, calls out something else.

The boy laughs, and then moves to get down. Vann obliges, then Lorien looks back at me, waving one last time before the elf riding the black dragon scoops him up into his arms.

Theren begins to shift Lorien in every which direction—probably looking for injuries—and Lorien starts to spin a tale in his quick, high voice. I can tell because the boy imitates the sound of the mountain cat, only pausing to point at me with a smile.

The man frowns. And then, he looks up and spits a few more violent-sounding words at Vann. At least, as violent as they can be in a language as beautiful as elvish.

"Come here, Firelocks," Vann shoots back at me gruffly. Then his hand scoops around my waist, pulling me close on the opposite side to Lorien.

I gasp at the sudden movement. But the rider atop the grey dragon bites out a few more lyrically harsh words.

Vann looks down at me and his grip tightens. *"Play along."*

Before I can protest, his head dips, and his lips brush the crown of my head.

Every ounce of sense in my body hones in on that action, and my skin burns slightly when he pulls back.

To any onlooker, it would seem intimate. Protective. But I can feel the tension in his body.

I don't like forced affection.

One of the elves narrows his eyes, lowering his bow slightly but still not at ease. The leader, now holding Lorien, tilts his head as if assessing the situation.

Vann switches to elvish, his tone controlled but firm. A low exchange passes between them, and I am surprised to pick out a few familiar words—travelers and Mrath.

The leader of the group laughs, but after a long pause, the one with the bow atop the green dragon lowers his weapon completely.

Theren gestures for us to move.

"We're in luck," Vann murmurs under his breath, his fingers still pressing into my waist. His mouth presses in a firm line. "Remember how Mrath told us to find a city in the mountains? That they would be able to take us to the witches? I think they are from there. They want us to come, that they might issue you a proper thank you and assist us as needed."

I swallow hard, my eyes flickering from him to the towering dragons, then back to the warriors who watch our every movement. "To thank me?" I echo, though my voice is hoarse. "I am just glad the boy is all right."

The man on the dragon, Theren, hears. He cocks his head to the side and furrows his brow as Lorien balances on his side.

"Ah, it is not often I can use the common tongue. It will be a delight to practice." His voice is so accented, it takes me a second to recognize the words.

I break into a smile. "I understand you!"

Theren grins, then says something else to Vann as he replaces his goggles over his eyes. I wait until he's ready to translate.

After a few more words tossed back and forth, Vann says, "Apparently, Mrath did tell them to look for our arrival. And you have saved their leader's only son. Lorien snuck onto a dragon, and strapped himself to one of their legs. He came here with the group waiting for us, but they expected us earlier. He ran away when they landed."

I look up at him. *"En serio?"*

He smiles. "Well done, Arlet. Come."

I suck in another breath, my core warming at his compliment. Then I let his hand guide me along. How strangely familiar his touch is, especially since I'd once thought he'd be the last man to hold me close. How comforting it is to have someone to care for me.

The last thought comes accidentally, but I don't push it away. In fact, I welcome it.

The elves mount their dragons with the ease of men stepping onto solid ground, their hands guiding the beasts with precise gestures. The leader turns back to us and motions for us to follow.

My gaze lingers on the dragons, on their massive wings and sharp talons. But deep inside me, something thrums with anticipation.

No, a rush *flows* through my veins. For so long, I wanted to stay home. I wasn't one to try to explore outside, but this? I am excited for this.

Vann releases me slowly, his touch lingering for just a moment longer than necessary, and I step forward, only for the men to gesture furiously at Vann. They take our packs, secure them in a net, and Vann steps forward.

I watch as he puts on another pair of spectacles and is helped onto the beast. Once he is firmly on the dragon's back, the massive creature blows out a hot breath from its nose, causing me to jump.

Vann holds out his hand, urging me toward him. He pulls me up. It's a blur of movement, and then my legs straddle the makeshift saddle, crafted from rough, woven fibers and tightly bound leather. The seat is uneven but sturdy, designed for function more than comfort.

I'm glad to have pants over a skirt, as the coarse material digs into my thighs.

The rider looks back and ignores me, handing a rope to Vann to hold onto and more eye coverings for me.

"What was all that about?" I ask, looking up at Vann as I position the spectacles.

He frowns.

"It appears that, for them, it's improper to touch another man's wife," he grumbles.

My jaw goes slack. "Wife? Do they think that I am your wife?"

Vann looks down, a hint of a smirk teasing his lips. "Yes. Mrath told them we were together, and they assumed marriage. This is good news, no? I thought you were looking for a husband."

I laugh. I am not angry—not even a little. In fact, something warm washes through me. It builds, coils, and concentrates between my thighs. Even the subtle shift in the saddle makes me nearly jump as it presses against my sex.

This is... a lot.

And yet, it feels normal.

Daniel wasn't half the man Vann was. His affection couldn't hold a candle to how I feel when Vann holds me close.

My cheeks flush, thinking of the last time he was behind me and he'd cradled me against him in his sleep. It's surprising, but a part of me is thrilled to be Vann's, even if only for a few days.

"Well, I suppose I could've chosen worse," I retort.

I feel his chuckle reverberate through his chest.

"I won't think less of you if you scream," he says. "I might actually prefer it."

And then, the dragon begins to move.

CHAPTER 26

VANN

The air is thin and crisp as we ascend into the high mountains. The wind whips past us, and my stomach lurches as the dragon cuts through the sky, flapping its wings only occasionally.

Arlet sits in front of me, taking to the air like a bird in flight. She shifts from side to side, looking down at the ground, impossibly fearless on this creature of death.

"Stop," I growl as she leans dangerously far over the side of her saddle. She lets out a laugh, strands of her hair blowing back, whipping me in the face.

"Look down!" she calls back. "Everything is so small!"

I decline with a firm, *"No."* I don't like heights, especially when all that holds us up are these leather scraps.

Arlet shakes her head. "Suit yourself! I feel lighter than a feather!"

She looks it too. I can see the worry, the panic, and the pain melt off her body as she lets out another whoop.

Good.

But then I catch another glimpse of the ground and groan, fixing myself firmly in the riding saddle to curl my tail tighter around her waist.

The elf leading us, Theren, lets out a high-pitched series of calls, ones that his dragon quickly repeats. Soon, the air is filled with the trilling sound, and slowly, the night shimmers.

Elven glamor.

Even I forget to be afraid as the city is revealed, its lights glittering against the dark cliffs.

“This is Dragon's Reach,” our rider turns back to say, his clipped voice carrying with the wind. He gestures toward the city sprawled across the mountain ahead, now laid bare in the moonlight.

I take it in, my gaze sweeping over the tiered city built into the rock itself.

Bridges of woven vines and reinforced stone span the gaps between cliffs, connecting a network of terraces carved into the mountainside. Buildings rise in elegant, twisting structures, their wooden spires curling like talons.

The scent of burning resin and crisp air fills my lungs as we descend the last ridge toward the city’s entrance.

As we approach, I see elves in sleek, layered garments rushing to the rails built into the cliffside. They point at us, completely awake despite the late hour. More dragons rest on nests above the city, their massive forms sticking out from the rock.

Gods on their stony thrones—*dragons*. What would Teo think of this? While it would be safe to assume that these elves are at least somewhat loyal to Mrath—did Arion have access to such creatures?

I’d never seen one. They weren’t used in the Great War. No, for us enduares, such a myth had been found in epic poems written by great lyricists from the past.

The crimson-colored dragon we ride stretches its wings out, swooping down toward a circular landing pad.

Arlet squeals in delight.

“It’s so beautiful!” she calls.

The onyx dragon lands first, and Theren leaps off, Lorien in his arms, in one smooth motion. His dragon flies away and they walk to the side of the landing area. A few other elves come to speak with them, each looking up at us before hurrying off.

The green dragon is next. And then the storm-grey one.

At last, it’s our turn, and we’re carried straight to the platform.

My stomach drops when the dragon lands, the height making my legs feel unsteady. The rider slips off first.

"Follow, same as me. Then help your wife," he says, his accent thick.

The word '*wife*' sends a jolt through me, and I turn back to Arlet. Seeing her illuminated by the lights from the city, I have the urge to pull out the sketchbook I'd brought from the Sisterhood's Enclave. I want to capture this moment for her to enjoy, too.

A part of me feels like she belongs to me. It's hard to describe—it's just *there*.

I look away, and shift my focus to getting off the damned dragon. Balancing my weight in the saddle, I grip the rope they gave us tightly and I swing my leg over. My hands shake as I lower myself, and when my feet finally hit the platform, I hit the stone hard enough to make my knees groan. The world around me tilts, as if I'd forgotten what it is like to be on solid ground.

The elf behind me snickers.

I shoot him a glare. Then hold out my arms for Arlet.

"Come, Firelocks. I'd like to get you away from the edge."

She grins down at me, windswept. As she slides forth, the rest of her hair comes out of its bun, spilling over her shoulders.

I marvel.

"That was... amazing," she breathes, her voice hoarse from calling into the wind.

"I thought you didn't like adventures," I tease as she falls into the space next to me.

I hold out my arm. She slides her hand through, and then takes in the city. Her head twists right and left, and she grins.

The tall, slender buildings are everywhere, and an arch marks the official entrance to Dragon's Reach.

After a moment, Theren and Lorien approach. Arlet stays at my side, her breath visible.

"It is my pleasure to escort you to your room for tonight," Theren says. "There should be food waiting for you."

"We would both appreciate a full night's rest," I respond.

The elf smiles and begins to escort us away. Lorien hangs back from his uncle's side, sneaking glances at us both.

"Did you get in more trouble?" I lean over and ask him.

Arlet catches my movement and smiles.

Lorien looks up at us. "Yes. My uncle is displeased."

The quick, matter-of-fact way he chirps his words makes me laugh, and then he goes to Arlet's side to hold her hand.

"You will have to forgive us, as we expected you much earlier. We had planned an evening of feasting. Everyone is quite eager to meet you both," Theren continues, pulling me away from Arlet and Lorien.

"Forgive us," I say. "We were... detained."

Theren glances over his shoulder. "One of our scouts saw the bodies."

I pause. "Do you not fear getting caught by Arion?"

He shakes his head. "Arion is a fool, and our magic is strong."

I consider this, remembering the heavy glamor that had been placed over the city. It might be some of the strongest magic I've seen in a long time.

What kind of artifact could hold such power?

"Fear not," Theren continues, "for we sent word to Vaer'Tharion Selric around noon. Preparations will have been made for tomorrow."

It takes a moment for me to place the title, the term roughly translating to *'High Warden.'*

"He is your brother?" I ask, wondering how old the king of these people would be if the elf at my side is already quite mature.

"Correct. Selric is Lorien's father," he says. Then, as if catching the way I stare at the buildings, he continues, "We are not a part of the Elven Dominion, so you can rest easy. They will not find you here. This land has been hidden for a very long time. Mrath is our only contact with the outside elven world. And, I must admit, I am quite eager to get to know you both. I know Lorien is too."

He gestures at the way his nephew points out dozens of buildings and sculptures to Arlet.

"Thank you," I say, my mind churning. "And that is good to know. We are not exactly friends with the current high king."

Theren laughs. "Who is?"

I smile, then return to gazing at the city. Visually, this place is different from the other elven factions I've encountered.

Unlike Mrath and her people, they do cut their wood—abundantly, in truth.

They bear no royal insignias to Arion's court, though. But, from what I can tell, they share many of his ideals. Their social structure must lean heavily toward a patriarchal order if they had laws around the treatment of women without a husband.

"If you are not allied with Arion, then is Selric your King? Or... is Mrath your queen?" I ask.

Theren turns his head slightly. "Selric is the leader of the Vaer'Saryth, similar to a king. Mrath is a very close ally."

High Saddles? Perhaps a council.

"And your ranking, that I might address you properly?" I ask, much to the chagrin of the man before me.

He smiles as he answers, "I am Theren Saryth'Vaan. I lead the Skyborne. But, the Vaer'Tharion rules over all, Skyborne and Grounded alike."

I nod thoughtfully as we step through the carved archway leading into the heart of the city. Immediately, we are surrounded by more elves—some curious, others wary.

"We are almost to the room we have prepared for you. In the morning, I will answer any other questions and ensure you are shown a proper tour of the dragons. They are something, no?"

I laugh inwardly. "They are. I am sure my wife will like that very much."

We fall back into silence as we walk through dimly lit halls carved from the mountain, the stone smooth beneath our boots. When we finally reach our assigned quarters, Theren pulls open a heavy wooden door and steps aside.

"Here we are. Thank you again for your service in saving this little hell-raised pup." Theren nods his head to Lorien. "Till morning."

I incline my head slightly and Arlet waves as he and Lorien leave.

Once the door is shut, we turn and look around. The room is sparse but warm, with a low-burning hearth and blankets folded neatly atop a stone-framed bed. Arlet releases a slow breath, then turns to me and smiles.

"Thrown together yet again," I murmur.

She laughs. Some of the post-dragon riding glow has dimmed, but she looks mostly fine. Just tired.

"I'm ready to know what happened as soon as you are ready to talk," she says.

I let out a long breath, pulling out one of the wooden chairs, and then sitting down.

"Well, he merely explained that we would be meeting Selric, their king, tomorrow evening. They are not affiliated with Arion, but they are allied with Mrath. Theren plans to give us a tour in the morning."

I hesitate, then say, "Since Mrath told us they could take us to the witches' island, in the middle of the ocean, I have been thinking that we will likely need—"

"A dragon?" she squeals excitedly.

"Yes," I grumble, but I turn my head to hide my smile as I start loosening my cloak.

"Gods, I can't wait," Arlet says.

"You won't be so excited when your ass is rubbed raw and your skin burns from the wind," I muse.

Her face falls, and I regret opening my godsdamned mouth.

"You didn't enjoy yourself," she states.

I purse my lips. The answer is, 'no.' But a twinge of guilt still radiates through my heartless chest at the thought of disappointing her.

"I don't like heights."

"Really?" she sits on the bed, and I'm struck by her unbound hair yet again. It cascades over her shoulders in wild waves of fiery red, the color almost glowing in the soft light.

"I live underground. Why would I need to worry about heights?"

She props her chin up with the heel of her hand. "I've seen enduares climb up the cave walls. It looks dangerous and it is, of course, very high up."

"Well, I don't perform those tasks, so," I let myself trail off.

She lays back for a second, then forces herself forward to remove her boots. I watch how unconcerned she is with the prospect of sleeping tonight, since the last time she'd been awoken, it was brutal.

And yet... I'm not inclined to remind her.

I'm not prepared to bind her, either.

Though, a thought pops into my head, not for the first time.

What Daniel had done was wrong. But why bind her? It is such a specific act, especially having read that story she kept near her at night.

I can't shake the feeling that her wound is deeper than she lets on. And I hunger to uncover its entirety.

When her eyes seek mine again, I catch her brow furrow.

"Vann, can I—" her lovely voice stops abruptly, as if she were gathering strength. "You had a wife once, didn't you? A mate?" she asks.

The question catches me off guard. It was a moment where two worlds clashed into each other. On the one hand, Adra was known by Teo and, therefore, Estela. Most if not all of the original two hundred and eighty enduares knew about Adra.

Arlet and I had floated around in similar circles. We knew a great deal about each other, and perhaps she even knew who she was. But *we* hadn't talked about this.

"You don't have to tell me," she says suddenly, and I realize just how long I've gone without speaking.

"No. I am sorry. Adra..." I pause, and my mind begins to flip through memories like a scroll keeper flips through the written word. Adra, with her grey-silver eyes and dark blue locks.

"Her name was Adra. Li'Adra." My throat bobs. "She was... Yes. We were together for many years. Around twenty, before the Great War ended."

Arlet waits patiently, a strange look on her face. It's bittersweet, perhaps tinged with something akin to jealousy.

It's wrong that should soothe me, but it does all the same.

"How did you meet?" Arlet asks, her voice careful.

I pause, flipping through old memories. It takes me a moment to continue.

"She was born into silk and song as a nobleman's daughter with soft hands and a sharper mind. But she never wanted the life that was laid out for her. She was restless, always looking beyond the walls of her father's home, craving something bigger than the fate of a well-bred wife."

Arlet raises her eyebrows. "I didn't know enduares thought that of women."

I shrug. "We were never as bad as the elves, but there were quiet customs observed by more traditional families that kept women at home. She didn't like it. "

Adra was so eager. So full of life.

My eyes find Arlet. Some might see similarities between their personalities and their ability to shine in any situation.

But Arlet was very different. She has a gentle calmness that Adra lacked.

Not better. Not worse. Just different. And my heart... Well. It doesn't matter what my heart says because it no longer beats in my chest.

"She ran away from her father to join the military and that is where we met. Service was not easy for her, but she worked hard. I remember how she looked at me—like I was a world she didn't understand but wanted to. Sadly, love isn't armor. And it wasn't enough to keep her safe," I finish.

Arlet's face grows serious. Then she reaches out, and places her hand over mine as it rests on my knee. It's like a flame lights over my entire skin.

"Lo lamento, Vann," she murmurs in her tongue.

I like the way she does that. Switching between words to suit the tone of the situation—enduar for sassing, human for soothing, and the common tongue for communicating.

There was a vastness under her smiling exterior that I crave to know.

Arlet shifts. "She sounds perfect. And..."

"Yes?"

"She was your mate?" she asks again.

I'd intentionally avoided the question before, but it's impossible to do so a second time.

I hesitate, my mind racing. If I tell her the truth, she'll know about the emptiness I carry with me, and she might press until I reveal my secret—that I don't have a heart. If she finds out, she'll want to help. She's always trying to fix things, but this can't be fixed.

Or worse... I'll have to admit that there was—or maybe still is—a mate for me, and I rejected the goddess's blessing to be with someone else. Someone long gone.

So, there were two options before me. Lie—a wrong thing that would save me trouble. Or tell the truth, and create more trouble.

I hate lies, but I don't think I can bear what comes with the truth.

Not with Arlet peering up at me. Our tentative relationship had grown so much in the time we'd spent together. A part of me is frightened by what we could be, and a larger part fears hurting her.

So I decide. A lie, however bitter, will keep things simple.

I force a smile, even though it doesn't reach my eyes. "Yes," I say, my voice a little rough. "She was."

"Oh," then she pauses. "For some reason, I had thought, since you attended the Mating Journey, you weren't—"

"I did that mostly to protect you," I say. That isn't a lie.

She nods, drawing in a breath.

"I'm sure it was a bond you cherished," she says, looking away, her hands folding in her lap. "Love is a strange thing. It can shape us, even when it's gone."

I can't stand the thought of her looking so down, so I reach for something—anything—to lift her mood.

"Hay heridas demasiado dulces como para borrarse," I respond, playing her own game.

There are wounds too sweet to be erased.

Her honeyed brown eyes snap to mine, and she smiles—slow and languid. For some reason, it strikes a heat inside me, and guilt twists in my chest.

I wait for the ice to come, for it to crawl up my limbs as it always does, but it doesn't. Instead, we sit there, staring at each other.

"That might be the first time you've ever said a full sentence in my tongue. Your pronunciation is good," she says, shaking off some of the sadness.

I want to take my lie back, but all the reasons for saying them still stand.

"Thank you for being so open with me," Arlet says, her voice quiet. "After last night, I don't think it's wise to sleep unbound... but we have no rope since I destroyed it."

"You wish to be tied again?" I ask. I'm not surprised at her bravery, but this time I worry it isn't just bravery, but more a way to create space between us. Space I am rapidly realizing I don't want.

She nods, subdued but resolute.

I retrieve a few spare garments from my pack, tearing one into long strips for makeshift bindings. As I approach her, she stands, turning her back to me. She lets me secure the bindings around her wrists, and the feel of her skin under my fingers is like silk. I push the sensation aside, focusing on the task.

"There." I step back to admire my work. "That should be enough for tonight."

Arlet turns around, her wrists fidgeting with the bindings, and I notice the room is cold.

As I go to light the fire, guilt for keeping secrets, protectiveness for her well-being, and a growing, dangerous fondness swell inside me. These feelings, I know, are a danger. They collide with memories I can't outrun, memories that pull me back when I want to keep moving forward.

As the fire crackles, casting shadows across the room, I see worry on her face.

"I'll be awake if you should turn. You have nothing to worry about."

The lines between her brows ease, and she breathes out slowly. "Very well. I trust you."

I blink, realizing that she means it. Truly. And I had to live with the fact I'd already broken that trust by lying to her.

CHAPTER 27
ARLET'S CURSE

The curse calls me awake once more. It's a stabbing pain that shoots through me as I realize we are even further from our mark. Much further.

So far I can hardly tell which direction to run.

Fuck.

The room is still. The fire in the hearth burns low, casting flickering shadows along the wooden walls. The air is filled with the scent of smoke and aged timber, and the furs beneath me are soft but cold, unable to hold the heat of my body. I lie on the bed, wrists bound.

"You were so close, little flower. Now I can hardly feel you."

I groan. Irritated, and reluctant to move. But the mark on my ankle burns. The room vanishes. The furs, the firelight, the walls—all gone.

Heat flares, burning through my limbs like wildfire. It spreads like a sickness, an aching, searing hunger. The shadows shift overhead.

"Come back to me."

His voice is velvet and steel, honey dripping over poison. The first voice pulls, wrapping around my thoughts, will, and breath.

I inch upright, chest rising and falling in frantic bursts. The air is thin, my skin is sweaty, and my mouth waters.

The hunger returns, along with my ability to see the room. I want blood.

I yank at the bindings on my wrists. My breath comes in sharp, shallow gasps. A snarl rips from my throat. My arms strain. I pull harder, but my body remains bound.

Bleed. I will make whoever did this bleed.

One more violent yank, and the fabric gives way, then falls.

I stagger forward, my vision swimming. I see nothing but the door. The way out. The way back to the voice, to be free of this task.

Vann is on the ground, and near him lies his weapon. I snatch it up. The blade hums against my palm, its power seeping into my bones, feeding the flame roaring through my blood.

Yes. My grip tightens. *Yes.*

Kill. The demand hisses through me.

Vann wakes, moving with the speed of a warrior. He crouches, across the room and takes me in.

He does not fear me, even though he should.

"Firelocks," he says. "Dammit. Put my weapon down."

I hiss at him. He was the one who tied me up.

Angling the weapon, I narrow my eyes in his direction.

His muscles shift under his shirt, preparing to charge. He is much larger than me. But I knew that I could kill someone larger than me—I'd done it before.

The second, ancient voice, chuckles.

I lift the weapon, and charge.

Somehow, Vann is faster. He tackles me.

The world tilts. I thrash. Light crashes into my eyes, a heat pulsing within my chest. I drop the weapon.

I kick him out of the way. My rage mounts, but Vann's voice is steady. "Stay. You are stronger than this."

Sweat beads on my forehead. I try to tear his hands off.

"Arlet," he begs.

That *name*. My fingernails dig into his flesh, scratching. I feel the blood well, feel the urge to kick. To bite.

He cries out.

Good.

But then, somehow, I am pushed to the side.

THE KNOWLEDGE THAT VANN WAS HURT CRASHES OVER ME LIKE A BUCKET OF ice water.

Despite it, the heat doesn't vanish entirely—it lingers, sitting inside me like an ember waiting to catch flame again. But the hunger ebbs. It no longer claws at my insides, no longer demands I run.

I breathe in—smoke and stone and leather.

And blood.

Vann.

He is on his knees before me, but the blood in question leaks from a wound that has already started to heal thanks to the glow coming from his Fuegorra.

"I'm all right, Firelocks. And you are too," he murmurs, his voice rough but calm. His breath is slow, steady, grounding.

I shudder, the last of the tremors shaking loose from my limbs. Then I turn, pressing my forehead against his chest. A choked sob escapes me.

My breath evens out as I press my fingers lightly over the gash I left on his arm, the wound already mostly healed. I pull back and bring his skin to my mouth, brushing my lips over the hurt. Soft, small, useless gestures against something almost fixed.

But the need is there—this quiet ache inside me, whispering that if I could take the pain back, I would.

I kiss the mark again.

Vann exhales sharply, but he doesn't pull away.

His hand goes behind my head, his thumb pressing lightly against my pulse.

"Firelocks," the name is too rough. Too ragged. All I know is that I wish to be closer to him.

I press my lips to his arm once more, the warmth of my breath spilling over his skin.

My fingers tremble where they rest against his forearm, and I close my eyes. I was more awake for that awakening than I had been for any of the others.

I could feel the curse inside of me, how it forced my body to work.

It is dangerous.

Vann's hand slips from my pulse to tilt my chin up. His silver eyes pierce mine, sharp as steel, unreadable as the night sky.

I swallow thickly, forcing myself to hold his gaze. "You pulled me back."

Something flickers behind his eyes—something reckless. His hand lingers at my jaw, thumb brushing over my cheekbone in the faintest ghost of a touch.

"You need to rest," he says, voice rough. His eyes drop to my lips.

I suck in a breath.

I recognize this moment from previous moments with lovers, and I know what comes next. My head spins, and I lean forward.

But things weren't so simple between us.

In a strange moment of clarity, I remember him talking about Adra, the woman he loved before.

His mate—enduares were only recorded to have one.

That leaves me in the same position I've been in before. Eventually, there would come a point between us where it would end. And it would hurt.

I was coming to rely on Vann. Our friendship is... important to me.

I need to stop putting myself in positions where I can get hurt.

Vann moves quickly, leaning in to brush his lips to mine.

At the last moment, I reach up, placing my hand over his mouth, though not so soon that he stops his trajectory.

My palm pushes into my lips as he kisses me through the barrier of my hand. I expect him to pull back, but he doesn't immediately.

There's too much pain in the action.

For a second, I think about letting my hand slide down, and opening myself for him, the rest of the world be damned.

But, finally, he pulls back.

His brows draw together and his mouth is parted. His chest heaves.

"Arlet," he groans. "Forgive me."

"I can't," I bite out. "Because you did nothing wrong."

He looks at me like a lost man. If he could, I don't doubt he would've tried to bolt. To run far from both this place and me.

But he can't. We have to stay here.

I sit there, waiting to see what would happen next. Would he try to kiss me again? Or skulk away to the fire?

His throat bobs.

"You need to sleep, Arlet. We both do. We're just tired," he chokes out.

I nod my head, then glance back at the bed. "Would you—"

"I'll be more attentive this time. I'll wake if you turn again," he says quickly. "No need for the bindings."

Accepting his answer, I dip my head once more, and push towards the bed. I slide under the blanket, and close my eyes.

My mind stays totally awake for hours.

CHAPTER 28
VANN

The night drags on, and sleep evades me.

I roll onto my side, blinking against the dim firelight. I let myself look up at the bed, and there she is. *Arlet.*

Her breathing is soft and steady, and her lips are slightly parted in sleep. A strand of her copper-red hair has fallen across her cheek. The memory of the warmth of her skin lingers on my fingertips.

We'd almost kissed last night.

And she rejected me.

It fucking hurt.

It hurts almost as much as my stupid lie, and I worry I made a mistake.

Love is vast, like the ocean. It has unknown depths. It gives and takes, ebbs and flows.

Was my maintained loyalty to Adra just a way to staunch the flow of the waves? Am I… a fool seeking to hold back something as mighty as the sea?

The woman before me is just starting to find herself. Even without a heart, plagued by the constant pain, I have warmed to her.

She makes me feel like I am alive. Like it is all right to be happy again.

Perhaps it is time to lay to rest the ghost of what once was, and let the earth cradle the remnants of your past, a voice whispers. *It is not too late to tell the truth.*

I grit my teeth, frustrated and pull out the small pad and charcoal. It takes time to flip past the endless drawings of her. Lying in bed beside me, walking through the mountain pass, her hair tearing free of her bun on the dragon to whip over my skin.

Now, I capture this moment. Letting the brush of my hand craft another memory. Trying to get this all right because it was possible that one day, we would return to Enduvida, and everything would sink into the dull patterns we'd followed before.

Another ache blossoms in my chest. I will miss the constant companionship if that happens.

Arlet shifts slightly, the furs rustling as she moves, and a new pang of guilt twists in my gut as my charcoal traces the rise and dip of her form. One bare foot has snuck out from under the blanket to cross over her covered shin.

I keep thinking of last night. When the curse takes hold, when the hungry, foreign thing claws through her veins, it is my voice that calls her back. My hands that keep her tethered to herself.

Suddenly, heat blazes over my skin, and I remember her lips against my flesh. There had been no thought behind it, no calculation, just instinct. A desperate attempt to heal what she had broken.

She should've let me kiss her. I would've returned her sweetness with passion.

I could imagine her enjoying herself. I could picture moaning at the onslaught of kisses I'd gift her in gratitude.

If she wanted release, I would be there for her. I would draw her out of her head. Make her forget her sadness.

She would give herself to me in trust, and it would be my job to ensure every twisted fantasy in her head was completed to her satisfaction. *I* could give her what she needs.

Heat snakes through me, oblivious to how cold I'd been throughout the years. The adrenaline rushes to my cock, and my fingers twitch, eager to stroke her flesh. She could have been soft and well-fucked right now. But she'd rejected my advance.

Likely, because I am a bastard.

Arlet shifts under the blankets, her lashes fluttering before her gaze meets mine. I close the sketch book, and cast it to the side where my blankets are strewn. Then I adjust my pants.

Awareness dawns slowly, her breath catching as the space between us seems to shrink.

She swallows, her throat bobbing. The lamp light paints her in warm hues, and I wonder if she's ever looked at herself the way I do.

"Good morning," she murmurs, sitting up, her back arching slightly as she stretches the remnants of sleep away. "Are they here?"

They? Ah, yes.

Morning. Breakfast. Theren.

Time moves differently in this room, expanding and folding over itself.

"Not yet," I say softly.

She reaches up, trying to comb through her locks, before giving up and falling back onto the bed.

So tired, little human.

"Would you like me to help you with your hair?" I ask, surprising myself.

She looks up at me, blinking rapidly.

"I—wouldn't that be inappropriate?"

I shrug. "I've already seen your hair down. I only do it for your sore arms."

She shifts on the bed, then reaches for her pack, wincing as she fishes out a stone comb. When her hand extends, holding it out to me, I smile.

Really smile. Perhaps she isn't so mad after last night.

She looks unsure. "It's simple. Just—"

"I know how to do such things," I murmur.

Silence falls over us as I untie the band around her locks, and let the red spill out over her shoulders. Gently, I work my way through the tangled tresses.

They are soft and carry her fragrance.

"Did... Adra teach you about these things?" Arlet asks.

I suck in a sharp breath. "Yes."

She doesn't respond again, as I twist the hair several times until it coils neatly around itself atop the crown of her head. She tucks a curl behind her ear, and I catch the scars over her fingers.

The ones I'd promised her such sweet things while holding.

"Lorien likes you very much," I say. "It is sweet. You are good with children."

I feel her soften at the compliment.

"I like them very much—and he is sweet."

"You like them enough to give up time you could spend weaving. I can imagine."

She shifts her head, and glances at me over the shoulder. "I haven't given up on weaving. I just... think that Lorepath is more important right now."

Lorepath. Hmm. "That is the name of your education project, no?"

"It most certainly is."

I pull the comb close to her hairline, smoothing the edges. "It is very important to you."

She hums.

Then, she takes a deep breath. "I think that proper education is one of the most important tools of a better life, you know? You probably learned practical skills like reading as a child, I was much older when I finally had the opportunity."

She sounds defensive, so I tap her shoulder.

"I wasn't trying to critique. You absorb information like no one I've ever met. You are witty."

She pauses, and it's like I can see the words tangling in her mind.

"I wish I could spend more time behind a loom... but I have the skills to make the program. I have the time. I want to give—to add so fiercely to the world around me that I won't have to search for my mark. It will be a deep gouge, brimming with good things. And when I've done that, I will rest. I will weave a thousand tapestries just for me."

When she talks, its like I can't fucking breathe. She is so good. So so sweet. Perfect.

"That doesn't sound like resting," I tease.

She laughs.

After tying her hair, I reach down, and grab her hand, holding it up to inspect. I line hers up next to mine and find my palm completely swallows her.

I smile.

"But, jokes aside, I think that is beautiful. I can picture it."

She relaxes against me, and it feels like a reward. Then her fingers expand, spreading my digits wide.

She looks up at me. "You know, I always wondered how you lost these."

I hesitate. "It's a gruesome tale, Firelocks. Not nearly as lovely as your gentle words."

"How gruesome?" she pries, our hands still touching.

"Very."

"I tell you my story if you tell me yours," she says, the silhouette of her cheek pulling up in a smile.

We'd had such a strange, heavy night. I find myself craving an easy moment.

I like talking to her, even if she will not let me have her.

"A giant bit them off while I tore his head in two."

She yelps and looks up at me. "Tore? How? His skull—"

"At the jaw," I murmur, touching the delicate hinge on the side of her face.

She frowns, then says, "The giants have always been cruel. One of the giant princes—"

"Cut yours off. Estela sewed them back on," I repeat. I'd asked about it the first week she came to Enduvida. "I already know."

A moment of silence follows, but she stares at me, her hand against mine. I see hurt flicker in her eyes, and I feel it reflected in my gut.

I'd hurt her with a lie she didn't know was a falsity. She'd hurt me with the kiss.

My sin is worse.

"Arlet, about last night—"

A small knock sounds. She drops her hand and moves away, so I stand, frustrated, and get the door.

When I open it, I find a man with a tray of bread, fruits I don't recognize, and water.

"Good morning," the elf says with a bow. "I bring you breakfast. Vaer'Saryth Theren will arrive soon to take you on a tour. Enjoy."

Arlet and I thank him and he leaves.

We eat in silence, and the discomfort grows.

Thankfully, it does not take long for Theren to make good on his promise. He arrives, dressed in dark leather and sporting a smile.

"Good morning, our honored guests," he says brightly, using the common tongue.

Arlet is delighted, and we exchanged pleasantries.

"So, you want to see the dragons, yes? It will be a fun outing before the feast tonight."

She looks up at me, surprised. "Can we?"

I make a funny expression. "Do you want to?"

She hesitates. "I thought you didn't like them."

"Yes or no, Firelocks."

"Yes, let's go," she responds, really smiling for the first time all morning.

Theren smiles and gestures us forward.

The cold rush of mountain air bites at my skin as we leave. The city is quiet but not asleep. People move through the streets, some with wares filling their arms, others hurrying off as if to make it to their jobs in a timely manner.

We walk through the rows of buildings, and her small hand nestles in mine. We move swiftly through the winding city paths until the buildings thin and the scent of smoke and beast fills the air.

Theren takes a deep breath. "Ah, you smell that? Dragons. Nothing compares to this. Smoke and scale, I like to call it."

I smile. The smell does cling to the wind, a heady mix of charred wood and molten rock.

"My wife is fascinated by them." I turn back to Arlet who has her head upturned to the sky.

Theren smiles. "I am glad." Then he switches to common tongue. "Did you enjoy the ride last night?"

She looks up, surprised again. Then nods.

His smile widens to a toothy grin, and he begins to spout off facts about the dragons. How long they live, what they eat, and even a description of the mating season.

I listen, translating as we walk and the ground beneath us changes from the smooth stone of the city paths to the rough-hewn trails carved into the cliffs. Ahead, the silhouettes of towering nests sit. Whereas the city is in the mountainsides, the nests are near the peaks.

They are massive structures, half-natural caves and half-elven craftsmanship, woven with thick ropes and reinforced with bones I don't care to identify. Low embers glow within the depths of some, like houselights.

Arlet sucks in a short breath. I hear her mutter something.

"What did you say?" I ask.

"Madre mía," she says, enunciating the words more clearly. "I'm just surprised."

Nodding, I tuck away more bits and pieces of her, and slow our pace. I draw Arlet closer to me as we press against the shadows of a stone wall.

When Theren mentions that a mating season had just completed not too long ago, Arlet beams.

"I wonder if we'll see any baby dragons," she whispers, clearly excited.

I don't answer. My focus remains on our surroundings, as we are close to the edge of the cliff. My tail instinctively wraps around her.

A soft rustle of wings draws my attention skyward. High above, a onyx black dragon from before shifts on its perch, its massive talons scraping against stone as it settles.

"There's my dragon. Perhaps you recognize him," Theren says. "Vyrenth."

Arlet's breath catches. "*Dioses míos*," she murmurs, pressing a hand to her chest. "It's so beautiful."

Beautiful isn't the word I would use. Terrifying, perhaps. Lethal.

I say the name to her and she tries to repeat it.

"The '*nth*' is lighter," Theren says in the common tongue.

When she gets it right, he laughs.

"How old is Vyrenth?" she asks kindly.

"I am his second rider," Theren continues. "He tells me maybe a thousand turns of the sun."

My eyebrows shoot up. "He speaks to you?"

Theren nods but doesn't elaborate. Instead he asks, "Are you interested in getting closer to the dragons?."

Arlet tenses beside me, but not in fear. "Yes."

I narrow my eyes. "I think it's too dangerous."

"No danger with me," Theren interjects.

"Come on, Vann, don't you like adventure?" she fires back.

I should argue, should put an end to this reckless idea before it forms further, but *damn me*, there's something about the way her eyes shine that makes my grip loosen just slightly.

I exhale sharply, pressing my fingers to my temples. "Fine. But if you get eaten, I'm leaving your body here."

Arlet beams. "I would expect nothing less, *mi cielo*."

"Fucking hell," I curse under my breath as she follows Theren..

We weave between the rocky outcrops, avoiding loose rock. Up close, I can see how the dragons rest within their nests. Their massive bodies are curled into a ball, and their breath causes the embers within to glow and fade with each exhalation.

Arlet stops abruptly.

"Are you well, human?" Theren asks.

I follow her gaze and my stomach tightens.

A dragon lies barely a dozen paces ahead, separated from the others, its body curled in a nest of dark stone and shattered eggshells.

"That dragon is... beautiful," she exclaims

Its golden scales shimmer, and its wings folded are neatly at either side, but its eyes cause me to pause.

Open. Watching.

It isn't sleeping. It knows we're here. And yet, it doesn't move.

"This is Seraph," Theren says. Then he tilts his head to the side, making a *tsking* sound.

The dragon watches us with something between curiosity and

patience. Its nostrils flare, inhaling, as if committing our scent to memory.

Then, a soft voice speaks.

"She doesn't fly anymore."

We all turn, and I spot a small figure stepping from behind a nearby boulder. Brown, wild hair, bright gleaming eyes.

"Lorien!" Theren laughs. "Your father told you not to sneak out today."

The boy grins, squaring his small shoulders with the kind of bravado only children can muster. "I wanted to see our visitors."

"Lorien!" Arlet repeats, drawing her attention from the dragon, and seeing the boy. "Hello again."

The child is confused, but Theren translates for him as he scoops him up, balancing his nephew on his shoulders.

"You sure you want to stay?" he asks.

Lorien nods.

"Very well. But we must be sure your father doesn't find out."

Arlet's attention goes back to the dragon, and I jerk my chin toward the beast. "What do you mean, it doesn't fly?"

Lorien glances at the dragon, his voice quieter now. "It is a mama dragon. Her babies died."

Theren casts him a weary glance. Then he clarifies, "We have a problem with hunting birds. They like to eat dragon eggs, and this past mating season was... difficult. We have not been controlling their growth as we should. Seraph killed the thieving creatures and put the eggshells back. She is mourning."

The words settle like a stone in my chest.

I turn to Arlet, who looks expectant. I hesitate. But I can't lie to her again.

When I finish the story, she looks as though she might cry. Instead, she chooses to be brave.

"May I touch her?" she asks Theren.

He purses his lips. "She does not let others touch her lately. But you can try. Put your hand up, and approach. If she doesn't look away, it should be fine."

"What happens if she looks away?" Arlet asks.

"Then you retreat," Theren says simply.

I watch her take a deep breath. That woman can't help herself but find a friend.

She steps forward, hand out.

The dragon, Seraph, watches. I keep waiting for the creature's head to turn so that I could bring Arlet back to my side, but she doesn't.

There were other things we needed to do, and being made to take a tour when the King of the Elves was hunting her seemed foolish.

But then, Arlet reaches the end of the nest. Her fingertips brush against golden scales. The dragon does not flinch. She only exhales, long and deep, as if waiting for something only Arlet can give.

"Very well done," Theren says. "Come, I will show you the training area."

Arlet reluctantly steps away, and then I fold her close to me again. I shouldn't be doing that, not after the kiss, but she doesn't fight me and I am on edge up here.

The trail narrows as we ascend, the air thinning with the climb. The city's noise fades, replaced by the rhythmic sound of wind rushing through the cliffs. Theren sets Lorien down and the boy moves with ease, his small frame darting around jagged rocks.

Other elves pass us, calling out common greetings. We move at a slow pace compared to them, but at last, we arrive.

The path leads to a rocky outcrop, half-shielded by a crumbling wall of stone. Beyond it, a plateau stretches out like an open hand.

Arlet's breath catches as she takes in the sight. Her neck tilts and she grins up at the clouded sky.

Five dragons—sleek, powerful creatures of varying sizes and colors—circle overhead. Their riders sit atop them with practiced ease, calling out commands in sharp, melodic elvish. The dragons respond in perfect harmony, banking left or right, climbing higher, then diving in breathtaking spirals.

Below, another group of riders stands in formation, their eyes skyward as they shout instructions to the airborne teams.

Lorien points upward. "I take lessons," he proclaims.

Arlet looks at me for meaning.

"They are teaching him how to ride a dragon," Theren says.

Her eyes go wide as stones. "Really? So young?"

Theren translates this time, and the boy puffs out his chest. "I'm going to be a Skyborne. Not like my father, who spends his time sitting on a chair."

I translate for Arlet as she watches an emerald green dragon break from formation and dives toward the plateau. Its wings flare at the last second, stirring the loose gravel at the edge of the cliff.

The rider gestures toward the sky, and the dragon launches into the air once more, beating its wings with thunderous force.

Theren grins. "Now comes the fun. You're own riding lesson."

The blood drains from my face, but Arlet practically vibrates with excitement.

I let out a long breath. We would be riding one of these things to the Witch's Isle anyway.

Better we learn now, surrounded by friendly faces.

"Excellent," I say. "What should we do first?"

"We'll get you suited. You'll need a harness that will connect you to the riding saddle," he gives an appraising look to Arlet, and I almost consider stepping in front of her.

Gods, I'm so on edge.

"Your wife will need new clothes. Enchanted leathers, so the scales will not cut into her skin," he declares over the sound of wing beats.

He turns to shout at one of the other elves. Another man. The newcomer nods sharply, and runs away.

Theren claps his hands and whistles. His dragon, Vyrenth, appears a little while later, hovering above him and casting rough gusts in our direction.

"Now watch me!" Theren makes another symbol and the beast zooms down, almost touching the stone. The elf grasps onto his saddle, jumping on.

Theren lets out a whoop and Lorien cheers as his uncle soars into the sky.

Perfect. This day might kill me.

CHAPTER 29

ARLET

Night drapes over Dragon's Reach, cloaking the city in a fading purple light that I watch from the window in our room.

Every muscle in my body protests as I shift on the narrow bed. My joints are stiff and my arms are sore from the dragon training earlier. The dragons had been magnificent to watch, but the hours spent learning the correct posture and balance on the practice saddles left me feeling like I'd been wrung out and left to dry.

The only thing that stirs me is Vann. I stealthily sneak glances at the way his muscles tense while he polishes his weapon, and the intense focus he applies to each swipe.

It's not good for my heart, but I can't stop thinking about our almost-kiss.

This morning, I'd been ready to avoid him forever. But his hands had been on me the entire time we were in the mountains.

It had been sweet. And I can't seem to let that go.

A knock sounds at the door.

Vann, who has been working on polishing his blade, stands and answers the sound. An elven woman with copper-brown skin waits on the other side of the entrance to our room, smiling.

"Hello," I call, standing up to slip on my shoes as Vann says something in elvish.

"We've been asked to assist you in preparation for tonight's feast," the woman says in accented common tongue. I'm surprised to hear another person other than Theren speaking it here—this place seems extremely secluded. "I will present you with your new clothes. And then I will take you to the royal bathing pools."

The door creaks open further, revealing a second person, a tall elf with braided hair woven through with thin chains of silver. His eyes, sharp and pale green, flick to me, then to Vann.

"We are ready when you are," he says.

"Thank you," Vann says with a bow. "Enter, please."

Both elves step inside, and the man, carrying a stack of fabric, dips his head. The scent of fresh fabric and mountain herbs wafts toward me as his bundle is set on the table.

Vann gestures me over, and I help him untie the twine, peeling back the waxed paper to reveal deep emerald-green fabric embroidered with silver thread.

I hold up the bodice of my dress. The material is heavy and smooth beneath my fingers. It's the kind of garment I'd seen worn by nobles. Beside it lies a matching tunic and pants, more utilitarian but no less exquisite.

"Not exactly a subtle gown," I say.

Vann huffs. "Elves aren't known for their subtlety."

The words draw a smile from me.

I trace the stitching along the hem—a pattern of curling wings and jagged cliffs.

"We can leave when you are ready," Vann says, standing quickly.

I nod. "Let's go now."

Picking up my new clothes, Vann and I follow the elves out of the room.

Together, the servants lead us through the winding halls, past narrow windows that spill pale moonlight across the polished stone floors.

We stop at a branching hallway. The elf gestures to me. "You will go that way."

Vann frowns. "Separately? We are married."

Butterflies take flight in my belly. He wants to bathe with me?

"The pools are divided," the elf explains. "It is our custom."

I hesitate, glancing at Vann, who gives me a small nod. His hand brushes my forearm as I pass. Heat snakes over my body.

It's so sudden, I can't contain it. Nor can I stop myself wishing he would come into my pool anyway. And... I shouldn't think of that right now.

"Don't drown," he says softly.

I bite my lip. "I'll try my best."

He sets off in one direction, and I continue alone down a narrower hall. Soon, the servant and I reach an arched doorway. Steam seeps from the crack at the bottom, carrying the scent of minerals and mint.

The door opens to reveal a cavernous bathing chamber, its walls carved from polished stone. Veins of luminescent ore snake through the rock, casting a soft glow over the steaming pools below.

A wave of homesickness takes over and I ache for Enduvida, or maybe, just Vann.

I shouldn't have asked about Adra.

The woman who had come to our door enters first. I descend the steps after her as she sorts through small vials of liquid. Her ears are long and pierced with several rings, each etched with delicate symbols of dragons and flames.

"You prefer me to call you Lord Vann's wife?" she asks.

"Just Arlet," I correct.

She gives me a sheepish smile as if she doesn't fully understand, so I drop the matter and smile back. She gestures to the nearest pool.

I step forward, removing my tunic and trousers with only a moment's hesitation. The water is blissfully hot as I lower myself in. Once submerged, I hiss as it soothes my aching limbs. My hair floats around me, and copper waves curling like tendrils of fire in the clear water fan out under my chin.

The woman kneels beside me on the ledge and pours something sweet, berry-scented concoction into the water. She bows her head and busies herself with bottles of soap, and then she stands.

"I will return soon."

When she leaves, I press my hand to my neck and think. Wearing a pretty dress tended to make me giddy. But I don't feel that right now. My relationship with Vann grows more complicated every day.

First, we avoided each other. Then we were friends. He *followed* me out of Enduvida.

Somewhere along the way, I started to feel safer at his side—started to imagine things in his presence. Perhaps it was the fact that travel is hard and I'd been so long without sexual affection, either alone or with someone else. In Enduvida, when tension coiled inside me, I had privacy.

Perfect stories. I liked reading about people falling in love, and a natural part of that was intimacy. The chase. The pull.

Safety has always been an important factor in my attraction.

Vann had mentioned reading one of my scrolls once.

My already hot skin pulses. He'd teased me, but there was heat behind it.

Some people could reduce the stories to scandalous words, but they were so much more for me.

It would be hard to explain to someone who hadn't experienced it, but replacing old, scarred memories with new ones—better ones—is how I heal.

Yes, being tied up led to one of the most traumatic experiences of my life.

But the truth was, I'd enjoyed those things before. And finding a story with that included that made me feel like I wasn't alone—wasn't broken.

The words made me feel like... if I tried it again, I could move on.

It didn't have to be about reliving sorrows. It could be about control. Safety.

Trust.

I didn't think it was wrong to want to experience that in a different way, with the right person.

Sometimes, I think so much about being a mother and motherhood, I forget the part of me that desires.

And Vann... well he couldn't be my mate. That title had been given to another. But I wondered if he could be the person I let myself explore with.

I soak until the heat dissolves the tension from my muscles and I'm able to scrub the sweat and dirt from my skin. But as I rub the wash rag over my arms and neck, my mind continues to spin.

When the cloth used for scrubbing scrapes over my nipple, I gasp.

Looking around, I don't see anyone near. The maid certainly hasn't returned.

A part of me is cautious, as I'm not sure when she will, and there is a festival to attend. But, the curse and the possession felt far away. In fact, we were closer than ever to breaking it.

I need this.

So I lean back, bracing myself against one of the stones. I use the cloth to scrape over my breasts and my wrists lightly.

Then I venture lower, and let myself do something I'd tried hard to avoid. I picture Vann.

I close my eyes, and pretend that the cloth was really his calloused hand. When I stroke over my lower belly, I shiver.

My cunt clenches and floods with heat.

"Vann," I murmur as I delicately rub the rough cloth against the sensitive bundle of nerves above my sex.

The skin on my neck and cheeks flushes and I swallow thickly.

It feels good.

I think of him, holding me so I can't move. So I have no choice but to give into his affection. When I imagine a ghost of his breath across my neck, whispering sweet words, I cry out and come.

I clamp my damp hand over my mouth.

Fuck.

That was loud. *And fast.*

I run my finger through my hair, panting. It'd been too long. I should've...

Steps echo in the hallway.

"Lady Arlet?" the servant calls out. "May I enter?"

"Yes," I say, voice high. I try to hide the meager evidence of what I'd done, as she comes in.

I help myself out of the pool, and she uses a cloth to dry my body. I stop her at one point, preferring not to be touched right now.

She seems confused, but helps me with my hair. She dries it with a brush and towel, and then starts braiding.

"I didn't take too long, right?" I ask.

She shakes her head. "Everything is all right. I am here to take care of our guest."

The plait she crafts gets twisted into a crown that coils atop my head. Then she helps me into the dress, and the sleeves are so long they nearly touch the floor. The leather slippers mold to my feet perfectly.

"Thank you," I say to the maid.

She reaches out, tapping the freckles on my cheeks. "You are an interesting beauty. I think your husband will be pleased."

She dips her head, and then I leave, feeling unsettled, not just because of what I'd done, but also because of how I look. The sun had made my spots more apparent.

Vann had once told me he liked them, but was that still the case as they stood out more and more?

It doesn't take long to be guided away from the pools, and I exit feeling wholly exposed. I rub the spot between my brows. What had I been thinking in there?

The warm water just made me feel so... desirable. Loose.

I am starving for affection.

Vann clears his throat, and I look up. The sight of him makes me stop mid-step. He's wearing the emerald tunic, its deep color setting off the silver of his hair and the blue of his skin. The fabric clings to his broad frame, and the silver embroidery at the collar catches the moonlight like frost.

His gaze sweeps over me, and heat flushes my skin. Images skitter over my mind, brought to life by the recent memory of my moment in the bath.

My core feels hollow, aching. For some reason, once I started to think about this, I couldn't stop.

His smile spreads and I can't breathe. I picture him picking me up, and carrying me somewhere to yank up my dress, expose my hot sex to the air and fill me to bursting. The...

"How lovely you are, Firelocks," he says gently.

What. The. *Hell.* Is going on?

Heat rushes to my cheeks, and I force my mind to stop picturing things. "You are too."

His eyes linger a moment longer before he holds out his arm. I take it, letting him guide me through the terrace doors and down a long, winding hallway.

At last, we exit the hallway and find ourselves in front of a structure built into the largest cliff. Its doors are reinforced with intricate carvings of dragons.

The guards on either side pull open the doors, revealing a grand hall bathed in flickering torchlight.

My senses are just as overwhelmed as my heart at the sight.

Long tables line the walls, laden with platters of roasted meats, honeyed fruits, and twisted breads shaped like dragons mid-flight. Musicians play in the far corner, their instruments unfamiliar. Some use thin, reed-like flutes that trill like birdsong, others beat drums that rumble like dragon wings.

Elves move through the space, some dressed in vibrant silks, others in more subdued hunting leathers. Their eyes follow us as we enter. Their skin varies from deep coppery brown to moonlight pale. Many hairstyles are woven into elaborate braids adorned with tiny metal dragons.

"They did this all for us?" I ask. A feast in Enduvida is always pleasant and beautiful, but nothing I'd ever seen matched the level of ethereal precision in Dragon's Reach.

"I'd wager this is just a regular day for the elves," Vann grunts. "Haven't you realized how much they love to show off? It doesn't seem to change, no matter what city or village I visit."

I laugh, and he pulls me closer.

Yes, my body hums.

The servants guide us past a crowd of dancers, and I see a tall throne is raised upon a platform. There, the sovereign of Dragon's Reach, Selric, is already awaiting.

We walk the length of the hall, the crowd pausing to watch our entrance.

At the bottom of the dais, Vann bows deeply, and I follow his lead.

Selric stands, positioning Lorien in front of him, and begins to speak in old elvish. The family resemblance is clear; they have the same deep skin tone with rounded features in their chin and noses.

Except, Selric appears younger than Theren. *Much* younger.

Hmm.

I do not catch most of the words, save the names of me and Vann.

A ripple of acknowledgment moves through the hall, and I catch sight of Theren near the throne. He smiles and nods his head. Strange man.

Selric continues, and Vann leans over to say, "He's welcoming us and thanking us at once."

Then, Selric raises his goblet.

"Arlet," he declares.

"Arlet," the crowd echoes.

I give a small bow. Glasses are lowered and conversations resume. In no time, the hall fills with the clink of goblets and the murmur of voices.

Selric nods in our direction, effectively dismissing us.

Vann leans over, whispering in my ear. "He thanks you, and says our dragon and rider will by ready by morning."

My brows raise. "So quickly?"

We were almost at the end of the journey. Compared to how hard the rest of it was, I'm shocked. A part of me feels this is too easy. But then, Vann huffs a laugh, and presses his hand to my lower back.

I suck in a sharp breathe. It is strange to suddenly and consistently feel so aroused. I was only human, I had my moments, but never this long.

Vann leads me toward a table near the edge of the room. He pours wine into two glasses, then holds out one to me. "To Firelocks."

I smile, and then hold up my own glass. "To *Mi Cielo.*"

Vann's eyes become impossibly warm at the compliment.

It's a silly action, but the rims of our glasses touch, and I think of our almost kiss. In my mind, I can picture him caging me against a wall, and kissing me for real. I can picture him seeking entrance to my mouth, and then making love to my mouth with his tongue.

What the hell is going on?

Before I can say another word, a low, resonant growl rolls through the air. The hall falls silent.

The sound comes from above.

I tilt my head back and freeze.

Through the open ceiling, dragons circle in the night sky, their massive forms silhouetted against the moonlit clouds. One dives, wings tucked tight, until it halts midair. Its eyes, molten gold, fix on me.

The hall watches as the dragon roars, the sound vibrating in my bones.

Selric smiles faintly, and shouts out another sentence that is rewarded with a cheer.

From the edges of the hall, elves step forward, each holding a torch. They move in unison, raising the flames high before casting them into the massive brazier at the center of the room. The fire leaps skyward, turning an intense, shimmering blue.

A scent I had barely perceived grows stronger.

The dragons above answer with a chorus of roars, their wings cutting through the night as sparks and embers rain down like stars.

Vann's hand finds mine beneath the table, his grip solid and reassuring.

A shadow falls over us, and we look up to find Theren approaching. He carries a goblet of wine and a lazy smile.

"Enjoying the spectacle?" he asks, slipping into the common tongue.

"It's remarkable," I reply honestly. "And unexpectedly nice."

Theren chuckles. "It's one of the few traditions that hasn't been twisted by politics. The dragons don't care for our schemes. They only care for the fire."

"And you?" Vann asks, leaning against one of the long tables. "Do you care for the schemes?"

Theren's smile widens. "I prefer the fire."

I glance at Vann, who arches a brow. "But your brother makes the decisions, no," Vann says carefully.

"He does," Theren agrees. "By my permission. And yes, I am the eldest. But the throne never suited me. Too many decisions about grain storage and trade routes. So I left it to Selric."

Vann's expression darkens. "That gives him reason to fear you."

Theren shrugs. "He bends, now and then, to my will. In return, I never consider taking the throne back."

Vann's lips twist in a knowing smirk. "He might try to get rid of you some day."

Theren's laughter is genuine and loud enough to draw a few curious glances. "I'd appreciate the challenge."

We are silent a while longer, and then his eyes land on me and stick. He swirls the wine in his goblet. "You know, I can see the magic around you, black like smoke, clinging to your skin like oil."

I open my mouth, not knowing enough about this Selric to trust him. My eyes flick to Vann.

He steps in. "Our business with the witches is our own."

Theren nods, and his expression fades. "Of course," he says, pouring more deep red liquid into our goblets. "Well, the night is young, and the fire demands to be fed. Drink with me."

This wine is different, it smells of smoke and berries, rich and tantalizing. It's the scent I smelled in the pools.

I raise my glass as Theren grins.

"To my nephew's savior," he says.

We drink, and the warmth of it spreads like molten flame through my chest as the dragons roar above us. Heat pools in my core, and I gasp at the sudden reaction.

Theren grins wickedly. "Welcome to Dragon's Reach. Lord Vann, watch your wife, and enjoy the fire," he says, before slithering away. Behind him, two of the elves begin to kiss passionately.

CHAPTER 30
ARLET

I blink. My skin is oversensitive, and most of the room turns to chaos.

The elves swirl around me, dancing closer than I'd seen two people touch. They kiss. They laugh.

It all scrapes against me. The heat in my core intensifies, spreading through my limbs like wildfire. Vann turns to me, concern spreading across his features as he sees the flush creeping up my neck.

"Are you all right?" he asks, leaning in closer.

The feel of his breath ghosting over my skin makes my breast ache. I want to kiss him, to feel his lips. To eliminate the space between our bodies, and explore the inside of his mouth with mine. I want him to touch me, and then to show him the fastest way to make my body come apart. I want him to hold me close and never let go. The sudden rush of desire is overwhelming, pulsing through my veins like a fever.

I force myself to look away, my cheeks burning with embarrassment at the intensity of my longing. I take a deep breath, willing the heat within me to simmer down.

"I-I think I just need some air," I manage to stammer out, pushing back from the table.

Vann's hand reaches out to stop me, his touch sending sparks of electricity through my body. “Let me come with you,” he offers, concern evident in his eyes.

I shake my head quickly, afraid to trust myself alone with him at this moment. “No, it's fine. I'll be back soon.”

With that, I turn, pulling my hand away, and practically run from the hall, desperate to escape the sensation of being consumed by flames from the inside out. The cool night air hits me like a balm as I step outside, trying to steady my ragged breaths and clear my head.

I walk briskly, putting distance between myself and the hall, hoping the cool night air will extinguish the fire raging within me.

As I wander through the moonlit path, I reach a fence protecting someone from going too close to the edge. My mind whirls. The touch of Vann's hand still lingers on my skin, and I still ache from head to toe.

When I shift, slickness spreads over my inner thighs.

Was something in that wine?

Lost in my tumultuous thoughts, I freeze as a shadow falls over me. My heart pounds, and there is a hollow ache in my lower belly. I turn to find Vann standing behind me, his eyes dark with concern.

"Arlet, you don’t seem well,” he asks, reaching out a hand towards me.

Before I can respond, a gust of wind brushes over my skin, almost painfully exquisite. I gasp, my head tilting back at the intense sensation.

The air between Vann and I feels thick. It’s hard to breathe.

“Did—did you drink the wine?” I ask, chest heaving from the heady sensation.

"I didn’t,” he admits softly, his gaze never leaving mine. "Arlet, what's happening to you?"

I try to form words, to explain the overwhelming desire coursing through me, but it feels impossible. The world around us blurs at the edges, narrowing down to just Vann and me in our own sphere of heated tension. A surge of panic shoots through me, fueled by the fire still burning within.

Need bleeds out of every pore. Without thinking, I spin on my heel and break into a sprint, desperate to get away from him. A new need blossoms—a desire that he would catch me. That he would hold me tightly, as tightly as he did in Mrath's enclave.

That I'd have new memories—sweet ones—to replace my nightmares.

To my delight, Vann is fast. With a few swift strides, he catches up to me and effortlessly lifts me over his shoulder, my half-hearted protests muffled against his back, as my heart pounds.

"Let me go!" I cry out, the world tilting around me as he carries me back toward our room.

As we near the entrance, a figure steps into our path, blocking Vann's way. The elf looks between Vann and me and then begins to laugh before stepping back. He says something taunting to Vann, who immediately snaps at him.

The cool air against my skin does nothing to ease the heat. The way that Vann holds me over his shoulder is uncomfortable, and doesn't allow friction in any of the right places.

Delicious images fill my mind of his hand pushing my skirts out of the way and then, finding just how wet I am.

My head spins as I use my hands to prop myself up, and look around. We're still not back at our small house. It would be inappropriate to—

Vann's hand goes around my ankle and I moan. My mind is foggy, but I can feel how his grip tightens, and he speeds his pace up. Dizzy, I let my head fall once more.

Before I know it, he is easing me off his shoulder, and placing me on the bed. I gasp out a breath and my chest heaves.

"What the fuck is wrong with these elves?" he grits out. I watch him light the fire, and then he begins pacing.

A fierce ache pulses within me as Vann walks away, his frustration palpable. I watch him, my heartbeat felt in my breasts, belly, and sex. The memory of his touch sends shivers down my spine.

"Vann," I call out softly, my voice barely above a whisper as I sit up unsteadily on the bed. He stops in his tracks, turning to face me. Those silver eyes that remind me of metal back home. I love to see them.

"Stop pacing and come here," I demand.

"This isn't right," he mutters, brushing hair out of his eyes. "None of this is right."

"What?" I demand, oversensitive. The wound of being not chosen surges within me. "Not right because I'm not your mate?"

My eyes fill with tears, and it is a dreadful thing to feel while aroused. Like I'm getting torn in half.

He freezes, then immediately comes to my side. "Oh gods, no Arlet. I'm sorry. I meant that..."

I reach for him.

"Come here," I say. The heat is so intense, it has gone from pleasurable to painful. My thighs rub together, and they slide with ease.

"Vann, please," I implore. I want to scream, to jump into ice water. "Help me."

He freezes, then turns. His chest rises and falls once, and then he comes to my side.

"Firelocks, I should've realized there was something wrong with the wine. This isn't you—this heat. Forgive me. I should've picked up on something when Theren kept going on and on about heat and fire," he says, holding my hand to his icy cheek.

I want to cry. His eyes flutter closed when I brush my fingers along his jaw.

He smooths his thumb over my knuckles, the gesture soothing and electric at the same time. "We should never have drunk anything that wasn't water. I won't let this happen again."

Another pulse of heat sweeps over me. I rock forward, desperate for a bit of friction. I trusted him so much.

He once had the power to break me, and he refused. He is safe. He has spent the last month teaching me how to trust.

I wanted to feel that connection on a deeper level. Wanted it to sizzle in the air between us. Wanted to give him pieces of me to care for.

But he is right—this isn't normal. I'd been heated all night. Something was off.

Except, this isn't the first time I'd been aroused by him. That he'd made my thighs slick and my lower stomach ache hollow.

But I didn't know how to do this.

"Vann—" I start, and a part of me can't believe I'm about to ask him, to beg him to come to me. To slide his hands up my legs and get me off. My head swims with sensation and fantasy. "I think I want the kiss now."

"Arlet," he growls. "No—your mind is altered. I would be taking advantage."

I suck in a sharp breath. "But what if I ask you to come to me, to put your hands on my body?"

"The heat will pass soon, Firelocks."

I focus on breathing and close my eyes. "It will pass soon?" I pant.

He nods. "Yes."

"And you won't touch me?"

"No," he says. "But I will stay if you want me to. Or—"

"Stay," I choke out. Reaching for his hands, I cling to him so tightly, it must hurt. "Tell me a story."

"I don't like telling stories," he says.

"Please? I need something to distract me—" a sharp burn licks at my stomach.

"Fine, I can tell you a story. I'll make it romantic, just for you," he says, sitting back so that he can face me on the bed.

"Once upon a stone," Vann starts, his voice low, "there was a man with an empty chest. His heart was gone, *traded away,* and wasted through tragedy. So he walked through life, untouched by warmth or wonder and bound only by duty, until the day he met a woman. A beautiful woman."

I hold my breath, my gaze locked on his face.

"He thought she was fragile," Vann continues, his eyes flicking to mine. "But he was wrong. She was fierce, and fought him when he acted like an ass. Everyone thought he hated her, even him."

The dim light reflects in his silver eyes, soft and searching. "But, in reality, he was afraid of her. Furious at her kindness and calming demeanor. More than any war or monster, she threatened the cold future he'd built for himself. Of course, that all changed when he found out she was in danger."

My mind is fully homed onto his words.

“Then what?”

“He followed her. She made him feel a lot of things, though it hurt like getting crushed by a fucking boulder. Then, slowly, it stopped hurting so much, not because of magic, but because of her. Through the way she saw the world. You see, she stopped looking at the world with fear. She found wonder.”

Vann’s mouth tilts into a small, crooked smile. “The fool watched as the woman who had only lived for others began to live for herself. It inspired him—made him want to live, too.”

The desire ebbs so harshly that I double over in pain. It takes a second for me to come to, but I find Vann leaning over me when I do.

I wince. Then ask, “Why was this man without a heart? Is that an expression or...?”

Vann’s expression shifts, the humor slipping away like mist burned off by the morning sun. His jaw tightens.

“It is literal. He traded it,” he says softly. “Long ago.”

The flames crackle, casting flickering shadows across his sharp features. I swallow against the lump in my throat.

“For what?” I ask, though I’m not sure I want to know.

Vann’s eyes return to mine, glacier-bright and filled with something raw and unspoken. "For a love he wasn't supposed to have. A promise made in a moment of myopic devotion." His voice dips lower, rougher. "Now, he's torn in half—haunted by a woman who no longer lives, and drawn to one he shouldn't be allowed to want."

The fire crackles. My breath catches. I don’t know what to say.

“Is that story real?” I manage.

“Are any stories real?” he responds. “You read quite a lot of them.”

I think for a second, but he interrupts my addled mind.

“Do you feel more like yourself yet?” Vann asks abruptly.

I open my mouth, trying to think back to the story, to my questions, but they become thin. Flying like severed cobwebs caught in a breeze.

“What did you say?”

“I said, do you feel better?”

I swallow, then nod my head.

He smiles. "The exhaustion will come soon. Rest, for we will travel in the morning."

And then he turns away and begins preparing his bed. He's right, soon, my limbs feel heavy and my lids droop.

A voice sounds in my ear.

"If you still want this after the heat passes, you know where to find me."

I try to open my eyes, but I feel heavy. Tired. All I can manage is a soft smile.

For the first time in a long while, I think of home. Of the blanket I'd been weaving in my room. I realize what is supposed to come next.

Daniel—a rocky river I couldn't cross.

Joso—a sun-soaked meadow that wasn't meant for me.

I'd started to weave an emerald forest. Vann is like that forest—a vast place I could spend a lifetime discovering.

CHAPTER 31
VANN

The fire burns low, casting a dim, crimson glow across the stone walls in our room. Outside, gusts of wind whistle through the mountain peaks, but here, in the shelter of the guest quarters, all is quiet.

I don't sleep, despite knowing we will leave in the morning.

Instead, I sit on the ground across from the bed and watch Arlet. I draw her again, charcoal scraping against a leaf of paper.

My body thrums with energy. Anticipation.

She sleeps as she usually does—on her side, her breathing soft and even. The light catches the curve of her cheekbone, the straight angle of her nose, the strands of copper hair that have escaped her braids and now fall across the pillow.

Something deep in my gut tightens.

I remember her running away from me. She had raced through the gardens, darting behind corners and jumping over a bench. I hadn't known she could move so fast. She'd told me to go and then begged for me to stay.

It was awful, but there was one thing she repeatedly called out for in distress. One person who put her at ease. One person she could trust.

Me.

I hope she will ask for me again when her mind clears.

I had told her to do so. But, like a coward, I only whispered the words after she had gone to sleep.

I shift against the wall. Not being near her hurts.

A soft sound breaks the silence.

I tense.

Arlet's breath catches. Her brows knit together, and her hands fist the blanket. Then she bolts upright with a gasp. Her chest heaves and her cheeks are flushed.

"Firelocks?" I ask, maneuvering onto my knees. For a second, I am cautious, but her eyes are brown and beautiful, not at all black. "What's wrong?"

She looks at me.

"Vann," she says and relaxes back into the cushion. "Yes. Sorry. I just... had a bad dream."

"I understand."

We share a smile, but then her easy expression fades. Her mouth goes slack, her eyes widen, and her shoulders rise.

Mild horror. Over last night?

"Are you well?" I ask.

"Yes," she breathes, and then rolls over, facing the window and wall. "I'm tired—we should both go back to bed."

From the rise and fall of her shoulders, it looks like her breath is short. She seems totally lucid. Evasive.

"What's wrong?" I ask.

She doesn't turn. Doesn't respond for a few minutes.

"I still feel... uneasy."

I sit forward. "Uneasy how? Is the wine still—"

"No," she says quietly. Definitively.

"Are you in pain? Is it your gown? I should've removed it, but I worried about touching you during..."

I trail off and she doesn't try to finish the thought.

This is clearly a point of pain—as is perfectly reasonable after the wine.

Giving us the drug doesn't feel like it was a deliberate attack against us—it feels more like a cultural misunderstanding.

But I wanted to leave this all behind. I think she does too.

"I am so sorry. But I hope you know it wasn't your fault."

She stares at the wall for a long time. *"Not my fault. Not in control."*

Her hand comes up to press against her eyes.

"I'm so tired of this," she murmurs.

"I know."

She turns to me, and each pop and crack of the fire punctuates my nerves as we stare at each other, suspended in something that stops time.

"I feel I must thank you again," she says.

"For not taking advantage of you?" I ask, bewildered.

"For, once again, upholding my trust."

Except, I had lied. I feel awful. Like I've sunk into the floorboards.

"I don't like it here," her voice sears through my thoughts.

"I don't either. It's around midnight, judging by the moon. We'll leave in the early morning, and then, we'll find your witches and go home," I say. "Just a few hours, Firelocks. Just—"

"Will you hold me?"

Relief floods over shoulders and down my arms. Without hesitation, I crawl over and climb onto the bed. Once there, I pull her against my shoulder.

Her skin is a normal temperature, not fevered like it had been last night. I let out a relieved breath as she presses her face into my chest.

"I'm here," I whisper, cradling the back of her head. "I've got you."

Her slender arms wrap around me, and her nails dig into my back. The scent of her hair, lavender and wood, fills my senses.

Her breathing slows, a soft rhythm that lulls me into the warmth of the moment. She shifts her body, curling into my lap like she's finally finding a place where she belongs. The blanket falls to the side. Firelight flickers and dances over her dress. And soon, it's just us. Arlet and Vann. Firelocks, and her sky.

There is utter abandon in how she holds onto me.

How could I have known that we would be here one day? That all the struggles, the misunderstandings, the walls we built between us

—would fall away like the blanket had, leaving two people who needed each other?

I'd been a fool for fighting her, for pushing her away when, all along, we could've had some version of this—this peace. I could've held her a long time ago. But I hadn't known how to let go, how to trust. And now...

She lifts her head. Her eyes meet mine. Then she flushes.

"Hostia," she winces. "I remember a few things, from before I fell asleep."

Me too. I remember how she smelled—sweat, heat, and something raw that lingered in the air. Gods, I can only imagine how embarrassing that must've felt for her. She's always put in twice the effort, fighting to keep a tight grip on the world around her, striving to make sense of it all.

Letting go of control is worlds apart from losing it. One feels like a gift, the other a violation.

When I look down at her, I wonder what exactly she's remembering.

"Put it from your mind, Arlet. It was the wine."

She sneaks another glance at me. "The story..."

I go back to holding my breath. Why had I told her that?

"It was lovely. Thank you," she whispers.

"You're welcome," I murmur, brushing my hand over her hair.

We stay like that for a long time, but she doesn't move. She doesn't go back to sleep, either.

Then she says the words I never thought I'd hear.

"There was something else you said—That if I still wanted you when I woke, I only needed to ask."

Heat floods through me. I am only aware of the places where our bodies are pressed together.

I swallow thickly, and pull back. She looks up at me with bright eyes.

"Aren't you tired?" I ask.

A dozen other reasons this is a bad idea parade through my mind. Adra, her curse, Teo, Estela, her hope for a child, matehood...

"Vann," she starts. "You seem to understand me. This journey has been hard. But right now, I am just me. You have to know—You must know that I care for you. Yesterday," she swallows, "wasn't the first time I wanted you."

I listen, repeating each word in my mind, as if to memorize her phrases. I scramble for my excuses, the ones that have served me well.

But she is warm. Soft. And, somehow, completely at my mercy. That level of confidence is rare. Precious. She deserves to know how sweetly I would honor that.

When she shifts in my arms, everything but two, bold words fade.

Fuck it.

I don't need excuses anymore. Not with her.

"Are you asking me?" I retort.

"What would you do if I was?"

I wait for her to look away, but she doesn't.

"You're staring," I murmur.

Her lips part, but she doesn't respond. Her gaze flits to my mouth, then back to my eyes. Her breath is sharp and shallow and quick.

"You do this from time to time," I murmur. "Watch me like you're trying to figure out what I am. Like you're unraveling a tapestry thread by thread." I tilt my head. "What do you hope to find?"

She swallows hard. "You're hard to read."

"Or perhaps," I drawl, "I'm not and you're simply afraid of what you see."

Her breath catches.

"Can I touch you?"

Her chest rises and falls.

Once.

Twice.

"Yes."

I dip my head, my breath fanning over her exposed neck.

"Good."

Letting go of her torso, I shift to the edge of the bed and she moves so her legs straddle my lap. She looks at me. Watching, again.

She still wears the gown from the night before, and my fingers graze over rough fabric, trailing up her thighs. Her pulse flutters at the hollow of her throat.

I can see it from here.

Then she draws her bottom lip between her teeth.

"I'm not afraid of you, Vann. If that's what you're implying."

"Maybe not of my blade, but you fear something. Maybe you fear to know what I think when you speak? What I feel when you look at me like that." I reach up, brushing a strand of hair behind her ear. My fingers linger at her jaw, thumb tracing the soft curve. "What runs through my mind when you bite your lip the way you're doing right now."

Her teeth release her bottom lip instantly, but it's too late. The damage is done.

"What do you mean?" she chokes out, breathless.

My thumb slides across her mouth, catching the faint warmth of where she'd been worrying the skin. I know she likes the written word. Likes it when I quote the poets. I can do that.

"For what feels like eternity, I have endured as my eyes seek you out."

Her eyes flutter closed.

"Arlet, if you still want what you wanted last night, I will be the warmth of the sun on a winter morning, the kind you didn't realize you were missing until it touches your skin." I splay my fingers over her stomach, and she gasps. "I will be the moment when the avalanche tumbles down the mountain—unyielding, just for you."

I press my teeth into the shell of her ear, barely enough to hurt.

"Last night, you begged me to kiss you. To make you come."

She freezes.

"Is that what you are asking from me now?"

Her eyes flutter open and closed. She threads her arms around my neck. "Yes."

A low sound escapes me—not quite a growl, not quite a laugh.

I reach out to cup behind her neck, guiding her mouth toward mine. I give her time to pull away. A chance to deny the electricity crackling across our skin. But she doesn't move.

“No hands between us tonight,” I practically purr.

When our lips meet, it's slow. Soft. A brush of breath and warmth, like the first touch of a flame to dry kindling. My body hums, arranging and rearranging my very essence to watch in awe. Her hands rise to my shoulders, tentative at first, but then her fingers dig into the muscles there, pulling me closer.

I oblige.

The kiss deepens. Her mouth parts beneath mine, and I taste her. Sweet, like sunshine. Her sigh melts into me as my free hand slides around her waist, anchoring her to me.

She shifts on the bed, her thighs spreading wider as I pull her closer. My body presses between her legs, and she gasps as I tear at the laces on the back of her dress.

Our lips crash together again. Heat burns my skin, but I don’t push away. I want more.

Her dress slides down her chest, and I take my time. Savoring. Exploring.

I’d already seen her bare, but a man didn’t tire of seeing a goddess twice. Especially in this context. One where she wanted me.

My hand slides over her ribcage, my thumb grazing the underside of her peaked breast.

"Arlet," I murmur against her lips. “I need you to answer one last question.”

“All right,” she says. Pliable in my grip. It makes my cock painfully hard.

“How do I make you come?”

She blinks, flushing harder. Then she squirms.

“Arlet,” I grunt when she brushes against my length, rocking once. White light fills the edges of my vision, but I don’t lose sight of her. Her brow, her neck, her eyes. They are warm and vulnerable and *worried.*

“There was a time when all I knew of you was gleaned through quiet observation. But we’ve moved past that. We talk—*of everything.”*

“Just do what you like,” she says quickly.

I shake my head, and put a finger under her chin, tilting her gaze to mine.

"No." The tip of my digit trails over her jaw. "No. That's not how this works."

Her eyes fill with tears. "But I... can't."

I keep tight pressure on her hip to remind her that all of this is safe. Then I notice when she moves to cover herself.

Ah. Her state of undress. She would feel more comfortable if I joined her.

Pulling my braid over my shoulder, I yank out the leather tie and let hair unwind. She watches, eyes shining. Then I pull my shirt over my head, letting it fall to the bed.

"Of all the things I've observed, the thing that has always made me the most sad is knowing that you deny yourself the most. You hide bits of yourself in plain sight. I can work with that, but we only get one first time. So tell me. It would be a gift."

Her bare chest rises once, causing her collarbones to become more prominent. The back of my knuckle traces one. *Lovely*.

"In the past, I have spoken," she says.

"But your partner didn't listen."

She shakes her head, agreeing.

"Do you think I would be so cruel?"

She blinks, warding the tears. "Well—no. I don't think so."

I pull her forward, giving her a moment to adjust to how we feel pressed together. My skin. My hands on her.

Our breath.

Rise, fall. Rise, fall.

"I want to be... overwhelmed," she breathes then stops. "I like pressure. Abandon. Surrender."

I muzzle my nose into the side of her neck. "Those are vague words." I graze my teeth against the column of her throat. "Be specific."

A shudder ripples through me when her hands tighten on my shoulders. Sizzling energy moves back and forth between us, crackling across my ribs.

"My mind is cluttered, full of work and life and worry. I want to be free of that with you. I want your touches to rip me away from my life. Be gentle, or don't. Just... take charge."

My mouth goes dry.

"You are so fucking perfect," I murmur into her hair. "But *you refuse to tell me exactly what is going through your mind."*

She lets out a stuttered breath. "I'm afraid."

"We go as far as you want."

She shudders against me. The foundations of her walls crack in the distance, and she seeks refuge right here. As she should.

"If there is one thing I am almost sure of, it is that you know how to do this. But I need you..." I hang on each word as she shifts her hips in my lap with another acclimating touch, "to make me stop. Hold me in place. Tie me to the bed. Force the world to go quiet. Give me a space where I can enjoy existing."

The heat pulses between us. Insistent. Maddening. It lifts me up, higher. Bolder. Something rests over us. A hum.

I had been right. I had read her like the back of my own hand—it was as if she'd been made just for me.

She misinterprets my silence. "I know it sounds strange—"

"No."

"—I've just always been like this. I shared it with Daniel and then... you know. Sometimes I wish I could replace those memories with happy moments. Ones that I could control."

"I think it is beautiful. I understand."

She pulls back, flushed. "Wait. What? You don't think me strange? *I think I'm strange* for wanting this. Sometimes I feel so scared. Scared of what I am, what I did, what I could do. Never having control again. But over the time I've spent with you, I've realized nothing scares me more than never being known completely. I want you... to be the one to know me."

I kiss her again. "Then let me. Let me help you fight the monsters. Let me patch up that scar. Do you want me to hold your wrists?"

She nods. "And my legs."

A smile spreads over my mouth.

"I will take care of you. Right now, you are mine to break. Mine to put back together."

I pull out the pins in her hair, letting it fall down. She watches me with wonder. Then I lock both of her wrists in one hand, and hold them above her head. My hand is so large it wraps around more than her wrist, covering her palms and fingers too. She tries to move, testing the strength of my grip.

"Is this still all right?"

Somehow. She manages to thread her small finger through mine and I stop breathing.

"I will tell you if I need you to stop."

Another promise.

Trust. It ripples off her in waves, giving me an endless supply of intoxicating power.

I guide her backward onto the mattress. Her hair fans across the pillow, and for a moment, I can only stare. The firelight paints her skin in shades of gold and rose, highlighting the delicate curve of her collarbone and the rapid rise and fall of her bare chest.

Under my gaze, she holds her breath.

"You are beautiful. Please don't forget to breathe."

And then I dip down to kiss her again. Starting at her throat, I touch each part of her arms, shoulders, and ribs, feeling the softness and the muscle, and listening to her perfect heart.

Rising, I use my shirt to tie her hands to the corner of the bed.

She sucks in a sharp breath, but doesn't tell me to stop. So, I push her dress down to where it snags on her hips, I trace words in her freckled skin that she would never identify. Sweet words in my language.

"You don't know what you do to me," I say hoarsely against her navel. "What you have always done to me."

"I trust you," she whispers, repeating those words once again.

Gods help me. I will follow her to the ends of the earth.

As the fire crackles and casts flickering shadows across the room, I continue my reverent exploration of her body—mapping every curve and angle. Then finally, I use my tail to push her dress to the floor.

I let myself take her in with total, undeterred admiration. My hand smooths over the funny little patch of curly hair that points toward her sex.

"Open."

Her legs shift, giving me a perfect, undeterred view of her glistening heat.

Fuck.

My tail moves forward, wrapping around her ankles as I watch her arch. She gasps as my thumb grazes the sensitive skin of her inner thigh. Her eyes flutter closed, a fresh flush painting her cheeks a rosy hue. The room is filled with the heady scent of arousal, mingling with the crackling fire that casts dancing shadows on the walls.

I lean in to capture her mouth in a searing kiss, pouring all the longing and desire I've held back into the fervent meeting of our mouths. The power of the moment sends shivers down my spine.

With practiced ease, I divest myself of my own pants, letting them fall to the floor in a forgotten heap. The cool air kisses my heated skin, but it's nothing compared to the scorching gaze she directs at me.

Heat, blessed heat, after an endless season of cold.

Then I cover her body with mine to kiss her again. Her neck. Her shoulders. One for each freckle. She gasps at my onslaught, writhing against her restraints.

"What do you prefer, mouth or fingers?" I murmur into her ears. The peaks of her nipples scratch against my chest.

"Fingers," she breathes, decided. Unapologetic. Gods, if I'd known she'd be decisive in this moment... my grip tightens.

Bringing my hand back to her curls, I trace the curves where her thighs meet her pelvis. And then, I seek out her warmth. The slickness coats my fingers. I take extra care to watch her movements. I look for where she takes a sharp breath, and what makes her squirm.

"Are you trying to torture me?" she chokes out after a second.

"You, my lovely Arlet, do not get to dictate how fast or slow this moment passes," I growl. "And right now, you are doing so well."

She freezes, and then a fresh wave of slickness coats my fingers.

"Nisera Hhalen," I murmur. "Beautiful woman."

She beams, and then I reward her by inserting one finger. She arches up, crying out.

Hmm. Sensitive. So beautifully sensitive.

I press my forehead to hers, breathing her in.

Then I use my thumb and finger to work. It only takes moments, for how tightly she was wound, for her to come apart around me.

I feel it. The way she flutters and dances. The shift in the air.

The feeling of guilt doesn't come, leaving me free from the pain. I just look at her, mouth parted.

I kiss her again. Fiercely. Our tongues tangle. She bites me. I groan.

"Again?" I ask.

"Yes."

It turns out that her body is made for mine, because I barely have time to insert a second finger before she spasms again.

She comes so hard she goes taut as a bow above the bed. My chest floods with pleasure. My cock strains against my under shorts, and I shift against the bed, enjoying the little bits of friction I can glean.

I haven't experienced anything like this ever.

The years alone, waiting, what were they for? I needed a woman under me.

I needed Arlet.

"It's like you've been waiting for me to do that since we met," I say into her throat. "You're soft and slick for me, Firelocks. Like a rainstorm beating on stone. Your body tells me stories your mouth would never dare utter."

She pants.

"Is this enough showing?" I nip at her neck, almost without thinking.

"Vann." Hesitation lingers in the last bits of her voice.

"Yes...?" I coax, still not thinking as I lavish wet kisses over her shoulder, down her sternum and up to a breast.

She takes a deep breath and her soft body goes rigid. I pull back immediately.

Her eyes glisten as she looks up at me. Her cheeks are flushed, and there is something akin to regret in her eyes.

And then tears fall down her temple.

“Firelocks, why do you cry?”

"Because this might be the first time I've ever felt completely, utterly known by another."

“I see you, and gods, it’s the most breathtaking sight.”

A smile breaks through her tears.

I shift our positions immediately. Propping her up, I reach for the folded nightgown she’s worn the past few nights and begin to slip it on, threading her arms through it.

She lets me do it all, and it fuels this need in my gut—an instinct to care for her, to be the sole person who would be hers.

A darker, more possessive thought creeps in. That all her passion and pleasure would be mine alone. As if I could make up for time lost being angry when we could’ve been this.

I would try.

I curl my body around her. Despite the moment of hesitation before, she pushes into me.

“Thank you,” she whispers.

I press my nose into her hair, loving how it brushes against my chest.

“Tavra sathen ri, fel avel'dras mivara.” I say into her essence, breathing it deep.

Sleepy eyes look up at me. “I’ve given you back a... piece of yourself?”

I smile down at her, throwing a leg over her hips.

“Yes. And now you own it, too.”

CHAPTER 32
VANN

I had fallen asleep almost immediately after Arlet and I finished. But my long-needed rest did not last long.

Arlet thrashes in my arms and I am forced back into consciousness.

"What's wrong?" I demand. I instinctively tighten my grip around her waist, pulling her closer as her body quakes.

At first, I think the threat is external. I seek out my cleaver—see it resting against the table—and press my hand to Arlet's chest.

Her breath comes in shallow bursts.

I sit up, still trying to make sense of what is happening. She falls flat on the bed.

Then, her eyes snap open, black and unblinking, and her voice changes.

"This is your last warning: let me take her."

Words spill out her mouth, cold and malevolent, as if someone else is speaking through her.

Fuck.

This has never happened, but I recognize the lilt of an elven accent. *Arion*. It has to be.

I snarl.

"She belongs to me now,"

My chest tightens. Fuck. *No.*

"Arlet?" I say, positioning myself over her immobile body.

"If you do not, she will leave a path of destruction in your wake. I will find her, no matter where you run. Any city that harbors you will burn."

The Elf King's presence moves through her like poison. When I uncover a stiff leg, I find her curse mark glowing.

It's activated and letting him in.

"Come on, Arlet," I growl. I refuse to let Arion poison what we've just built.

I shake her.

No response.

Then she kicks me. Her fingers curl into claws.

No.

I need her back—my Arlet—before that darkness hurts one of us.

Without any other options, I grab her shoulders and lean in. My lips find hers in a desperate, searing kiss.

Her body goes still. Then, slowly, like breaking through a fog, her trembling eases, and her eyes return to normal. She blinks, waking from the nightmare.

"Thank Endu," I breathe.

She pants through the pain. Her eyes find mine. They are sad. Tired.

So heartbreakingly weary.

"We need to go," she says, practically flinging off the bed. "Before it's too late. We can't let the city suffer."

I stand, trying to grab her wrist. "But we are supposed to leave in a few hours. We—"

"*We have to go now.* Arion is searching for me. He will find this place, and the whole city will be destroyed. Dragon's Reach has been hidden for hundreds of years and I will be the one to ruin it."

"They have glamor," I say. "We should go to Theren."

She shakes her head.

"No. *No more people.* No more permission. We need to leave. I need this to be over."

I grab her wrist as she freezes, finally looking up at me. I know she is afraid, but this is not wise.

"But we can only do so on the back of a dragon."

She takes a deep breath. "And it's a good thing they spent a day teaching us to ride."

"What? You can't believe that one riding lesson is enough to prepare us."

She rakes her fingers through her hair.

"Vann. Listen to me. When the darkness came, I saw Arion. Was in the room with him for a few moments. Remember the men that came to get me before we arrived? There are more. Two hundred archers. I can't—" she breaks off. "I don't want anyone else to die for me. We need to go."

I watch her, biting my lip and thinking. Enduvida's relationship with the elves was varied at the moment. We didn't need any more enemies.

If we stay and risk Arion's men finding us, then we could find ourselves in trouble with both Selric, and by extension, our only ally. Mrath.

But we couldn't leave this place without saying anything. Not after they'd welcomed us as a guest.

We need their blessing.

"All right, we will leave. But we *must* tell Selric."

She starts to protest, but I shake my head, cutting her off. "There is no reason why we shouldn't. They are not friends with Arion. They deserve to know what is happening."

Somehow, I find her in my arms again, seeking refuge. "I won't put you in unnecessary danger.

She takes a deep breath, pressing into me, and I can remember every moment we shared just hours before.

Does she feel how the air between us is different? Realize I can't stop touching her?

"Very well."

I hesitate, then say, "Get dressed."

She does so quickly, pulling on her tunic and boots before

reaching for her coat, the heavy fabric settling around her shoulders. She slips on her gloves, fingers still trembling.

I do the same, tugging my shirt on, donning my coat and securing the gloves.

We grab our packs. Without a word, we sling them over our shoulders, and leave our room.

The moonlight cuts through the cliffs as we step into the cold night. Our footsteps are muffled on the cobblestone streets. The Vaer'Tharion's mansion is nearby. We'd just had the party there hours ago. It's so different now. Dark. Clean. Silent.

As we approach the metal entrance, I find one guard. He spots us immediately, assessing us before his hand hovers near the hilt of his sword.

"What's your business?" he demands.

"We need to speak with Vaer'Tharion Selric," I say in my mediocre elvish. "It's a matter of life and death."

The guard hesitates, then enters the mansion, motioning for us to wait. Moments later, the door creaks open, and we are let inside. Selric awaits in a long, golden robe.

"Our guests—what is the trouble?"

"Vaer'Tharion," I saw with a bow. "Forgive the late hour, but it is urgent. My wife's curse. It has been activated. Arion spoke through her mouth."

Selric's expression darkens. "What did the snake say?"

"That he will come and burn down any city that harbors her."

The Vaer'Tharion sneers, his dark brown hair falling into his face. "Arion can not find us. He is a blind fool."

I shake my head. "We should leave. Now, not in the morning. We do not wish to endanger you or your people."

Selric steps forward, his eyes sharp and calculating. "I understand. But my son's savior is not leaving without proper provisions." He turns to a nearby attendant, his voice commanding. "Get the supplies ready. Dried meat and water. *A map.*"

The attendant nods quickly and disappears.

Selric begins to speak so fast, I can't pick up more than a few words. He talks to the guard, and if I didn't know better, it would almost sound like he was arguing.

The guard leaves, too, leaving the three of us alone in the room.

Selric breathes through his nose.

"If you had not saved my son, I would not be so kind in this moment," he informs.

I bow, and Arlet follows suit.

"We are grateful. We will not forget your generosity."

The first attendant that he had sent to retrieve supplies enters from a side room. They are stored in a medium-sized, woven sack.

Selric gestures for the man to hand it to me.

I take it, bowing again.

Then the High Warden looks at the entrance as it pushes open, letting in cold air. A guard waits for us.

"All is ready," Selric announces. "You will communicate with Mrath when you are finished, and we will make arrangements to meet again."

"Gods, that was fast. Faster than I would've imagined. Our thanks again."

Selric frowns. "Move quickly. And... thank you for the warning."

I take Arlet's hand, and begin to pull her out of the hall. We exit the mansion and step back into the cold night.

The pair of guards escort us to the edge of the city, where the high walls give way to the open landscape. They present us with the gear we'd used for riding lessons—dragonscale riding leathers and spectacles of some sort to protect our eyes.

The wind bites at our skin as we change. I put on my things first, and then help Arlet, shielding her from the eyes of the men. Something I fear I enjoy far too much.

Soon, a dragon appears in the sky. The emerald green beast is flying toward us, her wings slicing through the air with powerful strokes.

Familiar nerves build up inside of me.

The attendant who'd gone ahead meets us in the clearing, leading the emerald dragon down to place on a larger saddle.

"Come," he barks out.

Just as we prepare to climb onto the emerald dragon, the ground beneath us rumbles. A deep, thunderous growl cuts through the air, and a golden light glows faintly from the shadows.

Then, the massive form emerges completely from the darkness.

I freeze as the dragon flies into view, her molten eyes gleaming with an intensity I recognize. Her golden scales shimmer, and her black horns twist elegantly from her head. Her claws, dark as obsidian, gleam in the dim light.

She moves with force, pushing the emerald dragon aside. The other dragon staggers, nearly tumbling off the cliff. Seraph growls, her wings flaring slightly in warning as she asserts her territory.

Arlet steps forward, and the dragon retracts her wings. My fearless Firelocks extends her hand, and the creature bows its head. When flesh makes contact with scale, the dragon huffs.

"Seraph," I hear her say.

I turn to the guard. "Is this not the one who said she would no longer fly?"

The men watch.

"Yes."

I press my lips together. Eyes burning.

Arlet had a way of bringing people back from the darkness.

The men start moving. One of them takes our packs, and then secures them tightly to one of Seraph's legs.

"Is it all right to take her even though you had brought another?" I ask.

One nods. "If a dragon has a preference for a rider, it is against our customs to deny the beast."

The dragon's head is still hovering near Arlet. Watching. Studying.

The bond between them is palpable.

Once the saddle is placed correctly, Arlet climbs onto her back. I laugh, amused by her ease around monsters, then follow. I mount behind her, my heart racing as Seraph's muscles coil beneath us, preparing for flight.

Here we go.

She walks closer and closer to the edge.

I try not to look down.

Arlet grips the reins firmly, her posture calm, as if she were born to do this. Without a word, Seraph pushes off the ground. Her wings beat powerfully, the air rushing around us as we rise higher into the sky. The city below shrinks into the distance.

The wind howls past, but Arlet doesn't flinch. Her connection to Seraph is steady, unwavering, as we soar higher and higher.

We don't look back.

CHAPTER 33
ARLET

The world is ice and gold.

The wind howls against us, cutting mercilessly through my clothes. It numbs my skin until I can no longer tell if I am shivering or simply becoming one with the air.

The only warmth is trapped between me and Vann. He sits behind me, his arms locked tightly around my waist, his chest solid against my back. With him, I am safe. Cared for.

It's given me a much-needed reserve of confidence. Something necessary as we have been flying for hours.

Even when my back aches and my flesh burns under my enchanted clothes, I love flying. Seraph is a marvel in and of herself. She trusted me enough to take flight after months on the ground.

A part of me had worried she would not be strong enough, but her wings carve through the dawn, carrying us beyond anything I have ever known.

I adjust my riding goggles and look down. Beneath us, the continent unfurls in an endless, breathtaking sprawl—there are dense forests stretching into oblivion, rivers glistening like silver threads, and mountains rising to be crowned in mist.

We even pass over the Enduar Mountains. They rise up, the black peaks slicing into the sky. I long to return with Vann at my side.

Soon.

"Come back to us whole," Liana had told me upon leaving.

That is exactly what I am doing.

King Arion had used dark magic to twist my fate to suit his desires. The curse inside me is a leash, yanking me toward a master I never chose.

I am tired of being a tool.

A would-be wife to a king I hate. A vessel to bear something I cannot create.

So I will sever any connection between us.

I grit my teeth as the wind slashes against my skin, but I don't lower my head. I don't shrink back. Let it cut me. Let it freeze me. I will not be molded by their will.

The gods can demand. The kings can claim. The curse can pull *but I will not bow again.*

I lift my chin, defying the wind that howls around me. I want to rip the sky apart. I want to scream.

I want to be *free* again.

Eventually, the golden brilliance of sunrise washes over the clouds, spilling in great waves of radiance that bathe everything in shimmering warmth. Below us, the world stretches impossibly far, above oceans that crinkle and ripple like fabric carelessly thrown over a table.

"It's beautiful!" I shout over my shoulder, my voice barely carrying over the wind.

The arms around me tighten, a firm and steady anchor as the air rushes past, trying to steal me away. My head tips back, caught in the sheer expanse of it all—the vast, endless sky, and the golden light spilling over the clouds like molten fire.

"I will be if you stop squirming," Vann growls, his voice warm despite the gruffness. "You need to be careful!"

I laugh, remembering the way he held me last night. Bound me. Freed me in his care. It was the sweetest gift I've ever been given. Being around him now makes me feel bolder, happier.

Relieved that this will all be over soon.

"Vann?"

"Yes?" he calls, his voice rumbling through my ribs. His hands tighten just a fraction around my waist as Seraph crests another cloud, her great golden wings cutting through the endless white.

"We're just having fun, Vann. This is good!" I shout over the wind, my voice light with exhilaration.

Vann hesitates, his grip tightening for a moment. "It will be good when we land."

I laugh, feeling the rush of the air. "I don't want it to end."

He doesn't respond, but I can feel his tension behind me. Then, without warning, I turn slightly to face him, grinning.

"Will you help me with something else?"

His eyes narrow, studying me for a moment, concern flashing in them, but I can see the spark of trust too. "Hmm."

He shouts back, "What do you have in mind?"

"I want to feel the wind through my arms. To feel like I am really the one flying."

There's a beat of silence, then he nods slowly. *"Firelocks."*

"Please?" I ask. "We've been flying for hours without problem. Seraph is safe. She's excellent at flying."

Something grumbles against my back.

"Fine."

He takes the reins from me, carefully. His tail—strong and sure—wraps around my midsection, securing me without a word.

I take a deep breath, steadying myself against the wind, and slowly, I raise my arms. My fingers stretch wide, reaching for the sky itself. The wind rushes around me, the sun now beside me, instead of above. The world spins in a blur of clouds and light.

For a moment, I feel weightless, as though I am part of the sky. The wind sings in my ears.

Vann shouts something in enduar, but his grip does not loosen. Not once.

When I let out a bird-like call to the sky, he laughs. The sound of it is full, unrestrained. It carries the joy of the moment.

I can do anything.

I know without any shadow of a doubt, we've done the right

thing. We've done something challenging. Something impossible. And, for a few moments, the sky belongs to me. To us.

A deep rumble vibrates through Seraph's massive body, her wings tilting as she rides an air current.

My arms come back down and grip the reins with him.

Vann's voice is close, low against my ear. *"Hold on."*

I barely have time to react before the sky darkens, the clouds thickening into a dark gray. The wind changes, too.

Seraph lets out a low, warning growl, her golden wings flapping uneasily.

And then, in the distance, through the gloom—I see them.

The islands.

"Vann! Look!" I call back, pointing.

Below, a great crescent-shaped mass of land sits in the dark waters, its curved form like a moon resting upon the ocean's surface. Smaller islands are clustered nearby, scattered like broken pieces of a long-destroyed celestial body.

But beyond them, on the horizon, a storm brews. Fast. The sky churns with clouds so dark they swallow the dawn's glow. Flashes of lightning slither through the abyss, illuminating the massive, spiraling heart of the storm.

Fuck. I'd been so delighted, careless, up to now. But fear stabs into my heart. I lean forward, tightening my grip.

A deep, rolling thunder shakes the air, reverberating through my ribs. Vann leans forward, his grip firm.

"We don't have much time!"

The wind howls. Beneath us, the water rolls and pitches. I spot something dark bobbing atop a blue-gray wave.

My first glimpse of the boat is almost too strange to process.

At first, I think it's debris—driftwood. But then I see the movement. The frantic scrambling.

People.

We drop closer, and the ocean rises to meet us. I make out a man.

No tail.

No ears.

Short hair.

Not just any people, but, *humans.*

I suck in a sharp breath, my mind struggling to catch up with what my eyes are telling me. *"¡Mierda!"* I exclaim. "That's a human vessel."

Vann stiffens behind me. I feel his attention shift, following my gaze downward.

"They shouldn't be here," I say, barely able to find my voice over the roar of the wind. "This is too far—there's no land for leagues. What are they doing?"

His answer is lost.

The wind screams around us, a deafening, living force, snatching the breath from my lungs. Rain lashes against me, cold as needles, and Seraph fights against the gusts with every powerful beat of her wings.

Vann's grip around me is iron.

"We should try to go higher!" I shout over the roaring wind, but even as I say it, I know it won't matter.

The storm has us now.

A sudden gust slams into Seraph's side, sending us tilting violently. My stomach drops as we spiral. My vision spins and Seraph roars.

She struggles against the wind's relentless pull. My fingers claw at the saddle straps, gripping tight, and I feel Vann shift behind me, moving with the dragon's desperate attempt to steady herself.

The storm howls, pushing, forcing, dragging us toward the unknown. The rain covers my goggles, the wind howls through my bones, and Seraph—*Seraph fights.* Her wings cut through the air with everything she has.

It isn't enough.

The sky fractures into darkness, the ocean disappearing as the storm hurtles us forward. Then—through the blur of wind and rain, something looms ahead.

Land.

A jagged, dark shape rises from the mist, cliffs lined with shadowed trees. The sea crashes violently against its base, waves clawing at the rocks, and the wind shoves us toward it without mercy.

I wipe my hands at the goggles, trying to clear my vision.

"Seraph!" I scream, and she roars in response.

Her wings snap open at the last moment, straining against the force dragging us down, and for a single second, I think she'll right herself.

Then the wind changes direction again.

The island surges closer.

We hit.

Seraph's claws scrape across rock as she lands hard, skidding over soaked earth, her great body coiling to absorb the impact. I'm thrown forward, the saddle straps biting into my skin as I clutch onto anything to keep from being hurled off.

Vann's arms tighten around me, his breath a harsh curse against my ear.

Then everything stills.

My pulse thunders in my ears. My body is frozen and my lungs burn.

We crashed, but *we made it.*

Seraph lets out long, labored breaths and curls her tail to her torso. Vann unties both of us, and helps me to slide off.

I approach the dragon's front, checking for wounds. When I try to touch her, she muzzles into my hand. Almost as if to tell me, *I am all right. Just need rest.*

The rain continues to pour, soaking through my clothes, plastering my hair to my face. Salt and wet earth fill my nose. The trees are silhouetted against flashes of lightning.

Strong hands grip me from behind, and twist me around. Vann rips off his eyewear, tossing it to the side, and then picks me up.

My tall sky-blue enduar exhales sharply, his forehead pressing against my shoulder for the briefest moment before he straightens and sets me down. His hands brush down my arms, checking, solid and sure.

"Are you right?" His voice is rough. Eyes scorching.

I swallow hard. "Yes."

Then he grabs my face and starts to kiss me, hard and slow. I pull back, just long enough to remove my goggles, then I start to kiss him too.

Adrenaline floods through me.

We are safe.

Safe.

He pulls me down into the wet sand, the roughness of it against my skin a sharp contrast to the heat between us. His kisses grow harder, deeper, like he's trying to pull every bit of the tension from my body, to erase the storm that still shakes the world around us. The rain soaks us further, but it doesn't matter. Everything feels alive, urgent, and real.

His mouth trails along my neck, my jaw, and then, once he opens my coat and shirt, my breast.

It's overwhelming, in the best way.

The world fades, leaving only the sound of our breaths, the pounding of the rain, and my beating heart. He moves against me, grinding for a second.

Gods, this was a man who knew how to fuck. Sadly, something that would have to be discovered at a later time.

Who knows how much time passes, enough for me to be hot and wet in different ways across all of my body, but he releases me.

My forehead presses to him.

"Thank the gods you are all right," I whisper.

He holds my wrist and the adrenaline starts to wear off, little by little. He closes my shirt, fingers trailing lightly over my skin

Vann finally takes his eyes off me and looks around. "We should set up camp."

I nod, "Then we should use the map to see if we can find out which island we landed on."

CHAPTER 34
VANN

The rain slows, but it does not stop. Heavy drops patter against the thick canopy above in a rhythmic beat that mingles with the distant roar of the sea.

The trees here are ancient, and their vast, gnarled trunks twist into the ground, roots coiling over one another like serpents. Their fan-like leaves spread wide, forming a dense ceiling that provides some relief from the downpour.

Mist curls through the undergrowth, carrying the mingled scents of damp earth, salt, and the sharp tang of something unfamiliar.

I stand at the edge of the tree line, staring out at the ocean. The waves are still violent, rolling and crashing against jagged cliffs, their white froth building over the sand.

I watch the water for a long time, lost in the rhythm of the storm. It seems to match the chaos inside me.

Since we'd gotten here I'd kissed Arlet. Held her. Been half mad with worry.

And... I'm not in pain. Haven't been for the last day. Something is wrong.

Behind me, Arlet tends to Seraph. She runs her hands along the dragon's golden scales, whispering words too quiet for me to hear.

The beast exhales deeply, shifting her weight, her massive wings tucking closer to her body.

I take the packs from her leg, and return to the tree line. The underbrush of the jungle is dense, forcing me to hack through it with my cleaver.

Ferns as large as shields fan out before me, slick with moisture. Vines coil around the trees, some sprouting luminous flowers that pulse faintly like captured light. The land rises unevenly, jagged stone ridges carved by time and wind. Massive boulders, covered in moss, dot the landscape too.

Behind me, I hear Arlet's soft steps through the underbrush.

There's a brief pause, then she says, "Is—are we going to be okay?"

I can hear the uncertainty in her tone and imagine the tension in her twisting hands even without seeing them.

I glance over my shoulder and meet her eyes.

"Yes. We're together, Arlet. That's what matters."

A smile tugs at her lips. I turn fully toward her now, taking her hand. I pull her closer, wrapping an arm around her shoulders. Her head rests against my chest, and I feel her breath steady.

"Vann, I need to tell you something."

I still. "All right."

"I've never had something like this before, you know," she says. "And I just want to say that maybe I had been too focused on the wrong things. Matehood—"

She stops, and my nostrils flare.

"I just want you to know I am happy to have this. With you. Here." Her hand trails over my chest. "I wouldn't have been able to do any of this without you. Please tell me if I touch you too often, I know I can be greedy."

I sigh.

"Asking for what you need is not greedy. And I am happy to be here with you too."

As I hold her, guilt hits me again—buried, but still there.

"She was your mate?"

"Yes, she was."

After what we'd done the other night, I owed Arlet the truth about Adra. But maybe... not right now.

So I bury my feelings, just for a little while longer, because she needs me.

We are so close to finding the witches, to curing her, and going home.

"Want to help me set up?" I say softly, my voice a low murmur in the still air.

She smiles up at me and nods.

I squeeze her hand and guide her over to where I've cleared a space for our tent.

One of the poles has broken on our long journey and she sets off to find a replacement while I finish reinforcing the leather. Later, after she's returned and everything is arranged as well as it can be in the muggy weather, she starts cooking, and I turn to my pack.

I pull out the map from Selric, spreading it on my bedroll to prevent it from getting too wet. The ink is faded, but the markings are still clear. I trace the lines with my finger, calculate distances, and mentally map the terrain.

I mark the island I think we've landed on, just off the coast of the Witch's Isle.

"Good news. We're not far," I say.

Her face lights up. "Really?"

I nod, showing her where I think we've landed, and then I trace the distance to the next island.

"Seraph should be fine to fly tomorrow," she says. "I think she's mostly weary from how hard we pushed ourselves yesterday."

I agree quietly as Arlet hands me a plate of preserved mushrooms and meat from Dragon's Reach. We eat in relative silence, and then we head into the tent I've prepared.

We lie down together, and, despite the heat, I pull Arlet close. She doesn't protest

"Good night, *Mi Cielo*," she murmurs.

"Your sky?" I ask, curious and slightly starved for her conversation.

She smiles. "Yes. But for my people... it's a bit more like, darling. It can be affectionate. Or sarcastic."

I laugh. "Which one would you use for me?"

She turns. "Both." Then she kisses me.

It's soft. Slow. Gentle.

The jungle outside is alive with sounds, but inside the tent, we're in our own world. Nothing more happens after the kiss and she falls asleep first, as she often does. I focus on the steady sound of her breathing as my mind races.

What we shared two nights ago had not been trivial. It had marked a colossal shift in my heart. It was the first time I'd been with a woman in so long, and it had been unlike anything I'd ever experienced. I crave it—crave her.

I want to see her arch into my touch and cry out.

But we need to sleep. And more than that... I don't deserve to have her under me until I tell her the truth.

Soon.

For tonight, rest.

Not long after we fall asleep, the calm is broken. The sound of movement breaks through the quiet—a rustle in the underbrush, followed by a low growl.

My eyes snap open, looking down at the woman in my arms. Arlet is still sleeping, with no signs of any disturbance.

Ugh. For fuck's sake, what now?

I am, quite literally, exhausted. Everything feels slower. More sluggish.

Hopefully, this is just an animal.

I reach for a knife while I hold my breath, listening.

There is definitely movement—heavy, deliberate, footsteps. Leaves shaking against each other outside our space.

Something distorts my hearing, so I creep to the front of the tent to inspect the scene. Except, the second I come into view, a thick hand grabs me.

Before I can protest, a sharp, numbing wave of magic courses through me, I feel my limbs lock, my senses fade, and my last thought is of Arlet.

Then everything goes black.

CHAPTER 35
ARLET

I wake to the scent of herbs and the murmur of voices too low to distinguish. A sharp pain across my ankle makes me hiss. My head throbs, and I blink, my vision slow to adjust.

I'm lying on something hard, barely cushioned with a rough fabric. Something marginally softer props my head up. Above me is a rough stone ceiling, lit only by the flickering glow of firelight.

Stone.

For a moment, a sense of relief hits. I'm back in a cavern, safe. My journey is over.

Except... there are no crystals, nor is there a familiar hum. Around me is bare and silent.

The realization sends a rush of panic through me. If I'm not in Enduvida, then what is this place?

I push myself up onto my elbows, feeling another sharp throb in my skull. My throat is dry. "Where—?"

Shadows dance along the walls, elongating the figures standing around the stone slab where I lay.

My heart races.

Human women. The *brujas*.

They are draped in dark robes, their faces adorned with intricate black tattoos that twist and curve like living ink.

One is closer than the others, just near my exposed feet, but they all watch. Some of their eyes are dark as pitch, others unnervingly pale. All of them are fixed on me with unsettling intent.

This is it. This is where I have been trying to reach for weeks. My breath rushes in and out of my lungs.

The woman closest to me switches her position from my ankle, to my face. Her silver-streaked hair falls in full, straight locks over her shoulders, and her face is covered with intricate markings, curling over her cheekbones and down her throat.

She pulls something from her robes, a small vial with a thin, dark liquid, and then removes the small cap with her thumb.

My brows furrow, and she grabs my face. Before I can protest, she jerks on my chin and pours the bitter liquid inside.

I sputter.

"Swallow," she commands, her voice smooth. "This will be worse if you don't."

I do, blinking slowly.

The others hang back, apart from me and the witch. They watch her, and I wonder if she is their leader.

Her expression is unreadable, but there's a tension in the air, as if they are waiting for something.

"What did you give me?" I ask.

Silence.

If it had been poison, would my Fuegorra have detected it? It should have glowed, right? It does for many other things. It had worked last night, as my inner thighs are much less sore than they had been while flying.

But there is no heat, no rush of blood, no glowing light leaking through the fabric of my shirt.

Another possibility creeps up—that whatever she'd given me could inhibit the gem in my chest. I look for weapons around the room and see none.

"What is your name?" the woman asks.

"Arlet." My voice cracks, hoarse and weak. "Where is the man I travel with? We brought a dragon as well."

The woman's gaze sharpens, and her posture stiffens. "Your

companion and steed are being restrained." Her words are clipped, tight.

"Restrained?" I push myself to sit up fully, ignoring the dizziness that pulls at me. "No. Please. We are not a threat."

A different woman scoffs, arms crossed over her chest. "Dragons have voracious appetites and your man... He is an elf, and we do not harbor spies."

Confusion crashes into me like a wave.

"Spies? He's neither spy nor elf."

The leader looks away, waving her hand carelessly. "He looks like one of *them*."

"He is an enduar—a troll. His skin is blue," I insist.

"Perhaps he is sick."

"He has a tail! And there are no marks of the living wood on him," I continue.

The leader shakes her head, cutting me off. "Human, I do not know where you come from, but you seem confused. Elves have been testing our barriers for three days. Our sisters have caught them at the edges of the islands, searching for weaknesses. And now you arrive, with an elf-not-elf at your side. What is your true intent?"

More memories bubble up, this time of Arion using my body to kill. To run. To leave. And then, to speak.

I will find her, no matter where you run. Any city that harbors you will burn.

A wave of cold fear settles in my chest, but my tongue is loose. Compelled to speak.

"I mean no harm," I say quickly. "We came for help." I feel my heart pounding against my ribs. "I wasn't sent here to attack you."

The witches exchange quick glances. The leader leans down. Her gaze is piercing.

"Help?" she repeats, as if testing the word. "Or are you here as a scout, sent to find weakness in our defenses?"

Normally, I would hesitate, but whatever they have given me loosens my tongue again.

"I was cursed," I confess, the words coming slowly but resolutely. "By an elf, *the Elf King*. He wants me to be his wife. He gave me an object with dark magic—magic like what the witches on the mainland use. It burned that mark onto my ankle, and now it... it makes me run to him after I sleep. Makes me dangerous. I came to have it removed so I can sever his hold on me.

A heavy silence fills the cavern. The witches' expressions shift, their eyes flicking over the dark mark on my leg, which is already burning faintly.

The leader leans in, her fingers brushing lightly over my ankle. The contact sends a sharp jolt of pain up my leg, and I wince, pulling back instinctively.

"We have been studying this," she says sharply. "You carry the taint of Abhartach, but we have muted it."

The words freeze me. "You have?" I manage, my voice small.

"For a short time, nothing more. The demon god is not welcome here."

"Is he welcome anywhere?" I ask before thinking. It seemed to me that he was hated by most, but a necessary tool of power.

Another witch steps forward. I am surprised to see she is considerably older than the rest. Her hair is streaked with gray, and her hands are weathered, rough from a lifetime of work.

"Abhartach. The betrayer, the hungering void. His power seeps into the veins of kings and gods alike." She gestures to the ink scrawled across her throat. "There were some of our sisters who strayed from our path, turned their backs on the sisterhood. They were bound to him. The last we heard, they fell."

"Then you're not like them?" The question slips from my lips before I can stop it, and the witch who spoke before narrows her eyes at me.

"No," she answers, her voice thick with something ancient. "Unlike those who serve him willingly, we funnel what remains through our own goddess. A human goddess."

Her words land heavily. A flicker of recognition hits me like a jolt. "Ashra," I say quietly, unbidden—the name of one of Estela's patron deities.

The leader's expression darkens at the mention of the goddess. "Yes. But Ashra's power is worn thin. She is not enough to shield us from the gods who wish to claim us. Or the men who seek to cross our barrier. Your curse is a complication we cannot afford. We should cast you away."

The words hit me like a physical blow. My chest goes concave.

I remember being in the Sisterhood's Enclave.

"What if we get to the island and the witches refuse?" I had asked Mrath.

That is what they are doing right now.

"Then you had better learn how to be persuasive, little ruby."

A rush of heat floods my body, but I keep my voice steady, focused.

"You've been here, hidden away, untouched by the world for how long?" I ask, my voice low and fierce. "While I, and those I've known, were slaves. You've had your peace, your safety. The only time those I live with have seen dark magic in recent years is from your sisters. The tainted ones you mention. It is because of them that I am here at all."

The leader's eyes flicker with protest, but she doesn't interrupt.

"Please," I continue, rising to a sitting position despite the dizziness still clinging to me. "You must help me. We are of the same people. If you turn me away, you'll leave me bound to a god whose magic you've already said you despise. Is that what you want? More of his power, spreading and taking control among your own kin?"

The cavern grows deathly still as my words hang in the air.

"If you want less of his magic in the world, you must help me break free. I am already tainted, and by turning me away, you only leave the curse to fester. The elves may still attack you, just because I was here. If it will directly help the elf king, and the darkness will spread. It's not just my fate at risk—it's everyone's."

I don't know if that is exactly true, but Arion scares me. I don't want anyone here to be hurt, I just want to be cured and left alone. Enduvida waits for me. I want to go home. To see my students, my home, my loom, my friends... I want time to nurture whatever is budding between me and Vann.

Once removed from Arion's plans, those far more equipped to handle these situations will take the lead.

I need freedom from this like I need air.

The leader's face softens ever so slightly. For a long moment, the witches are silent, considering my words. Then the leader speaks again.

"Very well. Because you are human, and your curse is woven with the magic of a god we despise, we will help you, Arlet of the Enduares. If not for you, then for those of our kind who will fall victim to this darkness, this god you carry." She straightens, then looks back at the others. "Nighttime is close. There is only one ritual I know of that can sever a connection to your god. It requires blood—yours, freely given."

I swallow, my throat tight. "And Vann?"

She's silent for a moment before responding. "You may see him after the ritual."

I want to protest, but I know it is a bad idea to push. I cannot ask more of those who have already helped me. But if this is what it takes to free myself, I will endure it.

The leader gestures to two witches standing nearby. "You will bathe and be given fresh clothes. We will bring food to your companion."

The two witches step forward, one of them the elderly woman from before.

"Wait!" I say. "What is your name?"

The woman smiles, her lips twisting up at the corners.

"Maelira."

I nod my head. Strange, not at all like any of the human names I know. Despite everything, I feel giddy.

Just a few hours...

I can practically smell Enduvida. I was so full of new memories, ready to take back and apply to Lorepath. If the elves weren't so close by, I would ask to stay. To glean as much as I can from this place.

"Nice to meet you, Maelira," I say.

She gestures for the women to help me off the table. And I follow them, heart racing.

CHAPTER 36

VANN

The cavern is dark, lit only by the faint glow of bioluminescent fungi clinging to the walls like ghostly veins. The scent of damp earth and burning herbs filters through the air. Basil. Rosemary. It is strong enough to choke me.

"Hello?" I call out. "Good evening. Forgive me. I only—"

"Enter," a voice says in heavily accented enduar.

I walk through the stone passage and a room opens up. The witch with no name stands behind a rough, basalt table scattered with plants from the surface. She is draped in layers of black and wears a smooth, bone mask over her cheekbones and eyes. All that is left visible is the curve of her painted lips.

I do not falter as I set down the pouch of gold. It's heavy—weighted with the sum of my most recent promotion, enough to buy Adra a hundred gifts—enough to secure a better home.

Instead, I will use it for this.

Adra does not know I have come. She would kill me if she did, but she had been so unsure lately, so insistent that she felt our time was drawing to a close.

She called me foolish. Stubborn.

She has no idea how far I will go to sacrifice for her.

The witch plucks up the pouch with delicate fingers, testing the weight. She hums.

"This is a great sum of money, troll"

I meet her gaze, my voice steady. "The service I require is not cheap."

Another low hum vibrates from her throat, thoughtful.

She looks at me, and a light shines from her eyes through the mask. Then, as quickly as it had sparked, it dims and reveals dark, hazel eyes.

"You are not the first to come to me seeking to change what Endu or Grutabela have written." She bounces the pouch filled with gold once more. "Most who stand before me wish to find their mate. Some, after too many failed journeys, come begging for their fates to be forced. Others seek to undo a bond that has already begun."

She tilts her head, considering. "But you... you are different."

I clench my fists at my sides. "I am."

"You wish for no bond at all."

I nod once. "I have found a woman. She will always be my choice."

The witch sighs, almost as if she pities me. "And what if she finds her other half? Better yet, you look quite young—What if you do? What if one day, you wake and realize fate had planned otherwise?"

I scoff. She knew nothing of me, and less of Adra.

"This is the right choice. And I will have no reason to fear the fates," I growl. "Not if you do what I ask."

"What I ask," *she mocks. "If you wish such a brutal procedure, you must say the words."*

I take a breath and say, "I require the removal of my heart."

She exhales slowly, then extends her hand toward me, fingers curling. The air in the cavern presses against my skin.

"You do understand this is a wound that will not heal with time, yes?" she murmurs. "A loss you will suffer in every emotion that trickles through your veins for as long as you remain heartless."

I do not waver. "Will you do it?"

My heart hammers, as if it knows what is about to occur.

"You trolls have been given many gifts. Your home. Your magic. Those gems in your chest. You have it all, and still you want more."

I grit my teeth. "I don't need a lecture. I've brought good money. If you will not, I will find—"

Something cuts off my ability to speak.

She tilts her head, and for a long moment, there is silence.

"You are sure?"

The hold on my head loosens just enough for me to nod.

"Then I will take your gold." She whispers something—a word that slithers like ink into the air and curls around me.

And then the pain crashes into me. I am filled with agony unlike anything I have ever known.

A gasp tears from my lips as my chest seizes, a terrible wrenching that makes my bones feel as though they are being shattered from the inside. I stagger, my knees nearly giving way as something inside me rips.

I hear it before I feel it—an awful, wet sound, like flesh being torn apart. My hands fly to my chest, expecting to find a gaping wound, but there is nothing. No blood. No torn muscle. Just—emptiness.

She has taken it.

Floating between her palms, pulsing with a weak, flickering light, is a small, formless sliver of blue. A piece of me. My heart.

Or whatever had once been my heart.

The witch's fingers curl, and the light vanishes.

Gone.

The pain does not stop. It settles, deep and unyielding, inside my ribs, a cold void where warmth had once been. I gasp for breath, but air no longer satisfies my discomfort like it once had.

"You will live," the witch says, watching me. "But your heart—" she gestures toward my hollowed chest—"will need to be kept far away to ensure the survival of the spell."

The dream fades, but the ache in my chest does not. It is heightened by a haze that flows through my mind. I am suspended, and bound in my own head, every action punctuated by light measures of pain.

I feel my heartbeat in my stomach. My skull.

Thump. Thump. Thump.

My... heart. It pumps.

~

Two witches wake me in the late afternoon, bringing water and food. Their eyes linger on me as I sit up.

I have been placed in a dimly lit hut. A simple cot is beneath me, and a thatched roof with wooden crossbeams is above. The walls are rough, made from stone and clay, and a faint draft slips through the cracks.

Rosemary and basil.

My mind swirls with the dream.

The first one, a woman with milky eyes, stares at me. I cannot see the pupils within the orbs, but she tracks each of my movements with ease.

"Our leader, Maelira, has instructed us to care for you and answer your questions." She says.

"Where is the woman I came with? The flame-haired one?" I demand, my voice raw.

"She is being prepared for the ritual," the other, with bone-white skin replies.

I stand, fists clenched. "Have you done something to her?"

"You will not see her until the ritual is complete."

"I'm not waiting," I growl, stepping toward them. "I'm meant to protect her."

"You have no claim until the ritual ends," the first witch says, her gaze unwavering.

My fingers twitch at my sides. None of these answers are truly *answers*.

"What kind of ritual?"

The second witch speaks, cold. "She must be cleansed from the darkness."

I step closer. "Will you tell me where the dragon we came here with has been placed?"

"She is in the field near the ritual grounds. We will take you to see the creature when we are told it is safe for you to leave."

I inhale sharply, frustration flooding me. "And what is so dangerous that I cannot move freely through your village?"

The pale one smiles. "The magic on this island is more alive than you will ever know. Find yourself in the wrong place, and the it will rend you in two—tear your soul from your body."

I feel a chill creep up my spine as her words settle in. Their magic had always been powerful. Immensely so. Arlet shouldn't be alone right now.

But they are doing us a favor. If they have her, I cannot risk my actions ruining things for her, despite how I wish to charge out of this room and hunt her down.

I stay silent, frustration bubbling beneath the surface, and eventually, the quiet doesn't feel so tense.

They let me go to another room to wash, and the dream from earlier creeps back into my mind.

When I remember that my heartbeat was felt in my body, I press my hand to my chest.

I feel nothing.

This is, technically, good news. It was what I had wanted, and the lack of heart made up for the lie I had given Arlet. But another part of me sinks low.

I think it is the smell of rosemary that creeps in through the window. The woman who had attended to me long before had been so insistent that one day, I would regret my choice.

Six decades ago, and she had been right.

Once dressed, I return to the room, and sort through our packs. My weapon is placed on the ground in front of them, almost in warning.

I do not push to take it.

Time passes. The sun sets, and the witches remain in the shadows, their eyes never leaving me. The dream lingers, sharp and unsettling.

Finally, the witch speaks again. "It is time."

I stand immediately.

The witch gestures for me to follow. I move quickly, my heart pounding. The ritual is beginning, and I don't want to stand by any longer.

Last night, the assumption had been that we landed on the incorrect island. Clearly, I had been wrong. It was a kindness, and a part of me wonders if the gust of wind, the one that took us down was not Endu.

His tap on my shoulder from before was a rare moment. I followed it willingly.

Once we cross the threshold of the hut, I am surrounded by magic, wood and heat.

The Witch's Isle houses what they had called a village, but it seems more like another Enclave. It is a fortress made of the surrounding jungle. What a thing to discover a place few knew existed.

Hundreds of women move through the space, their inked faces flickering in the glow of floating spell flames. Their homes are woven onto the trees—huts of palm fronds and reeds perched among towering trees. Rope bridges connect them, swaying gently with each footstep.

Beyond the huts, the cliff sides are hollowed out into cavernous dwellings, their entrances covered with vines. Below, winding tunnels pulse with veins of bioluminescent fungi. Water drips from the stone, feeding underground pools that shimmer with an almost celestial light.

And at the heart of it all, open cenotes spread like glassy portals to the sky, deep and endless. The witches gather at their edges, their voices rising in whispered chants. Some of their bodies slip into the dark water below. The surface ripples, lilies shifting, their pale blossoms opening as if in offering.

I think of the warning I'd been given earlier—realizing just how powerful the energy of this place is.

The witches continue ahead, guiding me through the winding paths away from the cenotes. I breathe in deeply, letting the humid air settle against my skin.

A clearing comes into view, as does Seraph. Her golden scales gleam in the rising moonlight, the glow of the fire reflecting off her massive body. She watches me with sharp eyes. I can almost feel her disappointment that I am not Arlet.

When I approach her side, to be sure that she is being treated well, she exhales. It is a low rumble vibrating through her, accompanied by the restless twitch of her wings.

"Are you satisfied that she is well?" Pale-Eyes asks.

I walk around Seraph, making a show of checking for any less obvious ailments.

Once I return to my original spot, I nod.

"Come. The ritual is starting soon," Pale-Eyes continues.

We retrace our steps, and I try to memorize every turn, keeping track of where everything is, in case we need to make a quick escape.

A rhythmic beat of drums grows louder as we approach the ritual grounds. The witches' pace quickens, urging me to follow them toward the edge of the clearing. The flickering firelight casts long shadows, and the women gathered in formation sway in time with the drums. The intensity of the music builds, a pulse that resonates deep in my bones.

"You'll stay here," one witch says, her voice sharp. "Do not move forward, as you may ruin the magic our sisters weave."

I don't answer. My gaze is fixed on Arlet, who steps forward, bathed in the firelight. My heart clenches in my chest. I want to be closer, to be with her, but the witches block my way, forcing me to remain at the outskirts.

One of them speaks again, her voice colder now. "You are not to join. If you do, we will kill you. Remain here, or die. Do not test us."

I don't notice their formations and rite objects, my eyes land directly on Arlet as she steps forward.

Everyone is bathed in dark hues, but Arlet... she is radiant in the steaming air, a new green and pink dress clinging to her frame like water silk. The fabric gathers at her breasts, tapers at her waist, and flows down to the ground, the slit up one side revealing long, pale skin streaked with fire lit gold.

She moves like something untamed—wild and laughing, her hands slick with the berry-stained dye the witches have painted on her. The color is striking, strange against the deep red I've seen on her hands before.

Blood-red. War-red. The red of something taken, something stolen.

But this is different. This is hers. Given freely.

A smile spreads across her face, and my chest clenches with an ache I don't know how to name.

She's a wild, free thing.

One of the witches speaks, her voice rising above the drums, and the tempo quickens as the ritual shifts.

One steps forward with purpose. I assume it is the leader called Maelira. She carries a ceremonial dagger, its blade carved from dark obsidian, its handle wrapped in woven silver thread. The other witches slow their movements, circling around Arlet as Maelira approaches—the drumming changes, steady, low. It's a heartbeat against the night.

Arlet stills, chest rising and falling with exertion, her cheeks flushed from the dance. She meets Maelira's gaze as the witch takes her hand, turning her palm upward beneath the glow of the full moon.

"This is our covenant," Maelira murmurs, voice powerful. "Blood, given freely, under the eyes of those who came before us."

She presses the blade against Arlet's palm, and a thin line of crimson blooms. Arlet flinches but does not pull away.

Maelira lifts her own hand and slices a matching cut across her palm. Then, she presses their wounds together. A shiver runs through the air, a pulse of something unseen.

Arlet breathes out slowly.

The gathered witches murmur in unison, their voices weaving together, pulling at the air, at the night itself. Maelira tilts her head back, letting the blood drip from their joined hands into a small stone bowl. The liquid glows as it touches the surface, swirling with threads of gold and deep violet, magic laced within.

The earth hums beneath my feet.

Maelira releases Arlet's hand, lifting the bowl toward the moon. The light catches in the liquid, sending shimmering reflections across the gathered women.

"The first step is done," she declares, her voice carrying over the clearing. "In the morning, let Ashra show us the way to unmake it!"

Melodic grunts are chanted faster and faster as the blood moves up toward the moon, vanishing in the air.

The women break apart, their steps shifting into something more frenzied, something primal.

Their arms are thrown wide, hips swaying, feet pounding against the earth in rhythm with the song rising to the sky.

At first, Arlet hesitates, caught between watching and joining, but the hesitation doesn't last long. One of the humans grabs her hand and pulls her in, and instead of resisting, she laughs.

Gods, the sound of it.

Unbidden, I remember how she looked under me as I'd made her come. Red hair splayed over our shared bed, sweat trailing down the column of her throat and beading on her forehead. The pale cream of her skin had given way to a vibrant red flush.

A living flame.

I swallow hard, and she moves with them, untamed, her copper hair spilling over her shoulders, her bare arms lifting as she spins, feet kicking, and her voice rising to chant with the others as they call out to their goddess.

She twirls, her head tipped back. She looks like something otherworldly, a creature born of moonlight and fire.

And then, somehow, impossibly, she looks up and finds me in the shadows.

CHAPTER 37
VANN

Our eyes meet across the clearing.

Arlet's breath stutters, her chest rising and falling. The flush of exertion paints her cheeks.

She gestures me forward, and I shake my head, remembering the warning from the others.

I see the exact moment she decides to break away.

And, somehow, no one notices.

The witches are lost to the rhythm. Their bodies twist—hands grasping the air and feet pounding the earth in a fevered trance. The firelight pulses over their moving forms, their laughter curling into the night like mist. She could vanish, and they wouldn't see. Wouldn't care.

And she does.

She slips through them, her green and pink dress catching the light, flashing between bodies like a living ember. Then she's in front of me, her fingers catching my bicep and searing my skin.

But instead of gratitude, her eyes blaze.

"You shouldn't have come," she breathes. "They told me it would be dangerous. Uncontrolled magic can quickly turn malevolent."

"I wanted to make sure they didn't hurt you."

Her chest heaves and her pupils widen. She sways slightly when the rhythm shifts, as if the drumbeats had buried themselves beneath her skin.

As if they live inside her now.

She bites her lip, then smiles again.

“Then let’s get out of here before they see me with you,” she purrs.

Before I can speak, she grips my wrist and pulls.

No hesitation. No fear. Only movement.

“We need to be careful. They say it is dangerous without an escort,” I huff, bounding behind her.

“We won’t go into any houses or dark corners,” she responds over her shoulder.

The glow of exotic plants illuminates her bare shoulders and her unbound hair, which has curled in the humidity. She’s half-running, half-laughing as she moves.

I let her drag me deeper into the dark, past trees thick with hanging vines, the ground warm beneath our feet. When she finally stops, she turns to me, eyes gleaming in the low light.

"Do you remember what you said?" she murmurs.

I swallow hard. "I've said a lot of things to you."

“That I gave you back a piece of yourself.” She shakes her head, stepping closer, until I can feel the heat rolling off her skin. “I’ve never had anyone care about me the way you do. Never have I known someone to push me to be better. To voice what I want so they could... give it to me.”

My breath catches. I remember the feel of her coming apart as if she’d been crafted for my tastes. “I just—want you to be happy.”

She smiles so brightly I can hardly stand. “I am, Vann. And I want you to be happy to.”

“I... am.”

For a moment, she stares. Unraveling my soul. It makes my blood run hot—would make me lose my mind completely, if not for the guilt nagging in my gut.

And then she moves.

One second, she’s standing there, breathless and burning, and the next, her hands are in my hair.

Her lips crash into mine, wild and feverish, like she's trying to drink in the night, the fire, everything.

Her nails scrape against my scalp as she exhales into my mouth, half-mad.

"Gods, it's like I can still feel the drums in my skin," she laughs.

She bites my bottom lip, not hard, but enough to make me feel. Enough to make my whole body seize and thaw at the same time.

And then—she's gone.

Spinning away, arms high, feet kicking up the dirt.

She laughs, throwing her head back as she moves, the rhythm consuming her, owning her. Her hair whips around and her dress sways in time with the beat she makes.

I stand there, watching, wrecked.

"What are you doing, Firelocks?" My voice is rough, unsteady.

She smiles. "Dancing."

Then, she steps back, slowly, her fingers slipping away.

Her hips roll, the motion subtle, hypnotic, and then her hands slide up the sides of her dress, skimming her waist, her ribs, before lifting to let her fingers trail through her hair.

I stand there, utterly frozen.

She's playing with me.

"Your hands are still stained," I rasp, eyes flicking to the plum-colored dye on her hands.

She lifts them, flexing her fingers, watching the way the color catches the moonlight. "You don't like it?"

I growl, ignoring the voice that tells me to put distance between the two of us until I tell her the truth.

"I like everything on you."

She steps closer again, tilting her head. "Then you should dance with me."

I huff out a laugh. A part of me wants to, but another part has never seen her like this.

The last month has been torture for her. She's been so afraid, but right now, she looks unburdened. Happy.

A part of me is acutely aware that the only reason I am graced with this moment is because, somehow, by a stroke of cosmic luck, she forgave me—my rudeness and coldness—and then chose to trust me.

"I would but you look so beautiful in this light."

She grins. "Then you should watch."

She twirls, slow at first, and then faster, her laughter curling around me like a spell. The fabric of her dress sways, the slit revealing the long, freckled stretch of her thigh.

Then she stops abruptly, her chest rising and falling as she watches me. "I want you again. Want this moment, this night of good news, to be marked by you."

Her hands move to the knot at her shoulder, pulling it loose. The fabric shifts, the dress slipping slightly, baring more of her skin.

I go still.

"In the morning, the curse mark will be gone and we will leave together," she murmurs, fingers brushing the strap off her shoulder. "I don't want to go back to the Enduar Mountains and resume the life I had before. I want a new one. *With you*. Burn yourself onto my skin so that... matehood doesn't matter anymore."

My throat tightens.

Tell her.

She mistakes my pause for disagreement, and one of her steps falters. Unsure.

Absolutely fucking not.

I growl low in my throat, and reach out. My fingers wrap around her wrist, pulling her close, so close I can feel the heat of her breath against my jaw.

"You're playing with fire, Arlet."

She smiles, tilting her chin up, her lips inches from mine. "Burn me, *mi cielo.*"

Her gasp is lost in my mouth and her body molds against mine as I lift her and press her against the nearest tree. She clutches at me, legs wrapping around my waist and hands threading into my hair as the kiss deepens.

Grinning against her lips, I feel the heat pool between us. It is impossible not to savor the time I spend with her, free of pain.

She grinds against me once, and my tail wraps around the legs she's crossed behind my ass.

It is impossible to not be insane with lust around her, and my cock strains at my pants, pressing against the spot between her legs.

She pulls back, eyes wide, hungry.

When we'd been together before, I'd denied her this part—hadn't asked for anything more than to give her what she wanted. But now... she reaches down to undo the top laces of my clothing. She begins to rock as she undoes each tie, her mouth falling open and her breath turning to gasps.

I see white.

She's breathing heavily now—her cheeks flush pink.

I feel myself grow even harder at the sight.

"Can I touch you?" She whispers, licking her lips nervously. "Gods, have I dreamed about touching you. Causing your cock to go slick with your own seed. I want you to slide it between us. Inside me. Between my breasts. I want to smell so much like you that no man would come near. Your seed in my cunt. Your arm around my waist. A mark on my neck—two if you can manage."

I groan, my eyes heavy-lidded as I push against her. She grinds again. "Please let me touch you."

My hand goes around her neck. Begging, but in the most beautiful way. Begging for me. I would reward her for that.

"If you touch me now, I fear my plans for you won't last as long as I'd hoped," I grab her wrists again and she moans. Loud. "Do you know how long it has been since I laid with a woman?"

"How long?" she whispers, her voice just above a whisper as she looks at me with eyes full of lust and hope, wanting more.

"Half a century," I answer truthfully. "So let me savor this."

I move to undo the ties on her dress and feel a shiver run down her spine before my hands reach the last tie. "I was not even tempted by another, until you walked into the cave and shoved a finger in my face. You light me on fire. I've waited for this moment. For weeks, months... forever it feels like."

"Hate and desire feel confusingly similar," she confesses as I slide my hands down her body. "Forgive me for being confused."

She touches me again, as if she can't help herself. I grab her hand and hold it to my empty chest. I start to move, and she sucks in a sharp breath and squirms.

"Woman. I will need to hold you down unless you stop squirming," I pant.

Her eyes go wide. "Then do."

I blink.

Perfect, perfect creature.

"You are sure you want that?"

She places both hands on either side of my face.

"You are the man who promised me he would be the warmth of the sun on a winter morning." She presses a kiss to my nose. "I ventured halfway around the world. I've faced every fear, even the ones that threatened to break me, and soon, it will be over. You have been there every step. Come down this path with me, too."

As she speaks, I can feel my resolve weakening. Her words are a siren's song, and I'm powerless to resist.

"As you wish, Arlet," I say. "But I won't bind the knots so tight. We'll go slow. I am going to savor you until you tell me to stop."

Her chest heaves with each erratic breath, but she doesn't fight me. With her silken belt, I bind her hands and pull her arms above her head, securing them to the tree. She winced at the slight pull, but her eyes never left mine.

I lean down, my lips hovering over hers, and whispered into her ear, "I've got you—you are in my hands now, and you fit perfectly."

Another surge of lust flows through us as I kiss her again, our bodies pressed together. Her breasts rub against my chest.

Then I untie the final string of her dress. I run my hands down fabric, feeling the delicious curves beneath her dress and then finally... finally, I let my fingers glide over her skin.

I force myself to step back, instead deciding it is time to remove my own clothing.

I watch her as I begin to undress. I want her to see every part of me, know every inch. Her eyes rake hungrily over me as I pull off my shirt, revealing my labor-honed body, the faint scars that mark my years of service as a soldier.

She licks her lips.

Each movement brings the sound of rustling leaves and snapping twigs, until I stand before her, my tail twitching. In front of her stands a man transformed by time, both older and bolder than ever.

Her eyes widen as she takes in my cock, and something inside of me hums. I'd known her angry, sad, heartbroken, fiery, smart, and sleeping. But I hadn't really seen enough of her like this. Wanton. Sensual. Unapologetic.

I approach the tree, trailing my finger over her skin as she stands there, legs spread for me and waiting.

"Does this hurt?" I ask, touching her arms.

She shakes her head.

"You look so fucking good tied up and waiting for me," I praise. Then I cover her body with mine, kissing her again. She arches up. I begin to lay kisses along her neck, then trail downwards towards the valley between her breasts.

Each soft press of my lips and lick draws a sweet sound from her, urging me on. I am relentless in my pursuit. She is beauty incarnate, her light filling all empty corners of my empty chest

"Everything still all right?"

"Yes," she pants. When my hands trail between her thighs, she's soaked.

I feel like I've lost my mind. The possessive part of me rears its head again.

"I'm going to keep you forever, Arlet."

CHAPTER 38

ARLET

Vann's hand is between my legs and my wrists are above my head. I'm not in any danger of getting hurt.

Very much *in danger* of the way my breasts tighten and my lower belly tenses.

"Mine to break. Mine to put back together," Vann whispers. "Right?"

I nod.

"Are you ready to take me?" he asks.

I take a deep breath, a hum of pleasure sinking into my skin. "I'm ready."

Our bodies press together. His touch is both gentle and passionate—a masterpiece of emotion, skill, and desire.

"I want this to be perfect. I don't ever want you to feel anything but pleasure and warmth," Vann whispers, his breath warming my neck as he looks deep into my eyes.

He strokes his hand through my slickness, and then brings his wet hand to his cock to stroke himself once. Lining up our bodies, he enters me with a slow, deliberate motion. I gasp as he fills me completely, creating a sensation that leaves me breathless.

"Are you okay?" he asks, careful not to move.

I nod, unable to speak.

"Hostia puta," I moan, my head rolling back against the tree trunk as he begins to move in and out of me at a slow, steady pace.

Vann's eyes never leave mine as he continues to pump into me. His voice is a low rumble as he says my name over and over again, adding to the sensual symphony of our breaths and bodies colliding.

"Arlet," he says softly, "You feel so good. So warm..."

I moan, my hands pulling on the ties in response. Every thrust is a wave of pleasure crashing through my body. My senses are focused solely on Vann's touch—his lips on mine, his hands holding me close, the way he moves inside me.

My mind quiets. Sings.

“More,” I whisper.

He thrusts inside me harder, our bodies slapping against each other with each movement. My moans grow louder, and the leaves rustle around us with each gasp of pleasure.

My world becomes Vann and our connection. As if we are one entity, an amalgamation of emotions and desires. Each thrust brings us closer to the end.

“You are perfect,” he groans.

It takes me first, but he follows. The shock is an explosion of pure bliss that we will share together.

Vann's breath comes out in small gasps, his eyes locked onto mine. I’d had lovers. I’d had pleasure but this was something different. This was being seen. I didn’t need to ask what he feels.

I could see it in his eyes. Feel it in his actions.

For some reason, more tears well up and slide down my cheeks.

"I want to keep you forever, Vann," I say, repeating his words back to him.

The look of relief on his face is almost comical. Then he grins. Drawing me into his arms, and starting to rub my thoroughly stretched limbs.

As Vann unties me, a flash of light erupts in the sky, followed by a deafening rumble that shakes the earth beneath us.

“What was that?” I say.

Another boom shakes through the air. It hisses before impact, and then, there are screams. This isn’t a celebration.

"I will burn every city that harbors you."

"Fuck! That has to be the elves," I pant. "I thought they wouldn't make it through. Maelira told me that her barriers were secure. We have to do something, Vann. I don't want anyone else to be hurt because of me."

Vann's eyes harden with urgency. In a matter of seconds, he morphs from lover to warrior. The purpose is different, but the magnitude is the same.

"Let's go."

He pulls me along, his grip like iron as he helps me get to my feet. I scramble to put on my clothes, my fingers trembling, but he is fluid. He doesn't speak as he quickly pulls on his own gear.

Without another word, he tucks me close to him.

"First, we need to go to the hut where they kept me," he says. "I need my cleaver."

I nod, understanding, as we race toward the small hut where he keeps his weapon. The air crackles with tension, the rumble of distant explosions growing louder as we approach. Inside, Vann quickly retrieves his cleaver.

We don't stop. The destruction of the shore is already visible—bright balls of magical fire soaring through the air, crashing down into the water and setting the trees ablaze. The elves' boats skim across the darkened waters, their magic wreaking havoc on everything in their path.

In the distance, I see more ogres, their massive forms towering over the shoreline. They raise their hands, and huge rocks are lifted into the air, hurled back toward the elven boats with deadly precision. But the elves' barrage continues.

"Vann," I say, my voice high.

"Stay close," he orders, grabbing my arm and pulling me back toward the ritual grounds that is still full of witches casting spells. They launch red, black, and green trails into the air. The sound of battle is deafening, the shore in chaos, and I can feel the ground shake.

Together, we take cover in an alcove surrounded by trees.

I spot Maelira chanting, her arms swirling and pulling, drawing deep inside of herself before lightning crackles in the sky.

My mouth falls open as she directs a bolt to one of the ships.

It cracks and I flinch against Vann.

I don't know how to do this—how to be a part of any of this. The last time I was in a battle this big was with Arion.

He held me in place. Made me watch the death.

Vann *shields* me.

Another woman appears at my side and grabs my arm. I look up to see a tanned witch with dark brown hair. "What are you doing here? He may fight. You will not. Come."

I start to protest, but Vann's gaze hardens as he looks at me. Chaos and light rain around us.

"She's right," he calls over the roar. "You have no magic! You're not a fighter. Go!"

I pause. But then, with a reluctant nod, I agree. "I'll be fine," I whisper. I don't want Arion to take him from me. I can't bear it. "Just hurry back."

"I will. Stay hidden."

But as the witches start to pull me away, I turn back to Vann. For a heartbeat, everything freezes. He reaches out, pulling me close for another kiss. His hand cups my face, his thumb brushing the tear that I hadn't noticed.

"I will come for you soon," he whispers, his voice low, full of something raw.

I swallow hard, my heart aching.

"We need to go now!" the woman screams.

I reluctantly pull away, my eyes never leaving his. "Hurry back to me," I say, my voice strained with emotion.

He swallows. Then holds up his half-missing pinky.

"I will," he promises, his gaze never wavering.

And then, the witches move me forward, leading me toward the cave.

CHAPTER 39

VANN

When Arlet leaves, I feel cold. Chilled, but relieved. It's easier to fight without her here.

The shore is chaos. A dozen ogres tower over the landscape, hurling massive rocks at the elven ships, their strength shaking the ground. One ogre stumbles, crashing into nearby huts, splintering them. The thatched roofs burn quickly, and the walls crumble.

The witches stand firm, casting protective spells, but the elven fireballs are relentless. One witch's shield cracks as an explosion hits, and more huts fall as the shockwaves tear through the air. The walkways are broken, chunks of wood splintered and scattered.

A cenote nearby collapses with a deafening rumble. The ground shifts, and the water plunges downward, creating a violent whirlpool that sweeps away everything in its path. The once peaceful water is now a torrent, pulling trees and debris into its depths.

Smoke rises from the water as I race toward the battle. Three elven shoreboats, sleek and fast, speed toward the beach. Each boat is about twenty feet long, narrow, and with a sharply pointed prow.

The hulls are crafted from dark mahogany, streaked with silver veins that shimmer in the light. The wood has an ethereal sheen, catching the moonlight in strange, unnatural ways.

On the bow of each boat is a carving of a towering tree, its roots stretching out like delicate branches.

They would regret coming here.

I hold up my cleaver, it's familiar weight solid in my hand, the edge gleaming. My heart pounds, adrenaline coursing through me. There's no time for hesitation.

The first boat nears. Elves in dark, green armor stand along its sides. I don't give them a chance to strike. I run, my feet pounding against the earth, and launch myself toward the side of the boat.

I land hard, the wood splintering beneath me. The elves freeze for a second—just long enough for me to slash through the nearest one. He crumples to the deck, blood spraying across the planks. The others react too late, reaching for their weapons as I cut through another.

I'm a blur of movement, my focus narrowed to the kill. Every swing brings me closer to Arlet's arms. Elven magic crackles around me, but I'm faster. One elf raises his bow—but I'm already on him, cleaver slicing through his neck before he can release the arrow.

The second boat is close. I board it without hesitation.

The first elf I see is a woman, her eyes wide as she draws a dagger. She never gets the chance to use it—my cleaver cuts through her arm, disarming her with brutal efficiency.

The others hesitate, unsure whether to charge or retreat. They don't have time to decide. I'm on them, cutting and slashing, each blow sending another to the ground, their blood staining the deck. The sounds of battle—screams, clashing steel—are drowned out by the roar in my ear.

The third boat. It's here. Elves line up to fire, but I don't care. I charge, cleaver raised, and leap into the air. The boat's deck creaks beneath me as I land in the middle of their line, sending two elves flying with a single swing.

Blood coats the wood, slick beneath my feet.

Something thumps in my chest, and I push on.

I won't stop until they're all dead.

CHAPTER 40
ARLET

The witch with long brown hair leads me deeper into the cave, and farther from the battle. The entrance was wide when we walked in, but the path narrows quickly, and the stone underfoot is smooth and cool.

I'm shaky—*unsteady*—after leaving the shore. Vann has never done anything but prove he is a capable soldier, and yet my heart races, my head throbs, and *I fear.*

It has less to do with skill, and more with... something precious. The most precious thing in the world. We had just been together. I can feel his fingerprints on my skin, and hear the sounds he makes when he's pleased in my ear.

All my life searching for someone who understood me, and I had finally found that. It feels like catching a falling star moments before it burns out.

Come back safe, I repeat in my mind, over and over.

Thunderous crashes, rage-fed shouts, and metal sliding over metal roar behind me. I can't breathe.

When King Arion had been in Enduvida, there had been so much fear and death. I had lived through it before—whippings in Zlosa, being nearly kidnapped by the elves—but this... this is different. It's bigger. As uncontrollable as a storm tearing everything in its path. The sheer scale of it crushes me.

"Now you know what I do to those who have wronged me."

A cold, damp breeze brushes past us and I shiver. It's okay. The people up there know what they are doing. It will be over soon.

The cavern opens up, tripling in height from the tunnel. Being underground helps.

Reminds me of home. Especially because the walls glow with veins of blue and gold, pulsing in a steady rhythm.

I breathe out, grateful to be distracted by something—*anything*—as the zinging shocks crackling across my shoulders and hands.

Then the cavern shakes. Dust falls from the ceiling, and the ground beneath me trembles, making it hard to stay steady.

The witch who had brought me here glances over, her expression unreadable.

"They will need help—I must return. Will you be all right?" she asks, her voice steady, though an edge of urgency slips through.

"Of course. Thank you," I manage, but my legs tremble, and the words come out thinner than I intend.

Images of the shore flash through my mind—flaming balls of magic lighting up the night, the chaos and destruction, the screams still echoing in my head. The fight isn't over, and dread tightens in my chest for those still caught in it.

The escort calls something else at me.

"What?" I ask.

She uses a dialect of the human tongue, but the words blur together and I can't make out the meaning.

"You will be safe here," she reassures me, then hurries out, leaving me alone in the cavern.

I turn in a circle, my eyes darting around the dim space, but nothing seems solid. I can't shake the anxiety gnawing at my mind.

Suspended above me are shapes, delicate and flickering, trapped in something clear that catches the light, floating like stars in the dark. Some glow with a faint red hue, others silver or violet, each pulsing with its own beat.

The sight speaks to me. Feels... familiar. So much like the crystals back home. I just need Vann to return so we can leave.

Another woman steps into the light, and I yelp, startled. She holds up her arms.

"Easy! I'm here to help," she says.

Oh. My escort must have been telling her to watch me.

My cheeks heat a fraction. I didn't like that they saw me as such a fragile thing, but I also could acknowledge that I am not a war maiden.

Being useless stings.

I recognize her weathered hands. My gaze returns to her face. Yes, this is one of the women who had helped me bathe earlier before the ritual.

She is old, with tanned, white skin and grey hair falling in soft waves around her face, which is lined with the marks of time. Her hazel eyes are deep.

"Battle is not kind to those who do not fight," she says.

"I think it is cruel to everyone, just the same," I respond, holding my arms.

She hums. Thoughtful.

"I am sorry they came for you, but we are practiced in this. It will be over soon." She places a hand on my arm, and squeezes as another massive thud hits the ground and a tremor shakes the walls.

It isn't until she touches me that I realize how cold I am.

Breathe.

"I don't like that you are forced to do this. Why should you sacrifice for me?"

"You spoke elegantly when you first arrived. You reminded us of our duty to those of our kind who are not blessed with a channel to magic. Maelira does not speak much, but after our meeting, she told us that she felt we owe you," she says.

"I don't—"

"It was good you came. It has been so long since we have known anything about our kin."

I breathe. She makes it sound so easy to accept help.

It is not.

"Would it help if I showed you more of this place?" she asks, pointing up to the lights along the ceiling. "It might soothe the discomfort of not fighting."

I suck in a sharp breath, and nod. I am eager to get my mind off of what is happening outside.

"This place is called The Hollow. There used to be a dozen or so of these in the west," she starts.

"And what do you keep here?"

"In this one, we have over a thousand years of debts my sisters made with strangers across the continent," she says softly. "Each one a price, paid in memories or blood."

"Are they records?" I ask, thinking of the library in Enduvida.

She gives me a half smile. "Almost. Some are memories. Some are entire souls, or pieces of souls. Some..." she trails off as I look up again.

Each floating thing is pretty, but I don't know if I should be mesmerized or afraid by pieces of people flickering above.

"Thank you for telling me," I say. Then yelp *"fuck" as* another crash rumbles through the cave.

Vann. Be safe. Be safe. Be safe.

The old woman approaches and pats my back, waiting for the fear to ease with soft words. When the dust settles, she helps me up and smiles.

"You are kind," I murmur.

Something flickers behind her eyes, then she says, "Please excuse my frankness, but I am old and formalities are useless. I just need to tell you that when I saw you, I felt something," she says softly. "I felt a memory stirring in the cavern. A debt. Then they told me about your companion and I almost didn't believe them. It's been a long time since I've seen a troll."

My eyes widen. "You know of them? How?"

"I used to have a post near the city's capital. I was in charge of brokering more than a few of these debts." Her hand gestures above her.

I look around again. "For some reason, I thought people would only leave this place if they wanted to abandon your customs, like The Six had."

The woman laughs.

"We were much different when I was your age." Her brows draw together. "It's been nearly sixty years since I was there. Or perhaps more? Who knows. Time mixes with the humid air and addles my brain."

I smile, once again storing every bit of information. I want to ask more, but a new wave of dust shakes from the top of the cavern.

Nervous, I push away. Squeezing my hands, as if trying to pull out my worries through my palms.

The old witch, wizened and gentle, watches me as I pace, her eyes never leaving.

When I finally look up, I meet her dark hazel gaze, and to my shock, her eyes begin to glow. I gasp, stepping back, and bracing myself for her to speak with Arion's voice, or to attack me, or something totally unexpected, but decidedly worse.

But what I didn't expect was the pure sadness in her expression, a sorrow so deep it felt like it could swallow a mountain.

"Oh... no. I didn't realize... The man you bring with you... It was him. I told him he would live to regret it."

My heart skips a beat as she looks at me, and I realize she's talking about Vann.

"Vann? Regret what?"

"You," she continues, her voice firm, "are tied to him more deeply than you understand."

I open my mouth to speak, but she holds up a hand, silencing me as she turns away. "Come, kin sister," she urges, leading me deeper into the cavern. "There is more you must see."

Her pace quickens as we move further, the soft glow of the walls marking our path. Her words stay with me, gnawing at my thoughts. She said she felt something—a connection. What the hell does that mean?

More debts float around me.

And between them, written in light, are words that do not stay still. Promises, broken and unbroken, twisting like ink bleeding into water. Some flicker faintly, nearly faded, lost to time. Others burn so brightly I can barely look at them.

"It is unusual for a human to be with a member of a magical race," she says. "The world must be very different from how it was the last time I visited.

I hum. "Humans having mates is new, yes."

"Does that mean that you and him are...?"

"What? No. He... was mated before."

A part of me wonders why I am telling her everything, but I like her. And... I want to know what she's talking about.

"So he never told you."

I freeze.

"What?"

The old woman stops and looks at me.

"Is he still in pain?" she asks, her voice soft, but there's a sharpness to it that I can feel deep inside me. "Still cold? Still walking around without a heartbeat?"

My heart tightens, and I want to say something—anything—but the words catch in my throat.

Heartbeat... No heartbeat.

My eyes widen as I review all the moments I thought it was strange I couldn't hear his.

"You aren't one of us," she says, voice flat. "But you are human. A kin sister, of sort." She studies me carefully. "A human being with an elf or a giant or a troll, it is unwise. Before you stay with him, you should know the truth."

I swallow hard, uncertain of where this is going. "What truth?"

My pulse pounds in my throat and my hands go numb. It isn't her who makes me feel unsafe so much as it is the look in her eyes.

Her lips press together, her hand brushing against the curve of the cavern wall. She doesn't look at me for a moment, lost in thought. When she finally speaks, her voice is heavy with time, with things unsaid.

"Long ago, I met your troll. He was young then—different. He came here to make a deal. To remove his heart, so he would never have a mate."

"He did what?" My voice is raw with disbelief.

"He didn't want to be bound," she continues, the words coming slower now, like she's reluctant to say them. "He said he had a woman—that she was more important to him than the future."

Her gaze softens as she looks at me, almost protectively.

"Are you telling me... one of these debts is his?"

She nods once, then leads me into another room. More debts are swirling above us, but in the center of the small space, there is something deep purple. It's large, carved from crystal, but not still. It moves. It glows. It pumps.

Beats.

I look back at the witch, still unable to process what is happening. "You are saying that is—"

"His heart. He paid me. I took it, and sent it here for keeping."

I look back.

Vann's heart.

It hovers, caught in a web of light.

When I step completely inside the room, it sings.

The sound is not something I hear with my ears but something that moves through my bones, the Fuegorra in my chest humming in response. A call. A tether.

The stone embedded in my chest starts to glow brilliantly.

No. My eyes burn and I let out a sob.

The pull is undeniable. Because I know, I feel it.

I am his mate.

The truth slams into me, and the breath is ripped from my lungs. My knees give way, and I grip the nearest rock for balance. My vision blurs with unshed tears.

He had never told me about this. Not only had he hid this, he'd lied to me. He told me that he was mated. That we could never be.

"Did—"

I break off.

"Did he know that the other woman wasn't his mate?" I ask.

The old woman nods.

"How do you—"

Her hand reaches out and touches mine, and I am transported to a distant time. I watch the memory from her eyes, seeing Vann. I hear him insist on her services.

Watch her warn him, only for him to promise that he would never want another.

When the memory fades, my cheeks are wet.

The sting of not being chosen hurts. It burns and aches, but even then, I might be able to forgive it.

The lie, after all the trust we'd shared. After every secret I'd told him?

That... I cannot forgive.

The thought hits me as I stare at his heart, glowing and perfect, suspended in the air like a mockery.

I can't help but review each moment I poured out my soul. Did he know we were mates all along? He let me cry while I told him about children, and a future, and a happy, quiet life.

He listened, as if he had not been the one to rip those dreams away.

But it doesn't stop there.

More images push into my mind, relentless, cruel.

A home we built together, far from war and pain, with a fire that never goes cold. A child, *our child*, with blue skin and my dark eyes, gripping Vann's finger and giggling, babbling sounds that mean nothing and everything. I see him holding them the way he holds his weapons—as if they were both precious and powerful. I see laughter shared between us, quiet moments of warmth, safety. We could have had a love that would have been unbreakable.

I see a future that is now destroyed because he chose someone else. He gave his heart away before he ever met me, before he ever touched me, before he ever let me believe there could be something more.

He didn't stop me.

But he *let me* believe. Let me trust him.

My breath shudders, my hands shaking as I curl them into fists. I let him heal the wounds on my body, let his touch chase away the pain.

And now, he is the one who carves apart my soul. This is betrayal. This is the undoing of everything I thought I could be.

"It is in their nature to deceive humans. You should protect yourself, child. He won't protect you."

She was both wrong and right. Physically, he had saved me—many times. He'd paid dearly for some of those encounters. I think of the way he helped me open up. He'd been there, saving me from my own emotions. He'd brought me here to save me from myself.

And along the way, he had asked for total, utter honesty without returning it. It almost doesn't make sense—which is what scares me the most. If he had lied to me about something so big, then what else had he lied about?

The realization sinks into my ribs, sharp and unforgiving. I close my eyes, swallowing down the ache in my throat.

And I... I gave him everything.

If I return, I will always know what he did and what he hid from me. Like every man before him, he made promises, but when it came time to keep them—he chose to lie. He chose someone else.

Vann chose someone else.

And now, I have to make my own choice.

When I look down, I see my ankle. The curse mark is still there, a black snake burned into my lightly tanned skin.

The words of King Arion echo in my mind. I hear his promise to come for me, to destroy everything I've ever known. That threat won't go away, even if the curse mark fades in the morning.

And even being Vann's mate? He cannot protect me from that.

Arion had also offered peace in exchange for me. Lord Lothar had confirmed it was a binding political contract. Mrath would be upset, but they could smooth over that when the time came.

I think of all of my work. My position, the school, the children, the fabric... someone could pick up where I left off.

And then I think of that awful night spent in Zlosa, bound to my bed. The ache in my womb that has followed me for the last decade.

The childbearing aspect will be a problem. I don't have immediate solutions. Maybe, there will be a fix I haven't allowed myself to consider yet. Or maybe, Arion will do as I thought, and dispose of me.

But a *maybe* is better than a *definitely*.

If I go back to Enduvida with Vann, then the elves will follow us, as they did here—as they tried to do in Dragon's Reach—and they will burn the city.

How can I stay with Vann, knowing what he's done, and bear the weight of souls lost in my name?

I know what it is to kill. I know what it is to be powerless.

So I will choose.

If I cannot give my love to my mate, who is supposed to be my perfect partner, I will give it to others who depend on me in Enduvida.

They still deserve the bright, beautiful future I had hoped for in myself.

I wipe my face with the back of my hand, inhaling sharply. I turn to the old woman, my voice steady, even though my heart has been ripped open.

"I need to go back outside," I say, firm and resolute.

"That is unwise while the battle still rages," she responds.

One choking breath rushes out of me.

"Then help me end what is left."

Her lips press together. "I will not save you from one monster to give you to another. My words are not hollow."

My head shakes side to side.

"I am not afraid. Thank you for giving me the truth—I treasure it. But I have to do this to help as many people as possible. Can you understand that?"

Her head dips as she studies my face, then reaches for my hand.

"From what I see of your soul and heart, I know you are good. I hope you come to see that too," she says.

Good.

I want to be good—want it like air. At the very least, I want to not harm.

This decision will hurt. But at the end of the day, it will mostly only hurt me. And that is good enough.

CHAPTER 41
ARLET

The witch leads me away and the decision settles heavily on my shoulders. It locks into place around my heart.

I don't look back. Because if I do, I might think of Vann's heart. Or matehood. And then... I might break.

The way out of the cavern is quicker than I had anticipated, and soon, we reach the exit just as another explosion erupts on the shore.

At the mouth of the tunnel, I take it all in. We are on an incline from the beach, giving me a perfect view of the chaos. The wreckage of huts, broken bodies, and the scorched earth make my chest tighten. A pang of guilt shoots through me.

I feel small in the face of it, helpless.

"You will need to scream if you want them to hear you," the woman says. "I can help you with that."

She reaches out and places a weathered hand on my throat. I swallow, and then gasp in a deep breath.

"It is me! I am the one you seek! I will go with you!" The words spill from my lips, forced but final.

As soon as I am finished, the fighting falters for a heartbeat. The clashing of weapons slows, and a heavy silence fills the air. I feel the weight of every eye on me, and the pressure builds in my chest. I can't breathe. Not yet.

Without thinking, I scream again, my voice cutting through the quiet, raw and desperate. "I will go with you!" Miraculously, my plea works.

With a force that seems to ripple across the battlefield, Maelira raises her hand from over near a cluster of destroyed buildings. The air shivers under her power. Magic pulses outward, sweeping across the fighters, halting the chaos.

The battle stops.

I look around, my heart racing as I see the elves lower their weapons following the witches' retreat. A group of them starts to move toward where I stand near the cave.

"Be safe, kin sister," the witch says to me. "I am glad to have met you."

"Stop!"

The sound of Vann's voice snakes up my arms, curling around my neck, threading through my hair like lightning.

I begin walking toward the group of elves when the awareness comes over me. He hadn't been easy to spot from the incline, but now I feel him. The particles of my being seek him out.

Reach for his closeness.

There will be a few more quiet moments before the elves reach my path to the shore. In that silence, I see him.

Vann, his bloodied figure running from the other side of the hill. His pace is frantic, desperate. The sound of his boots hitting the earth carries over the stillness.

I wait for him, needing to see him—to give him this one last chance to say goodbye.

"What the fuck is going on?" he demands.

Up close, he's even more terrifying. He's utterly drenched. His clothes cling to his body, soaked through with the dark red stain. His silver braid sticks to his neck.

The elves approach on the other end, waiting for me, but he steps between me and them.

"Arlet, stop this," Vann says. He searches my face, likely seeing if my eyes are their normal color. When he realizes I haven't turned, he looks frantic. "*Arlet*. Don't be so self-serving. This is insanity."

A sharp voice from the group of elves interrupts, cold and commanding. "If she does not come with us now, we will attack."

I take a breath. I meet Vann's gaze, and I know—this is it.

My gaze shifts to the elf who spoke.

"I will come with you," I call back.

"You will not," Vann shouts, stepping forward. Crowding me. Choking me with the scent of blood.

I have just enough space to see one of the men raise their arrow.

"Wait! Just, a moment, please," I shout. "I am coming!"

The bow lowers.

Vann grabs my shoulders, the handle of his cleaver pushing into my shoulder bone. "What are you doing?" He shakes me once.

Tears spill down my cheeks.

"I saw it," I bite. "I saw your heart. What you did... you lied to me."

His face goes pale, and the lines of struggle fade into shock. His gaze locks with mine, a flicker of fear, but something deeper—guilt, maybe—crawls across his features.

"My what?" he whispers.

"The heart you traded to be with Adra. The woman who is not your mate!" I spit the words, bitter and sharp. "The one you lied to me about."

His eyes search mine.

"How?"

I shake my head. "It doesn't matter. You... you are my mate Vann. I saw your heart, and heard it sing. But you already made your choice. And now, I have to make mine."

"*No.* The last time I saw you, you were begging me to come back safely. Not even an hour ago we—"

"*Mi cielo,*" I press my hand against his soiled chest. "What... is one of the things I have wanted most?"

I wait for his answer. A family, a mate, a child, a quiet, happy life. Things he could have given me.

He presses his lips together. He knows. He knows me so well and *he didn't care.*

"I know I've made mistakes. Let me fix them."

I shake my head.

"Let me go," I whisper, the words breaking in my throat. "If you don't, I will never forgive you. And *I promise you,* I will find a way to leave again—but the lives lost between now and then will be on your head."

He holds me tighter.

"Firelocks."

"You lied to me," I said.

"But I didn't know—"

"Stop. Please. Let me go."

He doesn't move.

So I scream, *"Let me go!"*

"Arlet."

It's a name filled with the agony at the heart of every fallen civilization.

But then, with a sudden, shaky motion, he throws his cleaver to the ground, the blade clattering against the dirt and rock.

He steps back.

Surrenders.

Grants me one last gift—*listening to me.*

"Tell Estela I love her. Tell everyone I will miss them," I say, and then I walk past, to the elf waiting at the front of the group.

I know if I look I will break.

The elf does not speak, but his men create a tight circle around me. They do not restrain me or pick me up.

We just walk down the path. To the dark shore boat with Arion's tree insignia.

The world floats around me and I can hardly believe where I am. What is happening.

Someone helps me onto the boat.

I don't look back as they push us away from the sand, or cut through the water. The air feels cold now, unfamiliar. The soft hum of the boat is the only sound.

I try to breathe deeply, to find something that still feels like me, but there's nothing. Just the emptiness of moving forward, away from everything I thought I knew.

The shoreline grows distant, the sounds of battle muffled and fading. The ship looms large, its dark form rising from the water, and I can feel the eyes of the elves on me as we approach. Waiting for me.

So sure I would come.

The leading boat towers over the shoreboat as it docks. Its hull is dark, made of polished wood that gleams faintly in the moonlight, accented with silver trim. The sails are unfurled, shimmering like fine silk. The ship is sleek, with intricate carvings along the railings and a large, ornate tree sculpted into the stern, its roots sprawling across the back.

They throw down a ladder, and then I am made to climb up first. My legs shake, and my hands tremble.

Above me, more than twenty elves stand at attention, their postures stiff, their faces blank. So many. If I hadn't come... they would have kept sending more and more men.

Right choice. You made the right choice.

As I step onto the deck, they bow. One by one, each of them lowers their head to the floor in a single, coordinated motion.

I freeze.

They're bowing to *me?*

My chest tightens. I stand motionless, unsure of what to do. Their eyes are full of reverence, and yet, it feels like a trap.

My heart aches. I'm not ready, but there's no turning back now.

"Lady Arlet, betrothed of the King," one of the elves calls out.

The title is heavy and final. I hated getting a title in Enduvida... this is worse.

I close my eyes momentarily when something slick moves down my leg. I bite my tongue, holding back the sob.

The last piece of Vann I will ever touch.

This is what I chose. This is what I have to be now.

"Welcome aboard, Precious Cargo!" a familiar voice calls from behind. I turn, my heart racing, to see Emissary Thorne.

He stands tall, his short white hair catching the moonlight. His green eyes lock onto mine, he smiles brightly.

"What are you doing here?" I ask. "Are you taking me home?

His smile remains frozen on his lips, but his eyes change. They grow icy. They *harden.*

"No, my dear. We're going to Shvathemar."

What is he doing here?

My mind churns as I try to place him in a new light. My heart is still reeling from Vann. It rejects the possibility of more. Like another punch to the gut after getting slapped across the face.

I open my mouth, Thorne comes forward, grabbing my hand. I flinch, but his grip is unyielding.

"Come now, you should rest."

No one protests. No one even bats a fucking eye—like he belongs here.

He leads me firmly into the cabin at the end of the boat. The action is not overtly rough until the door is closed. Without warning, he shoves me forward. My hips him something solid—a table—and then I fall backward.

"Thorne!" I shout. Would anyone even come?

"You smell like basil. Trying to get this little curse mark removed? Wrong choice, lovely." Then his eyes narrow. "And you smell like... one of them. Have an eventful trip, then?"

I sneer, but he laughs. "You'll need to behave as the next queen now."

Then the elf pulls out a small, precise blade. He grabs my foot, restraining my attempt to kick him, and cuts across my curse mark. Pain lances through me, as a shockwave of power ripples beneath my skin. I arch off the table, gasping.

"What are you—" My voice falters as I try to steady myself.

Thorne watches me with an eerie calmness, his smile widening as he pulls at the air over my foot. Brilliant, white magic begins to flow from the wound.

My heart races.

"What is that?"

"Your gift to your future husband. I thought you would go to Arion quickly. He is unhappy with me."

"I thought you were working for Mrath," I say through gritted teeth.

A sharp, cold smile twists his lips. "Why serve the beast when you can serve its master?"

"All this time, we invited you into our home, showed you trust, we—"

"The Enduar King showed me that which he had to. There is no loyalty between us. And you, with your pretty projects. Your lovely devotion. You don't even lock your doors."

... What?

I don't think I voice the thought, but he smiles.

"A bit of glamor, and I could get near your house. A bit of persuasion, and it was easy to slip past your utter lack of protection."

I blink rapidly. Glamor?

The man at my door, Daniel.

"Are you telling me that you were—"

"Yes. Your last lover. I found him shortly after arriving in the city. It was easy to break his neck, simpler yet to steal his face. And it worked perfectly to be near you long enough to activate this little magical marvel."

He taps my leg.

I kick at him, and Vann's name freezes on my lips.

He's gone. It's just me.

One more slicing pain shifts over my foot.

"There," he murmurs, satisfied. "At last."

I pant, my body shaking as I clutch my side, blood soaking through my gown. "What did you—what did you do to me?"

Thorne does not meet my eyes.

Instead, he lets the white magic flow over my legs. A shifting mass of runes glows over my thighs, shins, and knees. Heat pours over my skin.

Hot, and powerful.

Then, in the back of my mind, a voice I haven't heard in days speaks.

Well done.

Not Arion's voice. The other one... the second voice. My eyes unfocus and refocus.

"The *Cumhacht na Cruinne* has been hidden for centuries. And somehow your people found it," he says, casually, as though he has not just carved something from my body, as though I am not trembling before him. "A force strong enough to destroy the unkillable."

My breath hitches. How long had this plan been in motion? He went to Enduvida to meet a human woman. And then he gave me a gift. During all that time, was he just waiting like a snake in the grass?

Thorne leans in, voice soft as silk.

"Strong enough to kill Mrath."

I stop breathing.

"When your queen first found it, I took back a part, just enough, and hid it. And now," he holds up the magic swirling in his palm, "I finally have a proper gift to give my king."

THE END... FOR NOW.

If you enjoyed A Cursed Bite, *please take a moment to leave a rating or review—it really makes a difference! If you are interested in preordering book two, you can do so here.*

If you'd like to read a few short chapters from the night Vann bit Arlet, click here or visit my website.

More by Daniela A. Mera

Check out my words below:

Prequel Novella: Bound by Shadows
The Stones of Fate
New Adult Monster Romantasy

Legends of Love
New Adult Urban Fantasy Romance
(co-authored by Daniela A. Mera and Elayna R. Gallea)

Entangled with the Enduar
New Adult Monster Romantasy

SUGGESTED READING ORDER

The Enduar World is an immersive Monster Romantasy experience. Some of the couples' stories are duets, others are standalones. While you do not have to read it in this order, it is recommended for maximum enjoyment.

(Note that not all books are out yet. Enjoy this sneak preview!)

Entangled with the Enduar:
1 To Steal a Bride
2 To Ignite a Flame
3 To Defend a Bride

Bound to Shadows:
3.5 The Stones of Fate

Bound to the Enduar:
4. A Cursed Bite (Coming April 2025)
6. Sequel (Coming Soon)

ACKNOWLEDGMENTS

As always, the biggest thank you will go to my smokeshow of a husband, Josué. You are the one who enables me to soar above the clouds. The last decade together has been the happiest of my life. You are a gardener, sowing seeds of peace and love, and I am the flower that blossoms under your care. Te amo con todo mi corazón. Eres mi media naranja.

Thank you to my writer friends Nisha, Ophelia, Elayna, Fleur, Demi, Cassie, Kourtney, and countless others. The gratitude for your love, support, and kindness is immeasurable. You make my life full.

Thank you to my family.

To my crusty white dog who single-handedly saves this señora's mental health.

To Margie, my fearless PA.

To the artists who have made pieces for Arlet and Vann, thank you for your care.

A notable mention goes to Andrew Hozier-Byrne—the man who's been making me cry for fifteen years. I wake up once a month and shake my fists at the heavens, cursing any god who will listen because it doesn't matter how romantic a line my little fingers tip-tap, you've written something better. I've been trying to emulate the depth and passion you pour into any song in my chosen media of novel writing without success. When I hear your music, I am filled with an indescribable and all-consuming rage for the sheer audacity you must have to be as good a lyricist/musician as you are. In my best Brian Cox voice, kindly "fuck off." (Actually, please don't.)

To the fans who have done so much to support and care for me.

As I've grown in popularity, it has become harder and harder to list each name—but know that I see and appreciate all you do.

About the Author

Daniela A. Mera was born into a royal Fae family in Scotland. She was a free spirit who loved traveling and cloud watching while laying velvet-soft grass. When she came of age, her Spanish Scottish mother forced her to travel to Las Vegas in order to kill a dragon and conquer a neighboring kingdom.

The dragon turned out to be a man, whom she fell wildly in love with. The couple ran away to the gentle hills of Mexico where Daniela ate lots of tacos and fruits the size of her head.

Something along those lines, anyway.

She writes whimsical tales full of lore all around the world, full of emotionally available men and women who run the world. She can be found listening to sappy romance ballads while writing scenes meant to emotionally damage her readers.

When not writing, Daniela can be found doing yoga and playing video games. Join her newsletter for freebies!

Visit: http://danielaamera.com/

facebook.com/AuthorDaniela.A.Mera

instagram.com/authordaniela.a.mera

amazon.com/~/e/B09JDDZQX7

goodreads.com/authordanieaamera

www.ingramcontent.com/pod-product-compliance
Lightning Source LLC
Chambersburg PA
CBHW020340310726
48979CB00015B/2448/J

* 9 7 8 1 9 6 0 3 4 3 2 6 0 *